Inés
of My
Soul

Inés
of My
Soul

ISABEL ALLENDE

Translated from the Spanish by Margaret Sayers Peden

HarperCollins*Publishers*

HarperCollins books may be purchased for educational, business, or sales promotional use. For information, please write: Special Markets Department, HarperCollins Publishers, 10 East 53rd Street, New York, NY 10022.

The illustrations preceding each chapter have been reproduced from an edition of Alonso de Ercilla's *La Araucana*, published by Gaspar y Roig (Madrid, 1852).

FIRST EDITION

Designed by Sarah Maya Gubkin

Library of Congress Cataloging-in-Publication Data

Allende, Isabel.
  [Inés del alma mía. English]
  Inés of my soul / Isabel Allende; translated from the Spanish by Margaret Sayers Peden.—1. Ed.
    p. cm.

ISBN-13: 978-0-06-116153-7
ISBN-10: 0-06-116153-5

  1. Suárez, Inés, 1507 (ca.)–1580. I. Peden, Margaret Sayers. II. Title.

PQ8098.1.L54I5413 2006
863'.64—dc22   2006043475

06 07 08 09 10 ID/RRD 10 9 8 7 6 5 4 3 2 1

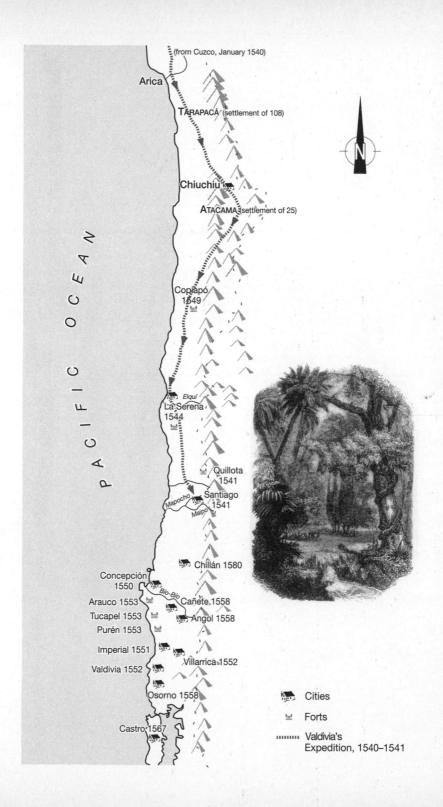

(from Cuzco, January 1540)

Arica

TARAPACÁ (settlement of 108)

Chiuchiu

ATACAMA (settlement of 25)

Copiapó
1549

Elquí
La Serena
1544

Quillota
1541

Mapocho Santiago
Maipó 1541

Chillán 1580

Concepción
1550
Arauco 1553 *Bío-Bío*
Tucapel 1553 Cañete 1558
Purén 1553 Angol 1558
Imperial 1551
Valdivia 1552 Villarrica 1552
Osorno 1558
Castro 1567

PACIFIC OCEAN

N

Cities

Forts

┈┈┈┈ Valdivia's
Expedition, 1540–1541

Inés
of My
Soul

ONE

Europe, 1500–1537

I AM INÉS SUÁREZ, a townswoman of the loyal city of Santiago de Nueva Extremadura in the kingdom of Chile, writing in the year of Our Lord 1580. I am not sure of the exact date of my birth, but according to my mother, I was born following the famine and deadly plague that ravaged Spain upon the death of Philip the Handsome. I do not believe that the death of the king provoked the plague, as people said as they watched the progress of the funeral cortège, which left the odor of bitter almonds floating in the air for days, but one never knows. Queen Juana, still young and beautiful, traveled across Castile for more than two years, carrying her husband's catafalque from one side of the country to the other, opening it from time to time to kiss her husband's lips, hoping that he would revive.

Despite the embalmer's emollients, the Handsome stank. When

I came into the world, the unlucky queen, by then royally insane, was secluded in the palace at Tordesillas with the corpse of her consort. That means that my heart has beaten for at least seventy winters, and that I am destined to die before this Christmas. I could say that a Gypsy on the shores of the Río Jerte divined the date of my death, but that would be one of those untruths one reads in a book and then, because it is in print, appears to be true. All the Gypsy did was predict a long life for me, which they always do in return for a coin. It is my reckless heart that tells me the end is near.

I always knew that I would die an old woman, in peace and in my bed, like all the women of my family. That is why I never hesitated to confront danger, since no one is carried off to the other world before the appointed hour. "You will be dying a little old woman, I tell you, *señorayyy*," Catalina would reassure me—her pleasant Peruvian Spanish trailing out the word—when the obstinate galloping hoofbeats I felt in my chest drove me to the ground. I have forgotten Catalina's Quechua name, and now it is too late to ask because I buried her in the patio of my house many years ago, but I have absolute faith in the precision and veracity of her prophecies. Catalina entered my service in the ancient city of Cuzco, the jewel of the Incas, during the era of Francisco Pizarro, that fearless bastard who, if one listens to loose tongues, once herded pigs in Spain and ended up as the marqués gobernador of Peru, but was crushed by his ambition and multiple betrayals.

Such are the ironies of this new world of the Americas, where traditional laws have no bearing and society is completely scrambled: saints and sinners, whites, blacks, browns, Indians, mestizos, nobles, and peasants. Any one among us can find himself in chains, branded with red-hot iron, and the next day be elevated by a turn of fortune. I have lived more than forty years in the New World and still I am not accustomed to the lack of order, though I myself have benefited from it. Had I stayed in the town of my birth, I would today be an old, old woman, poor, and blind from tatting so much lace by the light of a candle. There I would be Inés, the seamstress on the street of the aqueduct. Here I am Doña Inés Suárez, a highly placed señora, widow of the Most Excellent Gobernador don Rodrigo de Quiroga, conquistador and founder of the kingdom of Chile.

So, I am at least seventy years old, as I was saying, years well lived, but my soul and my heart, still caught in a fissure of my youth, wonder what devilish thing has happened to my body. When I look at myself in my silver mirror, Rodrigo's first gift to me when we were wed, I do not recognize the grandmother with a crown of white hair who looks back at me. Who is that person mocking the true Inés? I look more closely, with the hope of finding in the depths of the mirror the girl with braids and scraped knees I once was, the young girl who escaped to the back gardens to make love, the mature and passionate woman who slept wrapped in Rodrigo de Quiroga's arms. They are all crouching back there, I am sure, but I cannot seem to see them. I do not ride my mare any longer, or wear my coat of mail and my sword, but it is not for lack of spirit—that I have always had more than enough of—it is only because my body has betrayed me. I have very little strength, my joints hurt, my bones are icy, and my sight is hazy. Without my scribe's spectacles, which I had sent from Peru, I would not be able to write these pages. I wanted to go with Rodrigo—may God hold him in His holy bosom—in his last battle against the Mapuche nation, but he would not let me. He laughed. "You are very old for that, Inés." "No more than you," I replied, although that wasn't true, he was several years younger than I. We believed we would never see each other again but we made our good-byes without tears, certain that we would be reunited in the next life. I had known for some time that Rodrigo's days were numbered, even though he did everything he could to hide it. He never complained, but bore the pain with clenched teeth, and only the cold sweat on his brow betrayed his suffering.

He was feverish when he set off, and he had a suppurating pustule on one leg that all my remedies and prayers had not cured. He was going to fulfill his desire to die like a soldier, in the heat of combat, not flat on his back in bed like an old man. I, on the other hand, wanted to be with him, to hold his head at that last instant, and to tell him how much I cherished the love he had lavished on me throughout our long lives.

"Look, Inés," he told me, gesturing toward our lands, which spread out to the foothills of the cordillera. "All this, and the souls of hundreds of Indians, God has placed in our care. And as it is my obligation to fight the savages in the Araucanía, it is yours to protect the land and the Indians granted us to work it."

His real reason for leaving was that he did not want me to witness the sad spectacle of his illness. He wanted to be remembered on horseback, in command of his brave men, fighting in the sacred region to the south of the Bío-Bío river, where the ferocious Mapuche have gathered to build up their forces. He was within his authority as captain, which is why I accepted his orders as the submissive wife I had never been. They had to carry him to the field of battle on a litter, and there his son-in-law, Martín Ruíz de Gamboa, tied him onto his horse, as they had the Cid, to terrify the enemy with his mere presence. He rode in the lead of his soldiers like a man crazed, defying danger and with my name on his lips, but he did not find the death he was seeking. They brought him back to me on an improvised palanquin, mortally ill. The poison of the tumor had spread through his body. Another man would have succumbed long before, but Rodrigo was strong, despite the ravages of illness and exhaustion of war. "I loved you from the first moment I saw you, Inés, and I will love you through all eternity," he told me as he was dying, and added that he wanted to be buried without any fuss, though he did want thirty masses celebrated for the rest of his soul.

He died in this house, in my arms, on a warm summer afternoon. I saw Death, a little fuzzy, but unmistakable, as truly as I see the writing on this page. Then I called you, Isabel, to help me dress him, since Rodrigo was too proud to exhibit the decay of his illness before the servants. Only you, his daughter, and me, did he allow to outfit him in full armor and studded boots. Then we sat him in his favorite armchair, with his helmet and sword on his knees, to receive the sacraments of the Church and leave this earth with his dignity intact, just as he had lived. Death, which had not left his side and was waiting discreetly for us to finish our preparations, wrapped Rodrigo in her maternal arms and then made a sign to me to come receive my husband's last breath. I leaned over him and kissed him on the lips, a lover's kiss.

I could not fulfill Rodrigo's wish to be sent off without a fuss; he was truly the most loved and respected man in Chile. The entire city of Santiago turned out to weep for him, and from other cities in the kingdom arrived countless expressions of grief. Years before, the populace had come out into the streets to celebrate his appointment as governor with flowers and harquebus salvos. We buried him, with the honors he deserved, in the church of Nuestra Señora de las Mercedes, which he and I had had built to the glory of the Most Holy Virgin, and where soon my bones, too, will rest. I have left enough money to the Mercedarios that for three hundred years they can devote a weekly mass to the rest of the soul of the noble hidalgo Don Rodrigo de Quiroga, valiant soldier of Spain, adelantado, conquistador, and twice gobernador of the kingdom of Chile, caballero of the Order of Santiago . . . my husband. These months without him have been eternal.

I must not get ahead of myself. If I do not narrate the events of my life with rigor and harmony, I will lose my way. Chronicles must follow the natural order of happenings, even though memory is a jumble of illogic. I write at night, on Rodrigo's worktable, with his alpaca mantle wrapped around me. The fourth Baltasar watches over me, the great-grandson of the dog that came with me to Chile and lived beside me for fourteen years. That first Baltasar died in 1553—the same year Valdivia was killed—but he left me his descendants, all enormous, with clumsy feet and wiry coats.

This house is cold, despite carpets, curtains, tapestries, and the braziers the servants keep filled with live coals. You often complain, Isabel, that the heat here is suffocating; it must be that the cold is not in the air but inside me. That I can write down these memories and thoughts with paper and ink is owing to the good graces of the priest González de Marmolejo, who took the time, amid his labors of evangelizing savages and consoling Christians, to teach me to read. In those years, he was a chaplain, but later he became the first bishop of Chile, and also the wealthiest man in this kingdom. When he died, he took nothing with him to the tomb; instead, he left a trail of good works that had won him the people's love. At the end, Rodrigo, the most generous of men, always said that one has only what one has given.

We should begin at the beginning, with my first memories. I was born in Plasencia, in the north of Extremadura, a border city steeped in war and religion. My grandfather's house, where I grew up, sat at the distance of a harquebus shot from the cathedral, which was called La Vieja—the Old Lady—out of affection, not fact, for it had been there only since the fourteenth century. I grew up in the shadow of its strange tower covered with carved scales. I have never again seen it, or the wide wall that protects the city, the esplanade of the Plaza Mayor, the dark little alleys, the elegant mansions and arched galleries, or my grandfather's small landholding, where my sister's grandsons still live.

My grandfather, a cabinetmaker by trade, belonged to the Brotherhood of Vera-Cruz, an honor far above his social condition. Established in the oldest convent of the city, that brotherhood walked at the head of the holy week processions. My grandfather, wearing white gloves and a purple habit girdled with yellow, was one of the men chosen to carry the holy cross. Drops of blood spotted his tunic, blood from the flagellation he inflicted upon himself in order to share Christ's suffering on the road to Golgotha. During holy week the shutters of houses were closed to block out the light of the sun, and people fasted and spoke in whispers. Life was reduced to prayers, sighs, confessions, and sacrifices. One Good Friday my sister, Asunción, who was then eleven, awoke with the stigmata of Christ on the palms of her hands, horrible open sores, and with her eyes rolled up toward the heavens. My mother slapped her twice, to bring her back to this world, and treated her hands with wads of spiderwebs and a strict diet of chamomile tea. Asunción was kept in the house until the wounds healed, and my mother forbade us to mention the matter because she did not want her daughter paraded from church to church like a monster from the fair. Asunción was not the only stigmatized girl in the region. Every year during holy week some girl suffered the same thing. She would levitate, emit the fragrance of roses or sprout wings, and at that point she would become the target of exuberant devotion from believers. As far as I know, all of them ended up in a convent as nuns except Asunción who, because of my mother's precautions and the family's silence, recovered from the miracle without consequences, married, and had several children, among them my niece Constanza, who will appear later in this account.

I remember the processions because it was in one of them that I met Juan, the man who would be my first husband. That was in 1526, the year Charles V wed his beautiful cousin Isabella of Portugal, whom he would love his whole life long, and the same year in which Suleiman the Magnificent, with his Turkish troops, penetrated into the very heart of Europe, threatening Christianity. Rumors of the Muslims' cruelties terrorized the populace, and even then we thought we could see those fiendish hordes at the walls of Plasencia. That year religious fervor, whipped up by fear, reached the point of dementia.

In the procession, I was marching behind my family like a sleepwalker, light-headed from fasting, candle smoke, the smell of blood and incense, and the clamor of the prayers and moans of the flagellants. Then, in the midst of the crowd of robed and hooded penitents, I spied Juan. It would have been impossible not to see him since he was a handsbreadth taller than any of the other men. He had the shoulders of a warrior, dark, curly hair, a Roman nose, and cat eyes, which returned my gaze with curiosity.

"Who is that?" I pointed him out to my mother, but in reply received a jab of her elbow and the unequivocal order to lower my eyes. I did not have a sweetheart because my grandfather had decided that I would remain unmarried and take care of him in his old age, my penance for having been born in the place of a much desired grandson. He did not have money for two dowries, and had decided that Asunción would have more opportunities to make a good alliance than I because she had the pale, opulent beauty that men prefer, and she was obedient. I, on the other hand, was pure bone and sinew, and stubborn as a mule besides. I took after my mother and my deceased grandmother, who were not noted for sweetness. It was said that my best attributes were my dark eyes and filly's mane, but the same could be said of half the girls in Spain. I was, however, very skillful with my hands; there was no one in Plasencia and its environs who sewed and embroidered as tirelessly as I. With that skill, I had contributed to the upkeep of my family from the time I was eight, and I was saving for the dowry my grandfather did not plan to give me. I was determined to find a husband because I preferred a destiny of tilting with children to life with my ill-tempered grandfather.

That day during holy week, quite the opposite of obeying my mother, I threw back my mantilla and smiled at the stranger. So began my love affair with Juan, a native of Málaga. My grandfather opposed it at the beginning, and our home turned into a madhouse. Insults and plates flew, slammed doors cracked a wall, and had it not been for my mother, who put herself between us, my grandfather and I would have murdered each other. I waged such protracted war that in the end he yielded, out of pure exhaustion. I do not know what Juan saw in me, but it doesn't matter; the fact is that soon after we met we had agreed to marry within the year, a period that would give him time to find work and for me to add to my meager dowry.

Juan was one of those handsome, happy men no woman can resist at first, but later wishes another woman would win away because he causes so much pain. He never bothered to be seductive; in fact, he never bothered about anything. Being such a chulo—dressing so well and looking so handsome—was all it took for him to create a stir among the women. From the time he was fourteen years old, the age at which he began to polish his charms, he lived off his conquests. He used to laugh and say that he had lost count of the cuckolded men he had put the horns on, and the number of times he had given a jealous husband the slip. "But that's all over now that I'm with you, my pretty," he would add to soothe me, as out of the corner of his eye he would be eyeing my sister. His bearing and his pleasant nature won the admiration of men as well. He was a good drinker and cardplayer, and he had an endless repertoire of racy stories and fanciful plans for making an easy fortune. Soon after I met him, I realized that his mind was focused on the horizon and on tomorrow; he was never satisfied. Like so many men of his time, he fed on the fabulous stories about the New World, where great treasures and honors were within reach of brave men willing to take risks. He believed he was destined for great derring-do, like Columbus, who had set out to sea with courage as his only capital, and who ended up discovering the other half of the world. Or Hernán Cortés, who won the most precious pearl in the Spanish empire: Mexico.

"They say that everything has already been discovered in those parts of the world," I argued, wanting to discourage him.

"How ignorant you are, woman! There is more to *be* conquered than what has already been conquered. From Panama on to the south everything is virgin territory, and it contains more riches than all that Suleiman possesses."

His plans horrified me because it meant we would be separated. Furthermore, I had heard from my grandfather's own lips, who in turn knew through gossip in the taverns, that the Aztecs of Mexico made human sacrifices. Thousands and thousands of miserable captives formed lines a league long, awaiting their turn to climb the steps of the temples where the priests—wild-haired scarecrows covered with a crust of dried blood and dripping with fresh blood—tore out their hearts with an obsidian knife. Their bodies rolled down the steps and piled up at the bottom, hills of decomposing flesh. The city sat in a lake of blood. Birds of prey, sated with human flesh, were so heavy they couldn't fly, and carnivorous rats grew to the size of sheepdogs. There was no Spaniard who had not heard these stories, but none of it intimidated Juan.

While I embroidered and sewed from daybreak to midnight, saving for our marriage, Juan spent his days wandering through the taverns and plazas, seducing maidens and whores alike, entertaining the local residents and dreaming of setting sail for the Indies, the only possible destiny for a man of his rigging, he maintained. At times he was gone for weeks, even months, only to return without explanations. Where had he gone? He never said, but since he talked so much about crossing the sea, people made fun of him and called me the "bride of the Americas." I put up with his erratic behavior with more patience than was sensible because my thoughts were confused and my body flushed, as always happens when I'm in love. Juan made me laugh, he entertained me with songs and wicked poems, he mollified me with his kisses. He had only to touch me to turn my tears to sighs and my anger to desire. How accommodating love is; it forgives everything.

I have never forgotten our first embrace, hidden among the bushes in the woods. It was summer and the earth was pulsing, warm and fertile, filling the air with the fragrance of bay. We left Plasencia separately, to prevent talk, and went down the hill, leaving the walled city behind. We met at the river, and ran hand in hand toward the thicket, looking for a place far away from the road. Juan gathered leaves to make a nest. He took off his doublet and sat me down on it, then, in a leisurely way, instructed me in some of the ceremonies of pleasure. We had brought olives, bread, and a bottle of wine I had stolen from my grandfather, which we drank in naughty sips from each other's mouths. Kisses, wine, laughter, the warm earth, and the two of us in love. He took off my blouse and bodice and licked my breasts, saying they were firm as peaches, ripe and sweet, although I thought they looked more like hard plums. He explored me with his tongue until I thought I would die of pleasure and love. I remember that he lay back among the leaves and had me get on top of him, naked, moist with sweat and desire, because he wanted me to be the one to set the rhythm of our dance. So, little by little, like a game, without fear or pain, I lost my virginity. At one moment of ecstasy I lifted my eyes to the green canopy of the forest and to the burning summer sky above it, and shouted with pure and simple joy.

In Juan's absences, my passion cooled, my anger heated up, and I would determine to throw him out of my life, but as soon as he reappeared with some pale excuse and his wise lover's hands, I would surrender. And so would begin another identical cycle: seduction, promises, submission, the bliss of love, and the suffering of a new separation. The first year went by without our having set a date for the wedding, then a second and a third. By then my reputation had been dragged through the mud; everyone was saying that we were doing wicked things in every dark corner we could find. It was true, but no one ever had proof; we were very cautious. The same Gypsy who had predicted my long life sold me the secret for not getting pregnant: a vinegar-soaked sponge. I had learned, through the counsel of my sister Asunción, and my friends, that the best way to control a man was to deny him favors, but not even a martyred saint could deny pleasure to Juan de Málaga. I was the one who sought opportunities to be alone with him and make love. Anywhere, not just in dark corners. He had an extraordinary ability, which I never found in any other man, to make me happy, in any position and in very little time. My pleasure mattered more to him than his own. He learned the map of my body by heart, and he also taught me to enjoy it alone. "Look how beautiful you are, woman," he told me again and again. I did not share his flattering opinion, but I was proud of provoking desire in the most handsome man in Extremadura.

If my grandfather had had proof that we were making love like demented rabbits, even in the hidden corners of the church, he would have killed us both. He was very sensitive when it came to questions of honor. That honor was in large measure tied to the virtue of the women of the family, and therefore when the first whispers reached his hairy ears he exploded with rage, and threatened to beat me until I was where I belonged: with other devils. A stain on one's honor, he said, is cleansed only with blood. My mother stepped in front of him with arms akimbo and that look of hers that would stop a charging bull, and made him see that I was more than ready to be married. All he had to do was convince Juan. So my grandfather enlisted his friends in the Vera-Cruz brotherhood, all influential men in Plasencia, to twist the arm of my recalcitrant sweetheart, who had already been begged many times.

We were married one luminous Tuesday in September, market day in the Plaza Mayor, when the aroma of flowers, fruits, and fresh vegetables spread through the city. Juan took me to Málaga, where we moved into a rented room with windows overlooking the street. I tried to make it pretty with lace curtains and furniture my grandfather made for us in his workshop. Juan came to his role of husband with no wealth but his extravagant ambition, and with the brio of a stallion, even though we knew each other as well as an old married couple. There were days when we never got around to dressing because the hours flew by as we made love. We even ate in bed. Despite the excesses of passion, I soon realized that from the point of view of convenience, the marriage was a mistake. Juan had no surprises for me, he had shown me his character during all those years I had known him, but it was one thing to see his faults from a certain distance and something very different to live with them. The only virtues that I remember were his instinct to make me happy in bed and his toreador's good looks, which I never tired of admiring.

"This man is not good for much," my mother warned me one day when she came to visit us.

"As long as he gives me children, the rest doesn't matter."

"And who is going to provide for the little ones?" she insisted.

"I am, that's why I have my needle and thread," I replied defiantly.

I was used to working from sunup to sundown, and I did not lack for customers for my sewing and embroidery. In addition, I made onion- and meat-filled pies, cooked them in the public ovens at the mill, and sold them at dawn in the Plaza Mayor. After a lot of experimenting, I discovered the perfect proportion of lard and flour to obtain a firm, thin, malleable dough. My pies—or empanadas—became very popular, and after a while I was earning more from my cooking than from my sewing.

My mother brought me a gift of a small wood statue of the miraculous Nuestra Señora del Socorro, hoping she would bless my womb, but the Virgin must have had more important matters on her hands, because she ignored my pleas. I had not used the vinegar sponge for a couple of years, but there was no sign of a child. The passion I shared with Juan was becoming a source of vexation for both of us. The more I demanded of him and the less I forgave, the further away he drifted. Toward the end I was almost not speaking to him and he was speaking only to yell. He did not dare hit me, however, because the one time he lifted his fist, I swung my iron skillet at his head, the way my grandmother had with my grandfather, and then my mother with my father—which, they say, was why he left us and we never saw him again. In this respect, at least, my family was different: the men did not beat their wives, only their children. I had barely tapped Juan, but the frying pan was hot and it left a mark on his forehead. For a man as vain as he was, that little burn was a tragedy, but it made him respect me. The welt from the skillet put an end to his threats, but I admit that it did not help our relationship, because every time he ran his finger over the scar, I saw a criminal gleam in his eyes. He punished me by denying me the pleasures that once he had given with such magnanimity.

My life changed; the weeks and months dragged by like a sentence in the galleys, nothing but work and more work, always grieving over being sterile and poor. My husband's whims and debts became a heavy load that I assumed in order to avoid the shame of facing his creditors. Our long nights of kisses and lazy mornings in bed had ended; our embraces were further and further apart, brief and brutal, like rapes. I bore them only in hopes of a child. Now, when I can look back and observe my whole life from the serenity of my old age, I understand that the Virgin's true blessing was to deny me motherhood and thus allow me to fulfill an exceptional destiny. With children I would have been tied down, as we women are. With children I would have stayed in Plasencia, abandoned by Juan de Málaga, sewing and making empanadas. With children, I would not have conquered this Kingdom of Chile.

My husband continued to deck himself out like a chulo and spend like a hidalgo, assured that I would achieve the impossible in order to pay his debts. He drank too much and visited the street of the procuresses, where he tended to disappear for several days, until I paid some hefty men to go look for him. They would bring him back covered with lice and limp with shame. I would rid him of the lice and nourish the shame. I stopped admiring his torso and his statuesque body and began to envy my sister, Asunción, married to a man who looked like a boar but who was a hard worker and a good father to his children. Juan was getting bored and I was losing hope, which was why I did not try to stop him when finally he decided to go to the Americas in search of El Dorado, a city of pure gold, where children's playtoys were topazes and emeralds. A few weeks later, he left in the middle of the night, without a good-bye and with only a bundle of clothing and my last maravedís, which he took from the hiding place behind the hearth.

Juan had succeeded in infecting me with his dreams, even though I had personally never seen any adventurer return from America a wealthy man. To the contrary, they came back miserable, ill, and insane. The ones who made a fortune lost it, and the owners of the enormous haciendas it was said were available there could not bring them home with them. Nevertheless, these and other facts evaporated before the powerful attraction of the New World. Hadn't carts filled with bars of gold from the Americas been seen in the streets of Madrid? Unlike Juan, I did not believe there was any such thing as a city of gold, or magical waters that bestowed eternal youth, or Amazons who made merry with men and then sent them on their way laden with jewels, but I suspected there was something even more prized to be found there: freedom. In the Americas every man was his own master; he never had to bow to anyone, he could begin anew, be a different person, live a different life. There no one bore his dishonor for years, and even the humblest could rise in the world. "Higher than me, only my plumed cap," Juan used to say. How could I reproach my husband for that adventure when I myself, had I been a man, would have done the same?

Once Juan left, I returned to Plasencia to live with my mother and my sister's family, because by that time my grandfather had died. I had become another "widow of the Americas," like so many others in Extremadura. In accord with custom, I had to dress in mourning and wear a heavy veil over my face, renounce social life, and submit to the watchful eyes of my family, my confessor, and the authorities. Prayer, work, and solitude, that was my future, only that . . . but I do not have a martyr's nature. If the conquistadors found hard times in the Americas, their wives had it much harder in Spain.

I found ways to slip out of the custody of my sister and my brother-in-law; they feared me almost as much as they feared my mother, and to keep from having to confront me, they did not delve into my private life. They were satisfied as long as I did not create a scandal. I kept serving clients for my sewing and selling empanadas in the Plaza Mayor. I even gave myself the pleasure of attending fiestas. I also went to the hospital to help the nuns with the sick and the victims of plague and knife, because from the time I was young I had been interested in healing, with no idea that later in life that knowledge, along with my talent for cooking and locating water, would be indispensable. For like my mother, I was born with the gift of dousing. Often she and I would go out to the country with a laborer—or sometimes a señor—to show him where to dig his well. It's easy. You hold a long stick from a healthy tree loosely in your hands and slowly walk across the terrain until the divining rod, sensing the presence of water, dips and points to the ground. That is where to dig. People said that my mother and I could make ourselves rich with that talent because a well in Extremadura is a treasure, but we always did it for nothing. If you charge for that favor, you lose the gift. Much later it would help me save an army.

I waited for several years with very little news of my husband, except for three brief messages that came by way of Venezuela, which the priest read to me and helped me answer. Juan said that he was working hard and encountering danger, that vicious men were everywhere, that he was always looking over his shoulder and had to have his weapon ready anywhere he went, that there was gold in abundance, although he hadn't seen it yet, and that he would return a rich man and build me a palace and I would live the life of a duchess. In the meantime, my days dragged by, slow, tedious, always in want. I spent only enough to subsist, and hid the rest in a hole in the floor. I did not tell anyone—I did not want to fuel gossip—but I intended to follow Juan in his adventure, whatever the cost, not out of love, which I no longer had for him, not out of loyalty, which he did not deserve, but to follow the lure of freedom. There, far from everyone who knew me, I could take command of my life.

My body burned with impatience. My nights were a hell. I tossed and turned in bed, reliving the joyous embraces with Juan in the days when we desired each other, hot even in the depths of winter and furious with myself and the world for having been born a woman and being condemned to the prison of tradition. I brewed sleeping potions following the advice of the nuns at the hospital, but they had no effect. I tried prayer, as the priest urged, but I was unable to finish an Our Father without straying into dark thoughts, because the Devil, who weaves his way through every part of life, was venting his cruelty on me.

"You need a man, Inés. You can do anything if you're discreet," my mother sighed, always the practical one. For a woman in my situation, it was easy to get a man, starting with my confessor, a bad-smelling, lascivious priest who wanted us to sin together in his dusty confessional in exchange for indulgences that would shorten my days in purgatory. Vicious old man; it never happened. If I had wanted, men would never have been in short supply. Occasionally, pricked by the devil's pitchfork, I would embrace a man, but only out of need; there was no future for me there. I was tied to the ghost of Juan, and condemned to solitude. I was not truly a widow. I could not marry again; my role was to wait. Only wait. Wouldn't it be better to face the perils of the sea and savage lands rather than grow old and die without having lived?

Finally I obtained a royal permit to embark for the Americas, after negotiating for years. The Crown protected matrimonial ties and tried to reunite husband and wife in order to populate the New World with legitimate Christian families, but they did not rush to their decisions. Things move very slowly in Spain. They issued permits to married women to join their husbands only if a family member or another respectable companion went with them. In my case, that person was Constanza, my fifteen-year-old niece, the daughter of my sister, Asunción, a timid girl with a religious vocation, whom I chose as being the healthiest member of the family. The New World is not for the delicate. We did not ask her, but from the fit she threw, I have to believe that she was not attracted by the prospect of the journey. Her parents put her in my care with a promise, written and sealed before a scribe, that once I was reunited with my husband, I would send her back to Spain and would provide the dowry for her to enter a convent—a promise I was not able to fulfill, not for lack of honor on my part, but on hers, as will be seen later. To obtain my papers, two witnesses had to swear that I had no tainted blood—that I was not a Moor or a Jew, but an old Christian. I threatened the priest with revealing his lust before the Ecclesiastic Tribunal, and coerced him into writing a testimony of my moral quality. With my savings I bought what I needed for the journey, a list too long to detail here, although I remember it perfectly. Enough to say that I took food for three months, including a cage of chickens, in addition to the clothing and household utensils I needed to establish myself in the Americas.

———————

Pedro de Valdivia grew up in a timeworn stone house in Castuera, the land of poor hidalgos, more or less three days' march south of Plasencia. I regret that we did not meet in our youth, when he was a handsome lieutenant passing through my city on his way back from some military campaign. We may have walked its twisting streets the same day. He was already a man wearing the colorful uniform of the king's cavalry, and with a sword at his belt, and I still a girl with braided red hair—which color it was then, although later it grew darker. We might have passed each other in the church. His hand could have brushed mine at the holy water font, and we could have exchanged glances without recognizing each other. Neither that sturdy soldier, hardened by worldly travails, nor I, a young seamstress, could have divined all that fate held in store for us.

Pedro came from a family of military men, noble but without means, whose exploits went back as far as battles against the Roman army in the years before Christ, continued for seven hundred years against the Saracens, and kept producing males of great character for the endless wars among Christian monarchs. His ancestors had come down from the mountains to settle in Extremadura. He grew up listening to his mother tell of the feats of the seven brothers of the Valle de Ibia, the Valdivias, who once engaged an awesome monster in bloody combat. According to this inspired señora, it was not an ordinary dragon—body of a lizard, wings of a bat, and two or three serpents' heads—like the one Saint George slayed. This was a beast ten times larger and more ferocious, an ancient of centuries, which embodied all the evil of the enemies of Spain, from Romans and Arabs to the fiendish French, who in recent times had dared dispute the rights of our sovereign.

"Imagine, son! Us speaking French!" the good woman always interposed in her tale.

One by one the brothers Valdivia fell, scorched by the flames the monster spewed from its gaping jaws, or mauled by its tiger claws. When six of the clan had perished and the battle was lost, the youngest of the brothers, the only one left standing, cut a heavy branch from a tree, sharpened it on both ends, and drove it into the beast's maws. The dragon began to thrash about, mad with pain, and its formidable tail split the earth, raising a cloud of dust that reached to Africa. Then the hero took his sword in both hands and drove it into the dragon's heart, thus liberating Spain.

Pedro was descended in a direct maternal line from that youth, valiant among valiants, and as proof had two trophies: the sword, which had remained in the family, and the coat of arms on which two serpents on a field of gold were biting a tree trunk. The family motto was A Death Less Feared Gives More Life. With such ancestors, it was only natural that Pedro answered the call to arms at an early age. His mother squandered what remained of her dowry to outfit him for the undertaking: coat of mail and complete armor, a caballero's weapons, a page, and two horses. The legendary sword of the Valdivias was a length of oxidized iron, heavy as a club, its only value decorative and historical, so she bought Pedro another of fine Toledo steel, flexible and light. With that sword, Pedro would fight in the armies of Spain under the banners of Carlos V; with it he would conquer the most remote kingdom in the New World; and with it, broken and bloody, he would die.

Young Pedro de Valdivia, brought up by a doting mother, among books, went off to war with the enthusiasm of one who has seen nothing more gory than hogs butchered in the plaza, a brutal spectacle that attracted the entire town. His innocence lasted about as long as the brand-new pennant bearing his family coat of arms, which was shredded in the first battle.

Among the tercios of Spain, Spain's legendary infantry regiments, was another daring hidalgo, Francisco de Aguirre, who immediately became Pedro's best friend. The former was as blustering and bellicose as the second was serious, although both were equally courageous. Francisco's family was Basque in origin, but they had settled in Talavera de la Reina, near Toledo. From his earliest years, the young man showed signs of a suicidal boldness. He sought danger because he felt he was protected by his mother's gold cross, which he wore around his neck. Hanging from the same thin chain he wore a reliquary containing a lock of chestnut hair belonging to the young beauty he had loved since childhood, a love that was forbidden because they were first cousins. Since he could not marry his true love, Francisco had sworn to remain celibate, but that did not keep him from enjoying the favors of any female within reach of his fiery temperament. Tall, handsome, with an easy laugh and a ringing tenor voice that enlivened taverns and enchanted women, there was no one who could resist him. Pedro always warned him to be cautious, because the French illness did not exempt Moors, Jews, or Christians, but Aguirre had faith in his mother's cross. If it had been an infallible protection in battle, surely it would shield him against the consequences of lust.

Aguirre, amiable and gallant in society, became an uncontrolled beast in battle, in contrast to Valdivia, who was always calm and chivalrous, even in the face of gravest danger. Both young men knew how to read and write; they had studied, and they were more cultivated than the majority of hidalgos. Pedro had received a very thorough education from a priest, his mother's uncle, with whom he had lived in his youth, and who, it was whispered, was Pedro's true father, though he had never had the courage to ask. It would have been an insult to his mother.

Another thing Aguirre and Valdivia had in common was that they had come into the world in the year 1500, the same year as Holy Roman Emperor Charles V, monarch of Spain, Germany, Austria, Flanders, the West Indies, part of Africa, and an ever greater part of the world. The young men were not superstitious, but they were proud to have been born under the same star as the king and, therefore, destined for similar military triumphs. They believed that there was no better proposition in this life than to be soldiers under such a gallant leader. They admired the king's Titanic stature, his indomitable courage, his skill as a horseman and swordsman, his talent as a strategist in war and a scholar in peace. Pedro and Francisco were grateful for their good fortune in being Catholics, which guaranteed the salvation of their souls, and Spanish, that is, superior to the rest of humankind. They were hidalgos of Spain, sovereign over all the wide and beckoning world, more powerful than the ancient Roman Empire, chosen by God to discover, conquer, Christianize, found, and populate the most remote corners of the earth. They were twenty years old when they went off to fight in Flanders, and then the campaigns in Italy, where they learned that in war cruelty is a virtue and, given that death is a constant companion, that it is best to keep one's soul in a state of grace.

The two young soldiers served under the command of an extraordinary general, the marqués de Pescara, whose somewhat effeminate appearance could be deceptive, since beneath the gold armor and the pearl-embroidered silk finery he wore on the field of battle was a rare military genius, his acumen demonstrated a thousand times over. In 1524, in the midst of the war between France and Spain, disputing control of the Italian cities, the mar- qués and two thousand of the best Spanish soldiers disappeared in a mysterious manner, swallowed up by the winter fog. Word spread that they had deserted, and mocking couplets were circu- lated accusing them of treason and cowardice, while they, hidden away in a castle, were, in fact, part of a plan that hinged on great stealth.

It was November, and the cold turned to ice the souls of the hapless soldiers quartered in the courtyard. They did not understand why they were spending time there, numb and anxious, instead of being led to fight against the French. The marqués de Pescara was in no hurry; he was waiting for the right moment with the patience of an experienced hunter. Finally, after several weeks had passed, he sent word to his officers to ready the troops for action. Pedro de Valdivia ordered the men in his battalion to don their armor over wool undergarments, a difficult task since when they touched the icy metal it stuck to their fingers, and then he handed out sheets to use as covering. So, like white ghosts, they had marched the whole night in silence, shivering with cold, and by dawn had reached the enemy fortress. Lookouts in the merlons noticed some kind of movement on the snow but thought it was shadows from trees bending in the wind. Until the last moment before the attack was launched, they had not seen the Spanish soldiers pulling themselves forward in white waves across the snow-covered ground. Taken by surprise, the French were overwhelmed. That striking victory made the marqués de Pescara the most famous military man of his time.

One year later, Valdivia and Aguirre were in the battle of Pavía, the beautiful city of a hundred towers; there, too, the French had been defeated. The king of France, who was fighting desperately alongside his troops, was taken prisoner by a soldier in Pedro de Valdivia's company. He had tumbled the monarch from his horse and, not knowing who he was, had nearly slit his throat, ignoring proper protocol. Valdivia's timely intervention prevented that slaughter, thus changing the course of history.

Ten thousand dead littered the field of combat; for weeks the air was swarming with flies and the land with rats. They say that still today you can find splintered bones between the leaves of the cabbages and cauliflowers of the region. Valdivia realized that for the first time it was not the cavalry that had been essential to their triumph but, rather, two new weapons: the harquebus, complicated to load but long in range, and the bronze cannon, lighter and more mobile than the old ones of forged iron. Another decisive element had been the thousands of mercenaries, Swiss, and German Landsknechts, famous for their brutality, which Valdivia disdained. For him, war, like everything else in life, was governed by honor. The battle of Pavía left him pondering the importance of strategy and modern arms. The demented courage of men like Francisco de Aguirre was no longer enough. War was a science that required study and logic.

After the battle of Pavía, exhausted and limping from a lance wound in his hip that had been treated with boiling oil but tended to open with the least movement, Pedro de Valdivia returned to his home in Castuera. He was of an age to marry, to carry on the family name and take charge of his lands, which were barren following his long absence and lack of attention—as his mother never tired of reminding him. Ideal would be a bride with a substantial dowry, since the Valdivias' impoverished estate greatly needed replenishing. The family and the priest had lined up a number of candidates—all with money and a good name—whom he would meet during his convalescence, but plans did not work out as expected. Instead, Pedro's eye fell on Marina Ortiz de Gaete in the one place he had opportunity to meet her in public: on the way out of mass. Marina was thirteen and still dressed in the starched crinolines of childhood. She was accompanied by her duenna and a slave girl who held a parasol over her mistress's head even though it was a cloudy day: a direct ray of sun had never touched the girl's translucent skin. She had the face of an angel, gleaming blond hair, the unsteady walk of someone burdened with too many petticoats, and such an air of innocence that on the spot Pedro forgot his intention of improving the family fortunes. He was not a man of base calculations; he was honestly seduced by the girl's beauty and virtue. She had no fortune, and her dowry was far below her worth, but he began to court her the minute he learned she was not promised to another.

The Ortiz de Gaete family had themselves hoped for a union with monetary advantages but they could not reject a caballero with such an illustrious name, and proven valor as Pedro de Valdivia. Their only condition was that the pair wait to marry until the girl turned fourteen. In the meantime, though shy as a fawn, Marina accepted the attentions of her betrothed, and she let him know that she, too, was counting the days till they were married. Pedro was at the apogee of his virility; he was tall, well proportioned, and broad chested, with noble features: a prominent nose, an authoritative chin, and very expressive blue eyes. At the time, he wore his hair combed back and caught into a short pigtail at the nape of his neck. He shaved his cheeks, waxed his mustache, and wore a narrow little beard that would characterize him throughout his life. He dressed with elegance, acted unambiguously, spoke deliberately, evoked respect and conveyed certainty, but he could also be gallant and tender. Marina wondered, with awe, why a man with such great pride and courage had chosen her. The next year, after the girl had begun to menstruate, they married and moved into the modest property belonging to the Valdivias.

Marina entered the married state with the best of intentions, but she was very young, and that man of serious and studious temperament frightened her. They had nothing to talk about. She was embarrassed and upset when he suggested books to read, not daring to confess that she could barely handle basic sentences and signed her name with a squiggle. Her family had protected her from contact with the world, and wanted her to stay that way; her husband's perorations on politics or geography intimidated her. Her interests were prayer and embroidering ceremonial vestments for priests. She had no experience in managing a household, and the servants ignored the orders she issued in her baby voice. As a result, her mother-in-law continued to run the house, while Marina was treated like the child she was. She set about learning the boring household tasks, coached by the older women in the family, but there was no one whom she could ask about the other aspect of married life, one more important than planning meals or keeping books.

As long as Marina's relations with Pedro had consisted of sweet epistles and visits overseen by a duenna, she had been happy, but her enthusiasm evaporated when she found herself in bed with her new husband. She was completely innocent about what was to happen on her first night as a bride; no one had prepared her for the horrible surprise that lay in store. In her trousseau she had seen several ankle-length batiste nightgowns that tied at the neck and wrists with satin ribbons and had a cross-shaped opening in the front. It had never occurred to her to ask what purpose that keyholelike aperture served, and no one had explained that it was through it that she would have contact with her husband's most intimate parts. She had never seen a naked man, and believed that the differences between men and women were facial hair and tone of voice. When in the dark she felt Pedro's breath on her face and his large hands groping among the folds of her gown for that exquisitely embroidered opening, she kicked at him like a mule, jumped out of bed, and ran screaming down the corridors of the stone house.

Though he meant well, Pedro was not a thoughtful lover. His experience was limited to brief encounters with women of negotiable virtue, but he realized that he was going to need great patience. His wife was still a child, and her body was barely beginning to develop; it was not a good idea to force her. He tried to initiate her gradually, but soon Marina's innocence, which had attracted him so strongly in the beginning, became an insurmountable obstacle. Nights were a frustration for him and a torment for her, yet neither of the two dared speak of their feelings in the light of day. Pedro turned to his studies, and to supervising his lands and his laborers, burning off energy in fencing and riding. In his heart he was preparing, and saying farewell. When the call of adventure became irresistible, he again enlisted under the standard of Charles V, with the secret dream of equaling the military glory of the marqués de Pescara.

In the late winter of 1527, the Spanish troops, under orders from Charles de Bourbon, constable of France, were at the walls of Rome. The Spanish, backed by fifteen companies of ferocious German mercenaries, were awaiting their opportunity to enter the city of the Caesars and make up for many months without pay. They were a horde of hungry, insubordinate soldiers ready to lay claim to the treasures of Rome and the Vatican. They were not all rogues and soldiers for pay, however. Among the tercios of Spain, for example, were a pair of officers, Pedro de Valdivia and Francisco de Aguirre, who had met again after two years of separation. They embraced like brothers and caught up on everything that had happened in each other's lives. Valdivia showed his friend a medallion with a portrait of Marina painted by a Portuguese miniaturist, a converted Jew who had somehow escaped the Inquisition.

"We do not have children yet. Marina is very young, but there will be time for all that, if God wills it," he commented.

"What you mean is, if we aren't killed first!" his friend exclaimed.

Francisco, in turn, confessed that nothing had changed in his secret Platonic love affair with his cousin, who had threatened to enter a nunnery if her father insisted on marrying her to another man. It was Valdivia's opinion that that would not be such an outlandish idea. To many noblewomen the convent, where they could live with their full complement of servants, their own money, and all the luxuries they were accustomed to, was preferable to a forced marriage.

"In the case of my cousin, that would be a terrible waste, my friend," Francisco said emphatically. "A girl so beautiful and bursting with health, a woman created for love and motherhood, should not bury herself in a habit for life. But you are right about one thing. I would rather see her a nun than married to another man. I could not allow it; we would have to end our lives together."

"And condemn you both to the cauldrons of hell? I feel sure your cousin would choose the convent. And you? What plans do you have for the future?" Valdivia asked.

"I want to keep on soldiering as long as I can, and visit my cousin in her convent cell under cover of night," laughed Francisco, touching the cross and reliquary on his chest.

Rome was badly defended by Pope Clement VII, a man more adept at political intrigue than at strategies of war. Just as the enemy hosts approached the city gates in the midst of a dense fog, the pontiff escaped from the Vatican through a secret passageway to the Sant'Angelo castle, bristling with cannon. He was accompanied by three thousand persons, among whom was the famous sculptor and goldsmith Benvenuto Cellini, known both for his art and for his horrendous disposition, the man to whom the pope had delegated all military decisions. Clement had decided that if he himself trembled before this imperious artist, surely de Bourbon's armies would tremble as well.

During the first assault on Rome, Charles de Bourbon received a fatal musket shot in one eye. Benvenuto Cellini would later boast that he had personally fired the ball that killed him, though in reality he was nowhere near. But who would dare contradict him? Before the captains were able to impose order, the out-of-control troops pounded the defenseless city with iron and gunpowder, taking it within a matter of hours. During the first week, the massacre was so brutal that blood ran through the streets and puddled among the millenary stones. More than forty-five thousand fled the city, and the remainder of the terrorized population were condemned to a living hell. The voracious invaders burned churches, convents, hospitals, palaces, and homes. They killed right and left, madmen and hospital patients and domestic animals; they tortured men to force them to hand over everything they had hidden; they raped every woman and girl they could find; they murdered everyone from nursing babes to the aged and infirm. The looting, an interminable orgy, continued for weeks. Soldiers drunk from blood and alcohol dragged destroyed works of art and religious reliquaries through the streets, decapitated humans and statues alike, stole anything they could stuff into their pouches, and ground the rest to rubble. The famous frescos in the Sistine Chapel were saved because that was where Charles de Bourbon lay in state. Thousands of cadavers floated down the Tiber River, and the odor of decomposing flesh fouled the air. Dogs and crows devoured the corpses strewn throughout the city. Then came the faithful companions of war: hunger and plague, which attacked both ill-fated Romans and their victimizers.

During those apocalyptic days, Pedro de Valdivia went through the streets of Rome with sword in hand, furious, vainly attempting to stop the pillaging and killing and to impose some shred of order among the troops, but the fifteen thousand mercenaries recognized neither superior nor law, and were ready to kill anyone who stood in their way. By chance, Valdivia found himself at the gates of a convent just as it was attacked by a dozen German mercenaries. The nuns knew that no woman escaped being raped, and they had gathered around a cross in the patio and formed a circle around the young novitiates, who stood as frozen as statues, holding one another's hands, heads low, murmuring a prayer. From a distance, they resembled doves. They were asking God to save them from being stained, and to take pity on them by sending them a speedy death.

"Stand back! Anyone who dares cross this threshold will have to deal with me!" roared Pedro de Valdivia, brandishing his sword in his right hand and a short saber in his left.

Several of the Germans stopped out of surprise, calculating that the prize was not worth having to confront this imposing and determined Spanish officer, and that it might be more sensible to go to the next building, but there were others who rushed to the attack. Valdivia had in his favor that he was the only sober one among them, and with four well-aimed thrusts he incapacitated four Germans, but by then other men in the group had recovered from their initial befuddlement and they, too, were upon him. Even with their minds clouded with alcohol, the Landsknechts were as formidable as Valdivia, and soon they had surrounded him. That might have been the last day of the young Extremaduran's life had not Francisco de Aguirre happened by.

"Try *me*, you Teuton whoresons!" the enormous Basque shouted, red with rage and swinging his sword like a club.

The uproar attracted the attention of other Spaniards passing by, and when they saw their compatriots in grave danger, in less time than it takes me to tell it, a great free-for-all ensued. A half hour later the attackers fell back, leaving several of their own bleeding in the street, and allowing the Spanish officers to bolt the convent doors. The Mother Superior asked the nuns of stronger character to collect the ones who had fainted, and they all placed themselves under the orders of Francisco de Aguirre, who had offered to organize the defense by fortifying the walls.

"No one is safe in Rome. For the moment, the mercenaries have withdrawn, but I have no doubt that they will return, and when that happens it will be best for them to find you prepared," Aguirre advised them.

"I will round up some harquebuses," Valdivia said, "and Francisco will teach you to fire them." He had not missed the impish gleam in his friend's eyes when he imagined himself alone with a score of virgin novitiates and a handful of mature, but grateful, and still attractive, nuns.

Two months later, the horrible sacking of Rome was ended, bringing papal rule to a close. The carnage and destruction would go down in history as a shameful stain on the life of our emperor, Charles V, even though he was far away from the scene of the horror.

His holiness the pope was allowed to leave his refuge in Sant'Angelo castle, but he was arrested, and received the same treatment as a common prisoner. His pontifical ring was taken from him, and soldiers guffawed as he was given a kick in the seat that drove him to his knees.

Benvenuto Cellini could be accused of many things, but he was not one to forget a favor, which is why when the Mother Superior of the convent visited him to tell how a young Spanish officer had saved her congregation and had stayed on for weeks in the building to defend them, the renowned artist had wanted to meet him. Hours later, the nun accompanied Francisco de Aguirre to the palace. Cellini received him in one of the salons in the Vatican, amid piles of debris and furniture gutted by the marauding mercenaries. The two men exchanged brief, courteous greetings.

Then Cellini, who never beat about the bush, asked point blank, "What would you like, signor, in exchange for your courageous intervention?"

Red with anger, Aguirre instinctively put his hand to the grip of his sword. "You insult me, señor!" he exclaimed.

The Mother Superior stepped between them with all the weight of her authority, and separated them with a contemptuous gesture. This was no time for posturing. She was a member of the family of the Genoese condottiere Andrea Doria; the Mother Superior was a woman of fortune and breeding, accustomed to command.

"Enough! I beg you to forgive this unintentional offense, Don

Francisco. We are living in bad times; blood has flowed and terrible sins have been committed; it is not strange that good manners have been relegated to a secondary importance. Signor Cellini knows that you did not defend our convent out of any thought of reward but, rather, because you have a righteous heart. The last thing he wishes is to insult you. We would consider it a privilege if you would accept a sign of our appreciation and gratitude."

The Mother Superior gestured to the sculptor to stand back, took Aguirre by his sleeve, and led him to the far end of the salon. Cellini could hear them whispering for a long time. When his limited patience was wearing thin, they returned, and the Mother Superior presented the request as the young officer, with his eyes on the tips of his boots, sweated.

And that is why Benvenuto Cellini obtained authorization from Pope Clement VII—before he was sent into exile—for Francisco de Aguirre to marry his first cousin. The stunned young Basque ran to his friend Pedro de Valdivia to tell him the news. His eyes were moist and his giant's voice was trembling; he could not believe such a miracle.

"I am not sure that this is such great news, Francisco," Valdivia protested. "You collect conquests the way our holy emperor collects clocks. I cannot imagine you as a husband."

"My cousin is the only woman I have ever loved! The others are faceless creatures who exist only for a moment, and only to satisfy the appetite the Devil placed in me."

"The Devil is responsible for many different appetites in all of us, but God gives us the moral fiber to control them. That is what makes us different from animals."

"You've been a soldier all these years, Pedro, and you still believe we are different from animals," Aguirre joked.

"I have no doubt at all. Man's destiny is to rise above the beasts, to lead his life according to noble ideals, and save his soul."

"You frighten me, Pedro. You talk like a priest. If I did not know you for the man you are, I would think that you lack the primordial instinct that drives all males."

"I have no shortage of that instinct, I assure you, but I do not allow it to determine my behavior."

"I am not as noble as you, but I am redeemed by the chaste and pure love I feel for my cousin."

"I would say you have a small problem there, which is that you are going to marry the woman you have idealized. How will you reconcile that love with your 'primordial instincts'?" A sly smile crossed Valdivia's lips.

"That will not be a problem, Pedro. I will shower my cousin with kisses and lower her from her saintly altar, then make love to her with consuming passion," Aguirre replied, rolling with laughter.

"And faithfulness?"

"She will be the faithful one in our marriage, but I will not be able to renounce women, just as I cannot give up wine or the sword."

Francisco de Aguirre hastened to Spain to marry before the indecisive pontiff could change his mind. He must have somehow reconciled his Platonic feelings for his cousin and his unquenchable sensuality, and she must have responded without a trace of timidity, because the ardor of that couple came to be legendary. They say that neighbors gathered in the street before their house to wonder at the raucous sounds of revelry, and to make bets about the number of amorous assaults there would be that night.

After a long period of war, blood, gunpowder, and mud, Pedro de Valdivia, too, returned to his native land, preceded by word of his military campaigns. He brought with him hard-earned experience and a pouchful of gold, which he intended to use to restore his depleted patrimony. Marina was waiting for him, transformed into a woman; she had left her childish ways behind. She was sixteen, and her ethereal and serene beauty invited comparison with a work of art. She went about with the distracted air of a sleepwalker, as if she had foreseen that her life was to be an eternal waiting. On the first night they were together, the couple repeated the actions

and silences of old. In the darkness of their bedchamber, their bodies were joined, but joylessly: he feared he would frighten her and
she feared she would sin; he wanted to make her love him and she
wanted the night to end.

During the day they assumed their assigned roles; they inhabited
the same space but never touched. Marina treated her husband with
an eager and solicitous affection that annoyed more than flattered
him. He did not need such attentions, he needed a little passion,
but he did not dare tell her that because he supposed that passion
was not a proper emotion for a decent and religious woman. He
felt as if Marina were watching him, and as if he were a prisoner in
the invisible bonds of an emotion he did not know how to return.
He was repelled by her beseeching gaze as she followed him around
the house, by her unvoiced sadness when she said good-bye, by her
expression of veiled reproach when she welcomed him home after
a brief absence. He felt that he could not touch Marina, that he
could enjoy being with her only by observing her from a distance
as she embroidered, absorbed in her thoughts and prayers, and in
the golden light from the window resembling one of the saints in
the cathedral.

Their encounters behind the heavy, dusty hangings on their
conjugal bed, which had served three generations of Valdivias,
lost their attraction for Pedro. Marina refused to substitute a less
intimidating garment for the gown with the cross-shaped opening.
Pedro suggested that she talk with other women, but Marina was
unable to discuss such matters with anyone. After every embrace
she knelt for hours, praying, on the stone floor of that large, drafty
house, motionless, humiliated, suffering because she did not satisfy
her husband. Secretly, however, she took pleasure in the suffering
that distinguished her from ordinary women and brought her closer
to saintliness. Pedro had explained that lust cannot be a sin between
husband and wife, since the purpose of copulation was to conceive
children, but Marina could not help it that she turned to ice when
he touched her. Her confessor had been too busy filling her head
with the fear of hell and shame about her body. In all the years

Pedro had known her, he had seen nothing more than her face, her hands, and, once in a while, her feet. He was tempted to tear off the accursed nightgown, rip it to shreds, but he was stopped by the terror in his wife's eyes when he turned toward her, a terror that contrasted with the tenderness of her gaze during the day, when both were clothed. Marina did not take any initiative in making love, or in any other part of their life together. She never changed expression or mood; she was a quiet sheep. Her submission irritated Pedro, despite his belief that docility was a female virtue. He did not even understand his own feelings. When he had married her, and she was still a girl, he had wanted to keep her in the state of innocence and purity that had first seduced him, and now all he wanted was for her to rebel and defy him.

Valdivia had very quickly risen to the rank of captain because of his exceptional courage and his ability to command but, despite his brilliant career, he was not proud of his past. After the sacking of Rome, he had been tormented by recurrent nightmares in which a young mother embracing her children was preparing to leap from a bridge into a river of blood. He had witnessed the extent of human degradation and the dark depths of the soul. He had learned that men exposed to the brutality of war are capable of terrible acts, and he felt that he was no different from the rest. He went to confession, of course, and the priest always absolved him, giving him a minimal penance. Faults committed in the name of Spain and the church were not sins. Hadn't he been following his superiors' orders? Did the enemy not deserve the worst? *Ego te absolvo ab omnibus censuris, et peccatis, in nomine Patri, et Filii, et Spiritis Sanctis, amen.*

For anyone who has tasted the excitement of killing, there is no escape or absolution, Pedro thought. He had acquired a taste for violence. That was every soldier's secret vice, otherwise it would be impossible to wage war. The crude camaraderie of the barracks, the chorus of visceral roars the men uttered as they rushed into battle, the shared indifference to pain and fear, made him feel alive. The savage thrill of running a man through with his sword, the satanic power of cutting short another's life, the fascination of gushing

blood were very powerful addictions. One began killing as a duty
and ended up using violence as a way to satisfy one's penchant for
cruelty. Nothing could compare to it. Once unleashed, the instinct
to kill was stronger than the instinct to live, even in Pedro, who
feared God and prided himself on being able to control his appetites. Eating, fornicating, killing—that was what life was all about,
according to his friend Francisco de Aguirre. The only way to save
his soul was to avoid the temptation of the sword. On his knees
before the main altar of the cathedral, he swore to dedicate the rest
of his life to doing good, to serve the Church and Spain, not to
indulge his hungers, and to rule his life by strict moral principles.
He had been on the verge of dying more than once, and God had
allowed him to live in order that he might expiate his sins. He
hung his Toledo sword beside the ancient sword of his ancestor,
and prepared to live a quiet life.

The captain became a peaceful citizen, concerned with everyday
matters: his cattle and harvest, droughts and freezes, the intrigues
and jealousies of the townsfolk, and masses and more masses. As he
was interested in law, people consulted him about legal matters, and
even judicial authorities sought his counsel. His greatest pleasure
was books, especially chronicles of journeys, and maps, which he
scrutinized in detail. He had memorized the poem of the Cid, and
he had drawn pleasure from the fantasy chronicles of Solino and
the imaginary voyages of John Mandeville, but his true passion lay
in the stories published in Spain about the New World. The feats
of Columbus, Magellan, Vespucci, Cortés, and many others kept
him awake at night, staring at the brocade canopy over his bed,
dreaming while awake. Oh, to explore the far corners of the planet,
conquer them, found cities, carry the cross to barbaric countries for
the glory of God, and to engrave his name with fire and steel in the
annals of history. In the meantime, his wife embroidered chasubles
with gold thread and prayed rosary after rosary in a never-ending
litany. Even though Pedro ventured several times a week through
the humiliating opening in Marina's nightgown, the desired children
did not appear. And so the slow and tedious years went by in the

stupor of burning summer and in the sheltering by the fire of winter. Extreme harshness, Extremadura.

Several years later, when Pedro de Valdivia had resigned himself to growing old with his wife in the silent house in Castuera and never knowing glory, a traveler stopped by one day to deliver a letter from Francisco de Aguirre. The stranger's name was Jerónimo de Alderete, and he was a native of Olmedo. His agreeable face was framed by a thatch of honey-colored curls, the pomaded tips of his Turkish mustache turned upward, and he had the burning eyes of a dreamer. Valdivia received him with the hospitality that is the obligation of every good Spaniard, and offered him the welcome of his house, which had no luxuries but was safer and more comfortable than the inns. It was winter, and Marina had ordered a fire in the fireplace of the main room, though the flames did not mitigate either the drafts or the shadows. In that Spartan room, nearly empty of furniture and adornments, the couple passed their lives; it was there he read and she worked at her embroidery, there they ate, and there, before the altar set against the wall, they prayed on two prie-dieus. Marina served sausage, cheese, and bread, and the harsh wine of the house, then retired to a corner to sew by the light of a candelabrum as the men talked.

Jerónimo de Alderete was traveling around Spain recruiting volunteers to take to the Indies, and to tempt them he would exhibit in the taverns and plazas a necklace of heavy gold beads strung on fine silver. The letter Francisco de Aguirre had sent his friend Pedro was about the New World. Ebullient, Alderete told his host about the breathtaking possibilities of that continent that by now were common knowledge. He said that there was no longer any room for noble endeavors in a corrupt and war-weary Europe torn by political conspiracies, court intrigue, and heretical doctrines like those of the Lutherans, who were dividing Christianity. The future lay on the other side of the ocean, he assured Pedro. There was work to be done in the Americas—a name given those lands by a German cartographer in honor of Amerigo Vespucci, a swaggering sailor from Florence who had not been the one to discover them. That honor belonged to Columbus, known to the Spanish as Cristóbal Colón. According to Alderete, the new lands should have been called the Cristobals, or the Colonias. Ah well, what was done was done, and that was not the point, he added. What was most needed in the New World were hidalgos of indomitable heart, with a sword in one hand and the cross in the other, eager to discover and conquer.

It was impossible to describe the vast space of those places, the endless green of the jungles, the numbers of crystalline rivers, the depths of the lakes of calm waters, the opulence of the gold and silver mines. There a man could dream, not so much of treasure as of glory, he said; he could live a full life, combat savages, fulfill a higher destiny, and, with God's favor, found a dynasty. That and more was possible on the new frontiers of that empire, where there were birds with jewel-like feathers and naked, complaisant women the color of honey—"Begging your pardon, Doña Marina, that is merely a manner of speaking." There were not enough words in the Spanish tongue to describe the bounty of those lands: pearls as big as partridge eggs, gold that fell from the trees, and so much land, and Indians to work it, that any ordinary soldier could become the master of a king-granted hacienda the size of a Spanish province. Most important of all, he added, were all the peoples awaiting the word of the One True God and the gifts of our Spanish civilization. He added that Francisco de Aguirre, the friend they had in common, definitely wanted to go. In fact, his thirst for adventure was so great that he was prepared to leave his beloved wife and the five children she had given him in that same number of years.

"And do you believe there are still opportunities in that Terra Nova for men like us? It has been forty-three years since Colón landed, and twenty-six since Cortés conquered Mexico," Valdivia pointed out.

"And also twenty-six since Magellan set out to navigate the globe, Pedro. As you see, the earth is growing larger, the opportunities are infinite. It is not only the New World that is open to exploration, there is Africa as well, and India and the Philippine Islands, and much, much more," young Alderete insisted.

He repeated what was being talked about in every corner of Spain: the conquest of Peru and the extravagant treasures to be found there. A few years before, two soldiers no one had ever heard of, Francisco Pizarro and Diego de Almagro, had joined in the adventure of pushing forward to Peru. Defying Homeric perils on land and sea, they had made two voyages, starting from Panama and advancing along the ragged coastline of the Pacific, with no maps, feeling their way, heading south, always south. They were guided by rumors from Indians of several tribes who told of a place where cooking utensils and tools were crusted with emeralds, where the streams ran with liquid silver, and where beetles and tree leaves were living gold. Since they had no accurate idea of where they were, they had to anchor and leave their ships to explore land never before trod by a European. Many Spaniards died along the way, and others survived by eating snakes and insects.

On the third voyage, which Diego de Almagro did not participate in because he was recruiting soldiers and raising funds for another ship, Pizarro and his men finally reached the territory of the Incas. Walking dead, fatigued and sweating, wanderers strayed from sea and sky, the Spaniards debarked from their battered ships to find themselves in a benign land of fertile valleys and majestic mountains, very different from the noxious jungles farther north. They were sixty-two ragged, filthy cavalry and one hundred and six exhausted foot soldiers. They set out cautiously, clad in their heavy armor, cross in the lead, harquebuses loaded, and swords bared. They were met by a wood-colored people who dressed in colorful woven garments and spoke a language of sweet vowels. They were frightened because they had never seen anything like those bearded beings that were half man and half beast. The surprise must have been equally great on both sides, since the Spaniards had not expected to find a civilized people. They were astounded by the works of architecture and engineering, the textiles and jewels.

The Inca Atahualpa, the sovereign of that empire, along with thousands of his court, was at the time enjoying the curative waters of some hot springs, camped in a luxury comparable to that of Suleiman the Magnificent. One of Pizarro's captains went there to invite him to meet with the Spanish adventurers. The Inca, surrounded by his retinue, received him in a white tent decorated with flowers and fruit trees planted in pots of precious metals set amid the warm-water pools in which hundreds of princesses and swarms of children splashed and played. The Inca was hidden by a curtain, following the tradition that no one could look upon his face, but curiosity overcame protocol, and Atahualpa had the curtain removed so that he could observe the bearded stranger more closely.

The captain found himself facing a still-young monarch with agreeable features, seated on a throne of pure gold beneath a canopy of parrot feathers. Despite the strange circumstances, a flicker of mutual liking sparked between the Spanish soldier and the noble Quechua. Atahualpa offered the small group of visitors a banquet served on vessels of silver and gold inset with amethysts and emeralds. The Spaniard conveyed Pizarro's invitation to the Inca, secretly distressed, knowing that he would be leading the Inca ruler into a trap, the usual ruse of conquistadors. Within only hours he had come to respect the Incas, who were more civilized than many peoples in Europe. Amazed, he learned that they had an advanced knowledge of astronomy and had devised a solar calendar, that they had taken a census of the millions of inhabitants of their extensive empire, and that they commanded an efficiently run social and military organization. There were, however, strange omissions: they did not have a system of writing, their weapons were primitive, they did not use the wheel, and they did not have animals for riding or for labor—only a few delicate sheep with long legs and the eyes of a bride, which they called llamas. They worshipped the Sun, which demanded human sacrifices only during times of tragedies, such as an illness of the Inca or a defeat in war, when it became necessary to placate their god with offerings of virgins or children. Deceived by false promises of friendship, the Inca and his large court traveled without weapons to the city of Cajamarca, where Pizarro had set up the ambush. The Inca traveled in a gold palanquin carried on a platform by his ministers, and followed by his seraglio of beautiful maidens. After the Spanish killed the courtiers who had tried to protect him with their bodies, Atahualpa was taken prisoner.

"Peru's treasures are all anyone is talking about. It has spread like a fever, and infected half of Spain. Is it true what they say?" Valdivia asked.

"It is true, even though it sounds incredible. In exchange for his freedom, the Inca offered Pizarro all the gold that could be contained in a room twenty-two feet long, seventeen feet wide, and nine feet high."

"That's an impossible sum!"

"It is the highest ransom in history. It was paid in jewels, statues, and vessels, but it was melted down and turned into bars marked with the royal seal. And it was all for nothing that Atahualpa's subjects, like diligent ants, brought that fortune from every corner of the empire, because after Pizarro had kept the Inca a prisoner for nine months, he condemned him to be burned alive anyway. At the last hour, in exchange for the Inca's agreeing to be baptized, Atahualpa had his sentence commuted to a less horrible death: the infamous garrote," Alderete explained. He added that Pizarro believed he had good reason for what he did, since supposedly the captive had instigated an uprising from his cell. According to Pizarro's spies, there were two hundred thousand Quechuas on the way from Quito, along with thirty thousand Caribs—who were known to eat human flesh—all of them intending to engage the conquistadors at Cajamarca, but the Inca's death forced them to change their plan. Later it was learned that such an enormous army of insurgents had never existed.

"Whatever the case, Jerónimo, it is difficult to explain how a handful of Spaniards were able to defeat the advanced civilization you describe. And take control of a territory larger than Europe," said Pedro de Valdivia.

"It was a vast empire, but it was fragile and young. When Pizarro arrived, it had existed only a century. Furthermore, the Incas were real voluptuaries; they did not have a chance against our courage, our weapons, and our horses."

"I suppose that Pizarro aligned himself with the Inca's enemies, the way Hernán Cortés did in Mexico."

"He did. Atahualpa and his brother Huáscar were waging a fratricidal war, and first Pizarro, and then Almagro, who arrived in Peru a little later, took advantage of that to defeat them both."

Alderete explained that not a leaf stirred in the Inca empire that the authorities did not learn about; the ordinary Indians were all slaves. The Inca used part of the tribute paid him by his subjects to feed and protect orphans, widows, the ancient, and the ill, and also put part aside for bad times. In spite of these advanced social laws, which did not exist in Spain, the people detested the sovereign and his privileged court because they lived only to serve the military and religious castes, the orejones. According to Alderete, it didn't matter to the people whether they were dominated by Incas or Spaniards, and that is why they didn't offer much resistance to the invaders. In any case, Atahualpa's death gave the victory to Pizarro. When the head was cut off the body of the empire, the empire collapsed.

"Those two men, Pizarro and Almagro, bastards both of them, with neither education nor fortune, are a perfect example of what can be achieved in the New World, Pedro. They are not just wealthy beyond imagination, they have also had honors and titles heaped on their heads by our emperor."

"You hear only about their fame and their wealth, only about the ventures that succeeded: gold, pearls, emeralds, lands, and subjected Indians. No one ever mentions the dangers," Valdivia argued.

"You are right about that; there is no end to the dangers. It takes men of great character to conquer those virgin soils."

Valdivia blushed. Did Alderete have doubts about his character? But immediately he reasoned that if that were the case, the man was within his rights, since he himself had wondered. It had been a long while since he had put his courage to the test. The world was moving ahead with giant steps. It was his fate to have been born into a splendid age in which the mysteries of the universe were at last being revealed: not only was the earth round, there were those who suggested that it circled the sun and not the reverse. And what was he doing while all this was happening? He was counting sheep and goats, harvesting cork and olives. Once again Valdivia was aware of how bored he was. He was tired of tending cattle and tilling fields, of playing cards with his neighbors, of masses and rosaries, of reading the same books over and over—nearly all of them banned by the Inquisition—and of several years of obligatory, sterile embraces with his wife. Here before him stood destiny, embodied in that enthusiastic young man, come once more to knock at his door, as it had in the times of Lombardy, Flanders, Pavía, Milan, and Rome.

"When are you leaving for the Americas, Jerónimo?"

"This year, if God wills it."

"You can count on me," said Pedro de Valdivia in a whisper, so Marina wouldn't hear. His eyes were on the Toledo sword hanging above the fireplace.

In 1537 I said my good-byes to my family, whom I would never see again, and traveled with my niece Constanza to the beautiful city of Seville, perfumed with orange blossoms and jasmine, and from there down the clear waters of the Guadalquivir to the bustling port of Cadiz, with its narrow cobbled streets and Moorish cupolas. We set sail on Maestro Manuel Martín's ship, a three-master with a tonnage of two hundred and forty, slow and heavy but steady in the water. A line of men loaded on the cargo: barrels of water, beer, wine, and oil; sacks of flour and dried meat, live fowl, a cow, and two pigs to be eaten on the voyage, in addition to several horses, which were worth their weight in gold in the New World. I watched while my carefully tied bundles were delivered to the space Maestro Martín had assigned me.

The first thing I did as my niece and I settled into our small cabin was to set up an altar to Nuestra Señora del Socorro, the Lady of Perpetual Succor.

"You are very courageous to undertake this voyage, Señora Inés. Where will your husband be waiting?" Manuel Martín asked.

"In truth, I do not know, Maestro."

"What! He will not be waiting in Nueva Granada?"

"The last letter he sent came from a place they call Coro, in Venezuela, but that was some while ago, and it may be that he is no longer there."

"The Americas are a territory larger than all the rest of the known world. It will not be easy to find your husband."

"Then I shall look until I find him."

"And how will you do that, señora?"

"The usual way, by asking."

"Then I wish you luck. This is the first time I have carried women. I beseech you, you and your niece, to be prudent," the maestro added.

"What do you mean by that?"

"You are both young, and not at all bad looking. You must know what I am referring to. After a week at sea, the men begin to long for female companionship, and as you two are right here onboard, the temptation will be very strong. And another thing. Sailors believe that women aboard ship attract storms and other misfortunes. For your well-being, and my peace of mind, I would prefer that you and your niece have no dealings with my men."

The maestro was a stocky Galician with broad shoulders and short legs, a prominent nose, little rodent eyes, and skin weathered like saddle leather by the salt and wind of his years at sea. He had signed on as a cabin boy when he was thirteen, and could count on the fingers of one hand the years that he had spent on terra firma. His rough appearance contrasted with the gentleness of his manners and the goodness of his heart, which would be evident later when he came to my aid at a moment of great need.

It is a shame that I did not yet know how to write, otherwise I would have begun to take notes. Although I did not suspect that my life would be worth telling about, that voyage should have been noted down in detail, since so few people have crossed the salty ocean expanse: lead-colored water teeming with secret life, never-ending, terrifying, all foam, wind, and solitude. In this relation, written many years after the events it describes, I hope to be as meticulous as possible, but memory is always capricious, the fruit of all one has lived, desired, and fantasized. The line that divides reality from imagination is very thin, and at my age is no longer interesting, for now everything is subjective. Memory is also colored by vanity. Even with Death sitting in a chair near my table, waiting, I still am influenced by vanity, not just when I rouge my cheeks if visitors are coming, but when I am writing my story. Is there anything more vain than an autobiography?

I had never seen the ocean, and had thought of it as a very wide river, never imagining that I would not be able to see the other shore. I refrained from making comments, in order not to give evidence of my ignorance, and I hid the fear that froze my bones when the ship sailed into open waters and began to pitch and heave. There were seven of us passengers, and all of them, except for Constanza, who had a very strong stomach, were almost immediately seasick. So great was my misery that on the second day I begged Maestro Martín to allow me to take a boat and row back to Spain. He burst out laughing and forced a pint of rum down my throat, which had the virtue of transporting me to another world for thirty hours, at the end of which I revived, sunken cheeked and green. It was only then that I could sip the broth my sweet niece spooned into my mouth.

We had left terra firma behind, and were sailing through dark waters beneath an infinite sky, without shelter of any sort. I could not imagine how the pilot could know where he was in that never-changing vastness, with nothing to guide him but his astrolabe and the stars in the firmament. He assured me that I could rest easy, for he had made the voyage many times and the route was well known to Spaniards and Portuguese, who had been following it for decades. Navigation charts were no longer as closely guarded as they once had been; even the damned English had them now. He made it clear that it was a different matter when it came to charts of the Strait of Magellan, or the Pacific coast. Pilots guarded those with their lives; they were more valuable than any New World treasure.

I never grew used to the motion of the waves, the creaking wood, the grating iron, the incessant flapping of wind-whipped sails. By day I was tormented by the crowded conditions and, especially, the way the men stared at me with the eyes of dogs in heat. I had to fight for my turn to place our olla on the cookstove, as well as for privacy to use the latrine, a large box outfitted with a hole and suspended over the ocean. Constanza, in contrast, never complained, and even seemed content. After a month at sea, supplies began to grow scarce, and water, by now fouled, was rationed. Because the men stole the eggs, I moved the cage with my hens to our cabin, and took them outside twice a day with a string around their legs, like lapdogs being taken for a stroll.

On one occasion I had to use my frying pan to defend myself from a sailor more brash than the others, a certain Sebastián Romero, whose name I have never forgotten because I know we will meet again in purgatory. In the close quarters of the ship, this man seized the slightest excuse to fall against me, blaming it on the waves. I warned him again and again to leave me alone, but that merely excited him further. One night he found me alone in the small area beneath the bridge that served as a kitchen. Before he could get his hands on me, I felt his fetid breath on the nape of my neck and, without thinking twice, I half-turned and thumped him on the head with the frying pan, exactly as I had years ago to poor Juan de Málaga when he threatened to strike me. Sebastián Romero had a softer skull than Juan, and fell sprawling to the deck, where he lay for several minutes as if asleep, while I searched for rags to bandage his head. He did not lose as much blood as one might have expected, though later his face did swell and turn the color of an eggplant. I helped him to his feet, and since neither of us was eager to spread the truth about his injury, we agreed to say that he had banged his head against a beam.

Among the passengers on the ship was a chronicler and sketch artist, one Daniel Belalcázar, who had been sent by the Crown with the assignment of drawing maps and recording his observations. Belalcázar was a man of about thirty-five, slim and strong, with the angular face and dark skin of an Andalucian. He would trot from bow to stern and back again for hours, exercising. He combed his hair back into a short braid and wore a gold earring in his left ear. The one time that a member of the crew made some remark about him, he punched the man in the nose and no one bothered him again.

Belalcázar, who had begun his voyaging as a young man, and who knew the remote coasts of Africa and Asia, told us how on one occasion he was taken prisoner by Barbarrosa, the feared Turkish pirate, and sold as a slave in Algiers, from which he had escaped after two years of great suffering. He always carried a thick notebook wrapped in waxed cloth, in which he wrote his thoughts in little letters that tracked across the page like ants. He entertained himself in sketching the sailors performing their duties, and devoted a great deal of time to drawing my niece. In preparation for life in the convent, Constanza dressed like a novice, wearing a heavy cloth habit she had sewn herself. A triangle of the same cloth, tied beneath the chin, covered half her forehead and all her hair. This horrendous garb, however, was not able to hide her proud carriage or her splendid eyes, black and shiny as olives. Belalcázar first got her to pose for him, then he convinced her to take the scarf off her head, and finally, she agreed to undo her old woman's bun and allow the breeze to toss her black curls. No matter what the documents with official seals say about our family's purity of blood, I suspect that a good dose of Saracen blood runs through our veins. Constanza, liberated from her habit, resembled one of those odalisques on Ottoman tapestries.

A day came when we all felt the gnawing of hunger. That was when I remembered my empanadas, and convinced the cook, a black man from the north of Africa whose face was embroidered with scars, to provide me with flour, lard, and a little dried meat, which I set to soak in saltwater before cooking it. From my own reserves, I took olives, raisins, cooked eggs—minced so that they would go farther—and cumin, an inexpensive spice that adds a particular flavor to a dish. I would have given anything for some onions, the kind that are so plentiful in Plasencia, but there were none left in the ship's stores. I cooked the filling, kneaded the dough, and since there was no oven, prepared fried empanadas. They were a great success, and after that day everyone contributed some part of their provisions for the filling. I made empanadas with lentils, garbanzos, fish, chicken, sausage, cheese, octopus, and shark, and with them earned the gratitude of the crew and the passengers. I earned their respect when, after a storm, I cauterized wounds and set the broken bones of two of the sailors, as I had learned to do in the nuns' hospital in Plasencia.

That was the only event worthy of mention, aside from having escaped from French corsairs lying in wait for Spanish ships. Had they caught up with us, Maestro Manuel Martín explained, we would have met a terrible end, for they were very well armed. When we learned that danger was closing in on us, my niece and I knelt before the image of Nuestra Señora del Socorro and fervently pled for our salvation, and she sent us the miracle of a fog so thick that the French lost sight of us. Daniel Belalcázar said that the fog was already there before we began to pray; the helmsman had only to set a course toward it.

This Belalcázar was a man of little faith, but very entertaining. In the evenings he would delight us with tales of his voyages, and of the things we would see in the New World. "No cyclops, no giants, no men with four arms and the head of a dog, but you most certainly will meet evil-spirited primitives—especially among the Spaniards," he joked. He assured us that the inhabitants of the New World were not all savages: Aztecs, Mayas, and Incas were more refined than we, he said; at least they bathed and did not go around crawling with lice.

"Greed," he said. "Pure and simple greed. The day we stepped onto the soil of the New World, it meant the end of those cultures. At first they welcomed us. Their curiosity was stronger than their caution, and when they saw that those strange bearded creatures from the sea liked gold, the soft, impractical metal they had such quantities of, they handed it out with both hands. However, our insatiable appetite and brutal pride soon became offensive to them. And why not! Our soldiers abuse their women, they go into their homes and take whatever they want without asking permission, and if anyone dares get in their way, they dispatch him with one thrust of the sword. They proclaim that the land they've so recently come to belongs to a sovereign who lives on the other side of the sea, and they insist that the natives worship a couple of crossed pieces of wood."

"You must not let anyone hear you talking like this, Señor Belalcázar!" I warned him. "They will accuse you of being a heretic and betraying the emperor."

"I am simply saying what's true. You will find, señora, that these conquistadors have no shame. They arrive as beggars, they act like thieves, and then they behave as if they were lords of the world."

Those three months at sea were as long as three years, but they allowed me to develop a taste for freedom. There was no family—except for the timid Constanza—neighbors, or priests to observe me, I did not have to give an accounting to anyone, and so I shed my widow's black clothing and the undergarments imprisoning my flesh. In his turn, Daniel Belalcázar convinced Constanza to put away her nun's habit and wear my dresses.

The days seemed interminable and the nights even longer. The filth, the confinement, the limited, dreadful food, the men's bad humor, all contributed to the purgatory of the crossing, but at least we had escaped sea serpents capable of swallowing up the ship, monsters, tritons, the sirens that drive sailors mad, the ghosts of the drowned, phantom ships, and St. Elmo's fire. The crew had warned us of these and other dangers found at sea, but Belalcázar assured us that he had never seen any of them.

One Saturday in August we sighted land. The water that had been deep and black became clear and blue as the sky. The ship's dory took us to a beach of rippled sand licked by gentle waves.

Sailors offered to carry us, but Constanza and I lifted our skirts and waded to shore. We preferred exposing our calves to being slung like sacks of wheat over the men's shoulders. I had never imagined that the water would be so warm; from the ship it looked very cold.

The village where we came ashore consisted of a few cane huts with palm-leaf thatch. The single street was a mud pit, and there was no church—nothing but a wooden cross on a promontory. The few inhabitants of that godforsaken spot were an assortment of sailors between ships, black- and brown-skinned persons, and the Indians. It was the first time I had ever seen the natives of these new lands—poor, nearly naked, miserable people they were. All around us was dense greenery and sweltering heat. The humidity soaked even into one's thoughts, and the implacable sun bore down mercilessly. We could not endure the touch of our clothing, and took off as much as we could: collars, cuffs, shoes, and stockings.

It did not take long to find that Juan de Malága was not there. The only person who remembered him was Padre Gregorio, an unfortunate Dominican priest who had been stricken with malaria and was now a man aged before his time; he was barely forty years old, but he looked seventy. For two decades he had wandered through the jungle with the mission of spreading the Christian faith, and in his wanderings had twice come across my husband. He confirmed that, like many hallucinatory Spaniards, Juan was looking for the mythic city of gold.

"Tall, handsome, a good card player, likable," he said.

It had to be Juan.

"El Dorado is something the Indians dreamed up to get rid of the foreigners," the priest added. "Once they go looking for the gold, they end up dead."

Padre Gregorio offered his hut to Constanza and me. There we were able to rest while the sailors got drunk on a strong palm liquor and dragged the Indian girls, against their will, into the thicket that encircled the little settlement. Despite the sharks, which had followed the ship for days, Daniel Belalcázar steeped in that limpid water for hours. When he took off his shirt, we saw that his back was crisscrossed with the scars of lashings, but he offered no explanation and no one dared ask for one. On the voyage we had noticed that Belalcázar had a mania for washing, something he had learned in other lands. He wanted Constanza to go into the water with him, clothes and all, but I would not permit it. I had promised her parents that I would return her in one piece, not half eaten by sharks.

At sunset the Indians lighted fires of green wood to combat the mosquitoes that descended upon the village. The smoke blinded us and we could barely breathe, but the alternative was worse: the minute we moved away from the fire we were enveloped in a cloud of insects. For dinner we had tapir, an animal that looks like a pig, and a bland pap they call cassava, or manioc—strange tastes, but after three months of fish and empanadas, we thought the meal delicious. We also had our first taste of a foamy beverage made of cacao, a little bitter, in spite of the spices that had been added to it. According to Padre Gregorio, this cacao is so valuable to the Aztecs and other Indians that they use the seeds as we use coins.

That evening we listened to the adventures of Padre Gregorio, who several times had traveled deep into the jungle to convert the Indians. He admitted that in his youth he, too, had followed the terrible dream of El Dorado. He had traveled along the Orinoco, which at times was placid as a lake, but at others, a rushing, angry torrent. He told of enormous waterfalls born of the clouds that crash down in a rainbow of foam, of green tunnels through the forest, of the eternal dusk of vegetation barely touched by the light of day. He described carnivorous flowers that smell like dead meat, and others that are delicate and fragrant, but poisonous. And there are birds of sumptuous plumage, he said, and complete villages of monkeys with human faces that spy on intruders from among the leaves.

"For those of us who come from Extremadura, where it is so stark and dry, nothing but rocks and dust, such a paradise is impossible to imagine," I commented.

"But it is a paradise only in appearance, Señora Inés. In a hot,

swampy, voracious world infested with reptiles and poisonous insects, things decay very quickly, especially the soul. The jungle
transforms men into rogues and murderers."

"Those who go there only out of greed are already corrupted,
Padre. The jungle merely brings out in men what is already in
them," Daniel Belalcázar replied, then jotted down everything the
priest had to say in his notebook. He had every intention of following the course of the Orinoco himself.

That first night on terra firma, Maestro Manuel Martín and some
of the sailors went back to the ship to sleep—to guard the cargo,
they said, although it occurs to me that they were afraid of the
snakes and insects. Others of us, unable to face the confinement of
our cabins again, chose to stay in the village. Constanza, exhausted,
fell right to sleep in the hammock we'd been allotted, protected by
a filthy mosquito net, but I prepared for several hours of wakeful-
ness. The night was heavy and black, throbbing with mysterious
presences, filled with sounds, fragrant, and frightening. It seemed
to me that I was surrounded by every creature Padre Gregorio had
mentioned: enormous insects, snakes that could kill from a distance,
and unfamiliar beasts. However, more than those natural dangers, I
was concerned about the wickedness of the drunken men. I could
not close my eyes.

Two or three long hours went by, and just as finally I began
to doze, I heard something or someone outside the hut. My first
suspicion was that it was an animal, but I recalled that Sebastián
Romero had stayed ashore, and now that he was not under the
thumb of Maestro Manuel Martín, he was a man to be watched. I
was not mistaken. Had I been asleep, Romero might have accomplished his purpose in coming, but to his misfortune I was waiting
with a small, needle-sharp Moorish dagger I had bought in Cadiz.
The only light came from the reflection of coals dying in the fire
where the tapir had been roasted. An opening without a door was
all that separated us from the outside, and my eyes had become ac-

customed to the darkness. Romero crawled in on all fours, sniffing like a dog, and approached the hammock where I was supposed to be asleep beside Constanza. He got as far as reaching to pull back the netting, but froze when he felt the tip of my dagger against his neck, just behind his ear.

"You don't learn, do you, you pig," I said quietly, not wanting to create an uproar.

"Bitch! May the devil take you! You toyed with me for three months, and now you are pretending you do not want the same thing I want," he growled, furious.

That woke Constanza. Terrified, her cries brought Padre Gregorio, Daniel Belalcázar, and others sleeping nearby. Someone lighted a torch, and among them they dragged Romero from our hut. Padre Gregorio ordered them to tie him to a tree until the madness of the palm alcohol had passed, and there they left him, screaming threats and cursing. As dawn approached, he collapsed from fatigue, and the rest of us could sleep.

A few days later, after taking on fresh water, tropical fruits, and salted meat, Maestro Manuel Martín's ship set out for the port of Cartagena, which was already a thriving center because it was there that the treasures of the New World were loaded on to be taken to Spain. The waters of the Caribbean were as blue and clean as the pools in the palaces of the Moors. The air carried an intoxicating aroma of flowers, fruit, and sweat. The walls of Cartagena, constructed of stone and a mortar made from lime and bulls' blood, gleamed beneath an unrelenting sun. Hundreds of natives, naked and in chains, were transporting large stones, spurred by the whips of their overseers. The large wall and fortress protected the Spanish fleet from pirates and other enemies of the empire. Several anchored ships rocked in the bay, some of them warships and others merchantmen, including one carrying black cargo from Africa to be auctioned in the slave market. It was distinguishable from other ships by the stench of human misery and evil issuing from it.

Compared to some of the ancient cities of Spain, Cartagena was a village, but it had a church, well-laid-out streets, white-painted homes, substantial government buildings, storehouses for cargo, a market, and a number of taverns. The fortress, still under construction, presided over the bay from high atop a hill, its cannons already installed and pointed toward the bay. I noted a variety of people in the streets, and the women, bold and wearing deep décolletage, seemed beautiful to me, especially the mulatto women. After I learned that my husband had been there a little over a year ago, I decided I would stay awhile. In one shop Juan had left a bundle of clothes as pawn, with the promise he would pay the money he owed upon his return.

The one inn in Cartagena did not accept single women, but Maestro Manuel Martín, who knew many people, found Constanza and me a place to rent. It consisted of a fairly large, almost bare room with a narrow window and a door opening onto the street. Its only furnishings were a cot, a table, and a bench on which my niece and I arranged our belongings. My savings were melting away more quickly than I had planned, so I immediately looked for an oven in which I could make empanadas, and made it known that I wanted to offer my services as a seamstress.

Almost as soon as we moved in, Daniel Belalcázar came to call. Our room was crowded with bundles, so he had to sit on the bed, holding his hat. We had nothing but water to offer him, and he tossed down two glasses, sweating. He sat a long while in silence, tongue-tied, studying the tamped dirt floor while we waited, as uncomfortable as he.

"Señora Inés, I have come with the greatest respect to ask for your niece's hand," he blurted out at last.

Surprise nearly struck me dumb. I had never seen one thing between them that would indicate a romance, and for a moment I thought that the heat must have driven Belalcázar off his head, but the enthralled expression on Constanza's face forced me to reconsider.

"The girl is only fifteen years old!" I exclaimed, horrified.

"Girls marry at an early age here, señora."

"Constanza has no dowry."

"The dowry isn't important. I do not approve of that custom, and even if Constanza had the dowry of a queen, I would not accept it."

"My niece wants to be a nun!"

"She did, but not now," Belalcázar murmured, and in a loud, clear voice Constanza confirmed what he said.

I explained to them that I lacked the authority to give Constanza away in marriage, even less to some adventurer I knew nothing about. Belalcázar was more than twice her age, a man with no fixed residence who spent his life writing down tomfoolery in a notebook. How did he plan to support her? Did he perhaps intend for her to follow him up the Orinoco to sketch cannibals? Constanza, pink with embarrassment, interrupted me to announce that it was too late for me to object because in reality they were already married in the eyes of God, though not by human law. At that point it dawned on me that while I worked every night on the ship making empanadas, they were doing whatever their hearts desired in Belalcázar's cabin. I lifted my hand to deliver the slap I thought Constanza deserved, but Daniel caught my arm.

They were married the next day in the church in Cartagena, with Maestro Manuel Martín and me as witnesses. They moved into the inn while they made preparations to travel into the jungle, exactly as I had feared.

The first night I spent alone in the rented room a terrible thing happened that I might have managed to avoid if I had been thinking ahead. Although I could not truly afford the luxury of candles—they were very dear—I kept one lit a good part of the night, out of fear of cockroaches, which like to come out in the dark. I was lying on the cot, unable to sleep and barely covered by a thin gown, baking in the heat and thinking of my niece when I was startled by a kick at the door. There was a bolt I could shoot from the inside but I had forgotten to do it. A second kick burst the latch, and I saw Sebastián Romero silhouetted on the threshold. I started to sit up, but he pushed me back down on the bed and then was over me, muttering insults. I kicked and clawed, but he stunned me with a ferocious blow that left me breathless and seeing black for a few instants. When I recovered my senses, he was on top of me, flattening me with his weight, spraying me with saliva, and mumbling filth. I smelled his nauseating breath as his fingers dug into my flesh; he was trying to part my legs with his knee, and I felt his hard sex against my belly. Panic, and the pain of that blow, clouded my senses. I screamed, but he covered my mouth with one hand, smothering me, while with the other he was struggling with my shift and my underdrawers—not at all an easy task because I am strong and was twisting like a weasel. To keep me quiet, he slapped me hard in the face and then used both hands to tear at my clothing. I realized that I would not get anywhere with force. For an instant I contemplated the possibility of giving in to him and hoped that the humiliation would be brief, but I was blind with anger, and I was not sure that afterward he would leave me in peace; he might just as easily kill me to prevent my denouncing him. I had a mouthful of blood, but I was able to beg him not to hurt me and tell him we could both enjoy this, that there was no hurry, and that I was prepared to please him in any way he wished.

I do not remember very well the exact details of what happened next. I believe that I stroked his hair, murmuring a litany of obscenities learned in bed with Juan de Málaga, and that seemed to take the edge off his violence, because he let go of me and stood up to take off his breeches, which had fallen down around his knees. Feeling under the pillow, I found the dagger, which I had kept near me since arriving; I grasped it firmly in my right hand, hiding it by my side. When Romero again climbed over me, I allowed him to get comfortable, clasped both legs around his waist, and put my left arm around his neck. He grunted with satisfaction, thinking I had decided to cooperate, and prepared to seize the moment. In the meantime, I used my legs to immobilize him, locking my feet over his kidneys. I raised the dagger, taking it in both hands and calculating the precise spot that would inflict the greatest harm, and brought it down with all my strength, burying it to the hilt and closing him in a lethal embrace. It is not easy to drive a dagger into a man's strong back while in that position, but I was aided by terror. It was his life or mine. When for a moment Sebastián Romero did not react, as if he had not even felt the blow, I was afraid I had aimed poorly, but then he gave a visceral howl and rolled off me, tumbling to the floor among the piles of bundles. He tried to get up, but got no farther than his knees, with an expression of surprise on his face that quickly turned to horror. He reached behind him in a desperate attempt to pull out the dagger. What I had learned about the human body while tending wounds in the nuns' hospital had served me well, because my thrust had been deadly. The man kept flailing about as I sat upright on the cot and watched, as frightened as he, but ready to jump on him if he yelled and stop him however I could. He did not yell again; instead, a sinister little gurgle escaped his lips between rosy spurts of foam. After a time that seemed eternal, he shuddered as if possessed, vomited blood, and then lost consciousness. I waited a long time, until my nerves had calmed and I could think, and until I was sure that he was not going to move again. In the faint light of that single candle I could see that the blood was soaking into the dirt floor.

I waited the rest of the night beside the body of Sebastián Romero, first praying to the Virgin to forgive me for such a grievous crime, and then planning how to keep from suffering the consequences. I did not know the laws of that city, but if they were anything like those in Plasencia, I would be thrown into prison until it could be proved that I had acted in self-defense, something very difficult to do given that the judges always favored the man. I had no illusions. The blame for men's vices and sins always falls on us women. Who would expect justice for a young woman on her own? They would say that I had invited the innocent sailor to my bed and then murdered him in order to rob him. At dawn, I covered the corpse with a blanket, dressed, and went down to the port where Manuel Martín's ship was still anchored. The maestro listened to my story to the end, without interrupting, chewing his tobacco and scratching his head.

"It seems that I will have to take charge of this mess, Señora Inés," he declared when I had finished.

That night he came to my modest little room, bringing with him a sailor he could trust, and between them they carried Romero off wrapped in a length of sail. I never knew what they did with him. I imagine they threw him into the sea, weighed down by a rock, and that the fish took care of his remains. Martín suggested that I leave Cartagena as soon as possible. A secret like mine could not be hidden indefinitely, and so only a few days later I bid my niece and her husband good-bye and left with two other travelers for the city of Panamá. Several Indians carried our baggage and acted as guides through mountains, forests, and rivers.

The isthmus of Panamá is a narrow strip of land that separates our European ocean from the South Sea, which is now called the Pacific. It is less than twenty leagues across, but the mountains are precipitous, the jungle very thick, the water unhealthful, the swamps foul, and the air infested with fever and pestilence. There are hostile Indians, caimans, and water and land snakes, but the landscape is magnificent and the birds unbelievably beautiful. As we progressed, we were accompanied by the chatter of the curious and bold monkeys that liked to jump on us and steal our provisions. The jungle was a deep, dark, threatening sea of green. My fellow travelers carried their weapons in their hands and, just as Padre Gregorio had warned us, never took their eyes off the Indians who at the first careless moment would have turned on us. He had also warned us about the caimans that drag their victims to the bottom of the river; the red ants that come in waves of thousands and crawl into all your bodily orifices, devouring you from the inside in a matter of minutes; and the toads that can blind you with their poisonous spit. I tried not to think about any of that because it would have paralyzed me with fright. Just as Daniel Balalcázar said, it makes no sense to suffer in advance a misfortune that may never occur.

We made the first part of the trek in a boat rowed by eight natives. I was grateful that my niece was not present, for the men were totally naked. The truth is that despite the magnificent scenery, my eyes strayed to places they should not have gone. The third section of the trip was made on mule back, and when we climbed the last peak we could see the turquoise sea and the hazy outlines of the city of Panamá, suffocating in a hot mist.

TWO

America, 1537–1540

PEDRO DE VALDIVIA was thirty-five years old when he and Jerónimo de Alderete reached Venezuela—"Little Venice," the first explorers ironically called it when they saw its swamps, canals, and huts on stilts. Valdivia had left the delicate Marina Ortiz de Gaete behind, with the promise either to return a rich man or to send for her as soon as it was possible—little consolation for the abandoned young woman. He had spent everything he had, and gone into debt besides, to finance the voyage. Like everyone who came adventuring in the New World, he had invested his wealth, his honor, and his life in the undertaking, although all the conquered lands, and a fifth of the wealth—were there any to be had—belonged to the Spanish Crown. As Belalcázar had said, with the king's authorization, the adventure was termed a conquest; without it, it was armed assault.

The beaches of the Caribbean, with their blue waters, opalescent sand, and elegant palm trees welcomed travelers with deceptive tranquility, for as soon as they stepped into the undergrowth, they were absorbed by a nightmarish jungle. They had to slash a path with machetes, dazed by humidity and heat, constantly besieged by mosquitoes and animals they had never seen before. They slogged through swampy ground where they sank up to their thighs in stinking slime, weighed down, clumsy, covered with disgusting leeches that sucked their blood, but unable to remove their armor for fear of the poisoned darts of the Indians trailing them, silent and invisible in the undergrowth.

"We cannot be captured by these savages!" Alderete warned, and reminded the others that the conquistador Francisco Pizarro, on his first expedition to the south of the continent, had with a party of his men come across an empty village in which fires were still burning beneath a number of large clay pots. The starving Spaniards took off the lids and revealed the ingredients of the soup: human heads, hands, feet, and viscera.

"That happened west of us, when Pizarro was looking for Peru," put in Pedro de Valdivia, who considered himself well informed on discoveries and conquests.

"On this side the Carib Indians are cannibals too," Jerónimo insisted.

It was impossible to determine their location in the absolute greenness of this primitive world that predated Genesis, an infinite, circular labyrinth outside of time, outside of history. If they strayed a few feet from the banks of the rivers, the jungle swallowed them up forever—which happened to one of the men, who plunged into the tall ferns calling his mother, maddened by anguish and fear. The men were silenced, oppressed by an abysmal loneliness, a sidereal anguish. The river was infested with piranhas, which at the scent of blood rushed in schools to end a Christian's days in a matter of minutes, leaving nothing but clean white bones as sign that he once existed.

In all that lush growth, there was nothing to eat. Their provisions soon ran out, and hunger was added to their suffering. Occasionally they were able to catch a monkey and eat it raw—in that endless damp it was next to impossible to light a fire—nauseated by its human resemblance and its stench. They ate unfamiliar fruit, which made them deathly ill and for days kept them from making headway, weakened as they were by vomiting and watery bowels. Their bellies swelled, their teeth fell out, they were racked with fever. One man died bleeding through every orifice, including his eyes; another was lost in a pit of quicksand; and a third was crushed by an anaconda, a monstrous water snake as big around as a man's leg and as long as five lances laid end to end. The air was like hot steam, rotten, noxious—a dragon's breath. "This is Satan's kingdom," the soldiers swore, and it must have been so, for they grew quick to anger and fought at every turn. Their captains found themselves hard put to maintain discipline and force them to continue. Only one inducement kept them moving: El Dorado.

As they fought their way forward, Pedro de Valdivia's faith in the venture faded and his frustration mounted. This was not what he had dreamed of in the boredom of his family home in Extremadura. He was prepared to confront savages in heroic battles and to conquer remote regions for the glory of God and the king, but he had never imagined he would use his sword—the victorious sword of Flanders and Italy—to hack his way through a jungle. He was revolted by the cupidity and cruelty of his companions; there was nothing honorable or idealistic in that brutal group. Except for Jerónimo de Alderete, who had given more than enough proof of his nobility, his fellows were ruffians of the lowest sort, treacherous and quarrelsome. The captain at the head of the expedition, whom Valdivia immediately detested, was heartless: he stole, he treated the Indians like slaves, and he did not pay the *quinto,* the fifth owed to the Crown. "Where are we going, with such anger and desperation, when in the end none of us can take the gold with us to the tomb?" Valdivia wondered, but he kept on because he could not turn back.

This senseless adventure lasted several months, until finally Pedro de Valdivia and Jerónimo de Alderete were able to split away

from the ill-starred party and take a ship to the city of Santo Domingo, on the island of Española, where they took some time to
recover from the ravages of the trek. Pedro used the opportunity
to send Marina a little money he had saved, as he would continue
to do till he died.

They were in Santo Domingo when the news reached the island
that Francisco Pizarro needed reinforcements in Peru. His partner
in the conquest, Diego de Almagro, had gone off to the extreme
south of the continent with the idea of taming the barbaric lands
of Chile. The two men were unlike in temperament: the first was
somber, suspicious, and envious, though courageous, and the second
was frank, loyal, and so generous that he wanted a fortune only to
be able to share it. It was inevitable that men so different, though
equally ambitious, would have a falling out, even though they had
sworn to be loyal to each other before the altar, each taking half
of the same host. The Inca empire was too small to hold them
both. Pizarro, who had been given the title of marqués gobernador
y caballero de la Orden de Santiago, stayed in Peru, aided by his
fearsome brothers, while in 1535, Almagro, with an army of five
hundred Spaniards, ten thousand Yanacona Indians, and his own title
of Adelantado, started out for Chile, a still unexplored region whose
name in Aymará means "where the land ends." To finance the trip
he spent from his private fortune more than the Inca Atahualpa had
paid for his own ransom.

As soon as Diego de Almagro left with his men for Chile,
Pizarro was faced with widespread insurgency. Seeing the forces of
the *viracochas*—the Peruvians' name for Spaniards—divided, the
Indians rose up against the invaders. Without help, and soon,
the conquest of the Inca empire would be endangered, as well
as the lives of the Spaniards, who were forced to contend with
numbers far greater than their own. When Francisco Pizarro's call
for aid reached Española, Valdivia heard it, and without a moment's
hesitation decided to go to Peru.

For Pedro de Valdivia, the mere name—Peru—evoked visions
of inconceivable riches, along with a picture of the refined civilization his friend Alderete had described with such eloquence. In
fact, he had thought when he heard Alderete's account that it was
a civilization to be admired, even though not everything about it
was worthy of praise. He knew that the Incas were cruel, and that
they were ferocious in controlling their people. After a battle, if
the vanquished did not accept being absorbed into the empire, no
captive was left alive, and at the least hint of discontent entire villages were relocated a thousand leagues away. They tortured their
enemies, including women and children, in horrible ways. The Inca,
who wed his sisters in order to guarantee the purity of the royal
blood lines, was the divinity incarnate, the soul of the empire—past,
present, and future. Of Atahualpa it was said that he had thousands
of maidens in his seraglio and an uncountable number of slaves,
that he enjoyed personally torturing prisoners, and that he often
cut the throats of his ministers with his own hand. The faceless,
voiceless people lived in subjection; their destiny was to labor from
childhood to death to benefit the orejones—the priests, military,
and members of the court—who lived in Babylonian splendor while
an ordinary man and his family barely survived, living off a piece
of land they occupied but did not own. The Spanish reported
that many Indians practiced sodomy—a sin punished with death in
Spain—even though the Inca rulers had forbidden it. There were
many tales of sexual excess in the Inca society, proof of which could
be found in the erotic ceramics adventurers showed in taverns for
the entertainment of the customers, who had never suspected that
there were so many ways to disport themselves. It was also reported
that a mother broke her daughter's hymen with her finger before
giving her to a man.

Valdivia found nothing wrong in aspiring to the fortune he might
find in Peru. Riches, however, were not his incentive; that came
from feeling it his duty to fight beside his fellows and his desire
to achieve the glory that had until then been so evasive. A sense
of honor distinguished Valdivia from others who had joined the

expedition to go to Pizarro's aid; they were dazzled by the gleam of gold. This is what Valdivia himself told me, many times, and I believed him because his behavior would have been consistent with the other decisions of his life. Years later, driven by idealism, he sacrificed the security and wealth he had finally obtained in an attempt to conquer Chile, which Diego de Almagro had in the end failed to accomplish. Glory, always glory, that was the lodestar of his life. No one loved Pedro more than I did; no one knew him better than I, which is why I can speak of his virtues, just as later I must refer to his defects, which were not minor. It is true that he betrayed me and behaved in a cowardly fashion with me, but even the most valiant and honorable men sometimes fail their women. And I can speak with authority when I say that Pedro de Valdivia *was* one of the most valiant and honorable men among all those who have come to the New World.

Valdivia traveled to Panamá by land, and from there, in 1537, along with four hundred soldiers, sailed to Peru. The journey took a couple of months, and when he reached his destination the Indians' uprising had already been subdued by the opportune arrival of Diego de Almagro, who had returned from Chile in time to join his forces with those of Francisco Pizarro. Almagro had crossed icy peaks in his advance toward the south; he had survived incredible hardships and had returned across the hottest desert on the planet, a ruined man. His expedition to Chile had reached the Bío-Bío, the same river along which the Incas, seventy years before, had retreated when they had unsuccessfully tried to take the land of the Indians of the south, the Mapuche. The Incas, like Almagro and his men, had been stopped by these warring people.

Mapu-ché, "people of the earth," they call themselves, although now they are called Araucanos, a more sonorous name given them by the poet Alonso de Ercilla y Zúñiga, who took it from who knows where—perhaps from Arauco, an area farther to the south. I intend to call them Mapuche—the word has no plural in my language—until I die, since that is how they call themselves. It does not seem just that their name was changed only to make it easier to rhyme: *araucano, castellano, hermano, cristiano,* and on and on for three hundred quartos. Alonso was a runny-nosed boy living in Madrid when we first Spaniards fought on this soil. He came to the conquest of Chile a little late, but his verses will tell the epic story through the centuries. When there is nothing left of the spirited founders of Chile, not even the dust of our bones, they will remember us through the work of that young man who, in his eagerness to make his lines rhyme, is not always faithful to the facts. Furthermore, he does not always present us in the best light. I fear that many of his admirers will have a slightly erroneous impression of what the war of the Araucanía was.

Ercilla accuses the Spaniards of cruelty and an excessive hunger for wealth, while he exalts the Mapuche, to whom he attributes qualities of bravery, nobility, chivalry, a spirit of justice, and even tenderness with their women. I believe I know them better than Alonso because I have spent forty years defending what we founded in Chile, and he was here for only a few months. I admire the Mapuche for their courage and their deep love of their land, but I can tell you that they are not models of sweetness and compassion. The romantic love that Alonso so extols is quite rare among them. Every man has several wives, whom he prizes for their labor, and for bearing his children. At least this is what we are told by the Spanish women who have been kidnapped by them. The humiliations they suffered in captivity were so great that these poor, shamed women often choose not to return to the bosom of their families. On the other hand, I must admit that Spaniards do not treat the Indian women who serve them and satisfy their lust any better. The Mapuche do surpass us in some aspects. For example, they do not know greed. Gold, land, titles, honors, none of those things interests them. They have no roof but the sky, no bed other than moss. They roam free through the forest, hair streaming in the wind, galloping the horses they have stolen from us. Another virtue I celebrate is that they keep their word. It is not they who break pacts, but we. In times of war they attack by surprise, but not in betrayal, and in times of peace they honor accords. Before we came they knew nothing of torture, and they respected their prisoners of war. Their worst punishment is exile, banishment from the family and the tribe. That is more feared than death. Serious crimes are paid for with a swift execution. The condemned man digs his own grave, into which he throws small sticks and stones as he names the beings he wants to accompany him to the next world. When he has finished, he is dealt a fatal blow to the skull.

I am amazed by the power of Alonso's verses, which invent history and defy and conquer oblivion. Words that do not rhyme, like mine, do not have the authority of poetry, but in any case I am obliged to relate my version of events in order to leave an account of the labors we women have contributed in Chile; they tend to be overlooked by the chroniclers, however informed they may be. At least you, Isabel, must know the truth, for though you are not the child of my blood, you *are* the child of my heart. I suppose that statues of me will be erected in the plazas, and there will be streets and cities that bear my name, as there will be of Pedro de Valdivia and other conquistadors, but the hundreds of brave women who founded the towns while their men fought the wars will be forgotten.

But I have wandered. Let us return to what I was telling, because I do not have very long; my heart is weary.

Diego de Almagro abandoned the conquest of Chile, forced by the invincible resistance of the Mapuche, the pressure of his soldiers—disenchanted by the scarcity of gold—and the bad news of the Indians' rebellion in Peru. He returned in order to aid Francisco Pizarro and snuff out the insurrection, and then together to achieve the definitive defeat of the enemy hordes. The proud empire of the Incas, devastated by hunger and the violence and chaos of war, was broken. However, far from being grateful for Almagro's intervention on their behalf, Francisco Pizarro and his brothers turned against him; their sights were on Cuzco, a city granted to Almagro in the territorial division set out by Emperor Charles V. Their own vast holdings, with their incalculable riches, were not enough to satisfy the ambition of the Pizarro brothers. They wanted more. They wanted everything.

Pizarro and Almagro ended by taking up arms and facing off in a brief battle at Abancay that ended in Pizarro's defeat. Almagro, always magnanimous, treated his prisoners with unusual clemency, even the brothers of Francisco Pizarro, his implacable enemies. Because they admired Almagro's conduct, many of the defeated soldiers went over to his ranks, while his loyal captains begged him to execute the Pizarros and take advantage of his victory to claim all of Peru. Almagro ignored their counsel and opted for reconciliation with the ungrateful partner who had wronged him.

It was during this period that Pedro de Valdivia arrived in Ciudad de los Reyes and placed himself at the disposal of the person who had summoned him: Francisco Pizarro. Always respectful of the law, he did not question the authority or the intentions of the governor; he was the representative of Charles V, and that was enough. Nevertheless, the last thing Valdivia wanted was to be embroiled in a civil war. He had come to combat insurgent Indians, and it had never crossed his mind that he would have to fight other Spaniards. He tried to act as intermediary between Pizarro and Almagro and reach a peaceful solution, and at one moment believed he was about to achieve it. But he did not know Pizarro, who said one thing but in the shadows was planning another. While the governor was stalling, making declarations of friendship, he was preparing his plan to rid himself of Almagro, always with the single thought of governing alone and gaining Cuzco. He envied Almagro's virtues: his eternal optimism and especially the loyalty he inspired in his soldiers. He knew that he himself was detested.

After more than a year of skirmishes, broken agreements, and betrayals, the forces of the two rivals met again at Las Salinas, near Cuzco. Francisco Pizarro was not leading his army; he had placed it under the command of Pedro de Valdivia, whose military merits were widely respected. Pizarro had named Valdivia his field marshal because he had fought under the marqués de Pescara in Italy, and was experienced in European tactics. After all, facing badly armed, anarchical Indians was a far different matter from encountering disciplined Spanish soldiers. Also representing Pizarro was his brother Hernando, hated for his cruelty and arrogance. I want to make this part very clear, so that no one can blame Pedro de Valdivia for atrocities committed during those days. Of those I had conclusive proof, for it fell to me to tend the poor wretches whose wounds, months after the battle, still had not healed. Pizarro's troops had cannons and two hundred more men than Almagro. They were well outfitted with new harquebuses and deadly cannon shot; those iron balls, when fired, burst open and sprayed knife-sharp projectiles. Their morale was good, and they were well rested, while their opponents had just undergone great hardships in Chile as well as the task of putting down the Peruvian Indians' uprising. Diego de Almagro himself was very ill, and he, like Pizarro, did not personally take part in the battle.

The two armies met one rosy dawn in the valley of Las Salinas, as from the hillsides thousands of Quechua Indians observed the entertaining spectacle of *viracochas* killing one another like rabid beasts. They did not understand the ceremonies, or the reasons why those bearded warriors were fighting. First they lined up in orderly rows, displaying their polished armor and sleek horses, then they knelt on one knee while other *viracochas* in black robes performed some magic with crosses and silver vessels. They put a little piece of bread in their mouths, touched their fingers to their foreheads and chests, received blessings, bowed to their fellows across the field of battle, and finally, after about two hours of this dance, prepared to kill one another. And that they did with methodical and terrible cruelty. For hours and hours, they fought hand to hand, yelling the same words: "Long live the king and Spain!" and "Forward in the name of Santiago!" In the confusion and dust raised by the horses' hooves and the men's boots, it was impossible to tell one side from another; all their uniforms had turned the same clay color. In the meantime, the Indians whooped, laid bets, enjoyed their roasted corn and salted meat, chewed coca, drank chicha, got too hot, and finally rested because the battle was lasting too long.

At the end of the day, Pizarro's army emerged victorious, thanks to the military acumen of the field marshal, Pedro de Valdivia, hero of the day, but it was Hernando Pizarro who gave the last order: "Slit their throats!" His soldiers, animated by an enmity that they themselves could not later explain or the chroniclers set right, unleashed a bloodbath against hundreds of their compatriots, many of whom had been their brothers in the adventure of discovering and conquering Peru. They finished off the wounded in Almagro's forces and blasted their way into Cuzco, where they raped the women—Spanish as well as Indian and black—and robbed and pillaged until they had had enough. They were as savage in their treatment of the vanquished as the Incas were, which was saying a lot because the native Peruvians were not known to be merciful. It is enough to recall that among their habitual tortures were hanging a condemned man by his feet, with his guts wrapped around his neck, or flaying him, and then while he was still alive, using his skin to make a drum.

The Spaniards did not go that far because, as some survivors told me, they were in a great rush. Several of Almagro's soldiers who did not die immediately at the hands of their compatriots were massacred by the Indians who came down from the hills at the end of the battle, howling with jubilation because for once they were not the victims. They celebrated by desecrating the corpses, hacking them to bits with stone knives. For Valdivia, who from the time he was twenty had fought on many fronts and against many enemies, that was one of the most shameful episodes in his military career. He often awakened, screaming, in my arms, tormented by nightmares about his decapitated comrades, just as in dreams following the sacking of Rome he saw mothers with children in their arms leaping into the river to escape the marauding troops.

———————

Diego de Almagro, sixty-one years old and greatly weakened by illness and the Chile campaign, was taken prisoner, humiliated, and subjected to a trial that lasted two months. He was not given an opportunity to defend himself. When he learned that he had been sentenced to death, he asked that the enemy field marshal, Pedro de Valdivia, be witness to his last requests; he knew no one' more worthy of his trust. Diego de Almagro was still a fine-looking man despite the ravages of syphilis and his many battles. He wore a black patch over the eye he had lost in an encounter with savages before he discovered Peru. On that occasion he himself had pulled out the arrow with one tug—with the eye impaled on it—then continued fighting. When he lost the three fingers of his right hand, chopped off by a sharp stone hatchet, he shifted his sword to the left hand, and in that condition, blinded and dripping with blood, he fought until comrades came to help him. The wound was cauterized with a red-hot iron and boiling oil, which had scarred his face but not destroyed the charm of his generous laughter and amiable expression.

"I want him subjected to torture in the plaza, in front of everyone. He deserves special punishment," Hernando Pizarro ordered.

"I will not be a party to that, Excellency. The soldiers will not permit it. This fight between brothers has been difficult, let us not throw salt in the wound. We might have a revolt on our hands," Valdivia counseled.

"Almagro was born a peasant, let him die like a peasant," was Hernando Pizarro's retort.

Pedro de Valdivia refrained from reminding him that the Pizarros were of no higher birth than Diego de Almagro. Francisco Pizarro had been a bastard child himself; he had no education and had been abandoned by his mother. Both men had been dirt poor before a change of fortune had sent them to Peru and made them richer than King Solomon.

"Don Diego de Almagro bears the titles of adelantado and gobernador de Nueva Toledo. What explanation will you give our emperor?" Valdivia persisted. "I repeat, Excellency, with all respect, that it is not a good idea to stir up the soldiers. They are already on edge, and Diego de Almagro is an honorable military man."

"He returned from Chile trounced by a band of naked savages!" Hernando Pizarro exclaimed.

"No, Excellency. He returned from Chile to aid your brother, the honorable marqués gobernador."

Hernando Pizarro realized that the field marshal was right, but it was not in his nature to take back his words, and, even less, to forgive an enemy. His order was to behead Almagro in the main plaza of Cuzco.

In the days prior to the execution, Valdivia was often alone with Almagro in his dismal, filthy cell, his last dwelling place. He admired the adelantado for his heroic feats as a soldier and his reputation for generosity, although he was aware that he had weaknesses and had made mistakes. While a prisoner, Almagro told him what he had experienced during the eighteen months of that expedition to Chile, planting in Valdivia's imagination the prospect of conquest that Almagro himself would not be able to carry out to the end. He described the terrifying march across the high sierras, watched by condors circling slowly above their heads and waiting for them to drop so they could pick their bones. The cold killed more than two thousand auxiliary Indians—the ones they call Yanaconas—two hundred blacks, nearly fifty Spaniards, and quantities of horses and dogs. Even the lice and fleas could not endure the cold, but fell from the men's clothing like showers of little seeds. Though nothing grew there, not even lichen; everything was rock, wind, ice, and solitude.

"So great was our plight, Don Pedro, that we chewed the raw flesh of animals that had died from the cold, and drank the horses' urine. By day we marched at our quickest pace, to keep from being coated with snow, and by night we slept curled up with the horses. At dawn every day we counted the dead Indians and quickly

muttered an Our Father for their souls, for there was no time for
anything further. Bodies stayed where they fell, like ice monoliths
pointing the way for future lost travelers."

He added that the Spaniard's armor froze, imprisoning them,
and when they took off their boots or gloves, fingers and toes fell
off without pain. Not even a madman would have attempted that
route on the return, he explained, which was why they had chosen
the desert, never imagining how horrible it, too, would be. What
effort and suffering it costs men to conquer these lands, Valdivia
thought.

"During the day the desert is blazing hot, and the light is so
strong that it drives both men and horses mad, causing them to
see visions of trees and pools of fresh water," the Adelantado told
him. "As soon as the sun sets, the temperature plummets and the
camanchaca falls, a dew as icy as the deep snows that tormented us
in the peaks of the sierra. We were carrying a good supply of water
in barrels and wineskins, but soon it was nearly gone. Thirst killed
many Indians and made beasts of the Spaniards."

"In truth, Don Diego, it sounds like a journey to hell," Valdivia
commented.

"It was, Don Pedro, but I assure you that if I were to live, I
would try it again."

"But why, if the obstacles are so harrowing and the reward so
meager?"

"Because once the cordillera and the desert that separate Chile
from the rest of the known world have been crossed, you find
gentle hills, fragrant forests, fertile valleys, bounteous rivers, and a
climate more pleasant than any in Spain or anywhere else I know.
Chile is a paradise, Don Pedro. It is there we must found our cities
and prosper."

"And what is your opinion of the Indians in Chile?" Valdivia
asked.

"At first we encountered friendly savages, the ones they call
Promaucae. They are related to the Mapuche, but a different tribe.
Then they turned against us. They have mixed with Indians from

Peru and Ecuador, and are subjects of the Inca, whose domain reaches as far as the Bío-Bío. We got along with a few curacas, that is, Inca chiefs, but we could not go any farther south because that is the land of the Mapuche, who are very warlike. I must tell you, Don Pedro, that nowhere in any of my dangerous expeditions and battles did I encounter enemies as formidable as those savages armed with clubs and stones."

"That must be true, Adelantado, if they could stop you and your highly regarded soldiers."

"The Mapuche know only war and freedom. They have no king and they have no notion of hierarchies; they obey their toquis only during battles. Freedom, freedom—only freedom. It is the most important thing in their lives, and that is why we could not subdue them, and why the Incas failed in their attempt. The women do all the work while the men do nothing but prepare to fight."

Diego de Almagro's punishment was carried out one winter morning in 1538. At the last minute Pizarro reduced the sentence, fearing the reaction of the soldiers if Almagro were beheaded in public, as he had ordered. Instead they killed him in his cell. The executioner garroted him, slowly tightening a rope around his neck, and then his body was carried to the main plaza of Cuzco, where it was decapitated, though again the order was modified because they did not dare display the head on a meat hook as had been planned. By then Hernando Pizarro had begun to realize the magnitude of what he had done, and was worried about what the emperor's reaction would be. He decided to give Diego de Almagro a dignified burial, and he himself, dressed in severe mourning, led the funeral cortège. Years later, all the Pizarro brothers would pay for their crimes, but that is another story.

I have taken time to narrate these episodes in order to explain Pedro de Valdivia's determination to leave Peru, which was torn by intrigue and corruption, and conquer the still innocent territory of Chile, an undertaking in which I shared.

The battle of Las Salinas and the death of Diego de Almagro occurred a few months before my voyage to Cuzco. At that time I was awaiting news of Juan de Málaga in Panamá, where several persons told me they had seen him. People coming and going between the New World and Spain used that port as a meeting place. Many travelers passed through there—soldiers, employees of the Crown, chroniclers, priests, scholars, adventurers, and bandits—all sweltering in the humid breath of the tropics. I sent messages with them to the four cardinal points, but time was dragging by without any answer.

In the meantime, I was earning my livelihood with the trades I know best: sewing, cooking, setting bones, and treating wounds. I could do nothing to help those suffering from plague, fevers that turn blood to molasses, the French illness, and the incurable bites of the poisonous insects that abounded there. Like my mother and my grandmother, I am as strong as an oak, and I was able to live in the tropics without falling ill. Later, in Chile, I survived the desert, which I learned personally could be hot as fire itself, as well as the winter rains and the grippe that killed men more robust than I. All through the epidemics of typhus and smallpox, it was I who cared for and buried victims of those diseases.

One day, talking with the crew of a schooner anchored in the port, I learned that Juan had sailed for Peru quite some time before, as so many other Spaniards had done when they heard of the riches discovered by Pizarro and Almagro. I bundled up my belongings, took my savings, and since I was unable to get permission to go on my own, arranged to sail south with a group of Dominican priests. I imagine that those priests were associated with the Inquisition, but I never asked them; the mere word terrified me then and terrifies me still. I can never forget seeing heretics burned at the stake in Plasencia when I was eight or nine years old, but I wanted their help in getting to Peru. I went back to wearing my black dresses, and played the role of disconsolate wife. The priests marveled at the marital fidelity that led me through the world searching for a husband who had not sent for me and whose whereabouts I did not know. They could not suspect that my motive was not fidelity but the desire to end the state of uncertainty Juan had left me in. I had not loved him for many years. I barely remembered his face, and feared that when I did see him, I wouldn't recognize him. But I did not intend to stay in Panamá, where I was exposed to the appetites of idle soldiers and the unhealthful climate.

The voyage by ship lasted more or less seven weeks, skittering across the ocean at the whim of the winds. By then, dozens of Spanish ships were traveling the route back and forth to Peru, but their navigation charts were still a state secret. There were as yet no complete sets of charts, and on each sailing the pilots noted down their observations, from the color of the water and the clouds to any new landmark along the coast—when they were sailing close enough to view it. In that way they updated the routes that would later serve other voyagers. We experienced heavy seas, fog, storms, quarrels among the crew, and other unpleasantness that I will not detail here in order not to stray from my story. It is enough to note that the priests said mass each morning and made us pray the rosary in the evening to calm the seas and the contentious spirits of the crew. All voyages are dangerous. I am horrified when I am on a fragile ship at the mercy of the vast ocean, defying God and nature and far from human aid. I would rather find myself surrounded by savage Indians, as I have been many times, than board a ship again. Which is why I have never been tempted to return to Spain, even at times when the threat of attack by the natives forced us to evacuate cities and run like mice. I have always known that my bones would rest in American soil.

On the high seas I was once again hounded by men, despite the eternal vigilance of the priests. I could feel them circling around me like a pack of dogs. Did I emit the scent of a bitch in heat? In the privacy of my cabin, I washed with saltwater, frightened of that power I did not want because it could work against me. I dreamed of panting wolves, tongues hanging out and fangs dripping blood, ready to pounce on me—all of them at once. Sometimes the wolves had the face of Sebastián Romero. I spent my nights waiting and watching, locked in my cabin, sewing and praying, not daring, for fear of that constant male presence in the darkness, to go out into the cool night air to calm my nerves. I was frightened by that menace, it's true, but, I must confess, I was also fascinated. Desire was a terrible abyss yawning at my feet, inviting me to leap in and lose myself in its depths. I knew the festiveness and the torment of passion, as I had lived both with Juan de Málaga during the first years of our union. My husband had many faults, but I cannot deny that he was a tireless and captivating lover. That is why I forgave him again and again. Long after I had lost all love and respect for him, I continued to desire him. To protect myself from the temptation of love, I told myself that I would never find another man who could give me as much pleasure as Juan. I also knew that I had to guard against the illnesses men contract and spread. I had seen their effects, and healthy as I was, I feared them as I feared the Devil, since the least contact with the French illness is all that it takes to become infected. Or I might get pregnant. Vinegar-soaked sponges are not totally reliable, and I had so often prayed to the Virgin for a child that she might grant me the favor at the wrong time. Miracles can be inopportune.

These sensible precautions served me well during years of forced chastity in which my heart was snuffed out but my body continued to make demands. In this New World the air is warm, propitious to sensuality; everything is more intense: color, aromas, tastes—even the flowers, with their seductive fragrances, and the fruit, warm and fleshy, provoke lust. In Cartagena, and then in Panamá, I questioned the principles that had guided me in Spain. My youth was passing me by, my life was being wasted. Who cared about my virtue? Who was there to judge me? I concluded that God must be more compliant in the Americas than in Extremadura. If he forgave the abuses committed in his name against thousands of natives, surely he would forgive one poor woman's weakness.

I was elated when we reached the port of Callao safe and sound and I could leave the ship, where I was beginning to feel crazed.

There is nothing as oppressive as the confinement of a ship in the immensity of the fathomless, limitless ocean. "Port" was too ambitious a word for Callao in those years. They say that now it is the most important port in the Pacific, and that incalculable treasures leave from there for Spain, but at that time it was a miserable little pier. From Callao I accompanied the priests to Ciudad de los Reyes, which now is called Lima, not as graceful as the City of Kings. Since I prefer the former, I will continue to refer to it that way. The sky over the city Francisco Pizarro founded in a large valley seemed forever cloudy, and sunlight filtering through the humid air lent it the ethereal aura one sees in the hazy sketches of Daniel Belalcázar. Once there, I made the necessary inquries, and after a few days found a soldier who had known Juan de Málaga.

"You have come too late, señora," he told me. "Your husband died in the battle at Las Salinas."

"Juan wasn't a soldier," I corrected.

"Here there is no other occupation; even the priests take up the sword."

The man was frightful looking: a wild beard covered half his chest, his clothing was filthy and in tatters, his teeth had fallen out, and he seemed drunk. He swore to me that he had been a friend of my husband, but I did not believe him. First he told me that Juan was a foot soldier, deep in debt from gambling, and drained by the vices of women and wine, but then he went off on a tangent about a helmet with white plumes and a brocade cape. Then to top off my discomfort, he lunged forward as if to throw his arms around me, and when I pushed him away offered to buy my favors with gold.

Since I had already come so far—from Extremadura to the ancient territories of Atahualpa—I decided that I could afford to make one last effort, so I joined a caravan transporting supplies and a herd of llamas and alpacas to Cuzco. We were in the care of a group of soldiers under the command of a certain Lieutenant Núñez, handsome, boastful, and, it appeared, accustomed to indulging his whims.

Traveling with me, in addition to the soldiers, were two priests, a scribe, an auditor, and a German physician, all of us on horseback or mules, or carried in litters by the Indians. I was the only Spanish woman, but some Quechua Indian women with their children were following along behind the interminable string of bearers, carrying food for their husbands. Their clothing of brilliantly colored wool gave an impression of gaiety that was belied by the sullen, rancorous expression of subjected peoples. They were short, with high cheek-bones and small almond-shaped eyes, and their teeth were black from the coca leaves they constantly chewed to lift their spirits. I found the children enchanting, and a few of the women attractive, though none of them smiled. They followed us for several leagues, until Núñez ordered them to go back home; then they dropped off one by one, leading their children by the hand.

The bearers were very strong and, though barefoot and laden like beasts, they endured the vagaries of the climate and fatigue of the journey better than those of us riding on horseback. They could trot along for hours without changing their rhythm, silent and abstracted, in a kind of dreamlike state. They spoke only the most basic Spanish, plaintive, singsong, and always as if asking a question. The barking of Lieutenant Núñez's ferocious mastiffs, which had been trained to kill, was the only thing that seemed to penetrate their absorption.

Núñez began to harass me the first day of the march, and from then on never left me in peace. Prudently, I tried to hold him at bay by reminding him of my status as a married woman, knowing it did not behoove me to make an enemy of the man, but the farther we went, the bolder he became. He made much of being a hidalgo, something I had difficulty believing, given his behavior. He had made a small fortune, and kept thirty Indian concubines—half in Ciudad de los Reyes and half in Cuzco—"all very obliging," as he described them. In his town in Spain that would have been scandalous, but it is the norm in the New World, where Spaniards take Indian and black women at will. They abandon most of them after using them for their pleasure, but keep a few as servants, though rarely do they look after the children born of those subjugated mothers. And so these lands are being peopled with resentful mestizos. Núñez told me he would dismiss his concubines once I accepted his proposal, for he had no doubt that I would do just that as soon as I verified that my husband was dead—which he was certain was true. That pompous lieutenant was very like Juan de Málaga in his defects but he had none of the virtues, so why would I love him. And I am not one of those women who trips twice over the same stone.

At that time, the number of Spanish women in Peru could still be counted on one's fingers, and I knew of none who had come alone, as I had. They were wives or daughters of soldiers, and had come at the insistence of the Crown, which was attempting to reunite families and create a legitimate and decent society in the colonies. Those women wasted their lives behind closed doors, lonely and bored, though well cared for, since they had dozens of Indian women to carry out their least desires. I was told that Spanish ladies in Peru did not even wipe their own bottoms; their servants were charged with that duty.

Since the men in the caravan were not accustomed to seeing a Spanish woman without a companion, they made an effort to treat me with the greatest consideration, as if I were a person of high rank and breeding and not a poor seamstress. In that long, slow journey to Cuzco they tended to my needs, shared their food with me, lent me their tents and mounts, and gave me boots and a blanket woven of vicuña, the finest cloth in the world. In exchange they asked only that I sing them a song or tell them tales of Spain when we camped at night and their hearts were heavy with nostalgia. Without their help, I wouldn't have made it, for there everything cost a hundred times more than it did in Spain, and soon I had exhausted my last maravedí. Gold was so abundant in Peru that silver was scorned, and essential items—like shoes for horses or ink for writing—were so scarce that the prices were absurd. I pulled a rotten tooth for one of my companions, a quick and simple procedure. All I had needed were pincers and a prayer to Santa Apolonia but he paid me with an emerald worthy of a bishop. It is now set in the crown of

Nuestra Señora del Socorro, and is worth more than it was then, since precious stones are not plentiful in Chile.

After several days' march along the highways of the Incas, across dry plains and mountains, crossing gorges on hanging bridges woven of vines and reeds, and wading through streams and salt pools, upward, always upward, we eventually reached the end of the journey. Lieutenant Núñez, high atop his horse, pointed out Cuzco with his lance.

I have never seen anything like the magnificent city of Cuzco, the umbilicus of the Inca empire, a sacred place where man speaks with the divinity. Perhaps Madrid, Rome, or some of the Moorish cities that have a reputation for splendor can be compared to Cuzco, but I have not seen them. Despite the destruction and vandalism of war, it was a gleaming white jewel beneath a purple sky. I had difficulty breathing and for several days went about short of breath, not because of the altitude and thin air, as I had been warned, but because of the massive beauty of the city's temples, fortresses, and buildings. I was told that when the first Spaniards arrived there were palaces covered with sheets of gold, though now the walls were bare. At the north edge of the city sits a spectacular construction, Sacsahuamán, the sacred fortress, with its three lines of high, sharply zigzagging walls, the Temple of the Sun, a labyrinth of streets, towers, paths, stairs, terraces, cellars, and dwellings where fifty or sixty thousand people lived in comfort. The name means "satisfied hawk" and, like a hawk, it watches over Cuzco. It was built with monumental chiseled stone blocks put together without mortar, but with such perfection that a thin knife blade cannot be inserted between them. How did they cut those enormous stones without metal tools? How did they transport them so many leagues without wheels or horses? And I wondered, too, how a handful of Spanish soldiers managed so quickly to conquer an empire capable of erecting a marvel like that. The Incas may have been quarreling among themselves, and the Spaniards may have had thousands of Yanaconas to serve them and fight their wars, but their epic achievement still seems inexplicable today. The Spaniards would say, "We have God on our side, besides gunpowder and iron," grateful that the natives were defending themselves with stone weapons. "When they saw us arrive from the sea on houses fitted with great wings, they believed that we were gods," they would add, but it is my opinion that they were the ones who spread that very convenient story, and that both the Indians and they ended up believing it.

I walked through the streets of Cuzco, amazed, studying the throngs. Those copper-colored people never smiled at me or looked me in the eye. I tried to imagine their lives before we arrived, when entire families in their colorful clothing walked these same streets, along with priests with gold breastplates, and the Inca, bedecked with jewels and carried in a gold litter decorated with the feathers of fabulous birds, accompanied by his musicians, his pompous war-riors, and his interminable train of wives and virgins of the Sun. That complex culture survived, nearly intact, despite the invaders, but it was less visible. An Inca ruler was still enthroned, kept as a pampered prisoner by Francisco Pizarro, but I never saw him because I had no entrée to his sequestered court. Crowds filled the street, but they were silent. For each bearded Spaniard there were hundreds of smooth-skinned natives. The Spaniards, haughty and noisy, lived in a different dimension, as if the natives were invisible, mere shadows in the narrow cobbled streets. Indians stepped aside for the foreigners who had defeated them, but they maintained their customs, beliefs, and hierarchies, with the hope that one day, with time and patience, they would be free of the bearded ones. They could not conceive of their staying forever.

By then the fratricidal violence that had divided the Spaniards in the days of Diego de Almagro had calmed somewhat. In Cuzco, life was beginning again with a slow rhythm, the pace cautious because there was still unvented rancor and tempers were easily heated. The soldiers were keyed up over the merciless civil war, the country was impoverished and chaotic, and the Indians subjected to forced labor were storing up hatred. Our Emperor Charles V had ordered in his royal proclamations that the natives be treated with respect, that they be evangelized and civilized through kindness and good works, but that was not the reality. The king, who had never set foot in the New World, dictated his judicious laws in dark rooms in ancient palaces thousands of leagues away from the peoples he was endeavoring to govern, but never taking human greed into account. Few Spaniards respected his ordinances, least of all the marqués gobernador Francisco Pizarro. Even the lowest Spaniard had Indians for servants, and the rich landowners had them by the hundreds, since the land and the mines were worthless without men to work them. Under the overseer's whip, the Indians obeyed, although some chose a compassionate death for their families, and then killed themselves.

Speaking with the soldiers, I was able to fit together the pieces of Juan's story, and to learn, beyond a shadow of a doubt, that he was dead. My husband had reached Peru, after being worn down in his search for El Dorado in the steaming jungles farther north, and had enlisted in the army of Francisco Pizarro. He was not cut out to be a soldier, but he had somehow survived in his encounters with Indians. He obtained a little gold, since gold was everywhere, but again and again he lost it gambling. He owed money to several of his comrades, and a sizable amount to Hernando Pizarro, brother of the governor. To pay off that debt he had been forced to serve as the governor's lackey, and at his orders had been involved in several questionable activities.

In the battle of Las Salinas, my husband had fought with the victorious troops, where he was given a strange assignment, the last of his life. Before the battle, Hernando Pizarro ordered him to exchange uniforms with him, so while Juan was outfitted in orange velvet and fine armor, the brocade cape Pizarro usually wore, and a white-plumed helmet with a silver visor, his commander was blending in with the infantry, dressed as an ordinary soldier. It is possible that Hernando Pizarro might have chosen my husband because he was tall: Juan was exactly his height. Because his usual garb was so conspicuous, Pizarro expected that his enemies would seek him out during the battle, which is in fact what happened. The extravagant uniform was spotted by Almagro's captains, who slashed their way toward it with their swords, and taking the inconsequential Juan de Málaga for the brother of the governor, killed him. Hernando Pizarro's life was saved but that cowardice forever stained his name. His previous military feats were erased at one stroke, and nothing he ever did could restore his lost prestige. The shame of that ruse spilled over onto his fellow Spaniards—friends and enemies—who never forgave him.

A hasty conspiracy of silence was woven around Pizarro, whom everyone feared, but the despicable thing he had done during the battle circulated in whispers through taverns and wherever else men gathered. There was no one who didn't know and talk about it, and so I was able to verify all the details, though I never found my husband's remains.

From that day, I have been haunted by the near certainty that Juan did not receive a Christian burial, and that his soul is wandering in pain, seeking repose. Juan de Málaga followed me on my long journey to Chile; he was with me as we founded Santiago; he held my arm when I executed the caciques, the Indian chieftains; and he made fun of me when I wept out of rage and love for Valdivia. Still today, forty years later, he appears from time to time, although my eyes are failing now and I often confuse him with other ghosts from the past.

My large house in Santiago, with its patios, stables, and garden, occupies an entire block. Its walls are adobe, very thick, and oak beams support the high ceilings. There are many hiding places for errant spirits, demons, or Death, which is not a hooded skeleton with empty eye sockets, as the priests tell us to frighten us, but a large, roly-poly woman with an opulent bosom and welcoming arms: a maternal angel. I get lost in this mansion. It has been months since I've slept, I miss Rodrigo's warm hand on my belly. At night, when the servants have gone to bed and no one is up but the

outside guards and a chambermaid who stays awake in case I need
her, I roam through the house with my lamp, examining the large
rooms with lime-whitened walls and blue ceilings, straightening the
paintings and flowers in the vases, and peeking into the birdcages.
Actually, I go looking for Death. At times I have been so close to
her that I have caught her scent of freshly laundered clothing, but
she is clever, and a tease. I cannot catch her, she slips away and
hides among the multitude of spirits that inhabit this house. Among
them is poor Juan, who followed me to the ends of the earth, with
his rattling, unburied bones and bloody brocade rags.

It was in Cuzco that the last traces of my first husband vanished.
I have no doubt that his body, clad in Hernando Pizarro's princely
attire, was the first thing the victorious soldiers carried away at the
end of the battle, before the Indians swooped down from the hills
to make off with the spoils of the vanquished. The Spaniards must
have been surprised when they found the man beneath the helmet
and armor was not the enemy commander but an anonymous soldier, and I suppose that they grudgingly obeyed the order to hide
what had happened, because the last thing a Spaniard forgives is
cowardice. However, they hid it so well that they completely swept
away any trace of my husband's passage through life.

When the marqués gobernador, Francisco Pizarro, learned that
the widow of Juan de Málaga was going around asking questions,
he wanted to meet me. He had built a palace in la Ciudad de los
Reyes, and from there lorded it over the empire with pomp, per-
fidy, and an iron hand, but at that moment he was visiting Cuzco.
I was received in a salon decorated with carved furniture and Peruvian rugs of rich wool. The top of the large table, the chair backs,
the goblets, the candelabra and spittoons were solid silver. There
was more silver in Peru than iron. Several courtiers, clustered in the
corners, somber as vultures, were whispering and moving papers
around to look important. Pizarro was dressed in black velvet, a
tightly fitted doublet with slashed sleeves, a white ruff, a thick gold
chain upon his chest, gold buckles on his shoes, and a sable cape
thrown over his shoulders. He was a man of about sixty, haughty,

with sallow skin, a graying beard, sunken eyes with a suspicious gleam in them, and a disagreeable falsetto voice. He offered his brief condolences for the death of my husband, without mentioning his name, and then in an unexpected gesture handed me a pouch of money so that I could survive "until you can find a ship back to Spain." At that very instant, I made an impulsive decision, one I have never regretted.

"With all respect, Your Excellency, I do not plan to return to Spain," I announced.

A terrible shadow flashed across the face of the marqués gobernador. He walked to the window and for a long while stood contemplating the city laid out at his feet. I thought he had forgotten me, and I had started toward the door when suddenly he spoke to me again, without turning around.

"What did you tell me your name is, señora?

"Inés Suárez, Señor Marqués Gobernador, at your service."

"And how do you intend to make a living?"

"Honestly, Excellency."

"And discreetly, I hope. Discretion is greatly appreciated here, especially in women. The city officials in the ayuntamiento will find you a house. Good day, and good fortune."

That was all. I realized that if I wanted to stay in Cuzco, I had better stop asking questions. Juan de Málaga was dead and I was free. I can say with all certainty that my life began that day. The years that preceded it were merely training for what was to come.

I beg you to have a little patience, Isabel. You will soon see that this disorderly narrative will come to the moment when my path crosses that of Pedro de Valdivia and the epic I want to tell you about begins. Before that, I had been an insignificant seamstress in Plasencia, like the hundreds and hundreds of hardworking women who came before and will come after me. With Pedro de Valdivia I lived a life of legend, and with him I conquered a kingdom. Although I adored Rodrigo de Quiroga, your father, and lived with him thirty years, the only real reason for telling my story is the conquest of Chile, which I shared with Pedro de Valdivia.

I established myself in Cuzco, in the house the ayuntamiento lent me in accordance with instructions from Marqués Gobernador Pizarro. It was modest, but decent, with three rooms and a patio, well situated in the center of the city, and always fragrant because of the honeysuckle climbing the walls. They also provided me with three Indian servants, two of whom were young; the older woman had adopted the Christian name of Catalina, and she turned out to be my best friend. I began to practice my trade as a seamstress, a skill much appreciated among the Spaniards, who were having a hard time trying to make do with the few things they had brought from Spain. I also treated soldiers who had been crippled or badly wounded in the war, most of whom had fought at Las Salinas. The German doctor who had traveled with me in the caravan from Ciudad de los Reyes to Cuzco often called on me to help him with the worst cases, and I, in turn, always brought Catalina, for she knew many remedies and enchantments. A certain rivalry grew between Catalina and the doctor that did not always benefit their unfortunate patients. She was not interested in learning anything about the four humors that determine the state of bodily health, and he scorned sorcery, although at times it worked very well. The most difficult part of my work with them were the amputations, something that has always turned my stomach, but it had to be done because once flesh begins to rot there is no other way to save the life of the patient. In any case, very few survive those operations.

I know nothing at all about Catalina's life before the Spaniards arrived in Peru. Suspicious, mysterious, she never spoke of her past. She was short and square, the color of a hazelnut, and her two thick braids were tied behind her back with strands of bright wool. Her eyes were dark as charcoal, and she smelled of smoke; she could be in several places at the same time, and disappear in a sigh. She learned Spanish, she adapted to our customs, she seemed satisfied to live with me, and a couple of years later she insisted on accompanying me to Chile. "I wanting to go with you, then, *señorayy*," she begged me in her singing speech. She had agreed to be baptized in order to avoid problems, but she had not abandoned her beliefs. Just as she prayed the rosary and lighted candles at the altar of Nuestra Señora del Socorro, she recited her prayers to the Sun. This wise and loyal companion taught me about Peru's medicinal plants and their curative properties, which were very different from those in Spain. The good woman maintained that illness occurs when demons and malign spirits creep into bodily orifices and take shelter in the abdomen. She had worked with Inca medicine men who knew how to drill holes in the skulls of their patients to relieve migraine headaches and dementias, a procedure that fascinated the German doctor but that no Spaniard was willing to undergo

Catalina knew how to bleed the sick as well as the best surgeon, and she was expert in purges that alleviated colic and bloating, but she made fun of the German's pharmacopoeia. "You just killing with that, then, *tatay*," she would tell him, smiling, and revealing teeth black from chewing coca, and he ended by losing faith in the renowned remedies he had struggled so hard to bring from his country. Catalina knew powerful poisons, aphrodisiac potions, and herbs that created inexhaustible energy, along with others that induced sleep, stopped bleeding, and eased pain. She was magic. She could talk with the dead and see the future. At times she drank a concoction brewed from several plants that transported her to another world, where she was given advice by the angels. She did not call them angels, but she described them as transparent, winged beings able to strike a man dead with the fire of their gaze. They had to be angels. We were careful not to mention these matters in the presence of others; they would have accused us of witchcraft and of trafficking with the Evil One. It is not amusing to end up in the dungeon of the Inquisition. Many of those poor wretches burned at the stake for less than we knew. I have seen people die in that way, and I can testify to the cruelty of that torture.

Naturally, Catalina's spells did not always give the expected result. Once she tried to eject the spirit of Juan de Málaga, which was always around the houses, bothering us, but all that happened was that several hens died that same night, and the next day a two-headed llama appeared in the center of Cuzco. The animal fanned the discord between Indians and Spanish, because the former believed the llama was the reincarnation of the immortal Inca Atahualpa, and the latter ran it through with a lance to prove just how little immortal it was. An altercation ensued that left several Indians dead and a Spaniard wounded. Catalina lived with me many years; she looked after my health, she warned me of danger, and she guided me in important decisions. The one promise she did not keep was to stay with me through my last years. She died and I live on.

I taught the two young Indian girls the ayuntamiento sent me to mend, wash, and iron clothes, as I had done in Plasencia, another service greatly appreciated at that time in Cuzco. I had a clay oven built in the patio, and Catalina and I began making empanadas. Wheat flour was very dear, but we learned to make them with cornmeal. They never had time to cool after they came from the oven because the smell spread throughout the neighborhood and people came running to buy them. We always put some aside for beggars and the disabled, who were fed from public charity. The strong aroma of meat, fried onion, cumin, and baked dough soaked into my skin so deeply that I have never lost it. I will die smelling like an empanada.

I was able to make a bare living, but in that expensive and corrupt city a widow was hard pressed to rise out of poverty. I could have married, since there were many desperate unmarried men, some rather attractive, but Catalina always warned me against them. She often read my fortune with her beads and divining shells, and always told me the same thing: I would live a long life and I would become a queen, but that future was linked with the man in her visions. According to her, it was none of the ones who came knocking at my door, or hounded me when I went out. "Patience, *mamitayy*, your *viracocha* will be coming," she promised.

Among my suitors was the self-important Lieutenant Núñez, who had not given up on his quest to get into my petticoats, as he indelicately put it. He could not understand why I dismissed his petitions, since I no longer had a husband to use as an excuse. It had been confirmed that I was a widow, as he had assured me from the beginning. He had it in his head that my refusals were a kind of flirtation, and so the more intractable my rebuffs, the more he fancied me. I had to forbid him to let his mastiffs into my house; they terrorized my servants. Trained to subdue Indians, when they smelled the girls they began to tug at their chains, snarling and barking and showing their teeth. Nothing entertained the lieutenant so much as setting his beasts against the Indians, and he continued to ignore my pleas, and burst into my house with his dogs as he did everywhere he went. But one day his hounds waked with a green foam frothing from their snouts, and a few hours later they were stiff as boards. Their master, enraged, threatened to kill whoever it was who had poisoned them, but the German doctor convinced him that they had died of the plague and that he must burn their bodies immediately to prevent contagion. Núñez complied, fearing that the first victim would be himself.

The lieutenant's visits became more and more frequent, and, as he also stalked me through the streets, my life became a hell. "This white man, then, *señorayy*, he is not understanding with words. I say good that he go dying, like the dogs of him," Catalina announced. I preferred not to pursue further what she meant by that. On one of his visits, Núñez arrived, as always, with his macho scent and gifts I didn't want, filling my house with his noisy presence.

"Why are you tormenting me, my beautiful Inés?" he asked for the hundredth time, putting his arm around my waist.

"Do not make so bold, señor," I said, pulling away from him. "I have not given you permission to treat me in this familiar fashion."

"Well, then, my distinguished Inés. When shall we wed?"

"Never. Here are your shirts and breeches, mended and clean. Look for another washerwoman, because I do not want you in my house. Good-bye!" And I pushed him toward the door.

"Good-bye, you say, Inés? Good-*bye*? You do not know me, woman! No one insults me, and least of all a whore!" he shouted from the street.

It was the quiet hour of dusk when my neighbors gathered to wait for the last empanadas to come out of the oven, but I did not have the spirit to tend to them. I was trembling with anger and shame. I distributed a few empanadas to the poor so they would not go hungry, and then I closed my door, which usually I kept open until the cool of night fell.

"He is a pest, then, *mamitayy*, but do not hit the top. This Núñez, he will be bringing good luck," Catalina consoled me.

"The only thing that man can bring me is misfortune, Catalina! A blustering, vindictive man is always dangerous."

Catalina was right. Thanks to the ominous lieutenant, who went and sat himself down in a tavern to drink and boast about what he was going to do to me, that same night I met the man of my destiny, the one Catalina was constantly predicting would come along.

The tavern consisted of a low-ceilinged room in which a few window slits let in barely enough air to breathe. It was run by a good-hearted man from Andalucia who always gave credit to soldiers short of funds. For that reason, and because of the music—a black man playing some sort of stringed instrument and another with a drum—the place was very popular. The happy sounds of the clients contrasted with the somber figure of a man drinking alone in one corner. He was sitting on a bench before a small table on which he had spread out a sheet of yellowed paper and weighed it down with a carafe of wine to keep it from curling up. He was Pedro de Valdivia, Gobernador Francisco Pizarro's field marshal and hero of the battle of Las Salinas. He was by then one of the wealthiest encomenderos in Peru. In payment for his services, Pizarro had allotted him, for his lifetime, a silver mine in Porco, a fertile and productive hacienda in La Canela valley, and hundreds of Indians to work them.

And what was the famed Valdivia doing at that moment? Not calculating the amount of silver extracted from his mine, or the count of his llamas or sacks of maize; he was studying a map Diego de Almagro had hurriedly sketched in prison before his execution. Valdivia was bedeviled by the idea of triumphing where Adelantado Almagro had failed—in the far south of the hemisphere. It was yet to be conquered and populated, the one remaining place where a military man like himself could achieve glory. He did not want to live in the shadow of Francisco Pizarro and comfortably grow old in Peru. Neither did he intend to return to Spain, however rich and respected he might be. He was even less attracted to the idea of rejoining Marina, who had been faithfully waiting for years and never tired of calling him home in her letters, which always abounded with blessings and reproaches. Spain was the past. Chile was the future. The map showed the routes Almagro followed on his expedition and the most difficult points: the sierra, the desert, and the areas in which enemies were concentrated. "No one can go any farther south than the Bío-Bío river; the Mapuche will stop him," Almagro had repeated several times. Those words were like a thorn in Valdivia's side. I would have gone farther, he thought, although he never doubted the adelantado's courage.

That is what he was doing when above the noise of the tavern he heard the loud voice of a drunken man, and then, despite himself, listened to what the blusterer was saying. He was talking about someone to whom he planned to give a well-deserved lesson, a certain Inés, a prideful woman who dared defy an honest lieutenant serving the most Christian Emperor Charles V. The name sounded familiar to Valdivia, and he deduced that Núñez was talking about the young widow who washed and mended clothes in her home on Templo de las Vírgenes. He had not called on her services—he had his own Indian girls for that—but he had seen her a few times in the street and in church, and had noticed her because she was one of the few Spanish women in Cuzco. He had wondered how long a woman like that would be alone. On a couple of occasions he had followed some distance behind her for a few blocks, merely to enjoy the movement of her hips—she walked with the strong strides of a Gypsy—and to catch the reflection of the sun on her coppery hair. It seemed to him that she radiated assurance and strength of character, qualities he demanded in his captains but nothing he had ever thought he would appreciate in a woman. Up to that time, he had been attracted to sweet, fragile girls who awakened his desire to protect them; that was why he had married Marina. There was nothing vulnerable or innocent about this Inés. She was, in fact, intimidating: pure energy, like a contained cyclone, yet that was the very thing that made him notice her. At least that is what he later told me.

With the bits of what he could hear—most of the man's remarks were drowned out by the noise of the tavern—Valdivia was able to piece together the plan of the drunken lieutenant, who was shouting at the top of his voice for two volunteers to kidnap the woman by night and bring her to his home. The response to his request was a chorus of loud laughter and obscene jokes, but no one offered to help him. What he was asking was not only cowardly, it was also dangerous. It was all well and good to rape a woman in wartime, and to pleasure himself with Indian women—no one cared what happened to them—but it was something else for a soldier to assault a Spanish widow woman who had been personally received by the gobernador. Better to get that idea out of your head, his fellow drinkers advised Núñez, but he proclaimed that he would have no trouble enlisting strong arms to carry out his proposal.

Pedro de Valdivia kept a close eye on Núñez, and a half an hour later followed him outside. The man was staggering, unaware that anyone was behind him. He stopped a moment at my door, calculating whether he could handle the matter himself, but decided not to run that risk. However much the alcohol was clouding his reason, he knew that his reputation and his military career hung in the balance. Valdivia watched him stumble away, and took up a place at the corner, hidden in the shadows. He did not have long to wait. Soon a pair of stealthy Indians appeared and began to prowl about the house, trying the door and shutters of the windows that faced the street. When they found that they were all locked from the inside, they decided to climb the stone fence, which was only five feet high at the rear. Within a few minutes they had dropped down onto the patio, but not without the bad luck of tipping over and shattering a clay jug.

I am a light sleeper and I was awakened by the noise. For a moment Pedro did nothing, waiting to see how far the two marauders were willing to go, then leaped over the wall behind them. By then I had lighted a lamp and picked up the long knife I used to mince the meat for the empanadas. I was ready to use it, but prayed I wouldn't have to, since Sebastián Romero already weighed heavily on my conscience and it would have been painful to add another death. I went outside to the patio, with Catalina close behind. We were too late to catch the best part of the show, because the caballero had already corralled the two would-be kidnappers and was tying them up with the same rope they had brought for me. It all happened very rapidly, with no apparent effort on the part of Valdivia, who seemed more amused than angry, as if he had interrupted some boyish prank.

The situation was quite ridiculous: I in my nightdress with my hair hanging loose; Catalina cursing in Quechua; a pair of Indians shaking with terror; and an hidalgo dressed in polished leather boots, velvet doublet, silk breeches, with sword in hand, sweeping the patio with the feather on his hat as he bowed in greeting. We both burst out laughing.

"These miserable creatures will not bother you again, señora," he said gallantly.

"I am not worried about them, caballero, only the person who sent them."

"He will not be up to any further chicanery because tomorrow he will have to answer to me."

"You know who he is?"

"I have a good idea, but if I am mistaken, these two will confess under torture whose orders they were obeying."

At these words, the Indians threw themselves down and kissed the caballero's boots, pleading for his mercy, with the name of Lieutenant Núñez spilling from their lips. It was Catalina's opinion that we should slit their throats right then and there, and Valdivia agreed, but I stepped between the poor Indians and his sword.

"No, señor, I beg you. I do not want dead men in my patio. It would make a mess, and bring bad luck."

Again Valdivia laughed. He opened the gate and sent the men on their way with a good kick in the rear for each of them, warning them to disappear from Cuzco that very night or face the consequences.

"I fear that Lieutenant Núñez will not be as magnanimous as you are, caballero. He will move heaven and earth to find those men; they know too much and it would not be convenient for him if they talk," I said.

"Believe me, señora, I have the authority to send Núñez to rot in Los Chunchos jungle, and I assure you I will do just that," he replied.

At about that point, I realized who he was. He was the famous field marshal, the hero of many wars, one of the richest and most powerful men in all Peru. I had glimpsed him once or twice, but always from a distance, admiring his Arab horse and his innate sense of authority.

That night my life and that of Pedro de Valdivia were defined. We had wandered for years in circles, blindly seeking each other, until finally we met in the patio of that small house on Templo de las Vírgenes. Grateful for his aid, I invited him into my modest parlor. To welcome him, Catalina went to fetch a jug of the wine I always kept in my home. Before vanishing in thin air, as was her custom, she signaled to me from behind my guest's back, and that was how I knew that this was the man she had been seeing in her divining shells. Surprised—I had never imagined that fortune would send me someone as important as Pedro de Valdivia—I studied him from head to toe in the yellow lamplight. I liked what I saw: eyes blue as the skies of Extremadura; a frank, though severe expression; rugged features; a warrior's build; hands hardened by the sword but with long, elegant fingers. Such a man, unmarred, was an unusual prize in the Americas, where so many are marked by horrible scars or by missing eyes, nostrils, even limbs.

And what did he see? A slim, barefoot woman of medium height, with chestnut-colored eyes beneath thick eyebrows and loose, unruly hair, clad in a nightdress of ordinary cloth. Mute, we stared at each other an eternity, unable to look away. Although the night was cool, my skin was burning and a trickle of sweat rolled down my back. I saw that he was shaken by the same hunger; I could feel the air in the room grow heavy. Catalina emerged from nowhere with the wine, but when she saw what was happening, she disappeared and left us alone.

Afterward, Pedro would confess that he did not take the initiative in making love that night because he needed time to calm down, and to think. "When I saw you, I was afraid for the first time in my life," he would tell me much later. He was not a man for mistresses or concubines, he had no lovers, and he never had relations with Indian women, although I suppose that occasionally he visited the women who sell themselves. In his way, he had always remained faithful to Marina Ortiz de Gaete, to whom he felt indebted for having fallen in love with her when she was only thirteen; he had not made her happy and had abandoned her in order to throw himself into the adventure of America. He felt responsible for her before God. But I had no ties, and even if Pedro had had half a dozen wives, I would have loved him just the same. It was inevitable. He was nearly forty years old, and I close to thirty. Neither of us had time to waste, which is why I set about heading things along the right course.

How did we come to embrace so quickly? Who held out the first hand? Who sought the other's lips for a kiss? Surely it was I. As soon as I could get my voice back and break the charged silence in which we stood and stared at each other, I told him without preamble that I had been waiting for him for a long, long time, that I had seen him in dreams and in the beads and divining shells, and that I was prepared to love him forever—along with a number of other promises. All without holding anything back and without a touch of shyness. Pedro backed away, stiff, pale, until his back was against the wall. What woman in her right mind speaks that way to a stranger? But he did not believe that I had lost my mind, or that I was some common Cuzco whore, because he, too, felt in his bones and in the caverns of his soul the certainty that we had been born to love each other. He exhaled a sigh, almost a sob, whispering my name in a quavering voice. "And I have been waiting for you, forever," I think he said. Or perhaps he didn't. I suppose that as life passes we embellish some memories and try to forget others. What I am sure of is that we made love that very night, and that from that first embrace we were consumed in the same fire.

Pedro de Valdivia had been forged in the roar and tumult of war; he knew nothing of love but was ready to welcome it when it came along. He lifted me up and in four long strides carried me to my bed, which we fell onto, he atop me, kissing me, nibbling me, desperately struggling to get out of his boots and stockings, his doublet and breeches, with the fumbling ardor of a boy. I let him do it himself, to give him time to get his breath; perhaps it had been a long time since he had been with a woman. I pressed him to my breast, sensing the beating of his heart, his animal heat, his male smell.

Pedro had a lot to learn, but there was no hurry. We had the rest of our lives before us, and I was a good teacher. That, at least, is something I can thank Juan de Málaga for. Once Pedro realized that behind the closed door I commanded, and that there was no dishonor in it, he obeyed me with excellent humor. This took some time, let's say four or five hours, because he believed that surrender was the female's role and domination the male's. He had seen that in his animals and learned it as a soldier, but it was not for nothing that Juan de Málaga had spent years teaching me to know my own body, as well as a man's. I do not propose that all men are the same, but they are quite similar, and with a minimum of intuition any woman can make them happy. The reverse is not true: few men know how to satisfy a woman, and even fewer are interested in doing so. Pedro was wise enough to leave his sword on the other side of the door and surrender to me. The details of that first night are not important, just let me say that we both discovered what real love is. Until then we had never experienced the fusion of body and soul. My relationship with Juan had been carnal, and his with Marina had been spiritual. Ours was complete.

Valdivia did not leave my house for two days. During that time the shutters were never opened, no one made empanadas, my Indian servants tiptoed around silently, and Catalina saw that the beggars were fed corn soup. That loyal woman brought wine and food to our bed. She also prepared a tub with warm water so we could bathe, a Peruvian custom she had taught me. Like every Spaniard, Pedro thought it was dangerous to immerse the body in that way, that it caused weakening of the lungs and thinning of the blood, but I assured him that that Peruvians bathed every day and none had soft lungs or watery blood. Those two days went by in a sigh, as we told each other our pasts and made love in a blazing whirlwind, a giving that was never enough, a crazed desire to sink into each other, to die and die again. . . . Ay, Pedro! Ay, Inés! We would fall back together, our arms and legs still entangled, exhausted, bathed in the same sweat, talking in whispers. Then our desire would be reborn with greater intensity among damp sheets that bore a male scent—iron, wine, and horse—and a woman's—kitchen, smoke, and sea—*our* smell, unique and unforgettable, the breath of the jungle, our combined essence. We learned to rise to the heavens and moan together, lashed by the whip that drove us to the edge of death, and finally engulfed us in profound lethargy. Again and again, we awakened, ready to invent love all over again, until the third day dawned with its riot of roosters and the aroma of baked bread. Then Pedro, transformed, asked for his clothing and his sword.

Oh, how tenacious memory is! Mine never leaves me in peace; it fills my mind with images, words, pain, and love. I feel that I am living once more what I have already lived. The effort of writing this account lies not in the remembering but in the slow work of putting pen to paper. I have never had a good hand, despite the efforts of González de Marmolejo, but now my writing is nearly illegible. There is a certain urgency because the weeks are flying by and I have much left to tell. I am weary. My pen scratches the paper and I am spattered with ink. In sum, this labor is too much for me. Why do I insist on doing it? Those who truly knew me are dead. Only you, Isabel, have an idea of who I am, but that idea is colored by your affection and the debt you believe you owe me. You owe me nothing, I have told you that many times. I am the one who is indebted because you satisfied my deepest need: to be a mother. You are my friend and my confidante, the one person who knows my secrets, including some that, out of modesty, I did not share with your father. We get along well, you and I. You have a good sense of humor and we laugh together, that woman's laugh born of complicity. I am grateful that you and your children have moved here, when your own home is two blocks away. You tell me that you need company while your husband is away at war, as once mine was, but I do not believe you. The truth is that you are afraid that living as a widow I will die alone in this large old house, which very soon will be yours, as all my other earthly goods already are. I am comforted by the idea of seeing you become a wealthy woman. I can go to the other world in peace, since I have faithfully fulfilled the promise to protect you I made to your father when he brought you to my house. And though I was Pedro de Valdivia's lover at the time, that did not stop me from welcoming you with open arms.

By the time you came into my life, Isabel, the city of Santiago had begun to thrive, and we were giving ourselves certain airs, although Santiago was not truly a city, it was barely a village. Because of his merits and his spotless character, Rodrigo de Quiroga had become Pedro's favorite captain, and my best friend. I knew that he was in love with me—a woman always knows—but he did not betray his feelings by gesture or word. Rodrigo would not have been capable of admitting his love even in his secret heart, out of loyalty to Valdivia, his superior officer and his friend. I suppose that

I loved Rodrigo too—it is possible to love two men at the same time—but I kept that sentiment to myself in order not to damage his honor or his life. But this is not the moment to go into all that; it will come later.

There are things I have been too busy to tell you, and if I do not write them down now I will carry them with me to the tomb. Despite my desire to tell you everything, I have left out a lot. I have had to select only what is essential, but I am confident that I have not betrayed the truth. This is my story, and that of a man, Don Pedro de Valdivia, whose heroic feats were recorded by chroniclers in rigorous detail; his exploits will endure in those pages till the end of time. However, I know Valdivia in a way history could never know him: what he feared and how he loved.

My relationship with Pedro de Valdivia turned my life upside down. I could not live without him. One day without seeing him and I was feverish. A night without being in his arms was torment. At first, more than love, I felt a blind, reckless passion for him, which fortunately he returned. If not, I would have lost my mind. Later, when we were overcoming obstacles placed in our path by destiny, passion gave way to love. I admired him as much as I desired him; I succumbed totally before his energy; I was seduced by his courage and his idealism.

Valdivia exercised his authority matter-of-factly; his mere presence demanded obedience. He had an imposing, irresistible personality, but intimacy transformed him. In my bed he was mine; he gave himself to me with his whole heart, like a youth in his first love. He was accustomed to the rough life of war, and he was impatient and restless, yet we could spend days at a time in idleness, devoted to learning about each other, recounting the paths of our destinies with true urgency, as if our lives would end before the week was out. I kept count of the days and hours we spent together. They were my treasure. Pedro counted our embraces and kisses. It amazes me that neither of us was frightened by the passion that today, objectively, without love and seen from the distance of age, seems oppressive.

Pedro spent his nights in my house, unless he had to travel to Ciudad de los Reyes or visit his properties in Porco and La Canela. When that happened, he took me with him. I loved to see him on his horse—he looked so much the soldier—and to watch him issue orders to his subalterns and his comrades in arms. He knew many things I had no way of knowing. He would tell me about things he had read, and share his ideas and his plans. He was magnanimous with his gifts: sumptuous dresses, rich cloths, jewels, and gold coins. At first his generosity bothered me—it seemed an attempt to buy my affection—but I became accustomed to it. I began to put money away with the thought of securing my future. "You never know what can happen," my mother always said. She is the one who taught me to hide money. I had also come to know that Pedro was not a good administrator, and was not overly interested in his holdings. Like every Spanish hidalgo, he believed that he was above hard labor and vile cash, and that he could spend like a duke though he knew nothing about earning money. The land and mine given to him by Pizarro were a stroke of good fortune that he accepted with the same indifference with which he was disposed to lose them. Once, having had to earn my living from the time I was a girl and horrified by the way he squandered money, I dared say that to him, but he silenced me with a kiss. "Gold is for spending, and thanks be to God, I have more than enough," he replied. That did not calm me, just the opposite.

Valdivia treated his Indians better than other Spaniards did, but he was always strict. He had established work schedules, he fed his people well, and he obliged his overseers to use restraint in punishments, while in other mines and haciendas the encomenderos made women and children work with the men.

"That isn't my way, Inés. I respect Spanish law wherever possible," he replied haughtily when I commented on it.

"What determines up to what point it is 'possible'?"

"Christian morality and good judgment. Just as it is not good practice to work horses till they drop, one should not abuse the Indians. Without them, the mines and the land have no value. I would like to live in harmony with them, but you cannot subdue them without using force."

"I doubt that subduing them helps them in any way, Pedro."

"Do you doubt the benefits of Christianity and civilization?" he argued in turn.

"I know that sometimes mothers let their newborns die of hunger so they will not grow fond of them, knowing they will be taken from them to be slaves. Weren't they better off before we came?"

"No, Inés. They suffered more under the Inca than they do now. We must look to the future. We are here, and here we will stay. One day there will be a new race in this land, a mixture of our blood and that of the Indians, all of us Christians, united by Spanish law and tongue. When that day comes, there will be peace and prosperity."

Pedro believed that, but he died without seeing it, and I, too, will die before that dream is fulfilled; we have come to the end of 1580 and the Indians still despise us.

Soon the people of Cuzco grew used to thinking of us as a couple, although I imagine that malicious comments circulated behind our backs. In Spain I would have been treated like a kept woman, but in Peru no one denied me respect—at least to my face—which would have been to deny respect to Pedro de Valdivia. Everyone knew that he had a wife in Extremadura, but that was no novelty; half the Spaniards were in a similar situation, their legitimate wives a hazy memory. In the New World men needed immediate love, or a substitute for it. Besides, men have mistresses in Spain. The Spanish empire is strewn with bastards, and many of the conquistadors are bastards themselves.

Once or twice Pedro spoke to me of his regrets, not for having ceased to love Marina, but because that marriage was an impediment to marrying *me*. Once I could have wed any of the men who had courted me, he said, and now they didn't dare look my way.

However, I never lost any sleep over that. I realized from the start that Pedro and I could never marry unless Marina died, something neither of us wanted, and so I had torn that hope from my heart and instead rejoiced in the love and complicity we shared, never thinking about the future, or gossip or shame or sin.

We were lovers and friends. We often argued at the top of our lungs, because neither of us was calm by nature, but that did not drive us apart. "From this moment on, I have your back covered, Pedro, so you can concentrate on the battles you have before you," I told him on that second night of lovemaking, and he took me at my word and never forgot it. As for me, I learned to overcome the stubborn silence that determined my behavior when I got very angry. The first time I decided to punish Pedro with silence, he took my face in his hands, pierced me with his blue eyes, and forced me to confess what was bothering me. "I cannot read your mind, Inés. We can make this short if you will tell me what it is you want of me." Similarly, I did not hesitate to confront him when he became impatient and arrogant, or when a decision he'd made seemed questionable. We were alike: both of us strong, domineering, and ambitious. He wanted to found a kingdom, and I wanted to be part of that with him. What he felt, I felt; we shared the same illusions.

At first I simply listened in silence when he mentioned Chile. I did not know what he was talking about, but I hid my ignorance. I listened to the soldiers who brought me their clothing to wash, or came to buy empanadas, and in that way learned about Diego de Almagro's failed attempt. The men who survived that adventure and the battle of Las Salinas had ended up without a single maravedí in their purses. Their clothes were in tatters and often they crept up to the patio door to ask for charity, for food. That was why they were called the *rotos* of Chile, the down and out. They would not stand in the line of indigenous beggars, but they were just as poor. Chile, according to those men's descriptions, was an accursed land, but I had no doubt that Pedro de Valdivia had good reason to be going there. As I listened, I developed a keen interest in his plan.

"If it costs me my life, I will attempt the conquest of Chile," he told me.

"And I will go with you."

"This is not an undertaking for women. I cannot expose you to the dangers of that adventure, Inés, but it is also true that I can't be without you."

"Don't even think it! We go together or you go nowhere," was my reply.

We traveled to Ciudad de los Reyes, which had been founded on top of an Inca cemetery, for Pedro to obtain Francisco Pizarro's authorization to go to Chile. Though we spent every night together, we could not stay in the same house; we did not want to encourage gossip and provoke the priests, who stuck their fingers in every pie though they themselves were no paragons of virtue. I rarely saw the sun in Ciudad de los Reyes; the sky was always overcast. It didn't rain, but mist glistened in my hair and coated everything with a greenish patina. According to Catalina, who went with us, the mummies of the Incas buried beneath the houses wandered through the streets at night, but I never saw them.

While I was inquiring about what would be needed for an enterprise as complicated as marching a thousand leagues, founding cities, and pacifying Indians, Pedro was spending day after day at the palace of the marqués gobernador in social and political gatherings, both of which he found boring. The effusive show of respect and friendship that Pizarro lavished on Valdivia nurtured poisonous envy in the less favored military men and encomenderos. The city, still in its infancy, was already snarled in the gossip and machinations that characterize it today. The court was seething with intrigue, and everything had a price, including honor. Ambitious and fawning men outdid themselves to gain the favor of the marqués gobernador, the only person with the power to assign grants. There were incalculable treasures in Peru, but not enough to satisfy the greed of so many petitioners. Pizarro could not understand why, when everyone else had their hands out, grabbing everything they could, Valdivia was willing to give back his rich land and mine in order to repeat the error that had cost Diego de Almagro so dearly.

"Why are you so obstinate about this adventure in Chile, that worthless land, Don Pedro?" he asked more than once.

"To earn fame and leave memory of my name, Excellency," Valdivia always replied.

And in truth, that was his only reason. The road to Chile was the equivalent of crossing through hell; the Indians were indomitable, and, unlike Peru, in that territory there was little gold, but for Valdivia those negatives were positives. The challenge of getting there, and of battling ferocious enemies, appealed to him, and although he never disclosed it before Pizarro, he often explained to me that he liked the poverty of Chile. He was convinced that gold corrupts and defiles. Gold divided the Spaniards in Peru; it aroused evil and greed, nourished schemes, corroded customs, and destroyed souls. In his imagination, Chile, far from the courtiers of Ciudad de los Reyes, would be the ideal place to build a just society based on hard work and cultivating the land, not on the ill-gotten wealth bled from mines and slaves. In Chile, even religion would be simple, because he—who had read Erasmus—would personally recruit kind and gentle priests, true servants of God, and not an assembly of corrupt and odious men. The founders' descendants would be sober, honest, hard-working Chileans respectful of the law. Among them there would be no aristocrats; he had only disdain for them, he maintained, for the only valid title is not one inherited but one earned through a dignified life and a noble soul. Moist eyed, I spent hours listening to him speak of these things, my heart pounding with emotion, imagining the utopia we would found together.

After weeks in the salons and corridors of the palace, Pedro began to lose patience, convinced that he would never be granted his authorization, though I was sure that Pizarro would give it to him. Delay was standard with the marqués, who was not given to straightforward dealings. He feigned worry about the dangers "his friend" would undoubtedly encounter if he went to Chile, while in fact it was to his benefit that Valdivia be far away where he could not conspire against him or cast a shadow on his prestige. All the expenses, all the risks, all the hardship would be borne by Valdivia, while the territory gained would be under the control of the gobernador of Peru. He had nothing to lose in this audacious project, since he did not intend to invest a single maravedí in it.

"Chile sits there waiting to be conquered and Christianized, Señor Marqués Gobernador, a duty that we, the subjects of the emperor, cannot neglect," Valdivia argued.

"I doubt that you will find men willing to accompany you, Don Pedro."

"Among Spaniards, Excellency, we have never wanted for heroic men skilled in battle. When word spreads about this expedition to Chile, we will have more than enough men and arms."

Once the matter of financing was clear, that is, that the expenses would be assumed by Valdivia, the marqués gobernador, still feigning reluctance, granted his authorization, and quickly took back the silver mine and large hacienda that he had so recently bestowed upon his valiant field marshal. The field marshal felt no loss. He had assured Marina's well-being in Spain, and as for his personal fortune, he had no concern. He had nine thousand pesos in gold and the necessary documents for his undertaking.

"You are short one permission," I reminded him.

"Whose?"

"Mine. I can't go with you unless I have it."

So Pedro detailed to the marqués, in somewhat exaggerated form, my experience in treating the ill and the wounded, as well as my skills in sewing and cooking, attributes indispensable for a journey such as this, but again he found himself entangled in palace intrigues and moral objections. I insisted so strenuously that finally Pedro obtained an audience for me to speak with Pizarro myself. I did not want him to go with me, for there are some things a woman can do better alone.

I presented myself at the palace at the appointed time, but I had to wait hours in a room filled with people who, like myself, had come to ask favors. The salon was richly adorned and brightly lighted by rows of candles in silver candelabra. The day was grayer than usual, and a pale natural light sifted through the large windows. On learning that I came recommended by Pedro de Valdivia, the lackeys offered me a chair, while other solicitants had to remain standing. Some had been coming every day for months, and by now had an ashen air of resignation. I waited tranquilly, trying not to take personally the dark looks of a few who undoubtedly knew of my connection with Valdivia, and must have been asking themselves how an insignificant seamstress, a common concubine, dared seek an audience with the marqués gobernador.

At about midday a secretary appeared and announced that it was my turn. I followed him to an impressive room with an extravagant decor—curtains, shields, pennants, gold, silver—shocking to the somber Spanish temperament, especially to those of us who come from Extremadura. Guards in plumed helmets protected the marqués gobernador, and more than a dozen scribes, secretaries, lawyers, petty officials, and priests were busying around with large books and documents—which Pizarro could not read—and several Indian servants outfitted in livery, but barefoot, were serving wine, fruit, and pastries made by the nuns.

Francisco Pizarro, seated on a dais in a large silver chair with plush upholstery, did me the honor of recognizing me and mentioning that he remembered our previous interview. I had made a dress for the occasion, one appropriate for a widow, and I was all in black, with a mantilla and wimplelike affair that hid my hair. I doubt that the astute marqués was much deceived by my appearance. He knew very well why Valdivia planned to take me with him.

"And how may I be of service to you, Señora?" he asked in his high-pitched voice.

"It is I who wish to serve you, Excellency, and Spain as well," I replied, with a humility I was far from feeling, and I proceeded to show him Diego de Almagro's yellowed map, which Valdivia always kept with him. I pointed out the route through the desert that the expedition would have to follow, and then I told him that I had inherited from my mother the gift of finding water.

A perplexed Francisco Pizarro sat staring at me as if I was making fun of him. I think he had never heard of such a thing, even though it is a rather common skill.

"Are you telling me that you can find water in the desert, señora?"

"I am, Excellency."

"We are speaking of the driest desert in the world!"

"Some of the soldiers who were on the previous expedition have told me that they saw dry grass and brambles, Excellency. That means there is water, under the ground, of course, but if there is water, I can find it."

By then all activity had come to a halt in the audience hall, and everyone, including the Indian servants, was following our conversation openmouthed.

"If you will allow me to prove what I claim to be able to do, Señor Marqués Gobernador, I can go with witnesses to the driest place you know, and with a green switch show you that I am able to find water."

"That will not be necessary, señora. I believe you," Pizarro pronounced after a long pause.

He gave orders for me to be granted the requested authorization, and in addition, as a sign of friendship, he offered me a luxurious campaign tent, "To ease the sacrifices of the journey," as he put it. Instead of following the secretary who tried to lead me to the door, I took my place beside one of the scribes to wait for my document; otherwise I might have had to wait months. Half an hour later, Pizarro stamped it with his seal, and handed it to me with a wry smile.

All I lacked was the permission of the Church.

Pedro and I returned to Cuzco to organize the expedition, not an easy task, because in addition to expenses, there was the problem

that the marqués gobernador was right: very few soldiers wanted
to join us. The claim of well-armed men that Valdivia had so often
boasted about turned out to be an irony. Those who had marched
with Diego de Almagro had come back telling horrors of the place:
that it was called the "Spanish burying ground," and that, they assured anyone who would listen, it was a miserable place that would
not sustain even thirty encomenderos. The Chilean *rotos* had come
back with nothing, and were practically living off charity, more
than enough proof that Chile offered little but suffering. These tales
discouraged even the bravest of men, but Valdivia could be very
eloquent, and he assured them that once we lived through the obstacles of the journey we would come to a fertile and benign land,
a land of contentment, where we would prosper. And gold? the
men asked. There would be gold as well, he persuaded them; it was
a matter of looking for it. The only volunteers, however, were so
short of funds that just as Almagro had done with his men, Valdivia
had to lend them money to fit themselves out with weapons and
horses, knowing that he would never recoup his investment. The
nine thousand pesos were not nearly enough to acquire all the things
we had to have in order to leave, so Valdivia arranged financing
through an unscrupulous merchant to whom he agreed to pay 50
percent of everything he gained in the enterprise.

I went to the bishop of Cuzco for confession. I had smoothed the
way with gifts of embroidered cloths for the sacristy—I needed his
permission for the journey. I had Pizarro's document in my hand,
so I was more or less secure, but one never knows how priests, to
say nothing of bishops, will react. During confession, there was no
way to avoid revealing the naked truth of my love affair.

"Adultery is a mortal sin," the bishop reminded me.

"I am a widow, Your Eminence. I confess to fornication, which
is a terrible sin, but not to adultery, which is worse."

"Without repentance, and without the strong resolve not to sin
again, daughter, how do you suggest that I absolve you?"

"Just as you do all the other Spaniards in Peru, Your Eminence,
who without it would tumble headfirst into hell."

He absolved me and gave me my permission. In exchange, I promised that once I was in Chile, I would have a church built and dedicated to Nuestra Señora del Socorro, but he preferred Nuestra Señora de las Mercedes, who really is the same Virgin with a different name—but why argue with the bishop over that?

In the meantime, Pedro was struggling to recruit soldiers, sign up the Yanaconas, as the auxiliary Indians are called, and buy weapons, munitions, tents, and horses. I was put in charge of things of lesser importance, things that rarely distract great men, like food, work tools, kitchen utensils, llamas, cows, mules, hogs, hens, seeds, blankets, cloth, wood, and all the rest. These necessities were very costly, and I had to invest the money I'd saved and sell my jewels, which I didn't wear anyway and had put away for an emergency. It seemed to me that there was no emergency greater than the conquest of Chile. I have to confess that I have never liked jewelry, and certainly not the ostentatious pieces Pedro had given me. The few times I wore them, I thought I could see my mother, frowning, and reminding me that it is not seemly to attract attention or to cause envy.

The German doctor gave me a small trunk containing knives, pincers, and other surgical instruments, along with some medications: mercury, white lead, lunar caustic, powdered jalap, white precipitate, cream of tartar, salt of Saturn, basilicon, antimony, dragon's blood, silver nitrate, Armenian bole, cado, and ether. Catalina took one look at the vials and shrugged her shoulders scornfully. She was taking her pouches of native herbal remedies, and would add curative plants along the way. She also insisted on bringing the wooden tub for bathing, because nothing was as repulsive to her as the odor of *viracochas*, and also because she was convinced that nearly all illnesses are owing to filth.

I was deep in all these details when one day there came a knock at my door. It was a mature man with a boyish face, who introduced himself as Don Benito. He was one of Almagro's men, weathered by years of military life, the only soldier who had returned enamored of Chile, though he did not say that in public for fear of being considered deranged. He was as ragged as the other "Chileans," but he nevertheless had a great dignity about him, and he had not come to borrow money or set any conditions. Only to accompany us and offer us his help. He shared Valdivia's idea that in Chile it would be possible to found a just, and strong, society.

"That land runs a thousand leagues from north to south; the sea bathes the west side, while on the east there is a sierra more majestic than any seen in Spain, señora," he told me.

Don Benito told us stories of Diego de Almagro's disastrous journey. He said that the adelantado had allowed his men to commit atrocities that were not worthy of a Christian. They took thousands and thousands of Indians from Cuzco with chains and ropes around their necks to keep them from escaping. When one of them died, they simply cut off his head to save themselves the work of undoing the string of captives or holding up the endless line dragging across the sierra. When they lacked Indians to serve them, they descended like demons on defenseless villages, chaining the men, raping and kidnapping the women, killing or leaving the children behind; after they stole all the food and domestic animals, they burned the huts and maize. They made the Indians carry more weight than was humanly possible. They even strapped newborn foals onto their backs, along with the litters and hammocks in which they had themselves carried so as not to exhaust their horses.

Crossing the desert, in which water was unavailable, more than one *viracocha* tied to his mount an Indian woman who had recently given birth, in order to drink the milk of her breasts—having disposed of the newborn on the boiling sands. Indians who dropped from fatigue were beaten to death by the black work bosses, and hunger was so great that the miserable natives ate the corpses of their brothers. The Spaniard who was cruel, and killed the most Indians, was held to be good, and the Spaniard who didn't, a coward. Valdivia lamented such behavior, certain that he would have avoided it, but he acknowledged that these things happened in the chaos of war, as he had witnessed during the sacking of Rome. Pain and sorrow; blood everywhere; blood of victims, blood that makes monsters of the oppressors.

Don Benito knew the hardships of the Chilean venture because he had lived them, and he told us about crossing the Atacama Desert, the way they had chosen to return to Peru. That was the route we intended to follow to Chile, the reverse of Almagro's trek.

"We must not consider the soldiers' needs only, señora. The state of the Indians must also concern us. Like us, they require shelter, food, and water. Without them we will not get very far," he reminded me.

I had that very much in mind, but to provide for a thousand Yanaconas with the funds we had would take a magician.

Among the few soldiers who would come with us to Chile was one Juan Gómez, a handsome and courageous young officer who was a nephew of the deceased Diego de Almagro. One day he came to my house, velvet cap in hand, and shyly confessed his relationship with an Inca princess baptized with the Spanish name Cecilia.

"We love each other very much, Señora Inés, we cannot be apart. Cecilia wants to come with me to Chile."

"Well, have her come!"

"I don't think that Don Pedro will permit it, Cecilia is p-pregnant," the youth stammered.

That *was* a serious problem. Pedro had been very clear in his decision that on a journey of such magnitude he could not take women who were with child, it would create too many difficulties, but when I saw the depths of Juan Gómez's anguish, I felt obliged to help him.

"How far along is this pregnancy?" I asked.

"Maybe three or four months."

"You realize the risk it would be for her, don't you?"

"Cecilia is very strong. She will provide everything she needs, and I will help her, Señora Inés."

"A spoiled princess and her retinue will be a tremendous nuisance."

"Cecilia will not be any trouble, señora. I promise that you will scarcely notice her in the caravan."

"Very well, Don Juan. But for the moment, do not discuss this with anyone. I will decide how and when to mention it to Captain General Valdivia. Be ready to leave soon."

In gratitude, Juan Gómez gave me a black pup with hair as harsh and wiry as a boar's, and he became my shadow. I named him Baltasar, because it was Epiphany, January 6, the day of the three kings. He was the first in a series of identical dogs, his descendants, that have been my companions for more than forty years. Two days later, the Inca princess came to visit me. She arrived in a litter carried by four men and was followed by a number of female servants laden with gifts. I had never seen a member of the Inca's court at close range. I concluded that Spanish princesses would turn pale with envy if they saw Cecilia. She was young and beautiful, with delicate, almost childlike features. Short and slim, she was nonetheless imposing. She had the natural hauteur of one who has been born to a cradle of gold and is accustomed to being served. She was dressed in the style of the Inca court, with simplicity and elegance. Her head was not covered, and her hair, like a silky, shining, black mantle, fell to her waist. She told me that her family was prepared to contribute the supplies for the Yanaconas, as long as they were not chained. Almagro had done that, using the excuse that he was killing two birds with one stone: preventing the Indians from escaping, and transporting iron. More Indians died from the weight of those chains than from the rigors of the climate. I explained that Valdivia did not plan to fetter the Yanaconas, but she reminded me that *viracochas* treated the natives worse than they did their animals. Could I speak for Valdivia, and for the behavior of the other soldiers? she asked. No, I couldn't, but I promised to keep my eyes open, and, in passing, I congratulated her for her compassion, since concern for their subjects was not typical of the Inca nobility. She looked at me with surprise.

"Death and torture are normal, but not chains. They are humiliating," she clarified in the good Spanish she had learned from her lover.

Cecilia attracted attention because of her beauty, her clothing of finest Peruvian weaving, and her unmistakable royal bearing, but she managed to pass almost unnoticed during the first fifty leagues of our trek—until I found the right moment to speak with Pedro, whose first reaction was anger, as was to be expected since one of his orders had been ignored.

"Had it been I in Cecilia's position, I would have had to stay behind," I sighed.

"Are you?" he asked hopefully. He had always wanted a son.

"No, unfortunately, but Cecilia is, and she is not the only one. Every night your soldiers are getting the auxiliary Indian women pregnant, and we already have a dozen carrying offspring."

Cecilia survived the desert crossing, sometimes riding her mule and sometimes carried in a hammock by her servants, and her son was the first child born in Chile. And Juan Gómez repaid us with unconditional loyalty, a very useful gift in the months and years to come.

Just as we and the handful of soldiers who wanted to go with us were ready to leave, an unexpected complication arose. A courtier, one of Pizarro's former secretaries, arrived from Spain bearing the king's authorization to lead an expedition to the territories to the south of Peru, from Atacama to the Strait of Magellan. This Sancho de la Hoz was refined in his manners and friendly in speech, but false and vile in his heart. He was, it was true, always prettily garbed; he wore cascades of laces and sprayed himself with perfume. The men laughed at him behind his back, but soon began to imitate him. He turned out to be a greater threat to Valdivia's plans than the merciless desert and the Indians' hatred. He does not deserve mention in this chronicle, but I cannot avoid doing so, since he will appear later, and also because had he achieved his goal, Pedro de Valdivia and I would not have fulfilled our destinies.

Once de la Hoz arrived, there were two men vying for the same undertaking, and for a few weeks it seemed that ours was hopelessly blocked, but after much discussion and delay, Marqués Gobernador Francisco Pizarro decided that both should attempt the conquest of Chile—as partners: Valdivia would go by land, de la Hoz by sea, and they would meet in Atacama. "You must go watching much this Sancho, then, *mamitayy,*" Catalina warned me when she learned what had happened. She had never seen the man, but she knew through her divining shells what kind of person he was.

We finally set out one warm January morning in 1540. Francisco Pizarro had come from Ciudad de los Reyes, with several of his officials, to see Valdivia off. He had brought a few horses as a gift, his only contribution to the expedition. The clamor of the church bells, which had been tolling since dawn, startled the birds in the sky and the beasts of the earth. The bishop officiated at a mass we all attended and delivered a sermon about faith and the duty to carry the cross to the ends of the earth. Afterward, he went outside to the plaza to bless the thousand Yanaconas who were waiting with the supplies and animals. Each group of Indians took orders from a curaca, or chief, who in turn obeyed the black work bosses, who took their orders from the bearded *viracochas.* I don't believe that the Indians understood any of the bishop's blessing, but perhaps they felt that the bright sun that day was a good sign. Most of them were young men, but there were a few submissive wives disposed to follow them, even knowing that they would never again see the children they left behind in Cuzco. Of course the soldiers brought their women, and that number would be augmented during the expedition with girls captured in destroyed villages.

Don Benito described to me the differences between the first and the second expeditions. Almagro had set out at the head of fifteen hundred robustly singing soldiers in polished armor; banners and pennants were flying and priests were carrying large crosses; thousands and thousands of Yanaconas followed, laden with supplies and leading herds of horses and other animals—all of this to the sound of trumpets and kettledrums. By comparison, we were a rather pathetic group: only eleven soldiers in addition to Pedro de Valdivia—and me, for I was prepared to wield a sword if the occasion demanded.

"It is not important, señora, that we are so few, since we make up for our paltry numbers with courage and good spirit. With God's blessing, other brave men will join us along the way," Don Benito assured me.

Pedro de Valdivia rode in the lead, followed by Juan Gómez, who had been named constable, then Don Benito and the other soldiers. On Sultan, his valiant Arab mount, Pedro looked splendid in his armor, plumed helmet, and shining weapons. Catalina and I were farther back, also on horseback. I had set Nuestra Señora del Socorro on my saddle, and Catalina was carrying the pup Baltasar in her arms because we wanted him to get used to the scent of the Indians. We were planning to train him as a guard dog, not to kill. Cecilia's serving girls were invisible among the soldiers' women. Then came the endless file of animals and bearers, many shedding tears because they had been forced to come and were leaving families behind. The black work bosses flanked the long, snaking line of Indians. They were feared more than the *viracochas*, because of their cruelty, but Valdivia had given instructions that only he could authorize major punishment or torture. The bosses were to limit themselves to the whip, and to use that prudently. That order was watered down along the way, and soon only I would remember it.

We were under way, and to the sound of the bells still ringing in the church towers were added shouts of good-bye, the pawing of impatient horses, the rattle of harness, the long lament of the Yanaconas, and the dull thudding of their bare feet striking the ground.

Behind us, beneath an azure sky, lay Cuzco, crowned by the sacred fortress of Sacsahuamán. As we left the city, Pedro, in full view of the marqués gobernador, his courtiers, the bishop, and the inhabitants of the city that was bidding us farewell, called me to his side and in a loud, clear, defiant voice shouted, "Come here beside me, Doña Inés Suárez!," and when I had passed soldiers and officers to ride at his side, he added in a low voice, "We are off to Chile, Inés of my soul. . . ."

THREE

Journey to Chile, 1540–1541

OUR SPIRITED CARAVAN SET OUT, following the route through the desert that Diego de Almagro had taken on his return and guided by the map his predecessor had sketched on the brittle sheet of yellowed paper. Like a sluggish worm, our handful of soldiers and the thousand auxiliary Indians climbed and descended hills, crossed through valleys and forded rivers, always to the south. The news that we were coming had preceded us, carried by fleet messengers, the *chasquis* who raced down hidden paths in the sierra along a system of relief posts, covering the Inca empire from the extreme north to the Río Bío-Bío in Chile. From them, the Chilean Indians had heard about our expedition as soon as we left Cuzco, and by the time we reached their territory, several months later, they were well prepared to do battle. They knew that the *viracochas* had controlled Peru for some time, that the Inca Atahualpa had been executed, and

that his brother, the Inca Paullo, manipulated like a puppet, ruled
in his stead. This prince had delivered his people to the foreigners
and was living his life in the golden cage of his palace, surrendered
to pleasures of lust and cruelty. The Indians also knew that in Peru
a vast indigenous insurrection was brewing in the shadows, directed
by another member of the royal family, the fugitive Inca Manco,
who had sworn to drive the foreigners from the land. The Chilean
Indians had heard that the *viracochas* were ferocious, diligent, tenacious, insatiable, and, most unbelievable of all, that they did not
honor a spoken agreement. How could they live with such shame?
It was a mystery.

The Chilean Indians called us *huincas*, which in their language,
Mapudungu, means lying people and land thieves. I have had to
learn this tongue because it is spoken throughout Chile, from north
to south. The Mapuche compensate for their lack of a written
language with an enduring memory. The story of creation, their
laws, their traditions, the feats of their heroes are recorded in Mapudungu, in tales that have been passed intact from generation to
generation from the beginning of time. I translated some of them
for young Alonso de Ercilla y Zúñiga, whom I referred to earlier,
as inspiration for his epic poem, "La Araucana." I have heard that
it has been published, and is circulating in the court in Madrid, but
I have only the scribbled verses Alonso left me after I helped him
copy them. If I remember correctly, this is how he describes Chile
and the Mapuche, or Araucanos, as he calls them, in his eight-line
stanzas:

> *Chile, fertile, majestic province*
> *In the regions of the famous Antarctic,*
> *Respected in far-distant nations*
> *For being strong, paramount, and powerful;*
> *Its people are so illustrious,*
> *So proud, so noble, so brave in battle,*
> *That they have never been ruled by a king*
> *Or subjected to foreign domination.*

Alonso exaggerates, of course, but poets have license to do that; if not, their verses would not have the needed vigor. Chile is not that paramount or powerful, nor are its people as illustrious and noble as he portrays them, but I agree that the Mapuche are proud and brave in battle, and that they have never been ruled by a king or subjected to foreign domination.

They scorn pain; they can suffer terrible torment without complaint—not because they are less sensitive to suffering than we, but because they are so stoic. There are no finer warriors; to them it is honorable to die in battle. They will never conquer us, but neither will we be able to subjugate them, even if it means they all die in the process. I believe that the war will go on for centuries, since it provides the Spaniards with servants. Slaves, actually. It is not just prisoners of war who end up in slavery, but free Indians as well, whom the Spaniards lasso and sell at two hundred pesos for a pregnant woman and a hundred pesos for an adult male or healthy child. The illegal commerce in these peoples is not limited to Chile, it reaches as far as Ciudad de los Reyes, and involves everyone from encomenderos and mine overseers to ship captains. We will, as Valdivia feared, eventually exterminate the natives of this land, because they would rather die free than live as slaves. And if any of us Spaniards had to choose, we would not hesitate to make the same choice.

Valdivia was indignant about the stupidity of the Spaniards who were killing off the peoples of the New World. Without the natives, he always said, the land has no value. He died without seeing an end to the slaughter, which has been going on for forty years now. Spaniards keep coming, and mestizos keep being born, but the Mapuche are disappearing, exterminated by war, slavery, and the illnesses brought by the Spaniards, which they cannot withstand. I fear the Mapuche because of the troubles they have visited upon us. I am angered by the fact that they have rejected the word of Christ, and resisted our efforts to civilize them. I cannot forgive them for the cruel way they killed Pedro de Valdivia, although all they were doing was giving back what they had received, for he had committed many cruelties and abuses against them. As they say in Spain, he who lives by the sword, dies by the sword. I do, however, respect and admire the Mapuche; I cannot deny that. Worthy enemies: Spaniards and Mapuche, equally courageous, brutal . . . and determined to live in Chile. They were here long before we were, and that gives them the greater right, but they will never drive us out, and apparently we will never live together in peace.

Where did those Mapuche come from? It is said they resemble certain peoples in Asia. If they did originate there, I cannot understand how they crossed such tumultuous seas and such broad expanses of land to get here. They are savages; they know nothing of art or writing; they do not build cities or temples; and they have no castes, classes, or priests, only captains for war, their *toquis*. They roam from place to place, naked, free, with their many wives and children, who fight with them in battle. They do not practice human sacrifice, like other American Indians, and they do not worship idols. They believe in one god, not our God, but one they call Ngenechén.

While we were camped in Tarapacá, where Pedro de Valdivia planned to wait until reinforcements arrived and we recovered from our fatigue, the Chilean Indians were organizing to make it as difficult as possible for us to press on. We rarely met them face-to-face; they stole from us, or attacked, from behind our backs. I was kept busy treating the wounded, especially the Yanaconas, who fought without horses or weapons. Battle fodder, we called them. The chroniclers always forget to mention them, but without those silent masses of friendly Indians who followed the Spaniards in all their wars and other undertakings, the conquest of the New World would have been impossible.

Between Cuzco and Tarapacá more than twenty Spanish soldiers had joined our ranks, and Pedro was sure that more would come once word spread that the expedition was under way, but we had lost five men, which was a lot when you consider how few of us there were. One had been gravely wounded by a poisoned arrow, and when I was not able to cure him, Pedro sent him back to Cuzco, accompanied by his brother, two soldiers, and several Yanaconas. A few days later our field marshal woke in good spirits because he had dreamed about his wife, who was waiting for him in Spain, and because a sharp pain that had been stabbing his chest for more than a week had gone away. I served him a bowl of toasted flour with water and honey, which he ate greedily, as if it were a very special dish. "You are more beautiful than ever today, Doña Inés," he said with his usual gallantry, and his eyes glazed over and he dropped dead at my feet. After we gave him a Christian burial, I suggested to Pedro that we name Don Benito in his place; the old man knew the route and was experienced in setting up camps and maintaining discipline.

We had lost a few soldiers, but like ragged shadows came others who had been wandering through fields and mountains, Almagro's defeated soldiers, who found no friend in Pizarro's empire. They had been living on charity for years; they had little to lose in the Chile adventure.

We stayed several weeks in Tarapacá, to give Indians and beasts time to put on weight before we started across the desert, which, according to Don Benito, would be the worst part of our journey. He explained that the first part was arduous, but that the second, called the wasteland, was much worse. In the meantime, Pedro de Valdivia rode for leagues, scanning the horizon in hopes of sighting new volunteers. Sancho de la Hoz was supposed to meet us, bringing by sea the promised soldiers and supplies, but there was no sign of our pompous partner.

While I was having more blankets woven, and preparing dried meat, cereals, and other food that wouldn't spoil, Don Benito was working the blacks from sun up to sundown in the forges crafting munitions, horseshoes, and lances. He also sent out parties of soldiers to look for the foodstuffs the Indians had buried before abandoning their settlement of huts. He had made camp in the safest and most suitable spot, a place where there was shade, water, and hills where he could post his lookouts. The one decent tent was the one Pizarro had given me; made of waxed cloth, it was supported by a strong armature of poles, its two rooms as comfortable, actually, as a house. The soldiers made do however they could, with patched cloths that barely protected them from the weather. Some did not have even that, but slept beside their horses. The camp for the auxiliary Indians was separate from ours, and under constant guard, to prevent them from escaping. At night you could see the hundreds of little campfires where they cooked what food they had, and the breeze carried the lugubrious sound of their musical instruments, which had the power to sadden both men and beasts.

Our camp was near two abandoned villages where we had not found any food, though we had searched it thoroughly. We discovered that these Indians have the custom of living on good terms with deceased relatives: the living in one part of the hut and the dead in the other. In each dwelling, we found a room with well-preserved mummies, dark and smelling of moss: grandparents, women, infants, each with personal belongings, but no jewels. In contrast, in Peru the tombs had been stuffed with precious objects, including statues of pure gold. "Even the dead are hard up in Chile," the soldiers had groused. "Not a hint of gold anywhere." To vent their frustration, they tied ropes around the mummies and dragged them behind their galloping horses until the bindings burst open and bones spilled out. They celebrated this accomplishment with screams of laughter, while in the camp fear spread among the Yanaconas. After sunset, a rumor began to circulate among the bearers that the desecrated bones were reknitting, and that before dawn the skeletons would attack us like an army from beyond the tomb. Terrified blacks repeated the tale, which then reached the ears of the Spaniards. Those invincible vandals, who do not even know the word "fear," burst out sobbing like nursing babes. By midnight, teeth were chattering so loudly that Pedro de Valdivia had to harangue his men and remind them that they were Spanish soldiers, the strongest and best trained in the world, not a clutch of ignorant washerwomen. I myself did not sleep for several nights but passed them in praying because the skeletons were wandering around outside . . . and anyone who says the opposite was not there.

The soldiers, who were bored and discontent, wondered what the devil we were doing camped for weeks in that accursed place instead of marching on toward Chile, as planned—or returning to Cuzco, which seemed even more sensible. When Valdivia was losing hope that reinforcements would arrive, a detachment of eighty men showed up. Among them were several great captains, whom I did not know but whom Pedro had spoken of because they were so famous, men like Francisco de Villagra and Alonso de Monroy. The former was blond, ruddy-faced, and robust, with brash manners and a sneer on his lips. He always struck me as disagreeable because he treated the Indians badly, was miserly, and unkind to the poor, but I learned to respect him for his courage and loyalty. Monroy, who had been born in Salamanca and was a descendant of a noble family, was just the opposite: refined, handsome, and generous. We immediately became friends. Jerónimo de Alderete, Valdivia's old comrade in arms, who years before had tempted him to come to the New World, was with them. Villagra had convinced them that their best bet was to join Valdivia. "We will do better to serve his majesty, and not wander in lands where the devil runs loose," he told them, referring to Pizarro, for whom he had no respect. Also in their party was a chaplain from Andalucia, a man some fifty years old, González de Marmolejo, who would become my mentor, as I have mentioned before. This man of the cloth showed signs of great kindness throughout his long life, but I believe he would have made a better soldier than a priest, for he was too fond of adventure, wealth, and women.

For months, these men had been in the terrible jungle of Los Chunchos, in eastern Peru. Their expedition had set out with three hundred Spaniards, but two of every three had perished, and the rest had been turned into starving shadows drained by tropical illnesses. Of their two thousand Indians, not one was left alive. Among the men whose bones had been left in the jungle was the ill-starred Lieutenant Núñez, the man whom Valdivia had sent to rot in Los

Chunchos, as he had said he would do when Núñez tried to force his attentions on me in Cuzco. No one could give me specific details about his death; he simply faded into the undergrowth, leaving no trace. I hope he died like a Christian and not in the mouths of cannibals. The hardships Pedro de Valdivia and Jerónimo de Alderete had borne years before in the jungles of Venezuela were child's play compared with what these men suffered in Los Chunchos under the hot, torrential rains and clouds of mosquitoes: sick and hungry, they had walked through swamps and been chased by savages who ate one another when they failed to catch a Spaniard.

Before I continue, allow me to make special mention of the man who commanded this detachment. He was a tall, very handsome man, with a broad brow, aquiline nose, and brown eyes that were large and liquid, like those of a horse. He had heavy eyelids and a remote, slightly sleepy gaze that softened his face. This I was able to appreciate only on the second day, after the filth that crusted his body had been washed away and the hair and beard that gave him the look of a shipwrecked sailor had been cut. Although he was younger than the other renowned military men in the group, they had chosen him captain of captains because of his courage and intelligence. His name was Rodrigo de Quiroga. Nine years later, he would be my husband.

I took charge of restoring strength and health to the Los Chunchos soldiers, helped by Catalina and several Indian women in my service whom I had trained in the healing arts. As Don Benito said, those poor souls had left the humid, tangled hell of the jungle only to find that the dry, barren hell of the desert lay ahead. Just washing them, cleaning their sores, delousing them, and cutting their hair and fingernails took days. Some were so weak that the Indian girls had to feed them pap by the spoonful. Catalina whispered into my ear the Incas' remedy for extreme cases, and without telling them what it was—we were afraid it would nauseate them—we gave it to the worst cases. At night Catalina would slip up to a llama and bleed it through a cut in its neck. We mixed the fresh blood with milk and a little urine, and gave it to the sick men to drink. They recovered, and after two weeks were strong enough to join the others.

The Yanaconas readied themselves for the suffering that awaited; they did not know the terrain but they had heard about the terrible desert. Each of them carried a wineskin of sorts around his neck. Some had been made from the skin of an animal's leg—llama, guanaco, alpaca—skinned off in one piece and turned inside out like a stocking, hair inward, and some from animal bladders or sealskin. Prudently, they dropped in a few grains of toasted maize to disguise the smell. Don Benito organized ways to haul water on a larger scale, using the barrels they'd made, and also skin containers like those the Indians carried. We were aware that the water we were taking would not be enough for so many people, but the men and llamas had reached their limits. To top off our woes, the local Indians not only had hidden their foodstuffs, they had also poisoned the wells, as we learned through one of the Inca Manco's *chasquis*, who revealed that information under torture. Don Benito had discovered him among our auxiliary Indians and had asked Valdivia's permission to interrogate him. The blacks used a slow fire to persuade him to talk. I have no stomach for witnessing torture and I went as far away as possible, but the man's horrible screams, chorused by the Yanaconas' howls of terror, could be heard a league away. To end the torment, the messenger admitted that he had come from Peru with instructions for the natives of Chile to stop the advance of the *viracochas*. That is why the Indians had hidden in the hills with the animals they could take with them, after burning their maize. He added that he was not the only messenger, that hundreds of *chasquis* were running south with the same instructions from the Inca Manco. After he confessed, they burned him to death anyway, to serve as an example. When I berated Valdivia for permitting such cruelty, he was annoyed, and would not listen. "Don Benito knows what he is doing," he replied. "I warned you before we left that this undertaking is not for the squeamish. It is too late to turn back now."

How long and how cruel is the road across the desert! How slow and fatiguing our progress! What burning solitudes! The long days went by, one after another, nothing but that harsh landscape: barren land and stone smelling of burned dust and thornbush painted fiery colors by the hand of God. According to Don Benito, the colors indicated hidden minerals, and it was a diabolical joke that none was gold or silver.

Pedro and I would walk for hours and hours, leading our horses by their bridles to save their strength. We talked very little because our throats were burning and our lips were cracked, but we were together, and every step brought us closer, led us inward, to the dream we had dreamed and that had cost so many sacrifices: Chile. As protection, I wore a broad-brimmed hat with a cloth over my face that had two holes for my eyes, and I wrapped my hands in rags because I had no gloves and the sun was making them peel. The soldiers could not bear the touch of the hot armor, but dragged it behind them. The long line of Indians moved forward slowly, in silence, carelessly guarded by the beaten-down blacks, who never lifted their whips. For the bearers, things were a thousand times worse than they were for us. They were used to hard work and little food, to trotting up and down hills fueled by the mysterious energy of the coca leaves, but they could not endure thirst. Our desperation grew as the days passed and we had not found a clean well; the only ones we came across had been polluted by animal cadavers the furtive Chilean Indians had thrown into them. A few of the Yanaconas drank the putrid water anyway, and died writhing on the ground, their intestines on fire.

When we thought we had reached the limits of our strength, the color of the mountains and the ground began to change. The air stood still, the sky turned white, and every sign of life disappeared, from thistles to the solitary birds we had seen from time to time: we had entered the fearsome Despoblado, the wasteland. At the first light of dawn we would start forward; later the sun would be too strong. Pedro had decided that the faster we moved the fewer lives we would lose, though the effort of each step was brutal.

During the hottest hours, we rested in a dead landscape, stretched out upon that sea of calcined sand beneath a leaden sun. We would start again about five and keep going until night fell and we could go no farther in the darkness. It was a world of boundless cruelty. We lacked the spirit to set up tents and organize a camp, since it would be for only a few hours. We were not in any danger of being attacked; no one lived in or ventured into these solitudes.

At night the temperature changed abruptly, from the unbearable heat of the day it dropped to glacial cold. We lay wherever we could, shivering, ignoring the instructions of Don Benito, the only one who insisted on discipline. Pedro and I, embraced between our horses, tried to share our bodies' heat. We were very, very tired. We did not think of making love through all the weeks that part of the journey lasted. Abstinence gave us the opportunity to learn our weaknesses and to cultivate a tenderness that had been superseded by passion. The thing I admired most about that man was that he never doubted his mission: to populate Chile with Spaniards and to evangelize the Indians. He never believed for a minute that we would bake in the desert, as the others said; his resolve never wavered.

Despite the severe rationing Don Benito had imposed, the day came when we ran out of water. By then we were ill with thirst; our throats were raw from the sand, our tongues swollen, our lips covered with sores. Suddenly we would think we heard the sound of a waterfall, and see a crystalline lake bordered with ferns. The captains had to hold the men back by force so they would not die crawling across the sand after a mirage. Several soldiers drank their own urine, and that of the horses, which was meager and very dark. Others, maddened, attacked the Yanaconas and drank the last drops from their llama skins. I think they would have killed them and drunk their blood had Valdivia not kept them in line with strong discipline. That night, in the bright moonlight, Juan de Málaga came again to visit me. I pointed him out to Pedro, but he could not see him and thought I was hallucinating. My husband was looking terrible; his rags were crusted with dried blood and sidereal dust, and his expression was desperate, as if even his poor bones suffered with thirst.

The next day, when we had resigned ourselves to the fact that there was no salvation for us, a strange reptile scurried between my feet. We had not seen any form of life other than our own for many days, not even the thistles that are so plentiful in some stretches of the desert. Perhaps it was a salamander, the lizard that lives in fire. I concluded that however diabolical the little creature might be, it must, from time to time, need a sip of water.

"So now it's up to us, Virgencita," I told Nuestra Señora del Socorro. I took the tree switch from one of my cases and began to pray. It was high noon, when the multitude of parched humans and animals was resting. I called Catalina to come with me, and the two of us slowly set out, protected by a parasol, I with an Ave María on my lips, and she with her invocations in Quechua. We walked a good while, perhaps an hour, in ever larger circles, covering more and more ground. Don Benito thought thirst had driven me out of my mind, but he was so drained that he asked a stronger, younger man, Rodrigo de Quiroga, to go look for me.

"For the love of God, señora," the officer begged me with what little voice he had left. "Come rest. We will put up a cloth to make some shade—"

"Captain, go tell Don Benito to send me some men with picks and shovels," I interrupted.

"Picks and shovels?" he repeated, astonished.

"And tell him, please, to bring some large jugs and a number of armed soldiers."

Rodrigo de Quiroga left to advise Don Benito that I was much worse than they had supposed, but Valdivia heard him and, filled with hope, he ordered the field marshal to do as I asked. Not long after, I had six Indians digging a hole. Indians have less resistance to thirst than we do, and they could barely hold the tools, but the soil was loose, and before long they were in a pit neck deep. At the bottom, the sand was dark. Suddenly one of the Indians uttered a hoarse cry and we began to see seeping water. First it was only dampness, as if the earth were sweating, but after two or three minutes there was a small pool. Pedro, who had not left my side, ordered the soldiers to defend the hole with their lives; he feared, with reason, the maddened onslaught of a thousand men desperate for a few drops of water. I assured him there would be enough for everyone, as long as we drank in an orderly fashion.

And so it was. Don Benito spent the rest of the day distributing a cup of water for each individual, then Rodrigo de Quiroga, with the help of some soldiers, spent the night watering the animals and filling barrels and the Indians' llama skins. The water flowed with some force; it was dark, and had a metallic taste, but to us it seemed as fresh as the fountains of Seville. People attributed the well to a miracle, and called it Virgin's Spring in honor of Nuestra Señora del Socorro. We set up camp and stayed on for three days, quenching our thirst, and when we continued, a slight stream was still flowing across the blasted surface of the desert.

"This was not the Virgin's miracle, Inés, it was yours," Pedro told me, deeply moved. "Thanks to you, we will make it across this hell safe and sound."

"I can find water only where there *is* water, Pedro, I can't create it. I don't know whether there will be another spring farther on, and in any case, it will likely not be as free-flowing."

Valdivia ordered me to get a half-day's start and look for other sources; I was to travel protected by a detachment of soldiers, with forty auxiliary Indians and twenty llamas to carry the water jugs. The remainder of the caravan would follow in sections, separated by several hours so everyone would not rush at once to drink, should we locate a well. Don Benito designated Rodrigo de Quiroga to command the group that accompanied me. The young captain had earned Don Benito's total confidence in a short time. He was, furthermore, the one with the best vision; his large brown eyes saw even what wasn't there. Had there been danger on the hallucinatory desert horizon, he would have been the first to discover it. But there was nothing. I found several sources of water, none as bounteous as the first, but enough to get us through the wasteland alive. One day the color of the ground changed again, and two birds flew overhead.

When the desert lay behind us, I counted up the days and found that it had been nearly five months since we left Cuzco. Valdivia decided to make camp and wait, for he had word that his closest friend, Francisco de Aguirre, might be in the area. Hostile Indians kept watch from a distance, but they did not approach us. Once again I could set up the elegant tent Pizarro had given us. I covered the ground with Peruvian mantles and cushions, took my china tableware from the trunks—I did not want to keep eating off wood trenchers—and had a clay oven built so I could cook the way one is supposed to; we had been eating nothing but grains and dried meat. In the large room of the tent, which Valdivia used as his general headquarters, audience hall, and court to dispense justice, I placed his large chair and a few leather taborets for the visitors who showed up at all hours. Catalina spent her days wandering around the camp like a wraith, gathering news. Nothing happened among the Spaniards or the Yanaconas that I did not know. The captains who often came to have a meal tended to be unpleasantly surprised that Valdivia invited me to sit at table with them. It is possible that none of them had ever eaten with a woman in his lifetime; that was not done in Spain, but here customs are more relaxed. For light we burned candles and oil lamps, and we heated the tent with two large Peruvian braziers because it was cold at night. González de Marmolejo, who in addition to being a priest was something of a scholar, explained to us that the seasons were reversed here, and when it was winter in Spain, it was summer in Chile, and vice versa. No one could understand, however, and we continued to think that the laws of nature were erratic in the New World.

In the other room of the tent, Pedro and I had our bed, a writing desk, my altar, our trunks, and the tub for bathing, which had not been used in a long time. Pedro's fear of bathing had waned, and from time to time he agreed to get into the tub and let me soap and wash him, but he preferred a half bath with a wet cloth. Those were good days in which we were once again the lovers we had been in Cuzco. Before we made love, he liked to read me his favorite books. He had no idea, because I wanted to surprise him, that González de Marmolejo was teaching me to read and write.

Some days later, Pedro left with a handful of his men to ride over the region and look for Francisco de Aguirre, and also to see if it was possible to parley with the Indians. He was the only one who thought it might be possible to make an agreement with them. One night while he was gone, I bathed and washed my hair with *quillay,* a Chilean tree bark that kills fleas and keeps one's hair silky black to the tomb. I did not receive that last benefit; I have used *quillay* forever and my hair is white, but at least I am not half bald, like so many persons my age. The long trek, walking and riding, had hurt my back somehow, and one of my Indian girls had rubbed it down with a *peumo* balm Catalina had prepared. I felt much better when I went to bed, and Baltasar lay at my feet. The dog was ten months old now, and still puppyish, but he had grown to a good size and I could see he was going to make a guard dog. For once I was not tormented by insomnia, and fell fast asleep.

Baltasar's quiet growling woke me after midnight. I sat up in bed, with one hand feeling in the dark for a shawl to throw around me, and holding the dog with the other. Then I heard a faint noise in the other room, and had no doubt that someone was there. My first thought was that Pedro had come back, because the sentinels at the door would not have let anyone else in, but the dog's behavior put me on the alert. There wasn't time to light a lamp.

"Who is it!" I shouted, alarmed.

After a tense pause, out of the dark someone called for Pedro de Valdivia.

"He is not here. Who wants him?" I asked, now with irritation.

"Forgive me, señora, it is Sancho de la Hoz, loyal servant of the captain general. It has taken me a long time to get here, and I want to give him my greetings."

"Sancho de la Hoz? How dare you, caballero, come into my tent in the middle of the night!" I exclaimed.

By then Baltasar was barking madly, alerting the guards. In a matter of minutes, Don Benito, Quiroga, Juan Gómez, and others came running with lights and drawn swords to find in my quarters not only the insolent de la Hoz but another four men as well. The first reaction of my companions was to arrest them immediately, but I convinced them that it was all a misunderstanding. I begged them to leave, and as I quickly dressed ordered Catalina to concoct something for the new arrivals to eat. I poured them wine by my own hand, and served them food with the proper hospitality, eager to hear anything they wanted to tell me of the hardships of their voyage.

Between servings of wine, I stepped outside to tell Don Benito to send a messenger to look for Pedro de Valdivia. The situation was very delicate, for de la Hoz had a number of supporters among the slackers and malcontents in our expedition. A few of them had criticized Valdivia for having usurped the right to conquer Chile from the envoy of the Crown, arguing that Sancho de la Hoz's royal documents had more authority than the permission granted by Pizarro. De la Hoz, nevertheless, had no economic backing; he had squandered in Spain the fortune that was his part of Atahualpa's ransom, and had not raised funds or outfitted ships or soldiers for the enterprise. His word was worth so little that he had been imprisoned in Peru over debts and swindling. I suspected that he intended to get rid of Valdivia, take over the expedition, and continue the conquest of Chile alone.

I had decided to treat the five inopportune visitors with the greatest consideration, so that they would feel confident and lower their guard until Pedro got back. For the time being, I stuffed them full of food and put enough sleeping powders in the wine jug to fell an ox. I did not want any uproar in the camp. The last thing we needed was to have the men divided into two bands, as could happen if de la Hoz established any doubt about Valdivia's legitimacy. When they found me so amenable, I suppose those contemptible men must have laughed behind my back, satisfied that they had put one over on a stupid woman. Before an hour had passed, however, they were so drunk and drugged that when Don Benito and the guards came to take them away, they did not offer the least resistance. When they were searched, it was discovered that each of them carried a dagger with an elaborate silver handle—all alike. That left no doubt that they had hatched a theatrical plot to assassinate Valdivia. The identical daggers could only be the idea of the cowardly de la Hoz, who in that way distributed responsibility for the crime among all five. Our captains wanted to judge them then and there, but I convinced them that only Valdivia could make such a serious decision. It took wit and firmness to prevent Don Benito from stringing up de la Hoz in the nearest tree.

Pedro returned three days later, already informed about the conspiracy. The news, however, did not seem to squelch his good spirits; he had found his friend Francisco de Aguirre, who had been waiting for several weeks and had, in addition, brought fifteen horsemen, ten harquebusiers, a large number of Indians, and enough food for several days. With them our contingent swelled to one hundred and thirty-some soldiers, if I remember correctly. That was a greater miracle than Virgin's Spring.

Before discussing the matter of Sancho de la Hoz with his captains, Pedro took me aside to hear my version of what had happened. It was often said that I had Pedro bewitched with my spells and aphrodisiac potions, that I beguiled him in bed with Turkish abominations, that I drained his potency, annulled his will, and one way or other did whatever I pleased with him. Nothing further from the truth. Pedro was stubborn, and knew exactly what he wanted. No one could make him change direction with magic or a courtesan's arts, only with reason. He was not a man to seek counsel overtly, least of all from a woman, but in our private moments, pacing around the room, he held his tongue and listened until I got to the point of offering my opinion. I tried to give it in a subtle way, so that in the end he believed the decision was his. This system always worked well for me. A man does what he can; a woman does what a man cannot. I did not think it was a good idea to sentence Sancho de la Hoz. He obviously deserved it, but he had the protection of the king's documents, and he had connections at court in Madrid who could accuse Valdivia of sedition. My duty was to prevent my lover from ending up on the rack or the gallows.

"What do I do with a traitor like that?" Pedro fumed, striding around like a gamecock.

"You have always told me that it is good to keep one's enemies nearby, where they can be watched. . . ."

Instead of immediately judging the accused, Pedro Valdivia decided to take a little time to find out what the mood was among his soldiers, collect proof of the conspiracy, and unmask the accomplices hidden among us. To everyone's surprise, he gave Don Benito orders to break camp and continue south, leading the prisoners, who were still in chains and filled with dread—all except the featherbrained Sancho de la Hoz, who thought he was above the law and who, despite his chains, continued his campaign to win over followers to his cause and to array himself as if he were at court. He demanded an Indian serving girl to starch his neckpiece, iron his breeches, curl his hair, spray him with perfume, and buff his fingernails.

The men were not happy with the order to break up camp; they were comfortable there, it was cool, and there was water and trees. Don Benito dressed them down, reminding them that the decisions of their leader were not to be questioned. Valdivia had brought them this far with a minimum of losses; they had successfully crossed the desert, and had lost only three soldiers, six horses, one dog, and thirteen llamas. The missing Yanaconas didn't count, but according to Catalina probably thirty or forty had died.

When I met Francisco de Aguirre I immediately trusted him despite his intimidating appearance. Over time I learned to fear his cruelty. He was a huge, extravagant man, loud, tall, strong, and always ready with a boisterous laugh. He drank and ate for three, and, according to what Pedro told me, he was capable of impregnating ten Indians in one night and another ten the next. The years have gone by, and now Aguirre is an old man without a conscience or a grudge; he is still lucid and healthy despite having spent years in the pestilential dungeons of the Inquisition and the king. He lives well, thanks to the land my deceased husband granted him.

It would be difficult to find two persons more different than my generous, noble husband, Rodrigo, and that undisciplined Francisco de Aguirre, but they loved each other as soldiers in war and as friends in peace. Rodrigo was not going to let his companion in life's adventures end up as a beggar because of the ingratitude of the Crown and the Church, which is why he protected him until his own death carried him off. Aguirre, whose battle scars covered every portion of his body, is spending his last days watching the maize grow on his small estate, at the side of his wife, whose love brought her from Spain to join him, and his children and grandchildren. At eighty, he is not defeated; he continues to imagine adventures and to sing the risqué songs of his youth. In addition to his five legitimate children, he engendered more than a hundred known bastards, and there must be hundreds more that have not been recorded. He had the notion that the best way to serve his majesty in the Americas was to people it with mestizos. He went so far as to say that the solution to the Indian problem was to kill all males older than twelve, sequester the children, and patiently and methodically rape the women. Pedro always thought that his friend was joking, but I know that he meant it. Despite that outlandish taste for fornication, the one love of his life was his first cousin, whom he married thanks to a special dispensation from the pope . . . but I believe I have already told you that.

Be patient with me, Isabel; at the age of seventy, I tend to repeat myself.

After several days' march, we reached the valley of Copiapó, the beginning of the territory Pedro de Valdivia was to govern. A yell of jubilation rose from the Spaniards: we had arrived. Pedro de Valdivia called his men together, surrounded himself with his captains, called me to his side, and with great solemnity planted the standard of Spain and took possession of the land. He gave it the name Nueva Extremadura, the new Extremadura, since he, Pizarro, most of the hidalgos on the expedition—and I—had all come from there. Our chaplain, González de Marmolejo, immediately set up an altar with his crucifix, his gold goblet—the only gold we had glimpsed for months—and the small statue of Nuestra Señora del Socorro, whom we had adopted as our patron saint after the aid she lent us in the desert. The cleric celebrated an emotional high mass, and all of us took communion, our souls swollen with gratitude.

The valley was inhabited by a number of different tribes, all subjects of the Inca empire, though they were so far from Peru that the Inca's influence was not oppressive. Their curacas came out to receive us with modest gifts of food and welcoming greetings the interpreters we called "tongues" translated for us, but they were not pleased with our presence. Their houses were made of clay and straw, more solid and better arranged than the dwellings we had seen before. These people, too, had the custom of living with their dead ancestors, but this time the soldiers carefully avoided despoiling the mummies. We also discovered some recently abandoned villages belonging to the hostile Indians under the command of a Chief Michimalonko.

Don Benito oversaw setting up the camp in a strategic location; he feared that the natives would become more bellicose once they learned that we had no intention of returning to Peru, as Almagro's expedition had done six years before. Even though we needed foodstuffs, Valdivia forbade sacking the inhabited villages or molesting their dwellers, keeping in view the possibility of winning them as allies. Don Benito had captured other *chasquis*, who when questioned repeated what we already knew: the Inca had ordered all the populations to escape with their families to the mountains, and to hide or destroy their food, something most of the natives had done. Don Benito reasoned that the Chileans—as he called the inhabitants of the territory of Chile without distinction among tribes—must have hidden their food in sand, where it was easier to dig. He sent all his soldiers, except for the guard, to scour the area and search by thrusting swords and lances into the ground until they found the buried provisions. Following those directions, they found maize, potatoes, beans, and even some gourds containing fermented chicha, which I appropriated because it would help the wounded endure the brutality of cauterizations.

As soon as the camp was in order, Don Benito had a gallows built and Pedro de Valdivia announced that the next day he would judge Sancho de la Hoz and the other prisoners. That night, captains of proven loyalty sat around the table in our tent, each on his leather stool, and their leader in his armchair. To their general amazement, Valdivia called me and pointed to a chair at his side. I felt a little intimidated by the incredulous expressions of the captains, who had never seen a woman in a council of war. "She saved us from thirst in the desert, and from the conspiracy of the traitors. She, more than anyone, deserves to participate in this meeting," said Valdivia, and no one dared contradict him. Juan Gómez, who was visibly nervous—Cecilia was actually giving birth at that moment—placed the five identical daggers on the table, explained what he had found out about the attempted plot, and named the soldiers whose loyalty was in doubt. There was especially a certain Ruiz, who had allowed the conspirators to enter camp, and had distracted the sentinels at our tent. The captains discussed for some time the risks involved in executing de la Hoz, and finally the opinion of Rodrigo de Quiroga, which coincided with mine, prevailed. I was very careful not to open my mouth; I did not want to be accused of being a virago who led Valdivia around by the ear. I saw that wine was in the cups, I paid attention, and I nodded meekly when Quiroga spoke. Valdivia had already made his decision, but he was waiting for someone else to propose it, so he would not seem to be worried about the documents the king had given Sancho de la Hoz.

Just as announced, the trial was convened the following day in the prisoners' tent. Valdivia was the sole judge, assisted by Rodrigo de Quiroga, the court recorder, and another military man who acted as secretary. This time I was not there, but it was no trouble at all to get the complete version of events. They had placed armed guards around the tent to keep the curious at a distance, and the three captains sat behind a table, flanked by two Negro slaves who were expert in applying torture and conducting executions. The recorder opened his large books and readied his quill pen and inkwell as Rodrigo de Quiroga lined up the five daggers on the table. They had also brought one of my Peruvian braziers filled with red-hot coals, not so much to warm the air as to terrorize the prisoners, who were well aware that torture is part of any trial of that nature. Fire was used more with Indians than with hidalgos, but no one was sure what Valdivia might do.

The accused, standing before the table, heavily chained, listened to the charges against them for more than an hour. They had no doubt that "the usurper," as they had labeled Valdivia, knew every last detail of the conspiracy, including the complete list of Sancho de la Hoz's loyalists in the expedition. There was nothing to allege. A long silence followed Valdivia's pronouncement, while the secretary finished putting down notes in his book.

"Do you have anything to say?" Rodrigo de Quiroga asked at last.

At that point, Sancho de la Hoz's aplomb dissipated and he fell to his knees, loudly confessing to everything he had been accused of—except the intention to assassinate the general, whom all five respected and admired, and would give up their lives to serve. The matter of the daggers was absurd; one look was all it took to understand they were not serious weapons. The other four followed his example, begging forgiveness and swearing eternal loyalty. Valdivia silenced them. Another unbearable hush followed, and finally the captain general stood and dictated his judgment, which to me seemed unjust, though I was very careful not to comment on it later. I supposed he must have had reason to do what he did.

Three of the conspirators were sentenced to be exiled; they would have to undertake the return to Peru on foot, following the route through the desert with only a handful of auxiliary Indians and one llama. A fourth was set free without explanation. Sancho de la Hoz signed a written declaration—the first ever in Chile—that dissolved his partnership with Valdivia, and remained chained and a prisoner, with his sentence left for the moment in the limbo of uncertainty. Strangest of all that night was that Valdivia ordered Ruiz to be executed. He was the soldier who had acted as accomplice, but he had not been among the five who entered our tent with the famous daggers. Don Benito personally supervised the blacks who hanged and later quartered Ruiz. His head, and each hacked-apart quarter, were displayed on meat hooks at several points throughout the camp, to remind any who had not yet made up their minds how disloyalty to Valdivia was repaid. By the third day, the stench was so nauseating, and there were so many flies, that we had to burn the remains.

Cecilia, the Inca princess, had a long and difficult birth; her baby had not turned in her womb. If a child survives a breech birth, the midwives say that it will be blessed. Cecilia's baby was pulled and tugged from her and came out purple, but healthy and crying lustily. It was a very good augury that the first Chilean mestizo was born on his feet.

Catalina was waiting for Juan Gómez at the door of our tent while the captains deliberated over the fate of the conspirators. That man, who had suffered worse tribulations than any of his stalwart companions—in the desert he had yielded his ration of water to his wife, he had walked and given her his horse when her mule foundered, and he had acted as her shield during Indian attacks—burst into tears when Catalina placed his son in his arms.

"His name will be Pedro, in honor of our gobernador," Gómez announced amid sobs.

Everyone celebrated the decision, except Pedro de Valdivia.

"I am not your gobernador, only the lieutenant, the representative of Marqués Pizarro and his majesty," Pedro sharply reminded us.

"We are in the territory that was assigned to you to conquer,

Captain General, and we are all content in this valley. Why not found our city here?" Gómez suggested.

"Good idea," seconded Jerónimo de Alderete, who had not yet recovered from jungle fever and was exhausted by the mere prospect of moving on. "And Pedrito Gómez will be the first child baptized in the city."

But I knew that Pedro wanted to continue south, as far south and as far away from Peru as possible. His idea was to establish the first city where the long arms of the marqués gobernador, the Inquisition, and all the shit-eating pen pushers—as he privately called the mean-minded employees of the Crown who did everything they could to complicate things in the New World—could not reach.

"No, señores. We will go on to the valley of Mapocho. That is the perfect site for our colony. Don Benito, who was there with the Adelantado Diego de Almagro, has assured me of that."

"How many leagues is that from here?" Alderete persisted.

"Many, but fewer than we have already traveled," Don Benito explained.

As for the battered Cecilia, first we treated her with infusions of *huella* leaves, until she finally expelled the afterbirth, then stopped the hemorrhaging with a liquor prepared from *oreja de zorro* root, a Chilean elixir Catalina had just learned about and which gave immediate results. All during the times our soldiers were engaged in a number of skirmishes with Indians, Catalina was calmly leaving the camp to mingle with the Chilean women and exchange remedies. I have no idea how she got past the sentinels without being seen, or how she managed friendly exchanges with the enemy without having her skull crushed. The only bad thing was that all the curative herbs dried up Cecilia's milk, so tiny Pedro Gómez was raised on llama milk. Had he been born a few months later, he could have counted on any number of wet nurses, for there were many pregnant Indians. The llama milk gave him a sweetness that would be a serious impediment in his future, since it was his fate to live and fight in Chile, which is no place for men with tender hearts.

And now I must recount a different episode that has no signifi-
cance except to a poor young man named Escobar, but it serves
to illuminate the character of Pedro de Valdivia. My lover was a
generous man with splendid ideas, solid Catholic principles, and
well-proved courage—all good reasons to admire him—but he also
had defects, some of which were quite grave, and over the years
they had changed his character. The worst was surely his excessive
hunger for fame, which in the end cost him, and many others, their
lives. The most difficult trait for me to endure, however, was his
jealousy. He knew that I was incapable of being unfaithful; it is not
in my nature, and I loved him too much. So why did he doubt me?
Perhaps he doubted himself.

The soldiers took as many Indian women as they wanted, some
by force and others who were willing, but surely they must have
missed words of love whispered in Spanish. Men want what they
do not have. I was the only Spanish woman on the expedition,
the captain general's concubine, visible, present, untouchable, and
therefore desired. I have asked myself sometimes whether I was
responsible for how Sebastián Romero, Lieutenant Núñez, and that
boy Escobar behaved. I find no fault in myself other than being
a woman, but it seems that is crime enough. We are blamed for
men's lust, but does the sin not belong to the one who commits it?
Why must I pay for another's lapse?

At the beginning of the expedition, I dressed as I always had in
Plasencia—underskirts, corset, blouse, long skirts, head covering,
shawl, dress shoes—but very soon I had to adapt to the circumstances. You cannot ride a thousand leagues sidesaddle without
breaking your back; I had to straddle my horse. I obtained some
men's breeches and boots, put aside the whalebone corset that
no woman can abide, and soon abandoned my head covering and
braided my hair the way Indian women do; it was too heavy on my
neck. I did not ever, however, wear a low-cut blouse or allow famil-

iarities from the soldiers. During encounters with bellicose Indians, I put on a helmet and a light leather breastplate and leg protectors Pedro had ordered made for me. Otherwise, I would have died of arrow wounds in the first portion of the journey. If that inflamed the desire of Escobar and other men on the expedition, I cannot understand how the male mind functions. I have heard Francisco de Aguirre say that males think only of eating, fornicating, and kill-ing—it was one of his favorite sayings, although in the case of the human animal that is not the whole truth: they also think of power. I refuse to agree with Aguirre, despite the many weaknesses I have observed in men. They are not all alike.

Our soldiers talked about women a lot, especially when we had to camp for a few days and they had nothing to do but stand their turn at guard, and wait. They exchanged impressions about the Indian women, boasted of their conquests—rapes—and enviously recounted the exploits of the mythic Aguirre. Unfor-tunately, my name frequently appeared in those conversations; it was said that I was insatiable, that I rode like a man so I would be excited by the horse, and that I always wore trousers beneath my skirts. That last part was true; I could not ride astride with naked thighs.

The youngest soldier on the expedition, this young Escobar—only eighteen, having arrived in Peru as a cabin boy while still a child, really—was offended by the men's gossip. He had not been hardened by the violence of war, and had formed a romantic idea of me. He was at the age when one is in love with love. He got it in his head that I was an angel who had been dragged into perver-sion by Valdivia's appetites, forced to service him like a common whore. I learned this through my Indian servants, the way I have always kept informed about what is going on around me. There are no secrets from them because men do not guard what they say in front of women any more than they do in front of their horses or dogs. They assume we do not understand what we hear. Quietly, I observed the boy's behavior and confirmed that he was always somewhere nearby, whether using the excuse of teaching tricks to

Baltasar, who was never far from my side, or asking me to change the bandage on his injured arm, or teach him to make corn stew since his two Indian girls were very poor cooks.

Pedro de Valdivia considered Escobar to be little more than a boy, and I don't think he was concerned about him at all until the soldiers began to make jokes. As soon as the other men realized that Escobar's interest in me was more romantic than sexual, they would not leave him alone, teasing him until they drew tears of humiliation. It was inevitable that sooner or later their jokes would reach the ears of Valdivia, who began to ask me insidious questions. Then he began to spy on me, and set traps for me. He would send Escobar to help me in chores that were ordinarily performed by servants, and that he, instead of objecting to the order, as any other soldier would have done, would hurry to obey. I often found Escobar in my tent because Pedro had sent him to look for something when he knew I was alone. I suppose I should have confronted Pedro at the beginning, but I didn't dare; his jealousy turned him into a monster and he would have thought that I had hidden motives for protecting Escobar.

This satanic game, which began shortly after we left Tarapacá, had been forgotten during the ordeal of the desert, where no one had the spirit for foolishness, but it was renewed with greater intensity in the quiet valley of Copiapó. Escobar's slight arm wound became infected, even though we had cauterized it, and frequently I had to treat it and put on a new bandage. I came to fear that we would have to take a drastic step, but Catalina pointed out that the flesh had not putrefied and the boy did not have a fever. "He is just clawing it, then *señorayy*, you do not see?" she hinted. I refused to believe that Escobar would dig into his wound just to have reason to see me, but I understood that the moment had come to speak with him.

Dusk was the hour when one began to hear music in the camp: the soldiers' vihuelas and flutes, the mournful reed flutes the Indians called quenas, the work bosses' African drums. That evening I could hear Francisco de Aguirre's warm tenor voice lifted in a risqué song.

The delicious aroma of the one meal of the day floated on the air: roast meat, corn, warm tortillas. Catalina had disappeared, as she often did at nightfall, and I was in my tent with Escobar, whose wound I had just dressed, and my dog, Baltasar, who had taken a liking to the boy.

"If this doesn't get better soon, I'm afraid we will have to cut off the arm," I told him straight out.

"But a one-armed soldier is not good for anything, Doña Inés," he murmured, pale with fright.

"A dead soldier is worth even less."

I offered him a glass of prickly pear chicha to ease his fright and give me time to think how to broach the subject. Finally I opted for frankness.

"I am aware that you seek me out, Escobar, and as this could be extremely unpleasant for both of us, from now on Catalina will tend to your arm."

And then, as if he had been waiting for someone to open the door of his heart, Escobar poured out a string of confessions mixed with declarations and promises of love. I tried to remind him whom he was speaking to, but he would not listen. He threw himself on me, and bad luck would have it that as I stepped back I tripped over Baltasar and crashed to the ground with Escobar on top of me. Had anyone else attacked me that way, the dog would have mangled him, but he knew the youth well, thought it was a game, and instead of pouncing on him, he leaped about us, barking happily. I am strong, and I had no doubt I could defend myself, and for that reason I didn't scream. Only a waxed cloth separated us from people outside, and the last thing I wanted was to create a scandal. With his wounded arm, Escobar was holding me tight against his chest, while with his free hand he gripped the nape of my neck, and his kisses, wet with saliva and tears, rained over my neck and face. I invoked Nuestra Señora del Socorro, and gathered my strength to knee him in the groin, but it was too late: at that moment Pedro appeared, sword in hand. He had been there the whole time, spying from the other room.

"Noooo!" I screamed, horrified when I saw him ready to run the wretched young soldier through.

Making a desperate effort, I rolled over and covered Escobar, now beneath me, with my own body, trying to protect him from the naked sword, as well as from the dog, which by then had assumed his role as my guardian and was trying to sink his teeth into him.

There was no trial, no explanation. Pedro de Valdivia simply summoned Don Benito and ordered him to hang Escobar on the morning of the next day, after mass, before the entire camp. Don Benito took the trembling youth by one arm and left him in one of the tents, under guard, but not chained. Escobar was limp as a rag, not from fear of dying, but from the pain of a broken heart. Pedro de Valdivia went to Francisco de Aguirre's tent, where he stayed till dawn, playing cards with the other captains. He did not give me a chance to talk with him, and even if he had, I think that for once I would not have found any way to make him change his mind. He was possessed with jealousy.

In the meantime, González de Marmolejo tried to console me, saying that what had happened was not my fault but Escobar's, for desiring another man's wife—or some such nonsense.

"I hope you are not going to sit here twiddling your thumbs, Padre. You must convince Pedro that he is committing a grave injustice," I demanded.

"The captain general must maintain order among his men, child, he cannot allow this kind of offense."

"Pedro allows his men to rape and beat other men's women, but woe to them if they touch his!"

"He cannot retract it now. An order is an order."

"Of course he can retract it! That young man does not deserve to be hanged, you know that as well as I do. Go talk to Pedro!"

"I will go, Inés, but I warn you in advance that he will not change his mind."

"You can threaten him with excommunication . . ."

"That threat cannot be made lightly!" the priest exclaimed with horror.

"But Pedro can have a man's death on his conscience—lightly—and that is all right?" I replied.

"Inés, you lack humility. This is not your problem, it is in the hands of God."

González de Marmolejo went off to speak with Valdivia. He did so in front of the captains who were playing cards with him, thinking they would help convince Valdivia to pardon Escobar. He was wrong on both counts. Valdivia could not afford to have his arm twisted before witnesses, and besides, his companions thought he was right; they would have done the same in his place.

In the meantime, I had gone to the tent of Juan Gómez and Cecilia, using the excuse of visiting the newborn. The Inca princess was more beautiful that ever, lying on a soft pallet and surrounded by servants. One Indian girl was rubbing her feet, another was combing her coal black hair, and a third was squeezing llama milk from a cloth into the baby's mouth. Juan Gómez, enthralled, was watching as if he were standing before the manger of the baby Jesus. I felt a tug of envy; I would have given half my life to be in Cecilia's place. After congratulating the young mother, and kissing the babe, I took the father by the arm and led him outside. I told him what had happened and asked him to help.

"You are our constable, Don Juan. Do something, please," I begged.

"I can't go against Don Pedro de Valdivia's order," he answered, his eyes wide with alarm.

"I am embarrassed to remind you of this, Don Juan, but you owe me a favor. . . ."

"Señora, are you asking this because you have a special interest in the soldier Escobar?" he asked.

"How can you think that! I would ask the same for any man in this camp. I cannot allow Don Pedro to commit this sin. And don't tell me that this is a matter of military discipline, because we both know it is nothing but pure jealousy."

"What do you suggest?"

"The chaplain says that this in the hands of God. What would you think if we helped the divine hand along a little?"

The next day, after mass, Don Benito convoked a gathering in the central plaza of the camp; the gallows had already been used to execute the hapless Ruiz, and it was waiting with a new rope. That was my first time to attend a hanging, because up until then I had managed to avoid witnessing tortures or executions. The violence of the battles and the suffering of the wounded and ill I was responsible for were enough. I carried Nuestra Señora del Socorro in my arms where everyone could see her. The captains stood in front in a rectangular formation, then the soldiers, and behind them the work bosses and the throngs of Yanaconas, the Indian serving girls, and the concubines. The chaplain had spent the night praying, after having failed in his mission with Valdivia. His skin was sallow and there were dark circles under his eyes, as was often the case when he flagellated himself. His penance made the Indian girls laugh; they knew too well what a real lashing was.

The execution was announced by a town crier and a drumroll. Juan Gómez, in his role as constable, read the sentence: the soldier Escobar was guilty of a serious infraction of discipline; he had entered the tent of the captain general with malicious intent to stain his honor. No further explanations were needed; no one doubted that the youth would pay for his puppy love with his life. The two blacks charged with executions escorted the criminal into the plaza. Escobar was not chained; he walked head up, tranquil, eyes straight ahead, as if he were sleepwalking. He had asked to be allowed to bathe, shave, and put on clean clothing. He knelt, and the chaplain gave him extreme unction, blessed him, and handed him the holy cross to kiss. The blacks led him to the gallows, tied his hands behind his back and bound his ankles, then looped the noose around his neck. Escobar refused a hood. I think he wanted to die looking at me, to defy Pedro de Valdivia. I held his gaze, trying to console him.

At the second drumroll, the blacks pulled the support from

beneath the prisoner's feet and he dropped a short distance, hanging in the air. The camp was as silent as the tomb, the only sound
the drums. For a time that seemed eternal, Escobar's body swung
from the gibbet as I prayed desperately, clutching the statue of the
Virgin to my chest. And then the miracle happened: the rope parted
and the youth fell to the ground, where he lay as if dead. There
was a collective gasp of surprise. Pedro de Valdivia took three steps
forward, pale as an altar candle, unable to believe what had happened. Before he could give an order to the hangmen, the chaplain
came forward, carrying the holy cross on high, as dumbfounded as
everyone else.

"It is God's judgment! God's judgment!" he shouted.

As if it were a distant wave, I first sensed a murmur, then heard
the frenetic jabbering of the Indians, and as that wave crashed over
the rigid Spanish soldiers, one of them crossed himself and knelt
on one knee. Another followed his example, and then another,
until every one of us except Pedro de Valdivia was kneeling. God's
judgment . . .

Juan Gómez, acting as constable, pushed the hangmen aside, and
he himself removed the noose from Escobar's neck, cut the bonds
around his wrists and ankles, and helped him to his feet. I was the
only one who noticed that he handed the gallows rope to an Indian
who quickly carried it away before anyone thought to examine it.
Juan Gómez owed me no further favors.

Escobar was not set free. His sentence was commuted to exile. He would have to return to Peru, dishonored, on foot, with
a Yanacona as his only companion. Should he manage to elude the
hostile valley Indians, he would perish from thirst in the desert,
and his body, dry as a mummy's, would never be given a decent
burial. It would have been more merciful to have hanged him. One
hour later, he left camp with the same calm dignity he had shown
walking to the gallows. Soldiers who had teased him to the point of
madness formed two respectful lines, and Escobar walked between
them, not speaking, but slowly saying good-bye with his eyes. Many
of them, shamed and repentant, shed tears. One handed him his

sword, another a short hatchet, a third came leading a llama laden with a few bundles and skins for water. I observed from a distance, fighting the animosity I felt toward Valdivia, so strong it choked me. When the boy was already outside camp, I caught up with him, dismounted, and handed him my only treasure, my horse.

We stayed in that valley seven weeks, during which twenty more Spaniards were added to our numbers, among them two priests and a despicable man named Chinchilla. From the beginning, he had sedition on his mind, and conspired with Sancho de la Hoz to assassinate Valdivia. De la Hoz's fetters had been removed, and he roamed freely about the camp, perfumed and dressed like a prince, eager to have his revenge against the captain general but carefully watched by Juan Gómez. Of the one hundred and fifty men who now composed the expedition, all except nine were hidalgos, sons of rural or impoverished nobility, but acting the hidalgo to the hilt. According to Valdivia, that had no bearing—after all, Spain itself was swimming with hidalgos—but I believe that those founders bequeathed their arrogance to the Kingdom of Chile. To the haughty blood of the Spaniards was added the indomitable blood of the Mapuche, and from that mixture has come a people of demented pride.

Following the expulsion of young Escobar, it took the camp a few days to settle back to normality. People were quick to anger, you could feel it in the air. In the soldiers' eyes, the blame was mine. I had tempted an innocent boy, seduced him, driven him out of his mind, and led him to his death. I, the shameless concubine. Pedro de Valdivia was merely doing what was demanded: defending his honor. For a long time I felt the rancor of those men like a burn on my skin, as once I had felt their lust. Catalina advised me to stay in my tent until the men's mood changed, but there was much to be done to prepare for the journey, and I had no choice but to confront the slanderous talk.

Pedro was preoccupied with indoctrinating the new soldiers and with rumors of treachery circulating through the camp, but he had time to take his rage out on me. If he realized that he had gone too far in his desire to avenge himself against Escobar, he never admitted it. Guilt and jealousy fired his lust; he wanted to possess me at every turn, at any time of day. He would interrupt his duties or his conferences with other captains, and drag me to the tent in full view of the entire camp; there was no one who did not realize what was going on. Valdivia didn't care; he did it partly to establish his authority, partly to humiliate me and defy the gossipers. We had never made love with such violence. He would leave me with bruises and act as if that pleased me. He wanted me to moan with pain, seeing that I did not moan with pleasure. That was my punishment, to suffer the fate of a whore, just as it was Escobar's fate to perish in the desert. I bore Pedro's abuse for as long as I could tolerate it, thinking that at some moment his anger would cool, but at the end of a week I lost patience, and instead of obeying when he wanted to do with me what dogs do, I slapped his face, hard. I don't know how it happened, my hand acted on its own. Surprise left us both paralyzed for a long moment, and immediately the spell in which we were trapped was broken. Pedro put his arms around me, repentant, and I began to tremble, as contrite as he.

"What have I done! What have I done, my love?" he murmured. "Forgive me, Inés, we must forget this, please . . ."

We lay with our arms around each other, our hearts full, murmuring explanations, forgiving each other, and finally falling asleep exhausted, without making love. From that moment, we began to recover our lost love. Pedro courted me with the passion and tenderness of the first days. We took short walks, always with guards, because at any moment we might be attacked by hostile Indians. We ate alone in our tent; he read to me at night; he spent hours caressing me, to give me the pleasure that only a short time ago he had denied. He was as eager for a child as I, but I did not get pregnant despite the rosaries I prayed to the Virgin and the potions Catalina prepared. I am sterile. I had no children by any of the men I loved—Juan, Pedro, Rodrigo—or any with whom I enjoyed brief and secret encounters. But I believe that Pedro, too, was sterile, because he never had children, not with Marina or any other woman. "To earn fame and leave memory of my name" was his motivation for conquering Chile. That may have been his way of substituting for the family dynasty he could not found. He left his name to history, since he could not bequeath it to descendants.

Pedro had the foresight and the patience to teach me to use a sword. He also gave me a horse to replace the one I had given Escobar, and assigned his best horseman to train it. A warhorse must obey instinctively, for its rider is occupied with his weapons. "You never know what will happen, Inés. You have had the courage to come with me, so you must be prepared to defend yourself like any of my men," he warned me. It was a prudent move. If we had hoped to recover from our fatigue in Copiapó, we were soon disenchanted, for every time we dropped our guard, the Indians attacked.

"We will send emissaries to explain that we come in peace," Valdivia announced to his principal captains.

"That would not be a good idea," said Don Benito. "They undoubtedly will remember what happened six years ago."

"What are you saying? What was that?"

"When I was here with Don Diego de Almagro, the Chilean Indians not only offered us signs of friendship, they also brought us the gold intended for their tribute to the Inca—they had already learned that he had been overthrown. The adelantado, suspicious, and not satisfied, made them promises, and invited them to a meeting, and as soon as he had gained their trust he gave us orders to attack. Many died in the fray, but we captured thirty caciques, whom we promptly tied to stakes and burned alive," the field marshal explained.

"Why did you do that! Wouldn't peaceful dealings have been much better?" Valdivia asked indignantly.

"If Almagro hadn't acted first, the Indians would have done that to us Spaniards later," Francisco de Aguirre interrupted.

The thing the native Chileans wanted most were our horses, and what they most feared were the dogs, so Don Benito kept the first in corrals, guarded by the second. The Chileans were under the command of three caciques, who in turn were directed by the powerful Michimalonko. He was an astute elder, and he knew that they were not strong enough to rush the camp of the *huincas*, so he opted to wear us down. His stealthy warriors stole our llamas and horses, destroyed our stores of provisions, kidnapped our Indian women, and attacked the parties of soldiers who rode out to look for food and water. We lost one soldier in that way, and several of our Yanaconas, whom we had, out of necessity, taught to fight, for otherwise they would all have perished.

Then spring appeared in the valley and on the hills, which came alive with flowers. The air turned warm, and Indians, mares, and llamas began to give birth. I have never seen a more adorable animal than a baby llama. The spirit of the camp improved; the new births brought a note of happiness to the weathered Spaniards and bone-weary Yanaconas. Rivers that ran dark in winter became crystal clear, and very rapid with the snowmelt from the mountains. There was abundant pasture for the animals, hunting and vegetables and fruit for us. The air of optimism ushered in by spring caused us to relax our vigilance, and then when we least expected it, two hundred Yanaconas deserted, followed by four hundred more. They simply evaporated like smoke, and no matter how many lashes Don Benito ordered as punishment for the work bosses' carelessness, and to the Indians for helping, no one ever learned how they had escaped or where they had gone. One thing was obvious: they could not have gone far without the help of the Chilean Indians; without a previous arrangement they would have been slaughtered. Don Benito tripled the guard and kept the Yanaconas strung together day and night, with the work bosses constantly patrolling the camp with their whips and dogs.

Valdivia waited until the colts and baby llamas could travel, and then gave the order to continue south toward the Edenic place so highly praised by Don Benito: the Mapocho valley. We knew that

Mapocho and Mapuche meant almost the same thing. We would have to confront savages who had turned back Almagro's five hundred soldiers and nearly eight thousand auxiliary Indians. We had one hundred and fifty soldiers, and no more than four hundred Yanaconas.

We confirmed that Chile lay in the shape of a long, slim sword. It is composed of a string of valleys lying between mountains and volcanoes and crossed by plentiful rivers. Its coast is abrupt, with fearsome waves and frigid water, its forests are dense and aromatic, its hills unending. Frequently we heard a sigh from the earth and felt it move beneath our feet, but with time we became accustomed to the temblors. "This is how I imagined Chile, Inés," Pedro confessed to me, his voice breaking with emotion as he gazed at the virginal beauty of the landscape.

Everything was not contemplation of nature, however; our trek was demanding. Michimalonko's Indians trailed us relentlessly, constantly harassing us. As a result, we were able to rest only in turns; if we were careless for an instant, they were upon us. Llamas are delicate animals and can carry only a limited amount of weight; too much will break their backs. That meant that the Yanaconas had to carry the bundles of the Indians who had deserted. Although we discarded everything we did not absolutely need—including several trunks of my elegant dresses, something I had no use for anyway—the porters were bowed over by their burdens and, in addition, roped to prevent their escape. All these factors made our advance very laborious and very slow.

The soldiers lost faith in their serving girls, who had turned out to be less submissive and not as simpleminded as expected. The men continued to use them sexually but did not dare sleep when they were around, and some of them were convinced that their girls were poisoning them little by little. However, it was not poison that was corroding their souls and creeping into their bones, it was pure fatigue. Several of the men mistreated the girls as a way to vent their own misery, at which point Valdivia threatened to take the women away, and, in two or three cases, he lived up to his word. The soldiers rebelled because they could not accept that anyone, not even their leader, should intervene in something as personal as how they handled their women, but Pedro prevailed, as he always did. We must preach by example, he said. He would not allow Spaniards to behave worse than savages. In the long run, the soldiers obeyed, but with resentment, and only halfheartedly. Catalina told me that they were still beating their women, just not on the face or anywhere the marks would be visible.

As the Chilean Indians gradually became bolder, we all wondered how the unfortunate Escobar had fared. We supposed he must have died a slow and atrocious death, but no one dared mention him aloud, so as not to bring him bad luck. If we forgot his name and his face, perhaps he would become as transparent as the breeze, and could slip past the enemy without being seen.

We moved forward at a snail's pace. The Yanaconas were slowed by the additional cargo they had to bear, and there were many foals and other newborn animals. Rodrigo de Quiroga always rode first because of his amazing vision, and his courage, which never wavered. Guarding the rear was Villagra, whom Pedro de Valdivia had named his second in command, along with Aguirre, always impatient to stir up a skirmish with the Indians. He liked fighting as much as he liked women.

One day a messenger Quiroga had sent from the head of the caravan came racing down the line yelling, "Indians are coming!"

Valdivia immediately installed the women, children, animals, and me in a place more or less protected by rocks and trees, then organized his men for the battle—not in the manner of the Spanish tercios, three infantrymen for one horseman, because on this expedition nearly everyone was on horseback. When I say that our men were mounted, it might sound as if they formed a formidable squadron of a hundred and fifty cavalrymen capable of withstanding ten thousand attackers, but the truth is that the horses were worn to the bone by fatigue, and their riders were outfitted with ragged clothing, badly fitting armor, dented helmets, and rusted weapons. They were courageous, but disorganized and arrogant, each dreaming of winning glory for himself. "Why is it so difficult for Spaniards to be one of a group?" Valdivia often complained. "They all want to be generals!" Another drawback was that we had lost so many Yanaconas, and the ones remaining were so exhausted and resentful from the treatment they'd received that they were very little help; they fought only because the alternative was death.

In battle, Pedro de Valdivia always rode in the lead, even though his captains pleaded with him to be careful because without him, the rest of us would be lost. At the cry "In the name of Santiago! Attaaaack!" that Spaniards had used to invoke the apostle Saint James during centuries of fighting the Moors, Valdivia took his place at the forefront, while his harquebusiers, kneeling, with weapons at the ready, aimed toward the enemy beyond him. Valdivia knew that the Indians would rush into battle bare chested, without shields or other protection, indifferent to death. They do not fear the harquebuses because they are more noise than anything else; the only thing that stops them are the dogs, which in the furor of combat eat them alive. The Indians confront the Spanish swords en masse, suffering devastating losses as their stone weapons ring against metal armor. Atop their mounts, the *huincas* are invincible, but if they are dragged from their horses, they are massacred.

We were not entirely prepared when we heard the *chivateo,* the dreaded war cry that announces an Indian attack, a hair-raising yelling that fires them to the point of madness and paralyzes their enemies with terror. In our case, however, it has the opposite effect; we fly into a rage. Rodrigo de Quiroga's detachment managed to join Valdivia's moments before waves of enemies poured down from the hills. There were thousands and thousands of them, nearly naked, wielding bows and arrows, lances, and clubs, howling, exultant in ferocious anticipation. The discharge of the harquebuses wiped out the first rows, but it did not stop or slow the onrushing hordes. In a question of minutes they were close enough for us to see their bright war paint, and to be engaged in hand-to-hand combat. Our lances thrust through clay-colored bodies, our swords lopped off heads and limbs, the hooves of our horses crushed the fallen. If they could fight their way near enough, the Indians would stun a horse with their clubs, and as soon as it dropped to its knees, twenty hands would seize the horseman and tumble him to the ground. For a few brief instants, helmet and breastplate would protect the soldier, and sometimes that was enough to give time to a companion to come to his aid. The arrows that were useless against coats of mail and armor were very effective on the unprotected parts of the body. In the uproar and whirlwind of the struggle, our wounded continued to fight, without feeling pain or realizing that they were bleeding, and when at last they fell, someone would rescue them and drag them to me.

I had organized my tiny hospital, surrounded by my Indian girls and protected by a few loyal Yanaconas interested in defending the women and children of their tribe, and also by the black slaves, who feared that if they fell into the hands of the Indians they would be flayed to see whether the color of their skin was painted on—something that had happened in other places. We improvised bandages from available rags, applied tourniquets to stop hemorrhaging, hurriedly cauterized wounds with red-hot coals, and as soon as the men could stand, we gave them a drink of water or wine, handed them their weapons, and sent them back to continue the fight. "Blessed Virgin, protect my Pedro," I muttered every time the grisly task of treating the wounded gave me a moment to breathe. The wind carried the odor of gunpowder and horses to us, where it blended with the smell of blood and seared flesh. The dying pleaded for confession, but the chaplain and other priests were in the battle, so it was I who made the sign of the cross on their foreheads and gave them absolution, that they might go in peace. The chaplain had explained that in an emergency, if no priest is available, any Christian can baptize and give extreme unction, though he was not sure that was the case with a Christian *woman*. Added to the cries of death and pain, the Indians' *chivateo*, the horses' neighing and snorting, the exploding gunpowder were the terrified wails of the women, many of whom had infants bound to their backs. Cecilia, accustomed to being served like the princess she was, for once descended into the world of mortals and worked side by side with Catalina and me. That small and graceful woman was much stronger than she appeared. She worked with us until her fine wool tunic was soaked with the blood of the injured.

At one point, several of the enemy fought their way to within a short distance of where we were treating the wounded. All at once, the yelling was louder, and closer, and I looked up—I had been trying to extract an arrow from Don Benito's thigh, as other women held him down—and found myself face-to-face with savages who were rushing toward us with clubs and hatchets held high, driving back our ineffective guard of Yanaconas and black slaves. Without thinking twice, I seized the sword Pedro had taught me to use and prepared to defend our small refuge.

The attackers were led by an older man adorned with war paint and feathers. A scar cut down his cheek from temple to mouth. I must have registered these details in less than an instant, because things happened very quickly. I remember that we faced each other—he with a short lance and I with the sword I had to lift with both hands—each crouched in identical postures, each furiously yelling terrible war cries, each with eyes boring into the other's with identical ferocity. To my surprise, the old man suddenly made a sign and his companions halted. I could not swear to it, but I thought there was a trace of a smile on his earth-colored face as he turned and ran off with the agility of a youth—just at the moment that Rodrigo de Quiroga came up on his rearing horse and charged our aggressors. That old man was the cacique, Michimalonko.

"Why didn't he attack me?" I asked Quiroga much later.

"Because he could not bear the shame of fighting a woman," he explained.

"Is that what you would have done, Captain?"

"Of course," he replied without hesitation.

The battle lasted at least two hours, and those hours were so intense that they flew by without an instant to think. Suddenly, when the Indians had nearly won the day, they dispersed, vanishing into the same hills they had emerged from, leaving their wounded and dead behind but taking the horses they had been able to capture from us. Nuestra Señora del Socorro had saved us once again.

The ground was strewn with bodies, and we had to chain the dogs, which had tasted blood, so they did not devour our injured as well. The blacks walked among the fallen, killing any Chileans who were not yet dead, and bringing me our wounded. I prepared for what lay ahead. For hours the valley would ring with the cries of the men we had to minister to. For Catalina and me there would be no end to pulling out arrows and cauterizing wounds, a truly repellent task. People say that one gets used to anything, but that isn't true; I never got used to those blood-curdling screams. Even now, in my old age, after having founded the first hospital in Chile and having spent a lifetime working as a nurse, I still hear the laments of war. If the wounds could be sewed with needle and thread, like a rip in cloth, our task was more bearable, but only searing heat prevents excessive bleeding and putrefaction.

Pedro de Valdivia had several light wounds and bruises, but he refused any attention. He immediately met with his captains to take the count of our losses.

"How many dead and wounded?" he asked.

"Don Benito suffered a very ugly arrow wound. We have one dead soldier and thirteen wounded, one gravely. I calculate that they stole more than twenty horses and killed several Yanaconas," said Francisco de Aguirre, who was very poor at arithmetic.

"We have four blacks and sixty-three Yanaconas wounded, a number of them seriously," I corrected. "One black and thirty-one Indians died. I believe that two men will not make it through the night. The injured will have to be transported on horseback; we cannot leave them behind. The most serious will have to be carried in hammocks."

"We will mount a guard around the camp for a few days. Captain Quiroga, for the time being, you will replace Don Benito as field marshal," Valdivia ordered. "Captain Villagra, I want you to count the number of savages left on the battlefield. You will be responsible for our safety; I suspect that the enemy will return, sooner rather than later. Chaplain, you take charge of burials and masses. We will leave as soon as Doña Inés thinks it is possible."

In spite of Villagra's precautions, the camp was very vulnerable because we were in an open valley. The Chilean Indians occupied the hills, but they gave no signs of life during the two days we stayed there. Don Benito explained that after every battle they drank themselves senseless and did not attack again until they had recovered, several days later. To our good fortune. May they never run out of chicha.

FOUR

Santiago de la Nueva Extremadura, 1541–1543

FROM THE IMPROVISED LITTER on which he was being transported, Don Benito recognized Huelén hill from afar; it was where he himself had planted a cross on his journey with Diego de Almagro.

"There it is! That is the Garden of Eden I have longed for years to see," the old man shouted; he was burning with fever from the arrow that neither Catalina's herbs and spells nor the chaplain's own prayers had been able to subdue.

We had descended into a lovely valley filled with oaks and other trees unknown in Spain: *quillayes, peumos, coigúes,* and *canelos.* It was the middle of summer, but the towering mountains on the horizon were crowned with snow. Hills and more hills encircled the gentle, golden valley. Pedro needed only one look to realize that Don Benito was right: intensely blue sky, luminous air, exu-

berant forest, and fecund earth bathed by streams and a bountiful
river, the Mapocho. That was the site God had assigned for our first
settlement, for in addition to its beauty and plenty, it met the wise
guidelines issued by Emperor Charles V for founding cities in the
Indies: *"Do not choose to populate sites at high elevations because of the
annoyance of the wind and difficulties of service and transportation, and
neither in very low elevations because they tend to harbor diseases. Found
your towns in moderate altitudes that without shelter are comfortable in the
north winds and in the heat of the day. And if there be sierras or hills, let
them lie to the east and the west; and in case of building on the banks of
a river, situate the settlement in such a way that the rising sun will first
cast its rays upon the town, and then upon the water."* Apparently the
Indians of this land were in total accord with Charles V, because we
had seen large numbers of them, along with their villages, crops,
irrigation channels, and roads. We were not the first to discover
the advantages of this valley.

Captains Villagra and Aguirre rode ahead with a detachment
to feel out the reaction of the natives, while the rest of us waited,
under guard. They returned with the agreeable news that the Indians, although suspicious, had shown no signs of hostility. They
also found that the empire of the Inca had reached this far, and the
curaca Vitacura, who represented that power, had assured them that
he would cooperate with us, knowing that the bearded *viracochas*
controlled Peru.

"Do not trust those Indians, they are treacherous and bellicose,"
Don Benito insisted, but the decision had already been made to
settle in this valley, even if we had to subjugate the natives by
force. The fact that for generations they had set up their dwellings
here, and grown their crops, was a strong incentive for the enterprising conquistadors. It meant that the land and the weather were
favorable for their purposes. Villagra calculated that adding up the
huts we could see, or guess were there, there must be about ten
thousand Indians living in the region, most of them women and
children. "We have nothing to worry about," he said, "as long as
Michimalonko's hordes don't turn up again." What must the Indians

have felt when they saw us arrive, and later, when they realized that we intended to stay?

Thirteen months after having left Cuzco in February 1541, Valdivia planted the standard of Spain at the foot of Huelén hill—which he baptized Santa Lucía because it was the day of that sainted martyr—and took possession in the name of his majesty. There he proposed to found the city of Santiago de la Nueva Extremadura. After attending mass and taking communion, we proceeded to the ancient Latin ritual of marking the city's perimeters. Since we did not have a team of oxen and a plow, we did it with horses. We walked in a slow procession, carrying the image of the Virgin at the head. Valdivia was so moved that tears ran down his cheeks. He was not the only one, half of those brave soldiers were weeping.

Two weeks later, our master builder, a one-eyed man named Gamboa, set out the classic plan of the city. First he determined the location of the Plaza Mayor and the site of the gallows or the hanging tree. From there, using a cord and a rule, he projected the straight parallel and perpendicular streets divided into squares of one hundred and thirty-eight varas, a total of eighty blocks, each of them divided into four properties. The first stakes driven into the ground were for the church, the principal site on the plaza.

"One day this modest chapel will be a cathedral," González de Marmolejo promised, his voice trembling with emotion. Pedro reserved the block north of the plaza for us, and distributed the remaining properties according to the rank and loyalty of his captains and soldiers. With our Yanaconas, and a few of the valley Indians who had shown up of their own accord, we began constructing our wood and adobe houses—putting on straw roofs until we could make tiles—with the thick walls and narrow windows and doors that would provide a defense in case of attack, and also maintain a comfortable temperature. We knew that summer was warm, dry, and healthful. We were told that winter would be cold and rainy. Gamboa and his helpers laid out the streets while others directed the squads of laborers for the constructions. Forges blazed around the clock, producing nails, hinges, locks, rivets, and angle irons; the sound of hammers and saws was stilled only at night and during mass. The smell of recently cut wood filled the air.

Aguirre, Villagra, Alderete, and Quiroga reorganized our ragged military detachment, which had deteriorated substantially during the long journey. Valdivia and the war-hardened Captain Monroy, who prided himself on having a certain diplomatic ability, rode off to talk with the Indians. My responsibility was to nurse the wounded and ill back to health, and to do what I like best: founding. That was something I had never done before, but as soon as the first boards on the plaza were nailed together, I discovered my vocation and have never turned away from it. From that moment on, I have built hospitals, churches, convents, chapels, sanctuaries . . . entire towns, and if I live long enough, there will be a badly needed orphanage in Santiago. The number of wretched little children in the street is shameful; there are as many as in Extremadura. This land is fertile, and its fruits should provide enough for all.

I was dogged in the challenge of building a community, a task that in the New World was left to women. The men built temporary towns in order to have a place to leave us with their children while they continued the endless war against the Indians. It has taken four decades of dead, sacrifices, tenacity, and hard work for Santiago to become the vigorous center it is today. I have not forgotten the days when it was little more than a collection of rudimentary huts that we had to defend tooth and nail. I set the women, and the fifty Yanaconas Rodrigo de Quiroga allowed me, to making tables, chairs, beds, mattresses, ovens, looms, pottery, kitchen tools, corrals, henhouses, clothing, mantles, blankets . . . all the indispensable items needed for civilized life.

In order to save effort and foodstuffs, I established a system in which no one would go hungry. We cooked once a day and served large bowls on tables set up in the Plaza Mayor, which Pedro called the Plaza de Armas, though we did not have a single cannon to defend it. Besides empanadas, we women cooked beans, potatoes, corn, and stew made with whatever birds and hares our Indians were able to hunt. Occasionally the valley natives brought fish and seafood from the coast, but it had a bad smell. Everyone contributed what he could to the table, just as we had years before on Maestro Manuel Martín's ship. This communal system also had the virtue of uniting people and silencing the malcontents—at least for a while. We devoted a great deal of care to our domestic animals; it was only on special occasions that we sacrificed a fowl, since it was my goal to fill our pens within a year. The hogs, hens, geese, and llamas were as important as the horses . . . and certainly much more so than the dogs. The animals had suffered from the journey as much as we humans, and each egg and each new birth was reason for celebration. I had seedbeds constructed for spring planting on the small plots the master builder Gamboa had assigned outside the town: wheat, vegetables, fruit, even flowers, for one cannot live without flowers; they were the one luxury in our rough lives. I tried to imitate the valley Indians' method of sowing and irrigating, instead of reproducing what I had seen in gardens in Plascencia; I had no doubt they knew their terrain better than we.

I haven't mentioned the maize, or "Indian wheat," without which we could never have survived. This grain is sown without clearing or plowing the ground; all that is needed is to cut back the branches of nearby trees so there is ample sun. You make shallow scratches in the dirt with a sharp stone; if you do not have a hoe, cast the seeds, and they grow on their own. Mature ears can stay on the stalks for weeks without rotting; they can be broken off without damage, and there is no need to thrash or winnow the grain. Maize was so easy to cultivate, and the crop so abundant, that it fed Indians—and Spaniards as well—throughout the New World.

Valdivia and Monroy returned, exuberantly bearing the news that their diplomatic tentatives had been successful: Vitacura would make us a visit. Don Benito warned us that this same curaca had betrayed Almagro, and that we should be prepared for some sort of duplicity, but that did not dampen our spirits. We were weary of fighting. The men polished their helmets and armor, we decorated the plaza with standards, tethered the horses in a circle—the Indians were fascinated by them—and prepared to entertain with our limited musical instruments. As a precaution, Valdivia had the men load their harquebuses, and put Quiroga and a group of marksmen out of sight, ready to fire in an emergency.

Vitacura arrived three hours late, the traditional protocol among the Incas, Cecilia had told us, adorned with brightly colored feathers and carrying a small silver hatchet—a sign of his authority. He was accompanied by his family and various persons of his court, in the style of the nobles of Peru. They came unarmed. Vitacura made an endless, very convoluted speech in Quechua, and Valdivia responded with another half hour of flattering words in Spanish, both of which the tongues found themselves hard put to translate. As his gift, the curaca brought a few grains of gold, which he said had come from Peru; some silver objects; and alpaca wool blankets. He also offered to provide a number of men to help us erect the city. In return, our captain general gave him trinkets we had brought from Spain, and hats, which the Quechuas were very fond of. I served a bounteous meal, with liberal doses of prickly pear chicha and *muday*, a strong liquor of fermented corn.

"Is there gold in this area?" Alonso de Monroy asked, speaking in the name of the other men, gold being their only interest.

"No gold, but there is a silver mine in the mountains," Vitacura replied.

The men were thrilled with that news, but it cast a shadow over Valdivia's soul. That evening, as others made plans for the silver they did not yet have, Pedro bewailed it. We were on our own property, installed in Pizarro's tent—for we hadn't yet put up the walls or roof of our house—soaking in cool water in our wood tub, seeking relief following the sultry heat of the day.

"I truly regret the business of the silver, Inés! I would like it better if Chile were as impoverished as it was said to be. I came to found a colony of hard workers with sound principles. I do not want them to be corrupted with easy wealth."

"It remains to be seen whether or not the mine exists, Pedro."

"I hope it doesn't, but exist or not, it will be impossible to keep the men from going to look for it."

And so it was. By the next morning, several parties of soldiers had been organized to explore the region in search of the accursed mine. That was the best thing that could happen to our enemies: for us to break up into small groups.

The captain general designed the first council hall himself, named his most faithful companions as councilmen, and prepared to distribute sixty land grants, with Indians to work them, among the most deserving men on the expedition. To me it seemed early to hand out land and encomiendas we did not have, especially before we knew the true size and riches of Chile, but that was how it had always been done: plant a flag, take possession with paper and ink, and later solve the problem of converting writing into real property—and in doing that dispossess the natives and force them to work for the new masters. In spite of everything, I felt very honored, for Pedro considered me as first among his captains, and granted me the best land, with its Indian *encomenadados*, arguing that I had confronted as many dangers as the bravest of his soldiers and had saved the expedition on more than one occasion, and that if the travails of the expedition had been arduous for a man, they were doubly so for a fragile woman. There was nothing fragile about me, of course, but no one objected to Pedro's decision aloud. You may be sure, however, that Sancho de la Hoz made use of Pedro's recognition of my contributions to stir the coals of rancor among disloyal soldiers. But if one day those fantasy haciendas became a reality, I, a modest woman from Extremadura, would be one of the wealthiest landowners in Chile. How happy my mother would be!

In the following months the city rose from the ground like a miracle. By the end of summer there were a number of substantial houses, we had planted rows of trees along the streets for their shade and birds, people were harvesting the first vegetables from their gardens, our animals seemed healthy, and we had stored provisions for the winter. This prosperity agitated the valley Indians because it was unmistakable evidence that we were not just passing through. They supposed, and with good reason, that more *huincas* would come to take away their land and turn them into servants. So while we were making our preparations to stay, they were preparing to drive us out. They stayed out of sight, but we began to hear the lugubrious call of the *trutruca* and the *pilloi*, a flute the Indians make from the leg bones of their enemies. The warriors were careful to avoid us; all we saw around Santiago were old men, women, and children, but we were very much on the alert. According to Don Benito, Vitacura's only purpose in visiting had been to judge our military capacity, and he most surely had not been impressed despite the theatrical show we had put on for the occasion. He must have cackled with laughter when he compared our depleted contingent with the thousands of Chileans spying on us from nearby forests. Vitacura was a Quechua from Peru, a representative of the Incas, and he had no intention of becoming involved in a contest between the *huincas* and the Promaucae Indians of Chile. He calculated that if war did break out, he would come out the winner. A roiling river favors the fisherman, as they say in Plasencia.

Catalina and I, using sign language and words in Quechua, went out to trade in the surrounding areas. From those trips we brought back fowl and guanacos, llama-like animals that give fine wool, in exchange for fripperies I pulled from the bottom of my trunks, or for our services as healers. We had good hands for setting broken bones, cauterizing wounds, and helping as midwives; those talents served us well. In the natives' settlements we met two machis, or female healers, who exchanged herbs and enchantments with Catalina, and who taught us both the properties of Chilean plants that did not grow in Peru.

The rest of the "physicians" in the valley were witch doctors who would wave their hands and make a lot of noise, and then "extract" small reptiles and saurians from the bellies of the ill. They offered minor sacrifices and terrified their patients with their pantomimes, a method that sometimes gave excellent results, as I myself witnessed. Catalina, who had worked in Cuzco with one of these *camascas*, "operated" on Don Benito when all else had failed. Discreetly, helped by a pair of secretive Indian girls from Cecilia's retinue, we carried the old man to the woods, where Catalina conducted the ceremony. We stupefied the man with a potion of herbs, smothered him with smoke, and proceeded to knead the wound in his thigh, which had not closed well. For the rest of his life, Don Benito would tell anyone who would listen how, with his own eyes, he saw the lizards and snakes that had poisoned his leg pulled from his wound, and how afterward it healed completely. He was lame, it is true, but he did not die of gangrene, as we had feared he would. I did not think it necessary to explain to him that Catalina had the dead reptiles hidden up her sleeves. "If you can cure with magic, you keep on doing it," said Cecilia.

For her part, this princess who served as our bridge between the Quechua culture and our own established an information network through her serving girls. She even went to visit the curaca Vitacura, who fell to his knees and touched his forehead to the ground when he learned that she was the younger sister of the Inca Atahualpa. Cecilia discovered that things were very turbulent in Peru; there were even rumors that Pizarro had died. I hastened to inform Pedro, in the greatest secrecy.

"How do you know that's true, Inés?"

"That's what the *chasquis* report. I cannot be sure that it's true, but wouldn't it be best to take some precautions?"

"Fortunately, we are a long way from Peru."

"Yes, but what happens to your title if Pizarro dies? You are his lieutenant."

"If Pizarro dies, I am sure that Sancho de la Hoz and others of like mind will again question my legitimacy."

"It would be different if you were gobernador, wouldn't it?" I suggested.

"But I am not, Inés."

The thought hung in the air, since Pedro knew very well that I would not be content to leave things there. I took advantage of my friendship with Rodrigo de Quiroga and Juan Gómez and asked them to circulate the idea that Valdivia should be named gobernador. After a few days, that was all that was being talked about in Santiago, exactly as I had calculated. That was the situation when the first winter rains were unleashed; the Mapocho rose, overflowed its banks, and our infant city was turned into a mud pit—but that did not prevent the town council from meeting, with great solemnity, in one of the more substantial huts. The mud came up to the ankles of the captains who met and proclaimed Valdivia gobernador. When they came to our house to announce the decision, he seemed so surprised that I was frightened. Perhaps I had overplayed my hand in my desire to read his thoughts.

"Caballeros, I am deeply moved by this show of confidence, but I fear that this resolution is premature. We are not sure whether or not the Marqués Pizarro, to whom I owe so much, is dead. I do not wish to overstep his authority in any way. I am truly sorry, my good friends, but I cannot accept the high honor you have bestowed upon me."

As soon as the captains had left, Pedro explained to me that his refusal was an astute move to protect himself. Now no one could accuse him of having betrayed the marqués, and besides, he was sure that his friends would be back with their request. And in fact, the members of the council did return with a petition written and signed by all the townspeople of Santiago. Their argument was that we were a very long way from Peru, and still farther from Spain; we were isolated at the end of the world, with no communication, and for that reason they were imploring Valdivia to be our gobernador. Whether Pizarro was dead or not, they wanted Valdivia to serve in that capacity. They had to insist three times, until finally I put the bug in Pedro's ear that there had been enough pleading; his friends might become frustrated and name someone else. I had learned from Cecilia's servants that there were several honorable captains who would be happy to accept that charge. With that, Valdivia deigned to accept. Since the entire settlement had asked, he could not refuse; the voice of the people is the voice of God; he humbly accepted the will of the community that he serve his majesty in a higher capacity; and on and on. He accepted the pertinent document, which he put in safekeeping against any future accusation, and that was how he was named the first gobernador of Chile: by popular decision, and not royal appointment.

Valdivia designated Monroy to be his lieutenant, and I was elevated to the role of Gobernadora, written that way, with a capital *G*, and that is the position the people have given me for forty years. In practical terms, more than an honor, it has been a serious responsibility. I became mother to our small community; I had to look out for the well-being of each of its inhabitants, from Pedro de Valdivia down to the last hen in the henhouse. There was no rest for me. I spent my life tending to everyday details: food, clothing, planting, animals. Fortunately, I have never needed more than three or four hours of sleep, so that I had more time than others to do my work. I made it a point to know each soldier and each Yanacona by name, and I taught them that my door was always open to receive them and listen to their troubles. I kept an eye trained to see that there were no unjust or excessive punishments, especially in the case of the Indians. Pedro trusted my good judgment, and usually heard me out before deciding on a sentence. I believe that by that time most of the soldiers had forgiven me for the tragic episode of Escobar, and had come to respect me. I had healed many of their wounds and fevers; I had fed them at a communal table; and I had helped make their dwellings comfortable.

The news that Pizarro had died turned out not to be true, but it was prophetic. At that moment Peru was calm, but a month later a small group of the Chilean *rotos*, that is, former soldiers in Almagro's expedition, burst into the palace of the marqués gobernador and stabbed him to death. A pair of servants rushed to his defense, as his courtiers and sentinels fled through the balconies. The inhabitants of Ciudad de los Reyes did not lament what had happened; they were fed up with the excesses of the Pizarro brothers, and in less than two hours the marqués gobernador was replaced by the son of Diego de Almagro, an inexperienced youth who only the day before did not have a maravedí to buy food, and the next morning was master of a fabled empire. When the news was confirmed in Chile, months later, Valdivia was already secure in his post as gobernador.

"In truth, Inés, you are a witch," Pedro murmured, frightened, when he learned.

The hostility of the valley Indians was evident all through the winter months. Pedro gave the order that no one should leave the city without a justifiable cause and without protection. That ended my visits to the machis and the markets, but I think that Catalina kept in touch with the outlying villages, because her stealthy nocturnal disappearances continued. Cecilia learned that Michimalonko was preparing an attack, and that as an incentive to his warriors he was offering the horses and women of Santiago. His forces were swelling, and already he had six *toquis*, with their men, camped in one of his strongholds, or *pukaras*, waiting for a propitious moment to start the war.

Valdivia listened to the details from Cecilia's lips, conferred with his captains, and decided to take the initiative. He left behind the major portion of his soldiers to protect Santiago and set out with Alderete, Quiroga, and a detachment of his best men to engage Michimalonko on his own ground. The *pukara* was a construction of clay, stone, and wood encircled with a stockade of tree trunks. It gave the impression of having been hastily raised, as temporary protection. In addition, it had been erected in a vulnerable location and was badly defended, so that the Spanish soldiers encountered no great difficulty in approaching by night and setting fire to it. They waited as the warriors ran out, choking on the smoke, and massacred an impressive number of them. The rout of the natives was swift, and our men captured several caciques, among them Michimalonko himself. We saw them as they were led back to camp, on foot, tied to the captains' saddles, bruised and disgruntled, but proud. They ran alongside the horses without any signs of fear or weariness. They were short in stature but muscular, with delicate hands and feet, husky shoulders and limbs, and large chests. They wore their long black hair braided with strips of cloth, and their faces were painted yellow and blue. I knew that the *toqui* Michimalonko was more than seventy years old, but it was difficult to believe; he had all his teeth and he was as spirited as a boy. The Mapuche who do not die in accidents or war can live in splendid condition until well past a hundred. They are strong, courageous, and bold, and they can endure mortal cold, hunger, and heat. The gobernador issued an order to leave the *toquis* chained in the hut built as a prison; his captains planned to torture them to find if the curaca Vitacura had lied and that there were in fact gold mines in the area.

"Cecilia says that it is futile to torture the Mapuche, you will never make them talk. The Incas tried many times, but not even the women or the children break under torture," I explained to Pedro that night as he was removing his armor and bloodstained clothing.

"Then the *toquis* can be used as hostages."

"They tell me that Michimalonko is very proud."

"Little good that does him, now that he is in chains," he replied.

"If you cannot force him to talk, perhaps his vanity will loosen his tongue," I suggested. "You know how some men are."

By the next morning, Pedro had decided to interrogate the *toqui* Michimalonko in a rather unusual way, so unusual that none of his captains could understand what the devil he was doing. He began by ordering a guard to remove Michimalonko's chains, and then that he be taken to a hut a good distance from the other captives. There three of my most beautiful Indian serving girls bathed him and dressed him in clean clothing, after which they served him a fine meal and as much *muday* as he wished to drink. Valdivia had the *toqui* brought to him under escort of an honor guard, and received him in the office of the banner-lined town council, surrounded by his captains in gleaming armor and bright plumes. I was there in my amethyst velvet dress, the only one I had—the others having been strewn along the road from the north. Michimalonko gave me an appreciative glance, but I was not sure whether he recognized the ferocious woman who had confronted him with a sword.

Two chairs had been placed in positions of equal honor, one for Valdivia and the other for the *toqui*. We had the services of a tongue, but we knew that *Mapudungu* cannot really be translated because it is a poetic language created as it is spoken; words change, flow, combine, separate. It is pure movement, and cannot be written. If one tries to translate it word for word, no meaning emerges. At the most, the tongue can transmit a general idea of what is spoken. With the greatest respect and solemnity, Valdivia manifested his admiration for the courage of Michimalonko and his warriors. The *toqui* replied with similar courtesies, and so, flattery returned with flattery, Valdivia led the Indian along the path of negotiation as his perplexed captains looked on. The old man was proud to be speaking person to person with this mighty captain, one of the bearded ones who had defeated no less a power than the Inca empire. Soon he began to boast of his position, his lineage, his traditions, the number of his warriors, and his women—more than twenty, though there was room for more, including a Spanish *chiñura*. Valdivia told Michimalonko that Atahualpa had filled a room to the ceiling with gold to pay his ransom. The more important the hostage, he added, the higher the ransom. Michimalonko sat thinking for a while, wondering, I imagine, why the *huincas* had such a craving for that metal that had brought his people nothing but trouble. For years they had had to give their gold to the Inca as tribute. But now it suddenly was good for something: to pay his own ransom. If Atahualpa had filled a room with gold, he could do no less. He stood, straight and tall as a tower, beat his chest with his fists, and announced in a strong voice that in exchange for his liberty he was prepared to hand over the only mine in the region to the *huincas*, the Marga-Marga. And in addition, he offered fifteen hundred people to work it

Gold! There was jubilation in the city. At last the adventure of conquering Chile had meaning for the men. Pedro de Valdivia set out with a well-armed detachment, Michimalonko at his side on a handsome sorrel steed, Valdivia's gift to the Indian. It was pouring rain; they were soaked and shivering but in very good spirits, while in Santiago we were listening to the howls of fury from *toquis* still chained to their posts, and worse, betrayed by Michimalonko. From the forest, the long cane *trutruca* flutes answered the chiefs' Mapudungu curses.

A proud, boastful Michimalonko led the *huincas* through the hills to the mouth of a river near the coast, some thirty leagues from Santiago, and from there to the stream with the beds of gold his people had worked for many years to satisfy the greed of the Inca. As he had agreed, he put fifteen hundred souls at Valdivia's disposition, more than half of whom turned out to be women, though that was little cause for complaint since it was women who did the work among these Chilean Indians. A man's role was to make speeches and perform tasks that required muscle, such as war, swimming, and playing their ball games. The men Michimalonko had assigned were less than useful; they did not think it was worthy of a warrior to spend his day in the water washing sand through a small basket, but Valdivia expected that the blacks and their whips would make them more industrious.

Now that I have lived many years in Chile, I know that it is pointless to enslave a Mapuche; he dies or he escapes. They are not vassals, nor do they understand the concept of labor. They understand even less the reasons for washing gold from the river, only to turn around and give it to the *huincas*. They live from fish, game, some fruits, and nuts such as the piñon, their maize, and domestic animals. Their only possessions are what they can carry with them. What reason would they have to submit to the whip of the work bosses? Fear? They don't know what fear is. They value courage above all else, then the justness of reciprocity: you give to me, I give to you. They do not have prisons, constables, or any law other than natural laws. Punishment also follows natural law; the person who does something wrong runs the risk of having the wrong returned. That is how it is in nature, and it can be no different among humans. They have been at war with us for forty years, and have learned to torture, steal, lie, and cheat, but I have been told that with one another they live in peace. The women maintain a network of relations that unite the clans, even those separated by hundreds of leagues. Before our war, they made frequent visits among themselves, and as the journeys were long, each stay lasted weeks and served to strengthen bonds and their common language, Mapudungu; it was a time to tell stories, dance, drink, and arrange new marriages. Once a year the tribes gathered in an open field for a Nguillatún, to invoke the Lord of the People, Ngenechén, and to honor the Earth, goddess of abundance, fertile and faithful mother of the Mapuche people. They consider it a lack of respect to bother God every Sunday, as we do; once a year is more than sufficient. Their *toquis* enjoy a certain authority, but there is no obligation to obey them; their responsibilities are greater than their privileges. This is how Alonso de Ercilla y Zúñiga describes the way they are selected:

> *Not by rank, or by inheritance,*
> *nor for their wealth, or being better born,*
> *but by virtue of the strength and excellence*
> *that make them preferred among men,*
> *and that illustrate, qualify, perfect,*
> *and assay a person's worth.*

When we came to Chile we knew nothing of the Mapuche. We believed that it would be easy to subdue them, as we had much more civilized peoples: the Aztecs and the Incas. It took us many years to understand how wrong we were. There is no end in sight to this war because when we execute a *toqui*, another immediately emerges, and when we exterminate a complete tribe, another issues from the forest to take its place. We want to found cities and prosper, live with decency and comfort, while they aspire only to be free.

Pedro was gone for several weeks, because in addition to organizing the operation of the mine, he decided to start building a brigantine that would provide a way to communicate with Peru.

We could not continue to live in isolation at the ass end of the world, with no company but naked savages, as Francisco de Aguirre put it with his usual frankness. Valdivia found a well-situated bay, called Concón, with a wide, clean sand beach surrounded by a stand of good wood suitable for a ship. There he left the one man who had some vague notion of things maritime, aided by a handful of soldiers, several work bosses, his auxiliary Indians, and others provided by Michimalonko.

"Do you have a plan for the boat, Señor Gobernador?" the supposed expert asked.

"Don't tell me you need a plan for something as simple as this!" Valdivia challenged.

"I have never built a boat, Excellency."

"Then pray that this one doesn't sink, my friend, because you will make the first voyage," the governor told him, and said goodbye, very content with his project.

For the first time, Pedro was excited about the idea of the gold. He could imagine the faces of people in Peru when they learned that Chile was not as godforsaken as was said. He would send them a sample of the gold on his own boat. That would cause a sensation that would attract more colonists, and Santiago would be the first of many prosperous and populous cities. As he had promised, he let Michimalonko go free, and bid him farewell with a great show of respect. The Indian galloped away on his new mount, hard put to hide his laughter.

On one of his evangelizing excursions, which up to that moment had not been fruitful—the natives of the valley had shown a stunning indifference to the benefits of Christianity—González de Marmolejo returned with an Indian boy. He had found him wandering along the shore of the Mapocho, thin and covered with filth and scabs. Instead of running away, as the Indians did every time they saw him in his worn and dirty cassock, cross held high, the boy began to tag along after him like a dog, not saying a word, his burning eyes watching the priest's every move. "Scat, youngster! Shoo!" the chaplain shouted, making menacing gestures with the cross, but the boy paid no attention, and instead followed him all the way back to Santiago. Lacking another solution, the chaplain brought him to my house.

"What do you want *me* to do with him, Padre? I have no time to raise troublemakers," I told him. The last thing I needed was to become fond of a child of the enemy.

"You have the best house in the city, Inés. This poor little fellow will do well here."

"But . . . !"

"What do God's commandments tell us, Inés?" he interrupted. "We must feed the hungry and dress the naked."

"I do not remember that commandment, but if you say so. . . ."

"Put him to work taking care of the hogs and the hens. He is very docile."

My thought was that the padre could very well raise him himself, that was why he had a house and a woman; after all, this little Indian might grow up to be an altar boy. I could not, nevertheless, deny the chaplain; I owed him too many favors, among them giving me lessons. I could already read, on my own, without any help, one of Pedro's three books, *Amadis of Gaul*, which was filled with love and adventures. I didn't yet dare try the other two, *El Cid*, which was nothing but battles, and a book by Erasmus, *Enchiridion Militis Christiani*, a manual for soldiers that did not interest me in any way. The chaplain had other books I hoped to read one day—they, too, I'm sure, banned by the Inquisition.

So the youngster stayed with us. Catalina cleaned him up and we found that he wasn't covered with dried blood after all, only mud and red clay. Except for a few scratches and bruises, he was sound. He was about eleven or twelve years old, very thin, with his ribs poking out, but strong; a mat of black hair, stiff with filth, crowned his head. He was nearly naked. He wore an amulet on a leather cord around his neck, and when we started to take that off he tried to bite us. I was so deeply involved in the tasks of founding the town that I forgot all about him, but two days later, Catalina reminded me he was there. She said that he hadn't moved from the fenced pen where we had left him, nor had he eaten anything.

"So what are we doing with him, then, *mamitayy*?"

"We will send him back to his people; that would be best."

I went to see him and found him sitting inside the fence, motionless, as if sculpted in wood, with his black eyes fixed on the hills. He had tossed aside the blanket we'd given him; he seemed to like the cold and rain of winter. I explained to him with signs that he could go, but he didn't move.

"Well, he is not caring to go, then. Only to stay he is caring," sighed Catalina.

"So let him stay."

"And who will be watching to the savage, then, *señorayy*? Thieves and slackers are these Mapuche."

"He's only a boy, Catalina. He will leave; he has nothing to do here."

I offered the boy a corn tortilla, and he did not react, but when I handed him a gourd of water he seized it with both hands and drank the water with loud slurps, like a wolf. Contrary to my predictions, he stayed. Until we could sew something to fit him, we dressed him in an adult-size poncho and trousers cinched tight at the waist. We cut his hair and deloused him. The next day he began to eat with a voracious appetite, and soon he began to come out of the hen yard and wander through the house, and then through the town, like a lost soul. He liked animals better than people, and they responded to him. The horses ate from his hand, and even the fiercest dogs, trained to attack Indians, wagged their tails when they saw him. At first he was chased out of everywhere he went; no one wanted a strange little Indian boy under his roof, not even the good chaplain, who had so often preached to me about Christian duties, but soon everyone grew accustomed to having him around, and he became invisible, coming and going through our houses, always silent and attentive. The Indian serving girls gave him treats, and even Catalina ended up accepting him, though grudgingly.

It was at this point that Pedro returned, exhausted and sore from the long journey, but very content. He had brought the first samples of gold, good-size nuggets taken from the river. Before meeting with his officers, he put his arms around my waist and led me to the bed. "In truth, you are my soul, Inés," he sighed, kissing me. He smelled of horses and sweat; he had never seemed so handsome, so strong, so my own. He confessed that he had missed me, that each time it was more difficult to leave me, even for a few days, and that when we were apart he had bad dreams, premonitions, the fear that he would not see me again. I undressed him as if he were a child. I sponged him off with a wet cloth, kissed his scars one by one, from the large horseshoe shape on his hip and the hundreds of scratches and nicks of war that covered his arms and legs, to the small star on his temple, the result of a childhood fall. We made love with a new, slow tenderness, like a pair of grandparents. Pedro was so drained by those demanding weeks that he submitted to me like the meekest virgin. Sitting astride him, making love to him slowly, so that his pleasure would build gradually, I admired his noble face in the light of the candle: broad brow, prominent nose, feminine lips. His eyes were closed and his smile was tranquil; he had surrendered to me completely. He seemed young and vulnerable, different from the hardened and ambitious man who had left weeks before leading his soldiers. At one moment during that night, I thought I glimpsed the silhouette of the Mapuche boy in the corner, but it may have been only the play of the shadows.

The next day, when Pedro came back from his meeting with the council, he asked me who the young savage was. I explained that the chaplain had foisted him off on me, and that we assumed he was an orphan. Pedro summoned him, looked him over from head to toe, and liked what he saw. Perhaps the boy reminded him of himself at that age, equally as intense and proud. Realizing that the boy did not speak Spanish, he called for a tongue.

"Tell him he can stay with us, on the condition that he become a Christian. He will be called Felipe. I like that name; if I had a son of my own, that is what I would call him. Do we agree?" Valdivia asked.

The boy nodded. Pedro added that if he caught him stealing, he would first lash him and then drive him out of the city. He could consider himself fortunate at that, because anyone else in the town would cut off his right hand with a hatchet. Understood? Again the boy nodded, without a word, and with an expression that was more irony than fright. I asked the tongue to propose a deal: if he taught me his language, I would teach him Spanish. Felipe was not in the least interested. Then Pedro sweetened the offer: if he would teach me Mapudungu, he would have Pedro's permission to look after the horses. The boy's face immediately lit up, and from that instant he adored Pedro, whom he called Taita. He called me, formally, *chiñura*—for señora, I suppose. We had our agreement. Felipe turned out to be a good teacher, and I an apt pupil, so thanks to him I became the only *huinca* able to understand the Mapuche, but it would take nearly a year. I just wrote, "understand the Mapuche," but that is a fantasy. We will never understand one another; there is too much accumulated resentment between us.

It was still midwinter when two of the soldiers Pedro had left in Marga-Marga came racing into Santiago at a full gallop. Badly wounded, they were near collapse, streaming rain and blood, their horses barely able to stand. They told us that Michimalonko's Indians had rebelled, and had killed many of the Yanaconas and blacks and nearly all the Spanish soldiers; they were the only ones who had escaped with their lives. There was not a nugget of gold left. They had also killed the men on Concón beach and scattered their hacked-up bodies across the sand, and reduced the boat under construction to a heap of burned wood. We had lost twenty-three soldiers in all, and an uncounted number of Yanaconas.

"Damn Michimalonko, that Devil's spawn! When I catch him I will have him impaled alive!" roared Pedro de Valdivia.

We had not yet absorbed the impact of that news when Villagra and Aguirre arrived to confirm what Cecilia's spies had warned her of weeks before: thousands of Indians were grouping in the valley.

They were arriving in small parties of armed men in war paint, hiding in the forests, in the hills, underground, in the clouds themselves. Pedro decided, as he always did, that the best defense was to attack. He selected forty soldiers of proven valor and at dawn the next day rode off at top speed to teach the Indians at Marga-Marga and Concón a lesson.

In Santiago, we felt abandoned and vulnerable. Francisco de Aguirre's words defined our situation: we were at the ass end of the world, surrounded by naked savages. We had no gold and no boat; the disaster was total. Chaplain González de Marmolejo called us together for mass and delivered an exalted harangue about faith and courage, but he could not lift the spirits of the frightened populace. Sancho de la Hoz seized the excuse of the rebellion to blame Valdivia for our suffering, and so increased to five the number of his followers, among them, the malcontent Chinchilla, one of the twenty who had joined the expedition in Copiapó. I had never liked that man, for I judged him to be dishonest and cowardly, but I had never dreamed that he was a hopeless fool as well. His idea was not original—to assassinate Valdivia—though this time the conspirators did not have five identical daggers; those were well hidden at the bottom of one of my trunks. So sure was Chinchilla of the genius of his plan that he had a few drinks too many, dressed up as a clown, with bells and rattles, and went out and leaped about in the plaza, imitating the gobernador. Of course Juan Gómez immediately arrested him, and as soon as he showed him a few tourniquets, and explained on which part of the body he would apply them, Chinchilla peed his breeches and informed on his co-conspirators.

Pedro de Valdivia returned with greater haste than he had left; his forty soldiers were not remotely a large enough force to confront the unexpected numbers of warriors who kept arriving in the valley. He had managed to rescue the poor Yanaconas who had survived the massacres at Marga-Marga and Concón and taken cover in the dense undergrowth, faint with hunger, cold, and terror. He had met several enemy parties, which he had been able to scatter and, thanks to luck—which up to that point had never failed him—had taken three caciques prisoner and brought them to Santiago. With them, we had seven hostages.

For a town to be a town, you have to have births and deaths, but apparently in Spanish towns you must also have executions. We witnessed the first ones in Santiago that same week, after a brief trial—this time with torture—in which the conspirators were sentenced to death without appeal. Chinchilla and two others were hanged and their bodies exposed to the wind and the enormous Chilean vultures for several days on the top of Santa Lucía hill. A fourth man was beheaded in prison; he used his titles of nobility to escape being hanged like a commoner. To everyone's surprise, Valdivia again pardoned Sancho de la Hoz, the principal instigator of the revolt. That time, in private, I opposed his decision, because the documents from the king were no longer pertinent. De la Hoz had signed a paper renouncing his claim to lead the conquest of Chile, and had acknowledged that Pedro was the legitimate governor. But that agitator had already given us too much trouble. I will never know why Pedro saved his neck one more time. He refused to give me any explanation, and by then I had learned that with a man like Pedro, it is best not to insist. That year of disappointments and setbacks had embittered him, and he easily lost control. I had to keep my mouth shut.

In the most splendid natural setting in the world, in the depths of the cold forests of southern Chile, in the silence of fragrant roots, bark, and branches, in the haughty presence of the volcanoes and peaks of the cordillera, beside emerald lakes and foaming rivers of melted snow, the Mapuche tribes joined together in a special ceremony, a conclave of ancients, heads of clans, *toquis, lonkos,* machis, warriors, women, and children.

Day after day they came to the forest clearing, an enormous hilltop amphitheater the men had already outlined with branches of araucaria and *canelo*; sacred trees. Some of the families had traveled weeks through the rain to get there. Groups that arrived early had set up huts—*rukas*—so attuned to nature that even from a short distance they could not be detected. Those who arrived later improvised leaf shelters—*ramadas*—and hung their wool blankets. At night they all prepared food they exchanged with others and drank chicha and *muday*, but in moderation, so they would not tire themselves. They visited to catch up on news told in long, solemn, poetic narratives repeating the histories of their clans memorized from generation to generation. Talk, talk, talk; that was the important thing. In front of each shelter a small fire was kept burning and smoke drifted in the mist that rose from the earth at the first light. The flickering fires illuminated the milky landscape of dawn. The young men returned from the river where they had been swimming in frigid water, and painted their faces and bodies in ritual colors of yellow and blue. The caciques donned their blankets of embroidered wool, sky blue, black, white; hung around their necks their *toquicuras*, the stone hatchets that were symbols of their power; stuck heron, ñandú, and condor feathers in their headdresses, while the machis burned aromatic herbs and prepared the *rewe*, the spiritual ladder they climbed to speak with Ngenechén.

We offer you this trickle of muday, *it is the custom, to nourish the spirit of the Earth, which is always with us. Ngenechén made the* muday, *he made the Earth, he made the* canelo, *he made the kid and the condor.*

The women braided their hair with bright yarn: the maidens sky blue, the married women red; they adorned themselves with their finest blankets and silver jewelry, while the children, also dressed for a festival, quiet and serious, sat in a semicircle. The men formed a single body like wood, proud, pure muscle, black hair held back in woven headbands, their weapons in their hands.

With the first rays of the sun, the ceremony began. The warriors ran around the amphitheater yelling and brandishing their weapons to the tempo of drums and flutes, frightening away the forces of evil. The machis sacrificed several guanacos, after asking their permission to offer their lives to the Great Father. They poured a little blood on the ground, tore out the animals' hearts, smoked them with tobacco, then divided them into small pieces to be shared among the *toquis* and *lonkos*, in that way communing among themselves and with the Earth.

Ngenechén, this is the pure blood of the animals, your blood, blood that you give us so that we may live and move about. Great Father, with this blood we are pleading that you will bless us.

The women began a melancholy chant as the men filed into the center of the amphitheater and danced, slow and heavy, pounding the ground with naked feet to the sound of the *kultrun* drums and *trutrucas.*

And you also, Mother of the People, we greet you. Earth and the people are inseparable. Everything that happens to the Earth happens also to the people. Mother, we beg you to give us the piñon that sustains us, we beg you not to send too much rain, for the seeds will rot, and the wool, and we ask you please not to make the earth tremble or the volcanoes spit, because it awes the herds and frightens the children.

Then the women entered the circle and danced with the men, moving their arms, heads, and blankets like great birds. Soon the dancers felt the hypnotic effect of *kultruns* and *trutrucas*, of the rhythmic beat of feet on the damp earth, of the powerful energy of the dance, and one by one they began to utter visceral howls that gradually merged into a long cry: Ooooooohm—which echoed in the mountains and moved their spirit. No one could escape the spell of that Ooooooooohm.

We are asking you only, Great Father, that if it pleases you, you aid us in every moment here on this earth, and in this time that we are going through, we ask that you hear us. We are asking, Great Father, that you do not abandon us, that you do not cause us to feel our way in the darkness, that you give great strength to our arms to defend the land of our grandfathers.

The music and the dance came to a stop. The rays of the morning sun were sifting through the clouds, tinting the mist with golden dust. The most ancient of the *toquis*, wearing a puma skin around his shoulders, stepped forward to speak first. He had traveled an entire moon to be here, to represent his tribe. There was no hurry. He began in the most remote times, the story of Creation, how the snake Cai-Cai stirred up the sea and the waves were threatening to swallow the Mapuche, but then the serpent Treng-Treng saved them, carrying them to the peak of the highest hills that it made grow and grow. And the rain fell in such abundance that those who did not manage to climb to the hills perished in the flood. And afterward, the waters receded, and men and women occupied the valleys and the forests, never forgetting that the trees and the plants and the animals are their brothers, and that they must care for them, and that every time branches are cut to make a shelter, they are thanked, and when an animal is killed to eat, it is asked forgiveness, and is never killed for the sake of killing. And the Mapuche lived free in the blessed land, and when the Incas from Peru came, the Mapuche joined together to defend themselves and defeated the Incas, and did not let them pass the Bío-Bío, which is the mother of all rivers, but her waters were stained with blood and the moon was red in the sky. And a time passed, and the *huincas* came along the same roads as the Incas. Many came, and they smelled very bad, they could be smelled at two days' distance, and they were thieves; they had no country and no land, they took what was not theirs, women, too, and they wanted the Mapuche and other tribes to be their slaves. And our warriors had to drive them out, but many died, because their arrows and lances could not pierce the metal clothes of the *huincas*, while they could kill from afar with nothing but noise, or with their dogs. No matter, they were driven out. The *huincas* themselves left, cowards that they were. And several summers and several winters passed, and other *huincas* came, and these, the ancient *toqui* said, wish to stay; they are cutting trees, raising their *rukas*, sowing their maize, and planting their seed in our women, and thus are born children who are neither *huincas* nor people of the earth. And from what our spy tells us, they intend to take over the entire land, from the volcanoes to the sea, from the desert to where the world ends, and they want to found many towns. They are cruel, and their *toqui* Valdivia is very clever. And I say to you that never have the Mapuche had enemies as powerful as these bearded ones from far away. Now they are but a small tribe, but more will come, because they have houses with white wings that fly across the sea. And I now ask our people what we must do.

Another of the toquis came forward, waved his weapons in the air, and leaped and uttered a long cry of rage, then announced that he was ready to attack the *huincas*, to kill them, to devour their hearts to absorb their power, to burn their *rukas*, to take their women—there was no other way. Death to them all. When he had spoken, a third *toqui* occupied the center of the amphitheater to maintain that the entire Mapuche nation had to join together against that enemy and choose a *toqui* among *toquis*, a *ñidoltoqui*, and make war.

Great Father Ngenechén, we ask only that you give us aid in overcoming the huincas; *help us to tire them, badger them, and not let them sleep or eat, make them fear us, let us spy on them, set traps for them, steal their weapons, crush their skulls with our* macanas. *This we ask of you, Great Father.*

The first *toqui* again came forward to say that they did not have to hurry, they had to fight with patience, the *huincas* were like a bad weed that when cut sends out more vigorous shoots than before; this would be a war with them, with their children, and the children of their children. Much Mapuche blood and much *huinca* blood would be spilled before the end. The warriors lifted their lances and from their throats came a long chorus of approving yells. *War! War!* At that moment, the fine rain ceased, the clouds parted, and a magnificent condor slowly cruised across a strip of clear sky.

At the beginning of September we realized that our first winter in Chile had come to an end. The weather improved and buds came out on the young trees we had transplanted from the forest to line the streets. Those months had been hard not just because of the Indians' harassment and Sancho de la Hoz's conspiring, but also for the forsaken feeling that frequently overwhelmed us. We wondered what was happening in the rest of the world, whether there had been Spanish conquests in other territories, new inventions, what was the state of our emperor, who according to the last news to reach Peru a couple of years before was losing his sanity. Madness ran in the veins of his family; one had only to think of his unfortunate mother, Juana, the madwoman of Tordesillas.

From May to the end of August the days had been short; it had grown dark about five o'clock and the nights had seemed eternal. We used the last ray of natural light to do our work, after which we had to gather in one room of the house—masters, Indians, dogs, even the fowl from the hen yard—with one or two candles and a brazier. Each of us looked for a way to help pass the evening hours. The chaplain started a choir among the Yanaconas to reinforce the faith through chants. Aguirre entertained us with his outlandish tales of womanizing and his risqué soldier ballads. Rodrigo de Quiroga, who at first seemed quiet and rather timid, loosened up and revealed himself to be an inspired storyteller. We had very few books among us, and knew them all by heart, but Quiroga would take the characters of one story and insert them into a different one, ending up with an infinite array of plots. All the books in the colony, except two, were on the black list of the Inquisition, and as Quiroga's versions were much more audacious than the originals, they were a sinful pleasure, and for that reason much requested. We also played cards, a vice suffered by all Spaniards, especially our gobernador, who was also blessed with luck. We did not bet money, in order to avoid quarrels and not set a bad example for the servants, but also to hide how poor we were. We listened to the vihuela, recited poetry, and had spirited conversations. The men remembered their battles and adventures, applauded by everyone present. Pedro was asked again and again to recount the feats of the marqués de Pescara; soldiers and servants never tired of praising the marqués's cleverness the time he had camouflaged his troops with white sheets to blend into the snow.

The captains held meetings—also in our home—to discuss the colony's laws, one of the gobernador's basic concerns. Pedro wanted Chile's society to be based on legality and the spirit of service of its leaders. He insisted that no one should receive payment for occupying a public office, least of all himself, since serving was an obligation and an honor. Rodrigo de Quiroga fully shared this idea, but they were the only two imbued with such lofty ideals. With the land and encomiendas that had been distributed among the enterprising soldiers of the conquest, they would in the future have more than enough to live very well, Valdivia said, even if for the moment their rewards were only dreams. Those who had the most land would have to do the most for other people in return.

The soldiers were bored, because aside from practicing with their weapons, copulating with their concubines, and fighting when called upon, they had little to do. The work of building the city, growing food, and looking after the animals was done by the women and the Yanaconas. I did not have enough hours to do everything: taking care of my house and the colony, looking after the sick, the plantings, and the animal pens, along with my reading lessons with González de Marmolejo and the Mapudungu with Felipe.

The fragrant spring breeze brought with it a wave of optimism; the terrors recently unleashed by Michimalonko's warriors lay behind us. We felt stronger, even though following the slaughters at Marga-Marga and Concón and the execution of four traitors our small numbers had been reduced even further; we now had only one hundred and twenty soldiers. Santiago had emerged nearly intact from the mud and wind of the winter months, when we'd had to bail out water with pails; our houses had survived the deluge and our people were healthy. Even our Indians, who died if they caught a common cold, had come through the storms without serious problems. We plowed our garden plots and planted the seedlings I had so carefully guarded from the icy winds. The animals had mated and we prepared fenced pens for the piglets, foals, and llamas soon to be born. We decided that as soon as the mud dried we would dig the necessary drainage ditches, and even planned to build a bridge over the Río Mapocho to join the town with the haciendas that

one day would lie on the town's outskirts . . . but first we would
have to finish the church. Francisco de Aguirre's house was already
two stories high, and still growing. We teased him because he had
more Indian girls, and gave himself more airs, than all the rest of
the men put together, and evidently he intended for his house to be
higher than the church. "The Basque thinks he is above God," the
soldiers joked. The women of my household had spent the winter
sewing and teaching their domestic skills to others. The morale of
the Spaniards, always very vain regarding appearance, rose when
they saw their new shirts, patched breeches, and mended doublets.
Even Sancho de la Hoz, from his cell, for once interrupted his plotting. The gobernador announced that soon we would be building
another brigantine, returning to work the gold beds, and looking
for the silver mine the curaca Vitacura had reported—and which
had been the most elusive prize of all.

Our spring optimism did not last long, for in early September
the Indian boy Felipe brought us news that enemy warriors were arriving every day in the valley, and that they were forming an army.
Cecilia sent her serving girls to investigate, and they confirmed
what Felipe seemed to know by pure clairvoyance, adding that there
were some fifteen hundred camped fifteen or twenty leagues from
Santiago. Valdivia summoned his most faithful captains, and once
again determined to teach the enemy a lesson before they were
better organized.

"Don't go, Pedro. I have a bad presentiment," I pleaded.

"You always have bad presentiments at times like these, Inés," he
replied. I detested that tone he sometimes used, like a father
humoring a child. "We are used to fighting against a number a
hundred times larger than our own; fifteen hundred savages are
laughable."

"There may be more hiding in other places."

"With God's favor, we will deal with them; have no worry."

To me it seemed imprudent to divide our forces, which were
already quite thin, but who was I to object to the strategy of an
experienced soldier like Valdivia? Every time I tried to dissuade

him from a military decision, because common sense demanded it, he flew into a rage and we ended up furious with each other. I did not agree with him on this occasion, as I did not agree later, when he was inflamed with a fever to found cities we could neither populate nor defend. That hardheadedness led to his death. "Women cannot think on a grand scale; they cannot imagine the future; they lack a sense of history; they concern themselves only with domestic and immediate realities," he told me once, but he had to retract his statement when I recited the list of everything that I and other women had contributed to the mission of conquering and founding.

Pedro divided his forces: fifty soldiers and a hundred Yanaconas under the command of his best captains, Monroy, Villagra, Aguirre, and Quiroga, to protect the town, while he himself would lead a detachment consisting of a little more than sixty soldiers and the remainder of the Indians. They left Santiago at dawn, with trumpets, flying banners, harquebus fire, and enough uproar to give the impression that they were more than their actual number. From the flat *azotea* atop Aguirre's house, which had been converted into an observation post, we watched them ride away. It was a cloudless day and the snow-covered mountains that surrounded the valley seemed immense, and very near. Rodrigo de Quiroga was at my side, trying to veil his uneasiness, which was as great as mine.

"They should not have gone, Don Rodrigo. Santiago is very vulnerable."

"The gobernador knows what he's doing, Doña Inés," he replied, not entirely convinced. "It is better to go out to meet the enemy; that way he understands that we do not fear him."

This young captain was, in my opinion, the best man in our small colony—after Pedro, of course. He was courageous, experienced in war, silent in suffering, loyal, and selfless. He had in addition the rare virtue of inspiring confidence in everyone who knew him. He was building a house on a property near our own, but he had been so busy fighting in the constant skirmishes with

the Chilean Indians that his dwelling consisted of a few pillars, two
walls, some canvas, and a straw roof. His home was so inhospi-
table that he spent a lot of his time in ours, since the house of the
gobernador, the largest and most comfortable in the town, had
become a meeting center. I suppose my determination that no one
would want for food and drink contributed to our social success.
Rodrigo was the only one of the soldiers who did not keep a harem
of concubines and did not chase the other men's Indian girls to get
them pregnant. His companion was an Indian named Eulalia, one
of Cecilia's serving girls, a beautiful young Quechua who had been
born in Atahualpa's palace. She had the same grace and dignity as
her mistress, the Inca princess. Eulalia fell in love with Rodrigo
the moment he joined the expedition. When he arrived he was as
filthy, ill, shaggy, and ragged as the other surviving ghosts of the
Los Chunchos jungle, but with just one glance she was attracted
to him, even before they cut his hair and bathed him. She could
not stop thinking of him. With infinite cleverness and patience she
seduced Rodrigo, and then came to me with her woes. I interceded
with Cecilia and asked her to allow Eulalia to serve Rodrigo, using
the argument that Cecilia had enough servants, while that poor man
was skin and bones and might die if he was not cared for. Cecilia
was too clever to be deceived by such tales, but she was moved
by Eulalia's love. She released her servant, and Eulalia went to live
with Quiroga. They had a delicate relationship; he treated her with
a fatherly, respectful courtesy unusual among the soldiers and their
women, and she attended to his least wish quickly and discreetly.
She seemed submissive, but I knew through Catalina that she was
passionate and jealous.

Rodrigo de Quiroga and I, up on Aguirre's *azotea*, watched as
more than half our forces marched away from Santiago. For some
reason, I found myself wondering what Quiroga was like in his intimate moments, whether by any chance he satisfied Eulalia. I knew
his body because I had taken care of him when he returned from
Los Chunchos, and when he had been wounded in encounters with
the Indians. He was slim, but very strong. I had never seen him
completely naked, but according to Catalina, "You need to be seeing

his *piripicho*, then, *senorayy*. Frisky as a colt." The women servants, who never missed anything, agreed, assuring me that he was very well endowed; on the other hand, Aguirre, with all his woman chasing . . . well, what did it matter. I recall that my heart gave a little lurch when I remembered what I had heard about Rodrigo, and I blushed so violently that he noticed.

"Is something the matter, Doña Inés?" he asked.

I quickly said good-bye, perturbed, and went downstairs to begin my daily chores, while he went off to his.

Two days later, on the night of September 11, 1541, a date I have never forgotten, Michimalonko's men and their allies attacked Santiago. As was always the case when Pedro was away, I couldn't sleep. It was not unusual for me to be awake all night. After I sent everyone else to bed, I had stayed up late, sewing. In that ambiguous hour a little before dawn, I felt the tension double that had tied my stomach in knots since Pedro rode away. I had spent a good part of the night praying, not from an excess of faith, but from fear. Speaking directly with the Virgin always calmed me, but during that long night she had not eased the ominous premonitions tormenting me.

I threw a shawl around my shoulders and made my usual rounds, accompanied by Baltasar, who had the habit of following me like my shadow. The house was quiet. I did not meet Felipe, but I wasn't worried; he often slept with the horses. Like me, he was an insomniac. I often ran into him in my nighttime prowls through the rooms of the house. He would be in some unexpected place, motionless and silent, his eyes wide open in the darkness. It had proved pointless to assign him a straw mattress, or a specific place to sleep; he lay down anywhere, without even a blanket to cover him. I went out front to the plaza, and noticed the faint light of a torch on the roof of Aguirre's house, where they had assigned a soldier as lookout. Thinking that the poor man must be fainting with fatigue after so many hours on solitary guard duty, I warmed a bowl of soup and carried it to him.

"Thank you, Doña Inés. Can't you rest?"

"I am a bad sleeper. Anything new?"

"No. It has been a peaceful night. And as you can see, there is a little moonlight."

"What are those dark splotches over there by the river?"

"Shadows. I've noticed them for a while now."

I stood watching a moment; it was a strange effect, as if a great, dark wave were overflowing the riverbanks to join another coming from the valley.

"Those shadows are not normal. I think we should advise Captain Quiroga; he has very sharp eyes."

"I cannot leave my post, señora."

"I will go."

I raced down the steps, followed by Baltasar, and ran to the home of Rodrigo de Quiroga at the other end of the plaza. I waked the Indian guard, who was asleep across the threshold that would one day house a door, and ordered him to summon the captain immediately. Two minutes later Rodrigo appeared, half dressed, but with his boots on and his sword in his hand. We hurried back across the plaza and up the steps to Aguirre's *azotea*.

"No doubt about it, Doña Inés. Those shadows are humans creeping in this direction. I think they are Indians with something like dark blankets pulled over them."

"How can that be?" I exclaimed incredulously, thinking of the marqués de Pescara and his white sheets.

Rodrigo de Quiroga sounded the alarm and in less than twenty minutes the fifty soldiers, who in those days were always primed for action, met in the plaza, each wearing armor and helmet, with weapons ready. Monroy organized the cavalry—we had only thirty-two horses—and divided it into two small detachments: one under his command and the other under Aguirre's, both having decided to confront the enemy before they penetrated the town. Villagra and Quiroga, with harquebusiers and a few Indians, remained in charge of internal defense, while the chaplain, the women, and I prepared to supply the defenders and treat their wounds. At my suggestion, Juan Gómez took Cecilia, two Indian wet nurses, and all the nursing babies of the colony to the cellar of our house, which we had dug with the idea of storing provisions and wine. He handed his wife the small statue of Nuestra Señora del Socorro, kissed her on the lips, blessed his son, sealed the cave with some boards, and shoveled dirt over the entrance. The only way he had to protect them was to bury them alive.

Dawn came on that eleventh day of September. The sky was cloudless, and at the moment the timid spring sun illuminated the outlines of the city, the Indians' monstrous *chivateo* rang out, the war cries of thousands of natives rushing toward us in a solid mass. We realized that we had fallen into a trap; the savages were much cleverer than we had thought. The party of fifteen hundred men who formed the contingent supposedly threatening Santiago had been a lure to distract Valdivia and a large part of our forces; later the thousands and thousands hidden in the forest would use the shadows of night to approach the town under cover of dark blankets.

Sancho de la Hoz, who had been rotting for months in a cell, yelled to be released and given a sword. Monroy decided that all arms were desperately needed, including those of a traitor, and ordered the chains to be removed. And I give witness that the courtier fought that day with the same ferocity as the rest of the heroic captains.

"How many Indians do you calculate are coming, Francisco?" Monroy asked Aguirre.

"Nothing to upset us, Alonso! Maybe eight or ten thousand. . . ."

Our two parties of cavalry galloped out to confront the first attackers, furious centaurs lopping off heads and limbs and crushing chests beneath the hooves of their horses. In less than an hour, nevertheless, they began to fall back. In the meantime, thousands of yelling Indians were already racing through the streets of Santiago. Some of the Yanaconas, and several women trained by Rodrigo de Quiroga months before, loaded the harquebuses for the soldiers to shoot, but the process was long and clumsy; the enemy was on top of us. The mothers of the babies in the cellar with Cecilia were more valiant than the most experienced soldiers; they were fighting for their children's lives. A rain of fiery arrows fell on the straw roofs, which, even though they were damp from the August rains, burst into flames. I realized that we would have to leave the men to their harquebuses while we women tried to put out the fire. We formed lines and passed buckets of water, but we quickly saw that it was futile; arrows kept falling and we could not afford to waste water on the fire, since soon the soldiers would need it desperately. We abandoned the houses on the periphery and grouped in the Plaza de Armas.

By then the first wounded were arriving, soldiers and Yanaconas. Catalina, my helpers, and I had organized as usual: rags, hot coals, water, and boiling oil; wine to disinfect and *muday* to help bear the pain. Others of the women were preparing soup pots, water gourds, and corn tortillas; it would be a long battle. Smoke from burning straw covered the city; our eyes were burning and we could barely breathe. As men came in bleeding, we tended to their visible wounds; there was no time to remove their armor. We gave them a cup of water or broth, and as soon as they could stay on their feet, they staggered off to fight again. I do not know how many times the cavalry held off the attackers, but the moment came when Monroy decided that it would not be possible to defend the entire city; it was burning an all four sides, and Indians occupied nearly all of Santiago. He conferred briefly with Aguirre and they agreed to fall back and combine all our forces in the plaza, where the aged Don Benito had already sat himself down on a wooden stool. His wound had healed, thanks to Catalina's sorcery, but he was weak and unable to stand for long at a time. He had at hand two harquebuses and a Yanacona helping to load them, and all through that long day he wrought havoc among the enemy hordes from his invalid's perch. He fired so steadily that he burned the palms of his hands on the red-hot weapons.

While I was busy with the wounded inside the house, one group of assailants climbed over the adobe wall of my patio. Catalina gave the alarm, screeching like a stuck pig, and I ran to see what was happening. I did not get far; the enemies were so near that I could have counted the teeth in those ferocious, war-painted faces. Rodrigo de Quiroga and González de Marmolejo, who had strapped on a breastplate and taken up a sword, came to drive them back, since it was essential to defend the house where we had the wounded and children hidden in the cellar with Cecilia. Some of the Indians confronted Quiroga and the priest while others started burning my plants and killing my domestic animals. That was what drove me over the edge; I had cared for each of those animals as I would the children I never had. With a roar that rose from my entrails, I ran toward the Indians—though I was not wearing the armor Pedro had had made for me; I could not treat the wounded while immobilized inside that metal. I am sure my hair was standing on end, and I was foaming at the mouth and cursing like a harpy; I must have presented a very threatening picture because for an instant the savages stopped and stepped back in surprise. I have never known why they didn't crush my skull right there. I was later told that Michimalonko had given the order not to touch me because he wanted me for himself, but those are stories people invent after the fact to explain the inexplicable.

And then Rodrigo de Quiroga came to my aid, whirling his sword overhead like a windmill and shouting for me to run to safety, and also my dog Baltasar, snarling and barking, his lips drawn back to reveal sharp eyeteeth, looking the beast he never was under normal circumstances. The attackers scattered, chased by the mastiff, and I stood in the middle of my burning garden and the corpses of my animals, desolate. Rodrigo took my arm to pull me away, but when we saw a rooster with singed feathers trying to stand, I instinctively lifted my skirts and wrapped it up in them. A little farther along I saw a pair of hens stupefied by the smoke, and it was an easy task to catch them and put them in with the rooster. Catalina came to look for me and when she saw what I was doing, she helped me. Between us, we saved those fowl, a pair of hogs, and four handfuls of wheat. Nothing more, but those we put in a safe place. By then Rodrigo and the chaplain were back in the plaza fighting alongside the other men.

Catalina, several Indian women, and I went back to tending the wounded, who were being brought in alarming numbers to the improvised hospital in my house. Eulalia came leading a foot soldier covered in blood from head to foot. "My God, this one hasn't a chance," I remember thinking, but when we removed his helmet we found that although he had a deep slash across his forehead the bone beneath wasn't broken, only slightly caved in. Catalina and another women cauterized the wound, washed his face, and gave him water to drink, but they could not get him to rest, not even for a minute. Dazed and half blinded by monstrously swollen eyelids, he stumbled back to the plaza.

While they helped him, I was trying to remove an arrow from another soldier's neck, a man named López, who had always treated me with ill-concealed disdain, especially following the tragedy of young Escobar. The poor soul was deathly pale and the arrow was in so deep that I knew I could not remove it without enlarging the wound. I had decided to take that risk when he began to shudder and utter rasping death rattles. I knew there was nothing to be done for him, and called the chaplain, who came quickly to administer last rites. The floor of the main room in my house was littered with the bodies of wounded in no condition to return to the plaza, about twenty, most of them Yanaconas. We had run out of rags, and Catalina was tearing the sheets that we had lovingly embellished with embroidery during the lazy winter evenings; then we had to cut our skirts in strips, and finally, my one elegant dress. At that point Sancho de la Hoz came in carrying a soldier who had lost consciousness, leaving him at my feet. The traitor and I exchanged a glance, and I feel sure that in that instant we forgave each other the affronts of the past. To the chorus of howls of men being cauterized with red-hot iron was added the whinnying of the wounded horses the blacksmith was treating as best he could in the same room. On the dirt floor, the blood of Christians and animals flowed together.

Aguirre appeared at the door, without dismounting, bloody

from helmet to stirrups, announcing that he had ordered all homes
to be abandoned except those around the plaza, where we would
prepare to defend ourselves to the last breath.

"Get off your horse, Captain, and let me treat your wounds!"
I begged him.

"Not a scratch on me, Doña Inés. Take water to the men in
the plaza," he yelled with fierce jubilation, and disappeared on his
rearing horse, it, too, bleeding from the ribs.

I ordered several women to take water and tortillas to the
soldiers, who had been fighting since dawn, while Catalina and I
removed the armor from López's corpse; then, just as they were,
soaked with blood, I put on his coat of mail and breastplate. I picked
up his sword—I couldn't find mine—and went outside to the plaza.
The sun had passed its zenith some time ago; it must have been
about three or four in the afternoon. We had been fighting for more
than ten hours. I took a look around and saw Santiago burning to
the ground, the labor of months lost. It was the end of our dream
of colonizing the valley.

In the meantime, Monroy and Villagra had joined the surviving
soldiers and were fighting on horseback inside the plaza, which our
men were defending shoulder to shoulder, attacked from all four
directions. A part of the church was still standing, and Aguirre's
house, where we were holding the seven captive caciques. Don
Benito, black with gunpowder and soot, was firing methodically
from his wood stool, carefully aiming before pressing the trigger, as
if hunting quail. The Yanacona who had been loading his weapons
lay motionless at his feet, and Eulalia had stepped into his place.
I realized that the girl had been in the plaza all the time, in order
not to lose sight of her beloved Rodrigo.

Above the pandemonium of gunfire, whinnying horses, barking, and
the Indians' *chivateo*, we could clearly hear the voices of the seven
captive caciques spurring on their warriors at the top of their lungs.
I do not know what came over me then. I have often thought about

that fateful September 11, and have tried to make sense of events, but I don't believe that anyone can describe exactly what happened; each of the participants has a different version, according to his or her part in it. The smoke was dense, the confusion overwhelming, the noise deafening. We were beside ourselves, fighting for our lives, maddened by the blood and violence. I do not recall any details of that day and so necessarily have had to trust what others have told me. I do remember that at no moment was I afraid; rage had taken over completely.

I looked toward the cell where I could hear the captives yelling, and despite the smoke and flames, I clearly saw my husband, Juan de Málaga, who had been haunting me since Cuzco, leaning against the door frame, staring at me with the pained eyes of a wandering spirit. He made a gesture as if calling me to come. I pushed my way through soldiers and horses, evaluating the disaster with one part of my mind and with the other obeying the mute order of my deceased husband. The improvised cell was nothing more than a room on the first floor of Aguirre's house, and the door a few boards with a crossbar on the outside. It was guarded by two young sentinels with instructions to defend the captives with their lives, since they represented our only negotiating card with the Indians. I did not stop to ask permission, I simply pushed them aside and lifted the heavy bar with one hand, aided by Juan de Málaga. The guards followed me in, unwilling to confront me and never imagining my intentions. Light and smoke sifted through cracks in the walls, choking the air, and a reddish dust rose from the ground, making everything hazy, but I could see the seven prisoners chained to heavy posts, straining like demons as far as their chains would allow, and howling to their warriors. When they saw me burst in, accompanied by the bloody ghost of Juan de Málaga, they fell silent.

"Kill them all!" I ordered the guards in a voice impossible to recognize as my own.

Both prisoners and guards were struck dumb.

"Kill them, señora? They are the governor's hostages!"

"Kill them, I said!"

"How shall we do that?" one of the frightened soldiers asked.
"Like this!"

I lifted the heavy sword in both hands and swung it with all
the strength of my hatred toward the nearest cacique, beheading
him. The force of the swing threw me to my knees, where gushing
blood hit my face as a head rolled on the ground before me. The
rest I don't remember at all. One of the guards swore later that I
had decapitated the remaining six prisoners, but the second said no,
they had completed the task. It doesn't matter. The fact is that in
a question of minutes there were seven heads on the ground. May
God forgive me. I took one by the hair, strode out to the plaza
with giant steps, climbed to the top of the sacks of sand forming
the barricade, and threw my horrendous trophy through the air with
unnatural strength and a paralyzing cry of triumph that issued from
the depths of the earth, traveled through me, and escaped, echoing
like thunder, from my chest. The head sailed through the air, turned
several times, and landed in the midst of the throng of Indians. I
did not stop to see the effect, but went back to the cell, picked up
two more, and launched them from the opposite side of the plaza.
It seems to me that the guards brought me the remaining four, but
I am not sure of that either. Perhaps I went to get them myself. I
know only that the strength of my arms was as great with the last
heads as with the first. Before I had thrown the last of them, an
eerie quiet fell over the plaza; time stopped, the smoke dissipated,
and we watched the Indians, mute, terrorized, begin to retreat: one,
two, three steps, then, jostling and shoving each other, they began
to run, back along the streets they had just captured.

An infinite period of time went by, or perhaps only an instant.
Exhaustion hit me and my bones turned to foam; then I awakened
from the nightmare and realized the horror of what I had done. I
saw myself as those near me saw me: a tangle-haired demon covered with blood, voiceless from screaming so hard. As my knees
buckled, I felt an arm at my waist. Rodrigo lifted me in his arms,
held me tight against his armor, and carried me from the plaza in
the midst of absolute stupor.

———————

Santiago de la Nueva Extremadura was saved, although nothing was left but burned posts and ruin. Only a few pillars remained of the church; of my house, four blackened walls. Aguirre's was more or less standing, and the rest was ashes. We had lost four soldiers; all the others were wounded, several gravely. Half of the Yanaconas died during the combat, and in the following days five more died of infection and loss of blood, but the women and children hiding with Cecilia emerged unscathed because the attackers had not discovered the cave. I did not count horses or dogs, but of my domestic animals only the rooster, the two hens, and the pair of hogs that Catalina and I saved were left alive. There were nearly no seeds at all, only those four handfuls of wheat.

Rodrigo de Quiroga, like everyone else, believed the madness that had invaded me during the battle was irreversible. He had carried me in his arms to the ruins of my house, where the improvised infirmary was still operating, and carefully laid me on the ground. When he bid me good-bye with a light kiss on my forehead, to return to the plaza, he wore an expression of sadness and infinite weariness. Catalina and a helper took off my breastplate, the coat of mail, and my blood-soaked dress, looking for wounds I didn't have. They washed me as well as they could with water and horsehair rolled up like a sponge—we had no more rags—then forced me to drink half a cup of liquor. I vomited a reddish liquid, as if I had also swallowed blood.

The noise of the hours of battle was replaced by a spectral silence. The men could not move; they dropped where they were, and lay there, bleeding, covered with soot and dust and ash, until women came out to give them water, remove their armor, and help them up. The chaplain went around the plaza making the sign of the cross upon the brows of the dead and closing their eyes; then one by one he threw the wounded over his shoulder and carried them to the infirmary. On will alone, Francisco de Aguirre's noble horse, fatally wounded, stood on trembling legs until several women were able to help Aguirre dismount; then it bowed its neck and died before it hit the ground. Aguirre had several superficial wounds, and was so stiff and cramped that they could not remove his armor or take his weapons; they simply left him for more than half an hour, until he could move again. Then the blacksmith sawed both ends of his lance so they could pull it from his clenched fist, and several of us women undressed him—not at all an easy task because he was a large man and rigid as a bronze statue. Monroy and Villagra, in better shape than the other captains, and still fired up by the conflict, had the wild idea that they would take a few soldiers and pursue the disorganized Indians. They could not, however, find a single horse able to move, or a single man who wasn't wounded.

Juan Gómez had fought like a lion, thinking all through the day of Cecilia and his son, buried in my cellar, and the minute things quieted down he ran to open the cave. Desperate, he dug the dirt away with his hands; he couldn't find a shovel because the attackers had carried off everything. He ripped away the boards, opened the tomb, and peered into a black and silent hole.

"Cecilia! Cecilia!" he shouted, terrified.

The clear voice of his wife replied from the depths, "You've come at last, Juan. I was beginning to get bored."

The three women and the children had spent more than twelve hours underground, in total blackness, with no water, very little air, and no knowledge of what was happening outside. Cecilia assigned the wet nurses the task of nursing the infants in turn, all through the day, while she, hatchet in hand, stood ready to defend them. The cavern did not fill with smoke, thanks to the hand and grace of Nuestra Señora del Socorro, or perhaps because it was sealed by the soil Juan Gómez had shoveled over it to conceal the entrance.

Monroy and Villagra decided to send a messenger that very night to take the news of the disaster to Pedro de Valdivia, but Cecilia, who had emerged from underground as dignified and beautiful as always, said that no messenger would come out alive from such a mission; the valley was seething with hostile Indians. The captains, little accustomed to listening to a woman's opinion, ignored her.

"I beg you, señores, to listen to my wife. Her network has always been helpful to us," Juan Gómez intervened.

"What do you suggest, Doña Cecilia?" asked Rodrigo de Quiroga, whose two wounds had been cauterized and who was pale from exhaustion and loss of blood.

"No man can slip past the enemy lines . . ."

"Are you suggesting we send a homing pigeon?" Villagra interrupted sarcastically.

"No. Women. Not one, but several. I know many Quechua women in the valley; they will send the news to the governor, from one mouth to the next, more quickly than a hundred pigeons can fly," the Inca princess assured them.

As they did not have time for long discussions, they decided to send the message two ways: one by Cecilia's chain of women and the other by a Yanacona who was as nimble as a hare, and who would attempt to cross through the valley by night and find Valdivia. I regret to say that this loyal servant was caught at dawn and clubbed to death. Best not to think what his fate might have been had he fallen into Michimalonko's hands alive. The cacique was surely enraged by the failure of his vast army. He had no way to explain to the indomitable Mapuche of the south that a handful of bearded ones had held off eight thousand of his warriors. Much less mention a witch who threw heads of caciques through the air as if they were stones. They would call him a coward, the worst thing that could be said of a warrior, and his name would not be remembered in the epic oral tradition of the tribes but instead in malicious jests. Through Cecilia's network, however, the message reached the governor in twenty-six hours. The notice flew from one hut to another across the valley, through forests, and over mountains to reach Valdivia, who was scouting the area, vainly looking for Michimalonko and still unaware that he had been tricked.

After Rodrigo de Quiroga had walked through the ruin of

Santiago, and delivered his assessment of the losses to Monroy, he came to see me. Instead of the demented basilisk he had left in the infirmary only shortly before, he found a more or less presentable woman, as sane as ever, treating the many wounded.

"Doña Inés . . . all thanks to the Most High . . ." he murmured. He was so spent that he was about to burst into tears.

"Take off that armor, Don Rodrigo, and let us take care of you," I replied.

"I thought that . . . God in Heaven! You saved the city, Doña Inés. You sent the savages running . . ."

"Don't say that, it's unfair to these men who fought so bravely, and the women who backed them up."

"The heads . . . they say that all the heads landed with the eyes looking toward the Indians and they took that as a bad augury, and that was why they ran off."

"I do not know what heads you are talking about, Don Rodrigo. You must be confused. Catalina! Here, woman! Help this man off with his armor!"

I had time to weigh my actions during those hours. I worked without taking a breath all through the first night and the next morning, tending the wounded and trying to save what we could from the burned houses, but one part of my mind was in constant dialogue with the Virgin, asking her to intercede in my favor for the sin I had committed, and also with Pedro. I did not want to imagine his reaction when he saw the destruction of Santiago and learned that he no longer had the seven hostages, and that now we were at the mercy of the savages, and had nothing with which to negotiate. How could I explain what I had done, if I myself did not understand? To tell him that I had gone mad, and didn't remember what happened, was an absurd excuse. I was embarrassed, besides, to think of the grotesque spectacle I had presented in front of his captains and soldiers. Finally, at about two o'clock on the afternoon of September 12, fatigue caught up with me and I slept a few hours, lying on the floor beside Baltasar, who had come dragging back at dawn with bloody jaws and a broken leg.

The next three days went by in a breath. I worked along with everyone else to clear away debris, put out fires, and fortify the plaza, the one place where we could defend ourselves from another attack, which we assumed was imminent. Catalina and I also scratched through burned furrows and the ashes of the plantings, looking for anything edible to throw into the soup. Once we had disposed of Aguirre's horse, there was very little food; we had returned to the times of the communal pot, except that now it consisted of water with whatever herbs and tubers we could dig up.

On the fourth day, Pedro de Valdivia arrived with his detachment of fourteen cavalry; the foot soldiers were following behind as quickly as possible. Riding Sultan, the governor entered the ruin that we had once called a town, and with one glance absorbed the magnitude of the destruction. He rode along streets where weak columns of smoke were still rising, marking the sites of former houses, and into the plaza, where he found our meager populace in rags, hungry and frightened. The wounded were stretched out on the ground, bound with filthy bandages, and his captains, as ragged as the least of the Yanaconas, were helping wherever there was need. A trumpeter signaled the governor's entrance, and those able to stand up, calling on their last reserves of strength, formed lines to greet the captain general.

I stayed back, half hidden behind some canvas. From that vantage I saw Pedro, and my soul gave a leap of love and sadness and weariness. Pale with concern, Valdivia dismounted in the center of the plaza and, before embracing his friends, took in the devastation, looking for me. I took one step forward, to show him I was still alive. Our eyes met, and then his expression and his color changed. He spoke to the soldiers in that tone of reason and authority no one could resist. He praised the courage of each one, especially those who had died fighting, and gave thanks to the apostle Santiago for having saved the rest. The city was not important; they had strong arms and hearts to rebuild it from the ashes. We would have to begin again, he said; that was not a cause for discouragement but, rather, a challenge to spirited Spaniards, who never knew defeat, and to the loyal Yanaconas. "Santiago, and Spain!" he shouted, raising his sword in salute to Saint James. "Santiago, and Spain!" his men responded in a single disciplined voice, but in their tone was deep dejection.

That night, lying on the hard ground with a sliver of moon overhead and nothing to cover us but a filthy blanket, I wept with fatigue in Pedro's arms. He had already heard several accounts of the battle, and of my part in it. Contrary to what I had feared, however, he was proud of me, and so, according to what he told me, was every soldier in Santiago, for they would have perished without me. The versions he had heard were exaggerated, and in them, I have no doubt, lay the origin of the legend that I had saved the city.

"Is it true that you yourself decapitated the seven caciques?" Pedro had asked me as soon as we were alone.

"I don't know," I answered honestly.

Pedro had never seen me cry. I am not a woman given to easy tears, but that first time he did not try to console me, he merely stroked me with the distracted tenderness that was one of his ways. His profile was like stone, his mouth hard, his gaze fixed on the sky.

"I am very afraid, Pedro," I sobbed.

"Of dying?"

"Of everything. Not so much of dying . . . I have years before I get old."

He laughed quietly at the joke we shared: that I would bury several husbands and would always make a desirable widow.

"The men want to go back to Peru, I'm sure of that, though none of them dares say so; it would make them look like cowards. They feel defeated."

"And you? What you do want, Pedro?"

"To found Chile with you," he replied without a second thought.

"Then that's what we will do."

"That we will do, Inés of my soul."

My memory of the distant past is very vivid. I could tell step by step everything that happened in the first twenty or thirty years of our colony in Chile, but I don't have time for that. Death, that gentle mother, is calling, and I want to go with her and rest at last in Rodrigo's arms. I am surrounded by ghosts of the past: Juan de Málaga, Pedro de Valdivia, Catalina, Sebastián Romero, my mother and my grandmother, buried in Plasencia, and many others. Their outlines become more solid every day, and I hear their voices whispering in the corridors of my house. The seven beheaded caciques must be well settled in heaven, or in hell, because they have never come to haunt me. I am not daft, as the very old often are; I am still strong and have a good head on my shoulders, but I have one foot in the grave, and because of that I can observe and hear what others cannot perceive.

You get uneasy, Isabel, when I talk like this; you counsel me to pray. That will ease your soul, you say. My soul is already calm; I have no fear of dying. I had none then, when it was reasonable to have it, and less now, when I have lived longer than my time. You are the only one holding me in this world. I confess that I am not at all eager to watch my grandchildren grow up and suffer; I would rather go with the memory of their childish laughter. I pray out of habit, not as a remedy for anguish. My faith has never failed me, but my relationship with God has been changing with the years. Sometimes, not thinking, I call him Ngenechén, and I confuse the Virgen del Socorro with the blessed Mother Earth of the Mapuche—but I am no less a Catholic than before, God forbid! It is just that Christianity has worn a little thin, the way good wool cloth does after a lot of wear.

I have only a few weeks to live. I know that because at times my heart forgets to beat, I feel dizzy, I fall, and I no longer have any appetite. It is not true that I am trying to starve myself just to exasperate you, as you accuse me, daughter, but because food tastes like sand and I can't swallow it. That is why I take sips of milk for nourishment. I am thin, I admit; I look like a skeleton with skin stretched over it, as I did in the times of hunger—except that then I was young. A skinny old woman is pathetic; my ears have become enormous and the least breeze blows me off my feet. Any moment now I will fly away. I must cut this account short, otherwise too many dead will be left in the inkwell. My dead. Nearly all my loved ones are dead. That is the price for living as long as I have.

FIVE

The Tragic Years
1542–1549

FOLLOWING THE DESTRUCTION OF SANTIAGO, the town council met to decide the fate of our small colony, now threatened with extinction. Before the idea of returning to Cuzco—which the majority approved—could prevail, Pedro de Valdivia imposed the weight of his authority and rolled off a string of difficult to keep promises to win the argument for staying. The first, he decided, would be to send to Peru for help, then to fortify Santiago with a wall like those in European cities to discourage enemies. The rest would be solved along the way, but we should have faith in the future. There would be gold, silver, grants of land, and encomiendas of Indians to work it, he assured the meeting. Indians? I cannot imagine what Indians he was thinking of, because the Chileans had shown no signs of cooperation.

Pedro ordered Rodrigo de Quiroga to collect all the gold available, from the coins a few soldiers had saved through a lifetime and carried hidden in their boots to the one goblet in the church and the pittance sieved from the beds at Marga-Marga. He gave it all to the blacksmith, who melted it down and fashioned a complete set of trappings for a horseman: bit and stirrups for the horse, and spurs and sword guard for the rider. Our courageous Captain Alonso de Monroy, outfitted with pure gold to impress and attract colonists to Chile, was sent across the desert to Peru with five soldiers and the only six horses that were not wounded or down to pure bone. González de Marmolejo gave them his benediction, and we escorted them some distance and then said good-bye with heavy hearts because we did not know whether we would ever see them again.

That was the beginning of two years of indescribable hardships. I do not want to remember those years, just as I would like to forget the death of Pedro de Valdivia, but one cannot control memory, or one's nightmares. A unit of soldiers was formed to take turns standing guard day and night, as the others, turned into laborers and masons, sowed seed, rebuilt houses, and raised the wall to protect the city. We women worked side by side with the soldiers and Yanaconas. We had very little clothing left after the fire; the men worked in a kind of loincloth like the savages wear, and we women, modesty forgotten, in a shift. Those winters were very harsh, and everyone fell ill except Catalina and me. We had hides like a mule, González de Marmolejo always said, amazed. We had no food except what grew naturally in the valley: piñon nuts, bitter fruit, and roots, which all of us ate—humans, horses, and penned animals alike. The handful of seeds I had saved from the burning were used for planting, and the next year we harvested several bushels of wheat, which we again planted, so we did not see a loaf of bread until the third year. Bread, food for the soul. How much we missed it!

Now that we had nothing of interest to trade with the curaca Vitacura, he turned his back on us, and the sacks of maize and beans that we had once easily obtained were no longer available. Our soldiers had to raid Indian villages to steal grain, birds, blankets—whatever they could find—like bandits. I suppose that Vitacura's Quechuas were not wanting for anything, but the Chilean Indians destroyed their own plantings, determined to die of starvation if that would also mean the end of us. Driven by hunger, they migrated toward the south. The valley, once seething with activity, was emptied of families, but not warriors. Michimalonko and his legions never gave us a moment's peace, ever ready to attack with the speed of lightning and then fade away into the forests. They burned what we planted, they killed our animals, they attacked if we went out without armed protection, so that we became prisoners inside the walls of Santiago. I do not know how Michimalonko fed his men, because the Indians had stopped planting. "They eat very little; they can go months with only a little grain and piñons," Felipe, the Mapuche boy, informed me, and added that the warriors wore a little bag around their necks containing a handful of toasted grain; they could live for a week on that.

With his habitual tenacity and optimism, which never waned, the governor forced his exhausted and ailing people to work the ground, make adobe blocks, build the fortified wall and moat around the town, train for war, along with a thousand other duties, because he maintained that sloth is more debilitating than hunger. It was true. No one would have survived his dejection had he had time to think about his luck . . . but there was no time; everyone worked from dawn till late at night. And if there were hours to spare, we prayed; you can never pray too much. Block by block the great wall—as high as two men—grew around Santiago; board by board the church and the houses rose from the ground. Stitch by stitch we women mended the colony's tatters, which we did not wash for fear that they would fall into shreds in the water. We wore more or less "decent" clothing only for special occasions, for we had those, too, not everything was lamenting; we celebrated religious festivals, weddings, and sometimes a baptism. It was painful to see the wan faces of the population, the sunken cheeks, the clawlike hands, the dispiritedness. I was so thin that when I lay on my back in bed, my hip bones, ribs, and clavicle protruded, and I could feel my internal organs just beneath my skin. Outwardly I grew hard, my body dried up, but my heart softened. I felt a maternal love for those hapless people. I dreamed that my breasts held milk enough to feed them all. The day came when I forgot my hunger; I grew accustomed to the sensation of emptiness and lightheadedness that at times made me hallucinate. I did not see visions of roast pig with an apple in its mouth and a carrot up its ass, the way some of the soldiers did, who talked of nothing but food; my visions were of landscapes hazy with mist, where the dead walked. It occurred to me to veil misery by taking great pains to be clean, since we had water in abundance. I initiated a campaign against lice, fleas, and filth, but the result was that the mice, cockroaches, and other insects we put in the soup began to disappear . . . so we stopped soaping and scrubbing.

Hunger is a strange thing; it depletes energy, it slows and saddens us, but it clears the mind and whets the sexual appetites. The men, pathetic, nearly naked skeletons, relentlessly chased the women, and they, on the verge of starvation, were always pregnant. In the midst of famine, infants were born in the colony, although few of them survived. Of the first babies born in Santiago, several died during those two winters and the rest were nothing but bones, swollen bellies, and the eyes of old men. Cooking the thin soup shared by Spaniards and Indians came to be a much greater challenge than Michimalonko's surprise attacks. We boiled water in great cauldrons, threw in the herbs available in the valley—rosemary, bay, boldo, *maiten*—then added anything we had: a few handfuls of maize or beans from our reserves, which were rapidly dwindling, potatoes or tubers from the forest, an assortment of grasses and roots, and mice, lizards, crickets, and worms. By order of Juan Gómez, the constable of our small colony, I was given two soldiers armed day and night to prevent what little we had in the storeroom and the kitchen from being stolen, but a handful of maize or a few potatoes always managed to disappear anyway. I said nothing about these pitiful thefts, otherwise Gómez would have had to beat the servants as punishment and that would only have worsened our situation. We had enough suffering already, we did not need to add more. We tricked our stomachs with brews of mint, linden, and matico. If a domestic animal died, we used every scrap of it: we covered ourselves with its hide, used the fat in candles, made jerky from the meat, put the viscera in the stew, and saved the hooves for tools. We cooked the bones to give flavor to the soup, and boiled them again and again, until they dissolved in the cauldron like ashes. We boiled pieces of dried hide for children to suck on and ease their hunger. The pups that were born that year went directly into the pot as soon as they were weaned; we could not feed more dogs, but we did everything possible to keep alive the ones we already had; they were our first line of attack against the Indians. That is how my faithful Baltasar was saved.

Felipe was a born marksman; where he put his eye, his arrow followed, and he was always eager to go hunting. The smith made him iron-tipped arrows that were more effective than chipped stone, and the boy returned from his excursions with hares and birds, and sometimes even a mountain cat. He was the only one who dared go out to hunt alone; he blended into the forest, invisible to the enemy. The soldiers went out in groups, and in those numbers could not have caught an elephant, had there been any in the New World. Similarly, defying danger, Felipe would bring back armloads of grass for the animals, and thanks to him, though scrawny, the horses were on their feet.

It pains me to tell it, but I suspect that at times cannibalism was practiced among the Yanaconas, and perhaps even among some of our desperate men—just as thirteen years later it would be among the Mapuche, when hunger spread through the rest of the territory of Chile. The Spaniards used that excuse to justify the need to conquer, civilize, and convert them to Christianity, since there is no greater proof of barbarity than cannibalism. Before our arrival, however, the Mapuche had never fallen that low. In certain, very rare, instances they would devour the heart of an enemy in order to absorb his power; but that was a ritual, not a custom.

The Auraucan war created a famine. No one could cultivate the land because the first thing both Indians and Spaniards did was burn the plantings and kill the cattle of the other side. After that came a drought and the *chivalongo*, or typhus, which had a terrible mortality rate. Then as additional punishment came a plague of frogs, which poisoned the earth with a pestilent slobber. During that terrible period, the few remaining Spaniards survived on what they took from the Mapuche, while the Indians, thousands and thousands of them, wandered faint through the barren fields. Lack of food is what led them to eat the flesh of their fellows. God must know that those miserable people did not do it to sin, but because they had to. One chronicler, who in 1555 fought in the campaigns in the south, wrote that the Indians bought quartered humans, just as they would llama meat. Hunger . . . anyone who has not suffered it has no right to pass judgment. Rodrigo de Quiroga told me that in the hell of the steaming jungles of Los Chunchos, Indians ate their comrades. If necessity forced Spaniards to commit that sin, he did not mention it. Catalina, however, assured me that we *viracochas* are no different from any other mortal; some dug up the dead to roast the thighs, and went out to hunt the valley Indians for the same purpose. When I told Pedro, he cut me off short, trembling with indignation, for it did not seem possible to him that any Christian would do something so despicable. I had to remind him that because of me, he ate a little better than the rest of the colony, and that he was not in a position to criticize anyone. All you had to do was see the crazed joy of a person who had caught a mouse on the banks of the Mapocho to understand how a man can sink to cannibalism.

Felipe, or Felipillo, as the young Mapuche was called, turned into Pedro's shadow, and came to be a familiar figure in the town. He was the mascot of the soldiers, who were entertained by the way he could imitate the governor's gestures and voice—not out of any desire to mock him, but because he admired him. Pedro pretended not to notice, but I know that he was flattered by the boy's silent attention, and by how promptly he did his bidding. Felipe burnished Pedro's armor with sand, sharpened his sword, oiled his belts and straps if he could get his hands on a little fat, and, especially, he looked after Sultan as if he were his brother. Pedro treated the boy with the jovial indifference one bestows upon a faithful dog. He did not have to talk to him, Felipe divined his taita's desires. Pedro ordered one of the soldiers to teach the boy to use a harquebus, "So he can defend the women of the house in my absence," he said, which offended me, because I was always the one who defended not only the women, but the men as well.

Felipe was a contemplative boy, very quiet, able to spend hours without moving, like an elderly monk. "He is lazy, like all his race," they said of him. Using the pretext of the Mapudungu classes—a nearly intolerable imposition on him, since he scorned me for being a woman—I learned a good part of what I know about the Mapuche. They believe that the Blessed Earth provides; people take what they need and no more and give thanks for it, they do not accumulate goods. Work is beyond comprehension, since there is no future. What good is gold? The earth does not belong to anyone, the sea does not belong to anyone; the mere idea of possessing it or dividing it always provoked waves of laughter from the usually somber Felipe. People do not belong to others, either. How can the *huincas* buy and sell people if they do not own them? Sometimes the boy went two or three days without speaking a word, surly, and not eating, and when asked what was the matter, the answer was always the same: "There are content days and there are sad days. Each person is master of his silence." He did not get along well with Catalina, who did not trust him, but they told each other their dreams, because for both the door was always open between the two halves of life, night and day, and the divinity communicated with them through their dreams. To ignore such clear messages leads to great misfortunes, they assured me. Felipe never allowed Catalina to read his fate with her divining beads and shells; he had a superstitious fear of them, just as he refused to try her medicinal herbs.

The servants were forbidden to ride the horses, under threat of a lashing, but an exception was made in Felipe's case; he was the one who fed them, and was able to tame them without violence, speaking Mapudungu into their ears. He learned to ride like a Gypsy, and his prowess caused a sensation in our sad village. He sat the animal as if he were a part of it, moved to its rhythm, never whipping it. He did not use a saddle or spurs, and guided the horse with a light pressure of his knees, holding the reins in his mouth so that he would have two free hands for his bow and arrow. He could mount the horse when it was running, swing around and ride backward, or hang onto it with legs and arms so that he was galloping with his chest tight to the animal's belly. The men gathered around, but no matter how hard they tried, they were never able to imitate him. Sometimes he disappeared for several days on his hunting excursions, and just when we had given him up for dead at Michimalonko's hand, he would return with a string of birds over his shoulder to enrich our tasteless soup. Valdivia was uneasy when Felipe disappeared. More than once he threatened him with the whip if he left again without permission, but he never carried out his threat because we were happy to have the bounty of his hunts.

The bloody tree trunk where the lashings were carried out stood in the center of the plaza, but Felipe did not seem to have any fear of it. He had grown to be a slim adolescent, tall for someone of his race, pure bone and muscle, with an intelligent expression and astute eyes. He could shoulder more weight than any of the adult men, and he cultivated an absolute scorn for pain and death. The soldiers admired his stoicism, and some, to entertain themselves, liked to put him to the test. I had to forbid their challenging him to pick up a live coal in his hand, or to drive thorns soaked in hot chili into his skin. Winter and summer he swam for hours in the always frigid waters of the Mapocho. He informed us that icy water strengthens the heart, which is why Mapuche mothers submerge their babies as soon as they are born. The Spaniards, who fled from bathing as they would from fire, would climb up on the wall to watch him swim, and to make bets about his endurance. Sometimes he stayed under the rough waters of the river for as long as several

Our Fathers, and just when the watchers began to pay off their bets, Felipe would appear, safe and sound.

The worst thing about those years was the sense of helplessness and loneliness. We waited for help to come without knowing whether it would ever arrive; everything depended on Captain Monroy's success. Not even Cecilia's infallible network of spies could pick up any news of him and the five brave men with him, but we had no illusions. It would have been a miracle if that handful of men had slipped past hostile Indians, crossed the desert, and reached their destination. Pedro told me, in the privacy of our conversations in bed, that the true miracle would be for Monroy to find help in Peru, where no one wanted to invest money in the conquest of Chile. The gold trappings on his horse would impress the curious, but not the politicians and merchants. Our world was reduced to a few square blocks inside an adobe wall, to the same ravaged faces, to days with no news, to an eternal routine, to sporadic forays on horseback to look for food or to repel a group of daring Indians, to rosaries, processions, and burials. Even masses had been reduced to a minimum; we had only half a bottle of wine left to consecrate, and it would have been sacrilege to use chicha. At least we did not lack for water, because when the Indians prevented us from going to the river, or when they blocked the Incas' irrigation ditches with stones, we dug wells. My talent as a dowser was not needed; wherever we dug there was water in abundance. We had no paper to write down the proceedings of the town council, or the judicial sentences, so we used strips of hide; but in a careless minute the starving dogs ate them, so there are few official records of the hardships of those years.

Wait, and then wait some more. That was how those days went by. We waited for Indians, weapons in hand, we waited for a mouse to fall into our traps, we waited for news of Monroy. We were captives inside the town, surrounded by enemies, half dead with hunger, but we took a certain pride in our misfortune and poverty. For festivals, the soldiers wore their full set of armor over bare skin or, at best, skin cushioned by mouse or rabbit fur, because they had no clothing to wear underneath—but the armor gleamed like silver. González de Marmolejo's one last cassock was stiff with mending and filth, but to celebrate mass he wore over it a piece of lace altar cloth saved from the fire. None of us women had decent skirts, but Cecilia, the other captains' wives, and I spent hours combing our hair, and we painted our lips pink with the bitter fruit of a bush that, according to Catalina, was poisonous. No one died from it, but it is true that it turned our bowels to water. We always talked about our miseries in a joking tone because serious complaints would have been a sign of weakness. The Yanaconas did not understand this very Spanish form of humor; they went around like beaten dogs, dreaming of going home to Peru. Some of the Indian women ran off to offer themselves to the Mapuche, with whom at least they would not go hungry, and none returned. To prevent others from imitating them, we spread the rumor that they had been eaten, although Felipe maintained that a Mapuche is always happy to add another wife to his family.

"What happens to them when their husband dies?" I asked in Mapudungu, thinking of the mortality rate among warriors after a battle.

"What must be done: the oldest son inherits them all, except his mother," he answered.

"And you, my lad, aren't you about ready to marry?" I asked as a joke.

"It is not the moment for me to steal a woman," was his very serious reply.

In the Mapuche tradition, Felipe had told me, the groom-to-be, with the help of his brothers and friends, steals the girl he desires. Sometimes the party of young raiders would burst into her house, tie up the parents, and carry the struggling girl away; but then later, if the girl accepts the "proposal," the suitor sets things right by paying his future in-laws the proper sum in animals and other goods. In this way, the union is formalized. A man can have several wives, but he must give the same to each one, and treat them all equally. Often a man marries two or more sisters, so they don't have to be separated. González de Marmolejo, who often came to my Mapudungu lessons, explained to Felipe that such unbridled licentiousness was ample proof of the presence of the devil among the Mapuche, who without the holy water of baptism would roast in the coals of hell. The boy asked the priest if the devil was also among the Spaniards, who took a dozen Indian girls without paying their parents with llamas and guanacos, as should be done, and then in addition beat them, and did not give them all equal treatment, and, whenever it suited, exchanged them for new ones. Perhaps Spaniards and Mapuche would meet in hell, he suggested, where they would keep on killing one another throughout eternity. I had to run stumbling from the room to keep from laughing in the venerable priest's face.

Pedro and I were made for doing, not idling. The challenge of surviving another day, and keeping the morale of the colony high, filled us with energy. Only when we were alone did we allow ourselves to be discouraged; but it did not last long because soon we would be making fun of ourselves. "I would rather be eating mice here with you than dressing in brocade at court in Madrid," I would tell him. "Let's put it this way," he would reply. "You would rather be Señora Gobernadora here than be a seamstress in Plasencia." And we would fall onto the bed in each other's arms, laughing like children. We were never more united; we had never made love as passionately and knowingly as we did during that time. When I think of Pedro, those are the moments I treasure. That is how I want to remember him, the way he was at forty, emaciated from hunger but with a strong, determined spirit, and filled with dreams. And I could add that I want to remember him in love with me, but that would be redundant because he always was, even after we separated. I know that he died thinking of me. The year of his death, 1553, I was in Santiago and he was fighting in Tucapel, many leagues away, but I knew so clearly that he was seriously wounded, and dying, that when they brought me the news several weeks later, I shed no tears. I had already cried myself out.

In mid December, two years after Captain Monroy had left on his dangerous mission, as we were preparing a modest Christmas celebration with songs and an improvised crèche, an exhausted man caked with dust appeared at the gates of Santiago. He was nearly refused entrance because at first the sentinels didn't recognize him. He was one of our Yanaconas; he had been running for two days and had managed to reach the town by slipping unseen through forests filled with enemy Indians. He was one of the small group Pedro had left on the coast in the hope that help would come from Peru. Bonfires laid on a high cliff were kept ready to be lighted the instant a ship was sighted. And at last, the lookouts who had been scanning the horizon for an eternity saw a sail and euphorically sent the arranged signals. The ship, captained by one of Pedro de Valdivia's old friends, held the long-awaited aid.

"That you must be bringing men and horses to be carrying the cargo, then, *tatay*. This is what the *viracocha* of the ship is sending to tell you," panted the Indian, at the end of his strength.

Pedro and several captains galloped off in the direction of the beach. It is difficult to describe the jubilation that spread through the town. Our relief was so great that hardened soldiers wept, and our anticipation so consuming that no one paid any attention to the priest when he called for a mass of thanksgiving. The entire population of the town was up on the wall with their eyes on the road, even though we knew that it would take several days for the visitors to reach Santiago.

Horror was the overwhelming expression on the faces of the new arrivals when they first saw Valdivia and his men on the beach, and then later, when they reached Santiago and we went out to welcome them. That gave us an approximate measure of the magnitude of our misery. We had grown accustomed to looking like skeletons, to our rags and filth, but when we realized how they pitied us, we were profoundly shamed. Though we had done our best to spruce ourselves up, and to us Santiago looked splendid in the brilliant light of summer, we, and it, made a lamentable impression upon our guests. They wanted to give Valdivia and the other captains clothing, but there is no greater insult to a Spaniard than charity. What we could not pay was written down as a debt, and Valdivia signed for everyone since we had no gold. The merchants who had contracted the ship in Peru were well satisfied; they had tripled their investment and were sure that they would be repaid. Valdivia's word was more than enough guarantee. Among them was the same merchant who had lent Pedro money in Cuzco—at a usurer's interest—to finance the expedition. He had come to collect his money, multiplied many times over, but he had to agree to a fair settlement when he saw the state of our colony. Otherwise, he realized, he would not recoup anything. From the ship's cargo, Pedro bought me three linen blouses and one of fine batiste, everyday skirts and some of silk, work boots and dress shoes, soap, orange blossom cream for my face, and a bottle of perfume: luxuries I thought I would never see again in my lifetime.

The ship had been sent by Captain Monroy. While we were undergoing our trials and tribulations in Santiago, he and his five companions had gotten as far as Copiapó, where they had fallen into the hands of the Indians. Four soldiers were massacred on the spot, but Monroy, riding his gold-adorned steed, and one other man, had survived through an unexpected stroke of good fortune. They had been saved by a Spanish soldier who had fled from the law in Peru and had been living in Chile for several years. He had lost two ears for thievery and had run from all contact with people of his race and taken refuge among the Indians. The punishment for stealing is amputation of a hand, a custom that had prevailed in Spain since the time of the Moors, but when it was a soldier's hand, it was deemed preferable to cut off the nose or ears; in that way the accused could fight again.

This unexpected savior had intervened and convinced the Indians not to kill the captain, whom he supposed was very wealthy, judging from all the gold, or his companion. Monroy was a likable man and he had a silver tongue; he got along so well with the Indians that they treated him more as a friend than as a prisoner. After three months of agreeable captivity, the captain and the second Spaniard successfully escaped on horseback, but without the imperial trappings, naturally. The story goes that during those months Monroy had won the heart of the chief's daughter and had left her pregnant, but that may well be the captain's boast, or a popular myth—there are more than enough of those among us. The fact is that Monroy reached Peru and obtained reinforcements, gained the interest of several merchants, sent the ship to Chile, and himself started out overland with seventy soldiers and would arrive months later. This Alonso de Monroy, gallant, loyal, and of great courage, died in Peru a couple of years later under mysterious circumstances. Some say he was poisoned, others that he died of the plague or a spider bite, and there are those who believe he is still alive in Spain, to which he had returned without a word to anyone, weary of war.

The ship brought us soldiers, food, wine, weapons, munitions, clothing, household goods, and domestic animals—that is, all the treasures we had dreamed of. Most important of all was contact with the civilized world; we were no longer alone in the farthest corner of the planet. The five Spanish women who had come with them, wives or relatives of soldiers, added to the numbers of our colony. For the first time since leaving Cuzco, I could compare myself to women of my own race, and see how much I had changed. I decided to put aside my man's boots and clothing, to comb out my braids in favor of a more elegant hairdo, to indulge my face with the orange blossom cream Pedro had given me, and, not least, to cultivate the feminine graces I had discarded years before. Enthusiasm again swelled the hearts of our little community; we felt capable of confronting Michimalonko, or the Devil himself should he show up in Santiago. This must be what that unyielding cacique perceived from afar, because he did not attack the city again, though often we had to fight him if we went outside the walls, and chase him back to his *pukaras*. In each of those encounters, so many Indians were killed that one had to wonder where more came from.

Valdivia validated the encomiendas he had assigned to me and
some of his captains. He sent emissaries to ask the peaceful Indians
to come back to the valley, where they had always lived before
we came, promising them safety, land, and food in exchange for
helping us, for the haciendas were worth nothing without strong
arms to work them. Many of those Indians, who had fled out of
fear of the war and the raids of the bearded ones, returned. With
that turn of events, we began to prosper. The gobernador also
convinced the curaca Vitacura to send some Quechua Indians to us,
for they were much more efficient workers than the Chileans, and
with new Yanaconas he could reopen the mine at Marga-Marga,
and others he had heard of. No work demanded as much sacrifice.
I have seen hundreds of men, and an equal number of women,
some pregnant, others with babies strapped to their backs, work
from dawn to sunset in icy water up to their waists, washing sand
to sieve out the gold, exposed to illness, the overseers' whips, and
the soldiers' abuse.

Today, when I got out of bed, my strength failed me for the first
time in my long life. It is strange to find that the body is quitting
while the mind keeps inventing projects. With my servants' help,
I got dressed for mass, as I do each day, since I like to say good
morning to Nuestra Señora del Socorro, who now is mistress of
her own church and wears a gold emerald-studded crown. We
have been friends for a very long time. I try to go to the first
mass of the morning, along with the poor and the soldiers, because
at that hour the light in the church seems to come straight from
heaven. The morning sun beams through the high windows, and its
resplendent rays slice through the church like lances, illuminating
the saints in their niches. It is a quiet hour, favorable to prayer.
There is nothing as mysterious as the moment when the bread and
the wine are transubstantiated into the body and blood of Christ. I
have witnessed that miracle thousands of times during my life, but
it surprises me and moves me as much as it did the day of my first

communion. I can't help it, I always weep when I receive the host. I shall continue to go to church as long as I can get around, and I shall not abandon my obligations: the hospital, the poor, the convent of the Augustinians, the construction of chapels, the oversight of my encomiendas, and this chronicle, which may be growing longer than is advisable.

I am not yet defeated by age, though I admit that I've become clumsy and forgetful, and am not able to do well what I once did without thinking. It seems that time goes twice as fast as it once did. However, I have not given up my old discipline of bathing and dressing with care; I intend to be vain to the end, so that Rodrigo will find me clean and elegant when we meet on the other side. Seventy does not seem too old. . . . If my heart holds out, I could live ten more years, and in that case, I would marry again, because I need love to go on living. I am sure that Rodrigo would understand, just as I would if the situation were reversed. If he were with me, we would take our pleasure to the end of our days, slowly and calmly. Rodrigo dreaded the moment when we could no longer make love. I think that what he feared most was ridicule: men take such pride in performance. But there are many ways of making love, and I would have found one, so that even old as we were we could have loved as in our best days. I miss his hands, his scent, his broad shoulders, the soft hair at the nape of his neck, the whisper of his beard, his breath in my ears when we were lying together in the dark. My need is so great to hold him, to lie beside him, that at times I have to cry out. I can't hold it back. Where are you, Rodrigo? Oh, how I miss you!

But this morning I dressed and went out, despite the fatigue in my bones and my heart, because it is Tuesday, and I must go see Marina Ortiz de Gaete. Servants took me there in a sedan chair; she lives nearby and it is too much trouble to get out the coach. Ostentation is frowned upon in this kingdom, and I am afraid that the carriage Rodrigo gave me is sinfully conspicuous. Marina is a few years younger than I am, but I feel like a rosebud compared with her. She has become a fussy, ugly old woman who practically lives in the church—may God forgive my unkind tongue. "You need to button up your lips, Mamá," you counsel me, Isabel, laughing, when you hear me talk that way, although I suspect that my outrageous talk amuses you. And besides, daughter, I have won the right to say what others do not dare. Marina's wrinkles and her silly affectations give me a certain satisfaction, but I struggle against being so mean-spirited because I do not want to spend more days than necessary in purgatory. I have never liked sickly, weak people like Marina. I feel sorry for her; even the relatives she brought with her from Spain, now prosperous citizens of Santiago, have forgotten her. I do not blame them too much because this good lady is extremely boring. At least she is not living in poverty. She is blessed with a dignified widowhood, although that is little compensation for her bad luck in having been abandoned as a wife. How lonely this unfortunate woman must be; she anxiously awaits my visits, and if I am late, I find her sobbing. We drink cups of chocolate while I hide my yawns, and we talk about the only thing we have in common: Pedro de Valdivia.

Marina has lived in Chile for twenty-five years. She came sometime in 1554, ready to assume her role as wife of the gobernador, with a court of family and friends and fawning individuals eager to profit from the wealth and power of Pedro de Valdivia, whom the king had gifted with the title of marqués, and the Order of Santiago. But when she reached Chile, Marina was greeted with the surprise of finding herself a widow. Her husband had died a few months before at the hands of the Mapuche, never knowing about his honors. And as the last straw, Valdivia's treasure, which had been the subject of so much talk, was nothing but smoke. He had been accused of accumulating too much wealth, of taking the major share of fertile lands, of exploiting a small army of Indians for his own private use, but when all was said and done, he turned out to be poorer than any of his captains; his widow had to sell his house in the Plaza de Armas to pay off his debts. The town council did not have the decency to grant a pension to Marina Ortiz de Gaete, legitimate wife of the conqueror of Chile—ingratitude being so common in this land that a phrase has been coined for it: "Chile payment." I had to buy Marina a house and pay her expenses to prevent Pedro's ghost from pulling my ears. Never mind. I have my pleasures, such as founding institutions, having assured myself of a niche in the church for my burial, supporting a multitude of assorted dependents, leaving my daughter well placed, and holding out a hand to the wife of my former lover. What does it matter now if we were once rivals?

I have just realized that I have filled many pages and have yet to explain why this far-off territory of Chile is the only kingdom in the Americas. Emperor Charles V wanted to wed his son Philip to Mary Tudor, queen of England. What year would that have been? It was about the time that Pedro died, I think. The emperor's young heir needed the title of king to effect that union, and since his father was not yet ready to yield the throne to him, they decided that Chile would be a kingdom and Philip its sovereign—which did not improve our fortune, but gave us stature.

I remember that on the same ship with Marina—who was then forty-two years old and a little short on brains, but beautiful, with that washed-out beauty of mature blondes—came Daniel Belalcázar and my niece Constanza, whom I had bid farewell in Cartagena in 1538. I had thought I would never again see my niece, who instead of becoming a nun, as we had planned, had at fifteen suddenly married the chronicler who had seduced her on the ship. Our surprise was mutual. I supposed that they had been swallowed up by the jungle, and it was the farthest thing from their minds that I had founded a kingdom. They stayed nearly two years in Chile, studying the history and customs of the Mapuche—from afar, of course, because there was no chance of moving freely among them; the war was at its apogee. Belalcázar said that the Mapuche resembled some Asians he had seen in his travels. He considered them to be great warriors and did not veil his admiration for them—like the poet who later wrote the epic about the Araucans. Have I already mentioned him? Perhaps not, but it is a little late to worry about him now. Ercilla, his name was. When Belalcázar and my niece learned that they would never be able to approach the Mapuche to

sketch them and ask them direct questions, they resumed their pilgrimage across the world. They were perfect partners for scientific
undertakings; they shared the same insatiable curiosity and the same
Olympian scorn for the dangers of their preposterous ventures.

Daniel Belalcázar, however, planted in my head the idea of
starting a school, for he thought it was a ridiculous irony that Chile
pretended to be a civilized colony when you could count on the
fingers of one hand the number of persons who knew how to read.
I proposed the idea to González de Marmolejo, and we both fought
for years to create schools, but no one was interested in the project.
How backward they were! They were afraid that if people learned
to read they would fall into the vice of thinking, and from there to
rebelling against the Crown lay only a hair's difference.

But as I was saying, today has not been a good day for me.
Instead of focusing on the story of my life, I have been wandering.
Every day it is more difficult for me to concentrate on facts; I get
distracted. There is a constant activity in this house, although you
assure me it is the most tranquil in Santiago.

"That's all in your head, *mamita*. There is no activity here, just
the opposite, it's quiet, only ghosts wander here," you told me last
night.

"Exactly, Isabel, that is just what I was saying."

You are like your father, practical and reasonable, and that is
why you cannot see all the people wandering through my rooms
without permission. The veil that separates this world from the
next grows thinner with age, and I am beginning to see through
it. I suppose that when I die you will change everything; you will
give away my old furniture and paint the walls with a new coat of
whitewash; but remember that you have promised me to keep these
pages I have written for you and your descendants. If you would
rather, you can give them to the Mercedarians, or the Dominicans,
for they owe me some favors. Remember, too, that I am leaving a
fund to support Marina Ortiz de Gaete to the last day of her life,
and to feed the poor who are used to being given food every day at
the gate of this house. I believe I have told you all this; forgive me

if I am repeating myself. I am sure you will carry out my requests, Isabel, because you are like your father in that too. You have a good heart, and your word is sacred.

The fortunes of our colony took a turn for the better once we established contact with Peru and provisions and people eager to settle in Chile began to arrive. Thanks to the ships plying back and forth, we were able to order the items indispensable to our prospering. Valdivia bought iron, tools, and cannons, and I ordered trees and seeds from Spain—which grow very well in this Chilean climate—sheep, goats, and cattle. By mistake they sent me eight cows and twelve bulls, when one would have done. Aguirre tried to use the misunderstanding to inaugurate the first plaza de toros, but the animals were stunned by the sea voyage and not up to goring anyone. They were not wasted, however, since ten were converted to oxen and used for field work and hauling. The remaining two gallantly serviced the cows, and now we have large herds from the pastures of Copiapó to the Mapocho valley. We built a mill and public ovens, we have a quarry and sawmills, we made tiles and adobe, and set up a tannery and workshops to turn out pottery, wicker, candles, harness, and furniture. There were two tailors, four scribes, a doctor—who unfortunately was not good for much—and a stupendous veterinarian. At the rate the city was growing, the valley soon would be denuded of trees—such was the fervor of our construction. I can't say that life was easy, but at last we had enough food, and even the Yanaconas grew fat and lazy. We had no serious problems other than the plague of rats the Indian machis, using their black arts, sent to torment the Christians. We could not keep them out of the sown fields, our houses, our clothing; they ate everything except metal. Cecilia offered a solution they used in Peru: tubs half filled with water. At night we would set several in each house, and by dawn there would be five hundred drowned rats, but the plague did not end until Cecilia found a Quechua wizard able to counter the spell of the Chilean machis.

Valdivia urged his soldiers to send for their wives in Spain, as the king had ordered, and some did, but most preferred cohabiting with young Indian girls to living with an aging wife. In our colony there were more and more mestizo children who did not know who their fathers were. The Spanish women who came to rejoin their husbands looked the other way and accepted the situation, which, after all, was not very different from that in Spain, and even today in Chile the custom endures of the *casa grande*, where the wife and legitimate children live, and the *casas chicas* for the concubines and bastard children. I must be the only one who never tolerated that from her husband, although things might have happened behind my back that I don't know about.

Santiago was declared capital of the kingdom. It was the largest city in population, and the safest, now that Michimalonko's Indians kept their distance. That allowed us, among other advantages, to organize paseos, outdoor luncheons, and hunting parties on the banks of the Mapocho, which had once been forbidden territory. We designated feast days to honor the saints and others to entertain ourselves with music, in which Spaniards, Indians, blacks, and mestizos participated equally. There were cockfights, dog races, games of bocce and squash. Pedro de Valdivia, an enthusiastic player, continued the custom of organizing card games in our home, except that now they bet hopes and dreams. No one had a peso, but records were kept with a moneylender's meticulous care, even knowing the debts would never be collected.

Once mail service was established between Peru and Spain, we were able to send and receive letters, which took only one or two years to reach their destination. Pedro began to write long missives to the emperor Charles V, telling him about Chile, about the privations we were suffering, about his own expenditures and debts, about his way of dispensing justice, about how, as much as he regretted it, many Indians had died and strong arms were needed to work the mines and the land. In passing he would ask for the privileges and funding sovereigns may grant, but his just demands were unanswered. Pedro wanted soldiers, people, ships, the confirmation of his authority, and recognition for his accomplishments. He would read me the letters in a booming voice of command, pacing back and forth, his chest puffed out with vanity, and I would say nothing. How could I offer an opinion on his correspondence with the most powerful monarch in the world, the most sacred and most triumphant Caesar, as Valdivia called him? But I began to realize that my lover had changed; power was going to his head, he had become very arrogant. In his letters he referred to fabulous gold mines, more fantasy than reality. They were the lure to tempt Spaniards to come and settle in Santiago, because only he and Rodrigo de Quiroga understood that the true wealth of Chile was not gold and silver but its benign climate and fertile soil, which invite one to stay. The other colonists were still beguiled by the idea of getting rich as quickly as they could and returning to Spain.

To assure a more secure route to Peru, Valdivia ordered a city to be founded in the north, La Serena, and a port near Santiago, Valparaíso, and then turned toward the Bío-Bío river, with an eye to conquering the Mapuche. Felipe explained that that river is sacred because it regulates all watercourses; its coolness calms the wrath of the volcanoes; and everything from the strongest trees to the most secret, invisible, transparent mushroom grows within its purview. According to the documents Pizarro had given Valdivia, the area of his rule stretched as far as the Strait of Magellan, but no one knew with any certainty how far away the famous channel was that united the eastern ocean with that of the west. It was about the same time that a ship arrived from Peru under the command of a young Italian captain named Pastene, to whom Valdivia awarded the flamboyant title of admiral, and then sent on to explore the south. Sailing along the coast, Pastene caught glimpses of magnificent landscapes of dense forests, archipelagos, and glaciers, but he did not find the strait, which apparently lay much farther south than had been supposed.

In the meantime, very bad news was arriving from Peru, where the political situation had become disastrous; they were emerging from one civil war only to fall into another. Gonzalo Pizarro, one of the brothers of the deceased marqués, had grabbed power in open rebellion against our king, and there was so much corruption, betrayal, and deterioration in the viceroyalty that finally the emperor ordered an obstinate priest named La Gasca to restore order. I shall not waste ink trying to explain the complexities of the situation in Ciudad de los Reyes during those days because not even I understand them, but I mention La Gasca because that priest with the pockmarked face would make a decision that would change my destiny.

Pedro was seething with impatience, not just to conquer more Chilean territory, which the Mapuche were defending to the death, but to play a part in what was happening in Peru, and reestablish contact with civilization. He had been eight years away from the centers of power, and secretly he wanted to travel north in order to meet other military men, conduct business, be praised for the conquest of Chile, and offer his sword in the service of the king against the insubordinate Gonzalo Pizarro. Was he tired of me? Perhaps, but I did not suspect that then. I felt sure of his love, which for me was as natural as the falling rain. If I found him restless, I supposed that he was a bit bored with the sedentary life, now that the excitement of the first years in Santiago, when we had kept a sword in hand day and night, had given way to a more restful and comfortable existence.

"We need soldiers for the war in the south, and families to populate the rest of the territory, but Peru ignores my emissaries," Pedro told me one night, disguising his real reasons for wanting to go to Peru.

"Do you intend to go yourself? I warn you that if you leave for a single day, you will be inviting a calamity here. You know how your friend de la Hoz is," I said—pointlessly, since without my knowing, he had already made his decision.

"I will leave Villagra in my place; he has a strong hand."

"How do you intend to entice people in Peru to come to Chile? They are not all idealists like you, Pedro. Men go where there is wealth, not glory alone."

"I will find a way to do it."

It was his idea; I had no part in it. Pedro announced with great fanfare that he was planning to send Pastene's ship to Peru, and that any who wanted to leave and take their gold with them could do so. The response was delirious enthusiasm, for that was all anyone had been talking about in Santiago for weeks. Leave! Go back to Spain with money! That was the dream of every man who had left the old continent for the Indies: to return wealthy. Nevertheless, when the moment came to draw up the manifest, only sixteen colonists decided to take advantage of the opportunity. They sold their property for nothing, wrapped up their belongings, weighed their gold, and prepared to leave. Among the party traveling in the caravan to the port was my mentor, González de Marmolejo, who was now more than sixty years old and somehow had managed to get rich in the service of God. Señora Díaz was also going, a Spanish "lady" who had arrived in Chile a couple of years before on one of the boats. There was little *lady* about her; we all knew that she was a man dressed as a woman. "Balls and *piripicho* the doña is having between his legs, then," Catalina told me. "Where do you get such ideas! Why would a man dress as a woman?" I asked her. "Well, why would it be, *señorayy*? To be getting money from other men, then," she explained. But enough of gossip.

On the appointed day, the travelers boarded the ship, where they arranged their trunks, with their gold inside and nailed shut for good measure, in the cabins assigned to them. At that moment Valdivia and other captains appeared on the beach, accompanied by numerous servants, to send them off with a farewell meal: delicious fish and seafood fresh from the sea, all liberally washed down with wine from the governor's personal cellar. They set up canvas canopies on the sand, lunched like princes, and wept a little over the emotional speeches, especially the lady with the *piripicho*, who was very sensitive and sentimental. Valdivia insisted that to prevent any problems in the future, the colonists declare the amount of gold they were carrying, a wise measure that met with general approval. While a secretary was carefully noting in his ledger the numbers the travelers gave him, Valdivia climbed into the one available long-boat, and five vigorous sailors rowed him to the ship where several of his most loyal captains were waiting, all of whom planned to join him in placing themselves at the service of the king's cause in Peru. When the unwary would-be travelers realized they had been tricked, they stood howling with frustration, and several jumped in to swim after the longboat, but the only one who caught up to it received a thump from an oar that nearly broke his neck. I can imagine the desolation of the fleeced passengers as they watched the sails fill and the ship head off to the north, carrying with it all their earthly possessions.

It fell to Captain Villagra, a man of action, not contemplation, to take Valdivia's place as lieutenant governor, and to confront the furious colonists on the beach. His robust appearance, his ruddy face above well-set shoulders, his severe expression, and his hand on the grip of his sword imposed order. He explained to them that Valdivia had gone to Peru to defend the king, his lord, and to seek reinforcements for the colony in Chile. That was why he had found himself forced to do what he did, but he promised to return their last doubloon—with a corresponding sum from the mine at Marga-Marga. "Any man who is satisfied with that, well and good, and he who is not, he may settle with me," he concluded. None of which calmed anyone.

I can understand Pedro's motives; he saw in that deceit—so ill-befitting his upright character—the only solution to Chile's prob-lem. He weighed on the scales the harm he was doing to those sixteen innocents against the need to give impetus to the conquest, benefiting thousands, and the latter tipped the scales. If he had consulted with me, I'm sure I would have approved his decision, although I would have achieved it in a more elegant manner—and I would have gone with him—but the only ones he shared his secret with were three captains. Did he think that I would talk too much and spoil his plan? Never. In the ten years we had been together, I had demonstrated my discretion and my fierce defense of his life and his interests. I think, instead, that he was afraid I would try to keep him from going. When he left he took only what was indispensable, for if he had packed properly, I would have guessed his intentions. And he left without telling me good-bye, just as Juan de Málaga had done many years before.

Valdivia's trap, for there was no other word for it, however high-minded the cause, turned out to be a gift from heaven for Sancho de la Hoz, who now could accuse Pedro of a specific crime: he had swindled people, stolen the fruits of years of work and deprivation from his own soldiers. He deserved the death penalty.

When I learned that Pedro had gone, I felt much more betrayed than the deceived colonists. I lost control for the first and the last time in my life. For one whole day, I screeched with rage and destroyed everything within reach. I will show them who Inés Suárez is! No one tosses me aside like an old rag. I am the true gobernadora of Chile, and everyone knows how much they owe me. What would this accursed city be without me, anyway? I have dug irrigation ditches with my own hands; I have treated every sick and wounded person in the city; I have sown, harvested, and cooked so that no one would perish from hunger; and, as if it were nothing at all, I have wielded weapons like the best of the soldiers. Everyone knows that Pedro owes me his life; I have loved him and served him and made him happy; no one can handle his manias like I can . . . and on and on and on until Catalina and other women tied me to the bed and went to get help. I lay struggling in my bonds, possessed by the devil, with Juan de Málaga perched at the foot of my bed, making fun of me. Before long, González de Marmolejo appeared, extremely depressed. Being the eldest of the deceived, he took it for granted that he would never recover his losses, although in fact he not only recouped his wealth, with interest, but when he died several years later, he was the richest man in Chile. How had he done that? A mystery. I suppose that to some degree I had helped him, because we were partners in a horse-breeding enterprise, something that had been in my head from the first day I set out for Chile.

The priest had come to my house prepared to attempt an exorcism, but when he realized that the source of my ranting was nothing more than the indignation of a discarded lover, he limited himself to sprinkling holy water on me and praying a few Ave Marías, a treatment that brought me back to my senses.

The next day Cecilia came to see me. By that time she had several children, but neither motherhood nor the years had left a mark on her regal bearing and her smooth, Inca princess face. Thanks to her remarkable network of spies, and her position as the wife of our constable, Juan Gómez, she knew everything that happened behind every door in the colony—including my recent fit. She found me in bed, still exhausted by Pedro's desertion.

"Pedro will pay for this, Cecilia!" I said in greeting.

"I am bringing you good news, Inés. You won't have to take revenge; others will do it for you," she announced.

"What do you mean?"

"The many malcontents we have in Santiago plan to denounce Valdivia before the royal tribunal in Peru. If he does not lose his life on the gallows, he will at least spend the rest of it in prison. See what good luck you have, Inés!"

"That idea came from Sancho de la Hoz!" I exclaimed, leaping from the bed and starting to dress.

"Can you imagine that the fool would ever do you such a good turn? De la Hoz has circulated a letter asking for Valdivia to be removed, and many have already signed it. Most people want to get rid of Valdivia and name de la Hoz governor," she reported.

"That clown never gives up!" I muttered, tying my boots.

A few months earlier that fiendish courtier had tried to assassinate Valdivia. Like all the plots he dreamed up, that one, too, was quite colorful. He pretended to be very ill, took to his bed, sent out word that he was dying and wanted to bid farewell to friends and enemies alike, including the gobernador. He installed one of his followers behind a curtain to knife Valdivia in the back when he bent over the bed to hear the whispers of the supposedly dying man. These ridiculous details, and the fact that he boasted about them,

did de la Hoz in, because I had heard about his scheme without
even trying. Once again, I warned Pedro of the danger, and he at
first bellowed with laughter and refused to believe me, but later
agreed to have the matter thoroughly investigated. The result was
a guilty verdict; Sancho de la Hoz was sentenced to the gallows for
the second or third time—I had lost count. However, not to break
with tradition, Pedro pardoned him at the last hour.

I finished dressing, told Cecilia good-bye with an apology, and
ran to speak with Captain Villagra, repeating the princess's words
and assuring him that if de la Hoz were successful, the first to lose
their heads would be him and other men loyal to Pedro.

"Do you have proof, Doña Inés?" Villagra asked, flushed with
anger.

"No, only rumors, Don Franciso."

"That's enough for me."

And with that he arrested the plotter and had him decapitated
that very afternoon, not giving him time even to confess. Then
he ordered that the head be paraded through the city, held by
the hair, before setting it on the stocks as a lesson to anyone who
might be wavering—the normal procedure. How many heads have
I seen displayed this way in my lifetime? Impossible to count them.
Villagra made no move against the rest of the conspirators, who
were hiding like mice in their houses, because he would have had
to arrest everyone in Santiago, so great was the current animosity
against Valdivia. In a single night, the captain had wiped out the
germ of a civil war, and had also freed us from that vermin Sancho
de la Hoz. About time.

It took Pedro de Valdivia more than a month to reach Callao, stop-
ping at various ports in the north to await news from Santiago. He
needed to be sure that Villagra had skillfully handled the situation,
and was covering his back. He knew about Sancho de la Hoz's rebellion because a messenger had caught up with him carrying the
bad news, but he did not want to be directly responsible for his

demise since that might bring him problems with the law. He was extraordinarily pleased that his faithful lieutenant had solved the conspiracy in his way, although he feigned surprise and displeasure at the turn of events; he had not forgotten that his enemy had had important contacts at the court of Charles V.

To ask my forgiveness, Pedro sent from La Serena, by swift horse, a love letter and an extravagant gold ring. I tore the letter to bits and gave the ring to Catalina, under the condition that she keep it out of my sight; it made my blood boil.

On his way north, the governor gathered together a group of ten well-placed captains whom he outfitted with armor, weapons, and horses—using the gold of the fleeced citizens of Santiago—and then set out with them to enlist under the banners of the priest La Gasca, the king's legitimate representative in Peru. To find La Gasca's army, the band of hidalgos had to climb the icy peaks of the Andes, spurring on their horses, which collapsed in the thin air, while altitude sickness burst their own eardrums and made them bleed through various bodily orifices. They knew that La Gasca—who had absolutely no military experience, though he was a man of exemplary character and will—would have to confront a formidable army led by an experienced and courageous general. Gonzalo Pizarro might be accused of almost anything except being fainthearted. La Gasca's troops, who were ill from the exhaustion of the trek along the cordillera, paralyzed with cold, and terrified by the enemy's superiority, welcomed Valdivia and his ten captains as avenging angels. To La Gasca, those hidalgos who had miraculously come to his aid were the boost he needed. He gratefully embraced them, and turned over the command to Pedro de Valdivia, the mythic conquistador of Chile, naming him field marshal. The troops immediately regained their confidence, because with this general at their head, they felt the victory was theirs. Valdivia began by winning the goodwill of the soldiers with just the right words, the result of many years of dealing with his subordinates, and then pro- ceeded to evaluate their strengths and equipment. When he realized that he had an improbable task before him, he felt rejuvenated; his captains had not seen him so enthusiastic since the days of founding Santiago.

To approach Cuzco, where he would engage the army of the rebellious Gonzalo Pizarro, Valdivia followed the narrow paths the Incas had carved on the lip of sheer precipices. His advancing troops resembled a line of insects in the massive scene of purple mountains, rock, ice, piercing-the-clouds peaks, wind, and condors. From time to time petrified roots protruded from cracks in the rock, and the men held on to them to rest a moment in their terrible ascent. The beasts' hooves slipped on the cliff edges, and the roped-together soldiers had to grab their manes to keep them from tumbling into abysses. The landscape was one of overwhelming and threatening beauty, a world of refulgent light and sidereal shadows. Wind and hail had carved demons on the mountain spurs; the ice trapped in crevasses of the rocks glistened with the colors of the dawn. In the mornings, the rising sun, distant and cold, painted the peaks in tints of orange and crimson; in the evenings, the light disappeared as suddenly as it had dawned, sinking the cordillera into blackness. The nights were eternal; no one could move in the dark; men and animals huddled together, shivering, perched on the lips of dangerous overhangs.

To alleviate altitude sickness and energize his exhausted men, Valdivia provided them with coca leaves to chew, the drug Quechua Indians had used from time immemorial. When he learned that Gonzalo Pizarro had destroyed the bridges to prevent the attacking forces from crossing rivers and gorges, he ordered the Yanaconas to braid rope from the rushes and bunchgrass growing in the area, a task they accomplished with prodigious speed. He advanced with his band of courageous men, unseen under cover of fog, to one of the bridges Pizarro had rendered unusable; there he ordered the Indians to plait their traditional fiber ropes to make a suspension bridge. One day later, La Gasca arrived with the major part of the army and found the problem resolved. They were able to move nearly a thousand soldiers, fifty horses, countless Yanaconas, and heavy armament across blood-chilling gorges, swaying in the howling winds. After that, Valdivia had to drive his fatigued soldiers to scale two leagues of steep mountainside—carrying their supplies on their backs and pulling the cannons—to the spot he had chosen to challenge Gonzalo Pizarro. Once he had stationed the weapons at strategic points in the hills, he gave the men a day or two to regain their strength, while he, imitating his maestro, the marqués de Pescara, personally reviewed the emplacement of the artillery and harquebuses, spoke with each soldier to give him instructions, and prepared the plan of battle. It seems I can see him now, on horseback, wearing his new armor, charged with energy, impatient, calculating in advance the enemy's movements, plotting his offense like the good chess player he was. He was no longer young; he was forty-eight years old, he had put on weight, and the old wound in his hip bothered him, but even so he could ride two days and two nights without resting, and I know that in those moments he felt invincible. So sure was he of triumphing that he promised La Gasca they would lose fewer than thirty men in the battle; he lived up to his word.

The first round of cannon fire had barely echoed among the hills when Pizarro's forces realized that they were facing a formidable general. Many soldiers, uncomfortable with the idea that they were fighting against the king, abandoned Pizarro's ranks to join those of La Gasca. It is said that Pizarro's field marshal, an old fox with many years of military experience, immediately perceived the identity of his foe. "There is only one general in the New World capable of this strategy: Don Pedro de Valdivia, conquistador of Chile," he reportedly said. His enemy did not disappoint him, and neither did he give any quarter. At the end of several hours of battle, and of large losses, Gonzalo Pizarro had to surrender and hand over his sword to Valdivia. Several days later he was decapitated in Cuzco, beside his elderly field marshal.

La Gasca had fulfilled his mission of stamping out the insurrection and returning Peru to Charles V. Now he had to take the place of the deposed Gonzalo Pizarro, with all the enormous power that implied. He owed his triumph to the energetic Captain Valdivia, and he rewarded him by confirming the title of gobernador of Chile given to him by the citizens of Santiago, which until that moment had not been validated by the Crown. In addition, La Gasca authorized Valdivia to recruit soldiers and take them back to Chile, as long as they were not Pizarro's rebels or Peruvian Indians.

Did Pedro think of me as he rode triumphant through the streets of Cuzco, or was he so puffed up with pride that he was thinking only of himself? I have asked myself a hundred times why he did not take me with him on that adventure; if he had, our fate would have been very different. He went on a military mission, it's true, but I had always been his companion in war as well as in peace. Was he ashamed of me? Mistress, common woman, concubine. In Chile I was Doña Inés Suárez, the gobernadora, and no one recalled that we were not legally husband and wife. I myself tended to forget that. Women must have flocked to Pedro in Cuzco, and later in Ciudad de los Reyes. He was the great hero of the civil war, lord and master of Chile, supposedly rich and still attractive; any woman would have been honored to be seen on his arm. Besides, there was already talk of intrigue: assassinate La Gasca, a man of fanatic rigidity, and name Pedro de Valdivia in his place, but no one dared say that to Pedro's face. He would have been insulted. The sword of the Valdivias had always loyally served the king, it would never be turned against him—and La Gasca represented the king.

It is a waste of time, at my age, to conjecture about the women Pedro had in Peru, especially since my own conscience is not entirely clear, for it was during that time that my loving friendship with Rodrigo de Quiroga began. I must make clear that he did not take any initiative or reveal any sign of recognizing my ill-defined desires. I knew that he would never betray his friend Pedro de Valdivia, and for that reason I never acted on our mutual attraction, and neither did he. Did I turn to Quiroga out of spite? To get my revenge for having been abandoned by Pedro? I do not know; the fact is that Rodrigo and I loved each other like chaste sweethearts, with a deep and hopeless emotion that we never put into words, only glances and gestures. On my part, it was not the ardent passion

I had felt for Juan de Málaga and Pedro de Valdivia but, rather, a quiet desire to be near Rodrigo, to share his life, to look after him. Santiago was a small city in which it was impossible to keep a secret, but Rodrigo's reputation was irreproachable, and no one gossiped about us even though when he was not out fighting Indians we saw each other every day. We had every excuse, since he helped me in all my projects: building the church, the chapels, the cemetery, the hospital . . . and I had taken in his daughter.

You will not remember, Isabel, because you were only three years old. Eulalia, your mother, who loved you and Rodrigo very much, died that year during a typhus epidemic. Your father took you by the hand, brought you to my house, and said: "Look after her for a few days, I beg you, Doña Inés. You know that I have to go deal with those savages, but I will be back soon. . . ." You were a quiet, intense little girl with the face of a llama: the same sweet eyes and long eyelashes, the same expression of curiosity, and your hair was tied in two little tufts, like that animal's ears. You inherited the caramel skin of your Quechua mother and your father's aristocratic features: a good mixture. I adored you from the moment you stepped across my threshold clutching a little wooden horse Rodrigo had carved for you. I never gave you back to your father, and used different excuses to keep you with me until Rodrigo and I married. Then you were legally mine. Everyone said I spoiled you and treated you as if you were an adult; they said I was raising a monster—imagine those malicious women's disappointment when you turned out as you did.

During those nine years of the colony in Chile, we had survived several pitched battles and countless skirmishes with the Chilean Indians; nevertheless, we not only had established Santiago, we had founded new cities. We thought we were safe, but in truth the indigenous Chileans never accepted our presence in their land, as we would find out in the years to follow. Michimalonko's Indians, in the north, had for years been preparing a massive uprising but did not dare attack Santiago, as they had in 1541; instead, they concentrated their efforts on the small settlements to the north, where the Spanish colonists were nearly without defenses.

Don Benito died of a stomach ailment in the summer of 1549, from eating bad oysters. He was much loved by us all; we thought of him as the patriarch of the city. We had come to the Mapocho valley on the strength of that old soldier's dream, his vision of Chile as the Garden of Eden. He always treated me with exemplary loyalty and gallantry, which made me despair when I was not able to help him in his agony. He died in my arms, writhing with pain, poisoned to the marrow of his bones. We were in the midst of his funeral, which all the inhabitants of Santiago attended, when two ragged soldiers arrived, stumbling with fatigue, one of them badly wounded. They had come from La Serena, traveling by night and hiding during the day to avoid the Indians. They told us that several nights before, the only lookout for the recently founded town of La Serena had barely sounded the alarm before masses of Indians swarmed over it. The Spaniards could not defend themselves, and within a few hours nothing remained of La Serena. The attackers tortured men and women to death, killed children by smashing their heads against rocks, and reduced the houses to ashes. During the confusion, these two soldiers had slipped away, and despite great adversity had brought the horrendous news to Santiago. They assured us that this was a widespread uprising; all the tribes were on the verge of war, preparing to destroy every Spanish outpost.

Terror spread through Santiago; we seemed to see hordes of savages leaping the moat, climbing the city wall, and falling upon us like the wrath of God. Once again we found ourselves with our forces divided; some of our soldiers had been assigned to those villages in the north, Pedro de Valdivia was away and had several of the captains with him, and the promised reinforcements had not arrived. There was no hope of protecting the mines and the haciendas, which people abandoned to take refuge in Santiago. The women, despairing, gathered in the churches and prayed day and night, while the men, including the elderly and the ill, made ready to defend the city.

The town council, in full session, decided that Villagra should take sixty men and go meet the Indians in the north, before they organized to move on Santiago. Aguirre was left in charge of defending the capital, and Juan Gómez was authorized to use any measure to get information about the war—which, in a word, meant to wring it out of anyone who seemed suspicious. The howls of tortured Indians added to our frayed nerves. My pleas for compassion, and my argument that truth was never obtained by torture because the victim confessed what the executioner wanted to hear, went unheeded. The colonists' hatred, fear, and desire for revenge was so strong that they celebrated when they heard of Villagra's punitive raids—even knowing that his cruelty equaled that of the savages. His ferocious campaign succeeded in snuffing out the insurrection; he dismantled the indigenous force in fewer than three months and saved Santiago from being attacked. He forced a peace accord with the caciques, though no one believed the truce would last. Our one hope was that the governor would return soon with his captains, bringing more soldiers from Peru.

Months after Villagra's military campaign, the town council sent Francisco de Aguirre north with the mission of rebuilding the cities destroyed by the Indians, and of enlisting allies, but the Basque captain used the opportunity to give free rein to his impulsive and cruel temperament. He swooped down upon the Indian settlements without mercy, rounded up all the men—from children to elders—locked them in wood barracks, and burned them alive. He was on the verge of completely exterminating the indigenous population; and once that was done, as he would say, laughing, he would have to impregnate all the widows himself to repopulate it. But I will not add further details; I fear that these pages already contain more cruelty than a Christian soul can tolerate. In the New World, no one has scruples when the moment calls for violence. But what am I saying? Violence like Aguirre's exists everywhere, and has throughout the ages. Nothing changes; we humans repeat the same sins over and over, eternally.

All this was happening in the Americas, while in Spain Charles V was promulgating the Leyes Nuevas, new laws in which he affirmed that the Indians were subjects of the Crown. He warned the encomenderos that they could not force the indigenous peoples to work or subject them to physical punishment; they must be given written contracts and be paid in hard coin. And beyond that, the conquistadors should approach the Indians on their best behavior, asking them with gentle words to accept the God and the king of the Christians, hand over their land, and put themselves at the orders of their new masters. Like so many well-intentioned laws, these went no further than putting ink to paper. "Our sovereign must be softer in the head than we imagined, if he thinks that is possible," Aguirre commented. He was right. What did we Spanish do when foreigners came to *our* land to impose their customs and religion? Fight them to the death, of course.

In the meantime, Pedro had managed to pull together a substantial number of soldiers in Peru and had started back overland, following the known route across the Atacama Desert. When they had been traveling for several weeks, a hard-riding messenger from La Gasca caught up with them and told Pedro to return to Ciudad de los Reyes, where there was a voluminous file of accusations against him. Valdivia had to leave the troops under the command of his captains and return to face the law. When he did, the aid he had given the king and La Gasca by defeating Gonzalo Pizarro and restoring peace in Peru counted for nothing; he was tried anyway.

Besides Valdivia's envious enemies in Peru, there were other detractors who traveled from Chile for the sole purpose of destroying him. In total, there were more than fifty charges against him, but I remember only the most important, and those that concerned me. He was accused of naming himself gobernador without the authorization of Francisco Pizarro, who had only given him the title of lieutenant—teniente gobernador—and of ordering the death of Sancho de la Hoz and other innocent Spaniards, such as young Escobar, who had been condemned out of jealousy. It was claimed that he had stolen money from the colonists, but it was not clarified that he had already repaid nearly all that debt with gold from the

Marga-Marga, as he had promised. It was said that he had appropriated the best lands and thousands of Indians but never mentioned that he bore many of the colony's expenses, financed the soldiers, lent money without interest, and had acted as treasurer of Chile using money from his own pockets. It could never be said that he was miserly or greedy.

In addition it was charged that he had extravagantly enriched a certain Inés Suárez, with whom he lived in scandalous concubinage. What made me most indignant, when later I learned the specifics, was that those villainous accusers maintained that I could make Pedro do my least bidding, and that to obtain something from the gobernador one had to pay a commission to his mistress. I suffered many hardships in the conquest of Chile, and I have devoted my life to founding this kingdom. I do not have to list here what was achieved through my efforts, because it is recorded in the archives of the town council, and anyone who doubts can go there to consult them. It is true that Pedro honored me with valuable lands and encomiendas, which produced rancor in mean-spirited people with short memories, but it is not true that I earned them in bed. My fortune has grown because I administered it with a country woman's good sense, which I inherited from my mother—may she rest in peace. "Less should go out than comes in" was her philosophy in regard to money, a formula that cannot fail. Like the Spanish hidalgos they were, Pedro and Rodrigo never paid the least attention to managing their lands or their business interests. Pedro died poor, and Rodrigo lived a wealthy man, thanks to me.

Despite sympathizing with the accused, to whom he owed so much, La Gasca carried out the judgment to the last consequences. It was all anyone talked about in Peru, and my name traveled from mouth to mouth: I was a witch, I used potions to madden men, I had been a whore in Spain, and then in Cartagena; I kept my youth by drinking the blood of newborn babies, and other horrors I blush to repeat. Pedro proved his innocence, defusing the charges one by one, and in the end the only person who came out losing was I. La Gasca once again confirmed Valdivia's appointment as

governor, his titles and his honors; his only demand was that Pedro
pay off his debts within a prudent time. But in regard to me, this
clergyman—may he roast in hell—was hard as steel. He ordered
the governor to divest me of my lands and divide them among the
captains, to separate from me immediately and send me to Peru
or back to Spain, where I would have the opportunity to atone for
my sins in a convent.

Pedro was away for a year and a half, and returned from Peru
with two hundred soldiers, of which eighty came with him by ship
and the remainder overland. When I learned that he was coming,
I flew into a fever of activity that nearly drove the servants mad. I
set everyone to painting, washing curtains, planting flowers in the
flowerpots, preparing sweets that he liked, weaving blankets,
and sewing new sheets. It was summer, and in the gardens
around Santiago we were growing the fruits and vegetables of
Spain—except ours were more delicious. Catalina and I cooked
conserves and Pedro's favorite desserts. For the first time in several years I thought about my looks; I even made myself exquisite
blouses and skirts to welcome him like a bride. I was nearly forty
but I felt young and attractive; that may have been because my body
had not changed, which is often the case with childless women, and
also because I saw myself reflected in the timid eyes of Rodrigo de
Quiroga. I was nevertheless afraid that Pedro would notice the fine
wrinkles around my eyes, the veins in my legs, my hands callused
by work. I had decided not to greet him with reproaches: what was
done was done. I wanted to make my peace with him and return
to the times when we had been legendary lovers. We had a long
history together, ten years of struggle and passion that could not
be erased. I removed Rodrigo de Quiroga from my imaginings, a
futile and dangerous fantasy, and went to visit Cecilia to learn her
beauty secrets, the subject of much speculation in Santiago. It was
a true marvel how that woman, unlike the rest of the world, grew
younger with the years.

Juan and Cecilia's house was much smaller and more modest that ours, but it was splendidly decorated with furnishings and adornments from Peru, including some from the former palace of Atahualpa. The floors were covered with several layers of many-colored wool rugs with Inca designs; my feet sank into them as I walked across the room. Cecilia's home smelled of cinnamon and chocolate, which she managed to acquire while the rest of us made do with maté and infusions of local herbs. During her childhood in the palace of Atahualpa, she had grown so accustomed to her chocolate drink that in times of the disturbances in Santiago, when we went through periods of severe hunger, she never cried because she was hungry for bread; her tears were for chocolate. Before we Spaniards came to the New World, chocolate was reserved for royalty, priests, and the upper echelons of the Inca military, but we quickly adopted it.

When we took a seat on cushions, Cecilia's silent serving girls brought us that fragrant beverage in silver cups fashioned by Quechua artisans. Cecilia, who in public always dressed like a Spanish woman, at home followed the mode of the Inca court; it was more comfortable: a straight, ankle-length skirt and an embroidered tunic cinched at the waist with a sash woven of brilliant colors. She was barefoot, and I could not help comparing her perfect, princess-bred feet with mine, those of a rough country girl. She wore her hair loose and her only adornment was a pair of heavy gold earrings she had inherited from her family; they had reached Chile through the same mysterious channels as her furnishings.

"If Pedro notices your wrinkles, it will be because he does not love you, and nothing you do will change his feelings," she advised me when I told her of my worries.

I don't know whether her words were prophetic or whether she, who knew even the most closely guarded secrets, was already informed about something I did not as yet know. To please me, she shared her creams, lotions, and perfumes, which I applied for several days as I impatiently awaited my lover. However, a week passed, and then another, and another, and Valdivia had not shown his face in Santiago. He was on a ship anchored in the bay at Concón, and was governing through emissaries, but there was no message for me. I could not comprehend what was happening; I debated with myself, torn between uncertainty, anger, and hope, terrified by the thought that he had stopped loving me, and waited for the tiniest positive sign. I asked Catalina to read my fortune, but for once she found nothing in the shells, or else she did not dare tell me what she saw.

Days and weeks went by with no news of Pedro; I stopped eating, and could scarcely sleep. During the day I worked until I was exhausted, and at night I paced like a wild bull through the galleries and rooms of my house, my heels striking sparks from the floor. I did not cry, because in fact I wasn't sad, I was furious, and I didn't pray because it seemed to me that Nuestra Señora del Socorro would not understand my problem. A thousand times I was tempted to go visit Pedro on the ship and find out once and for all what he was doing—it was only two days by horseback—but I didn't dare. My instinct warned me that in this particular circumstance it would be best not to confront him. I suppose that I foresaw my misfortune but out of pride did not put it into words. I did not want anyone to see me humiliated, least of all Rodrigo de Quiroga, who fortunately did not ask questions.

Finally, one very hot afternoon, González de Marmolejo turned up at my house looking exhausted. He had gone to and returned from Valparaíso in five days' time, and had bruised buttocks from the ride. I greeted him with a bottle of my best wine, apprehensive, because I knew he was bringing me news. Was Pedro on the way here? Was he calling me to come join him? Marmolejo did not allow me to ask further questions but handed me a sealed letter, then with bowed head went out to drink his wine beneath the bougainvillea on the gallery while I read it. In few, and very precise, words, Pedro communicated the gist of La Gasca's decision to me. He reiterated his respect and admiration for me—without mentioning love—and urged me to listen carefully to González de Marmolejo. The hero of campaigns in Flanders and Italy, of revolts in Peru and the conquest of Chile, the most courageous and famous soldier in the New World did not have the nerve to face me. That was why he had hidden for two months on the ship. What had happened to him? I could not possibly comprehend his reasons for running away from me. Perhaps I had become a dominating witch, a virago; perhaps I had trusted too much in the solidity of our love. I had never asked myself whether Pedro loved me as much as I loved him; I had assumed that our love was an uncontestable truth. No, I decided finally. The blame was not mine. I was not the one who had changed; it was he. Feeling that he was getting old had frightened him, and he yearned to be the heroic soldier and youthful lover he had been years ago. I knew him too well. At my side, he could not reinvent himself or begin again with new trappings. Beside me, it would be impossible to hide his weaknesses or his age, and as he could not deceive me, he was tossing me aside.

"Read this, please, Padre, and tell me what it means," I said and held the letter out to the priest.

"I know what it contains, daughter. The gobernador did me the honor of confiding in me and asking my counsel."

"Then this wickedness is your idea?"

"No, Inés, those orders come from La Gasca, the supreme authority of the king and the church in this part of the world. I have the papers here; you can see them for yourself. Your adultery with Pedro is the source of scandal."

"Now, when I am no longer needed, my love for Pedro is a scandal, but when I found water in the desert, treated the ill, buried the dead, and saved Santiago from the Indians, then I was a saint."

"I know how you feel, my daughter—"

"No, Padre, you do not have the least idea how I feel. It is devilishly ironic that only the concubine is guilty, she being a free woman and he the married adulterer. I am not surprised by La Gasca's baseness—I would expect that. I am horrified by Pedro's cowardice."

"He had no choice, Inés."

"A well-born man always has a choice when it comes to defending honor. I warn you, Padre, I will not leave Chile, because I conquered it and I founded it."

"Be careful, Inés! That is your pride speaking. I can't believe that you would prefer for the Inquisition to come and resolve all this in its own fashion."

"Are you threatening me?" I asked with the shudder the name of the Inquisition always evokes.

"Nothing further from my mind, daughter. I have brought the gobernador's message, proposing a solution that will allow you to stay here in Chile."

"And what is that?"

"You could marry," the cleric managed to get out, clearing his throat several times and squirming in his chair. "That is the only way you can remain in Chile. There are many men who would be happy to wed a woman with your merits, and with a dowry like yours. Once you put your worldly goods in your husband's name, they will not be able to take them from you."

It was some time before I could speak. I could not believe that he was offering me this tortuous solution, the last that would have occurred to me.

"The gobernador wants to help you, even though it means giving you up. Can't you see that his is a selfless act, a proof of his love and gratitude?" the priest added.

He was nervously fanning himself, waving away the flies of the summer, while I strode back and forth on the gallery, trying to calm myself. This plan was not the fruit of sudden inspiration. Valdivia had suggested it to La Gasca back in Peru, and he had approved it. In other words, my fate had been decided behind my back. Pedro's betrayal seemed contemptible to me, and a wave of hatred washed over me like dirty water, as my mouth filled with bile. At that moment I wanted to kill the priest with my bare hands and I had to make an enormous effort to remind myself that he was merely the messenger. The person who warranted my vengeance was Pedro, and not this poor old man whose cassock was wet with the sweat of fear.

The next instant I was struck by something like a dagger in my breast; it took my breath and made me sway on my feet. My heart was leaping like a wild pony, something I had never felt before. Blood rushed to my head, my knees buckled, and everything went dark. I managed to fall into a chair; had I not, I would have crumpled to the ground. This swoon lasted only an instant; almost immediately I came to my senses and found myself with my head resting on my knees. I waited in that position until the beating in my chest became regular and I was breathing normally. I blamed that brief faint on anger and the heat, never suspecting that my heart had broken, and I would have to live thirty years more with the damage.

"I suppose that Pedro, who wants so badly to be of help, also went to the trouble of choosing a husband for me?" I asked Marmolejo when I could speak.

"The gobernador has a name or two in mind . . ."

"Tell Pedro that I accept his arrangement, but that I myself shall choose my future husband because I intend to marry for love and be very happy."

"Inés, I must warn you again that pride is a mortal sin."

"Tell me one thing, Padre. Is the rumor true that Pedro brought two women with him?"

González de Marmolejo did not answer, confirming with his silence the gossip that had reached my ears. Pedro had replaced a forty-year-old woman with two twenty-year-olds, a pair of Spanish women: María de Encio and her mysterious servant, Juana Jiménez, who also shared Pedro's bed, and, they said, controlled both of them with the arts of sorcery. Sorcery? That was what they had said of me. At times, all a woman has to do is dry the sweat from the brow of a weary man and he will eat from the hand that caresses him. You don't have to cast spells to do that. You have only to be loyal, and happy to listen—or at least pretend to be listening—and be a good cook to keep him, without his realizing, from doing

anything foolish, to revel, and make him revel, in every embrace
. . . those, and other equally simple things are the recipe for total
devotion. It can be summed up in two phrases: iron hand, velvet
glove.

I remember that when Pedro told me about the nightdress with
the opening in the shape of a cross his wife, Marina, wore, I made
myself the secret promise that I would never hide my body from the
man who shared my bed. I held to that decision, and so naturally
that up to the last day I lay beside Rodrigo, he never noticed that
my flesh had grown flabby, like any old woman's. The men I have
lived with have been naive: I acted as if I were beautiful, and they
believed it. Now I am alone and I have no one to make happy with
my love, but I know that Pedro was happy when he was with me,
and Rodrigo as well, even when illness kept him from taking the
initiative in our lovemaking. Forgive me, Isabel, I know that these
lines will be disturbing for you, but you need to learn. Pay no attention to the priests; they know nothing.

Santiago was by then a town of five hundred inhabitants, but gossip
circulated as quickly as in a hamlet; for that reason I could not fiddle
around, though my heart continued cavorting for several days following my conversation with the priest. Catalina prepared *cochayuyo*
water, dried sea algae she set to soak overnight. For thirty years I
have drunk this viscous liquid upon awakening, and am accustomed
to its foul taste—and thanks to that I am still alive. That Sunday I
dressed in my best clothes, took you, Isabel, by the hand, because
you had been living with me for several months, and at the hour
when people were leaving mass, so everyone would be sure to see
me, crossed the plaza in the direction of Rodrigo de Quiroga's
home. Catalina came with us, wrapped in her black mantle and
muttering Quechua spells, which are more effective in such matters
than Christian prayers. Baltasar brought up the rear, trotting along
like the fine old dog he was.

An Indian servant opened the gate and led me into the sala,

while my companions stayed behind in a dusty patio covered with chicken shit. Looking around I realized that it would take a lot of work to convert that bare, ugly military billet into habitable quarters. I suspected that Rodrigo did not have a decent bed but slept on a soldier's cot; it was no wonder that you, Isabel, had adapted so quickly to the comforts of my home. I would have to replace the wood-and-leather furniture, paint, buy something to cover the walls and floors, build galleries for sun and shade, plant trees and flowers, put fountains in the patio, take off the straw roof and put on tiles—in short, I would have projects for years. I like projects. Minutes later Rodrigo came down, startled, because I had never visited him in his house. He had taken off his Sunday doublet and was wearing breeches and a white, full-sleeved shirt, open at the throat. He looked very young, and I was tempted to turn and flee the way I had come. How many years younger than I was that man?

"Good day, Doña Inés. Is anything the matter? Is Isabel all right?"

"I have come to propose matrimony, Don Rodrigo. How does that sound to you?" I blurted it straight out; this was no time to beat about the bush.

I must say, to Quiroga's credit, that he took my proposal with theatrical gusto. His face lighted up, he lifted his arms to the heavens and let out a long Indian whoop, unexpected in a man of such sobriety. Of course he had already heard the rumor of what had happened in Peru with La Gasca, and of the bizarre solution that had occurred to the gobernador; all the captains were talking about it, especially the bachelors. Perhaps he suspected that he would be my choice, but he was too modest to take it for granted. I tried to spell out the terms of the agreement, but he did not allow me a single word; he swept me up in his arms with such verve that he lifted me off the floor and, without further ado, closed my lips with his. I realized that I myself had been waiting for that moment for almost a year. I grabbed his shirt in both hands and returned the kiss with a passion that had been there for a long time, dormant or disguised, a passion I had reserved for Pedro de Valdivia and that clamored to be lived before my youth deserted me. I felt the strength of his desire, his hands at my waist, at the back of my neck, in my hair, his lips on my face and neck; I caught his young man's scent, heard his voice murmuring my name, and I felt blessed. How could I in less than a minute go from the sadness of having been abandoned to the joy of feeling loved? At that time I must have been very fickle. I swore at that instant that I would be faithful to Rodrigo till the day he died, and not only have I fulfilled that oath to the letter, I have loved him for thirty years, more every day. It was so easy to do; Rodrigo was always an admirable man, everyone agreed about that, but the best men can have serious defects that are revealed only in intimacy. That was not true with that distinguished hidalgo, that soldier, friend, and husband. He never tried to make me forget Pedro de Valdivia, whom he respected and loved; he even helped me assure that an ungrateful Chile did not forget, but remembered him as he deserved. Rodrigo did, however, set out to make me love him, and he succeeded in that.

When finally we broke apart and caught our breaths, I went out to give instructions to Catalina, while Rodrigo greeted his daughter. A half hour later, a line of Indians were carrying my trunks, my prie-dieu, and the statue of Nuestra Señora del Socorro to the home of Rodrigo de Quiroga, while the citizens of Santiago, who had been waiting in the Plaza de Armas following mass, applauded. I needed two weeks to make plans for our wedding; I did not want to marry quietly, but with pomp and ceremony. It was impossible to decorate Rodrigo's house in such a short time, so we concentrated on transplanting trees and shrubs to his patio, constructing arches of flowers, and setting up tents and long tables for the feast.

Padre González de Marmolejo married us in what today is the cathedral, but was at the time under construction, before a large assembly of whites, blacks, Indians, and mestizos. We altered one of Cecilia's virginal white dresses to fit me, since there was no time to order cloth. "Marry in white, Inés, because Don Rodrigo deserves to be your first love," Cecilia advised me, and she was right. The wedding was accompanied by a high mass, and afterward we celebrated with some of my special dishes: empanadas, a casserole of game birds, corn cakes, stuffed potatoes, beans with chili peppers, lamb and roast kid, vegetables from my country gardens, and a variety of desserts I had planned for Pedro de Valdivia's arrival. The feast was duly punctuated with wines I took from the governor's cellar with a clear conscience, for it was also mine. The gates of Rodrigo's house were open the entire day, and anyone who wished to eat and celebrate with us was welcome. Among the crowd were dozens of mestizo and Indian children, and seated in chairs arranged in a semicircle were the elders of the colony. Catalina calculated that three hundred people filed through the house that day, but she was never good at numbers; there may have been more. The next morning, Rodrigo and I, along with you, Isabel, and a train of Yanaconas, left to spend a few weeks of love at my country estate. We also took soldiers to protect us from the Chilean Indians, who often attacked unwary travelers. Catalina and the faithful serving girls I had brought from Cuzco stayed behind to do what they could with Rodrigo's house, and the remainder of a large cadre of servants stayed where they had always been. Only then did Valdivia dare come ashore with his two concubines and return to his home in Santiago, which he found clean, orderly, and well stocked, with no trace of my presence.

SIX

The Chilean War, 1549–1553

IT IS OBVIOUS THAT THE WRITING is different in the last part of this account. For the first months I wrote in my own hand, but now I grow tired after a few lines and I prefer dictating to you. My handwriting resembles fly tracks, but yours, Isabel, is fine, and elegant. You like the brown oxide ink, a novelty from Spain that I have trouble reading, but since you are doing me the favor of helping, I can't impose my black inkwell on you. We would move along more quickly if you did not waylay me with so many questions, child. I love to hear you. You speak the singsong, gliding Spanish of Chile. Rodrigo and I no longer try to instill in your speech the harsh *h* sounds and lisping *th* of Spain. That is how Bishop González de Marmolejo spoke, since he was from Seville. He died long ago; do you remember him? He loved you like a grandfather, poor old man. At the last he admitted to being seventy-seven, although he reminded me of a biblical patriarch of a hundred, with his white beard and the way he was constantly predicting the Apocalypse, a quirk he acquired in his old age. His obsession with the end of the world did not, however, prevent him from engaging in material concerns; he seemed to have received divine inspiration in his financial dealings. Among his grand enterprises was the horse breeding in which we were partners. We experimented with mixing breeds, and obtained strong, elegant, and docile animals, the famous Chilean horses that now are known across the continent for being as noble as Arabians but with better endurance. The bishop died the same year as my Catalina; he from a disease of the lungs no medicinal plant could cure, while she was killed by a tile that fell during a temblor and struck her on the back of the head. It was deadly accurate; she never even knew there was an earthquake. Villagra also died during that same period, so frightened by his sins that he dressed in the habit of Saint Francis. He was governor of Chile for a time, and will be remembered among the most powerful and bold of military men, but no one appreciated him because he was so miserly. Avarice is a flaw repugnant to Spaniards, who are known for their generosity.

I must not linger on details, daughter, because if we dally, this account may be left unfinished, and no one wants to read hundreds of quartos only to find that the story has no clear ending. What will the ending of this one be? My death, I suppose, because as long as I have breath I will have memories to fill pages; there is much to be told in a life like mine. I should have begun these memoirs some time ago, but building and bringing prosperity to a town takes a lot of time. I began writing only when Rodrigo died and stirred my memories. Without him, I spend sleepless nights, and insomnia is very conducive to writing. I wonder where my husband is, whether he is waiting for me somewhere or if he is right here in this house, observing from the shadows, discreetly watching over me, as he always did in life. What will it be like to die? What is on the other side? Only night and silence? It occurs to me that to die is to fly like an arrow through dark reaches toward the firmament, toward infinite space, where I must look for my loved ones. It amazes me that now, when I am thinking so much about death, I still feel the urgency to accomplish projects and satisfy ambitions. It must be pure pride: to "earn fame and leave memory of myself," as Pedro always said. I suspect that in this life we are not going anywhere, and even less in haste; one merely follows a path, one step at a time, toward death. So let us keep going, Isabel, and tell this story as long as we have days left; there is still much I want to recount.

After I married Rodrigo, I determined to avoid Pedro, at least in the beginning, until I had lost the feeling of animosity that had replaced the love I'd held for him for ten years. I detested him as deeply as I had loved him; I wanted to hurt him, where before I had defended him from harm. His defects were magnified in my eyes; he no longer seemed noble, but, rather, ambitious and vain. Once he had been strong, astute, and severe; now he was fat, false, and cruel. I expressed those feelings only to Catalina because my resentment of my former lover embarrassed me. I was able to hide it from Rodrigo, whose own rectitude prevented him from noticing my unworthy sentiments. As he was incapable of base thoughts, he could not imagine them in others. If it seemed strange to him that I did not go out when Pedro de Valdivia was in Santiago, he didn't tell me. I dedicated myself to improving our country houses, and extended my stays there as long as possible, using the pretexts of sowing, cultivating roses, and breeding horses and mules, although in truth I was bored and missed my work in the hospital. In the meantime, Rodrigo traveled between town and the country every week, beating his kidneys to a pulp on a fast horse in order to see you and me. The fresh air, physical work, your company, Isabel, and a litter of pups, offspring of old Baltasar, helped me.

During that period I prayed a lot. I carried Nuestra Señora del Socorro into the garden, settled us both beneath a tree, and told her my woes. She made me see that the heart is like a box; if it is filled with rubbish, there is no space for other things. I could not love Rodrigo and his daughter if my heart was choked with bitterness, the Virgin informed me. According to Catalina, bitterness turns one's skin yellow and produces a bad odor; for that I began drinking cleansing teas. With prayers and teas I cured myself of my rancor against Pedro in two months' time. One night I dreamed that I had grown talons like a condor's, and that I swooped down on him and tore out his eyes. It was a stupendous dream, very vivid, and I awoke avenged. At dawn I got out of bed and confirmed that the pain in my shoulders and neck that had tormented me for weeks was gone; the pointless weight of hatred had dissipated. I listened to the sounds of awakening: roosters, dogs, the gardener's brush broom on the terrace, the voices of the servant girls. It was a warm, clear morning. Barefoot, I went out to the patio, and the breeze caressed my skin beneath my nightdress. I thought of Rodrigo, and the need to make love to him made me shiver, as it had in my youthful days when I escaped to the orchards of Plasencia to lie with Juan de Málaga. I yawned a great yawn, stretched like a cat with my face lifted to the sun, and immediately ordered the horses so I could return with you to Santiago that very day, with no luggage but the clothes we had on, and weapons. Rodrigo did not allow us to leave the house without protection, out of fear of the bands of Indians that roamed the valley, but we went anyway. We were lucky, and reached Santiago by nightfall, with no misadventures. The town sentinels sounded the alarm from their towers when they sighted the dust raised by our horses. Rodrigo came out to meet me, frightened, fearing some misfortune, but I threw my arms around his neck, kissed him on the mouth, and led him to the bed.

That night was the true beginning of our love; what had gone before was practice. In the months that followed we learned to know and give pleasure to each other. My love for Rodrigo was different from the desire I had felt for Juan de Málaga and my passion for Pedro de Valdivia; it was a mature, joyful sentiment, without conflict, that became more intense with the passing of time . . . until I could not live without him. My solitary trips to the country came to an end; we were apart only when the demands of war called Rodrigo away. That man, so serious before the world, was in private tender and playful. He spoiled us; we were his two queens, do you remember? And so the prophecy of Catalina's magic shells, that I would be a queen, came true. In the thirty years we would live together, Rodrigo never lost his good humor in our home, no matter how grave the external pressures. He shared problems concerning the war, matters of government and politics, his fears, his cares, but none of it affected our relationship. He had confidence in my judgment, sought my opinion, listened to my counsel. I never had to tread lightly to avoid offending Rodrigo, as I had with Valdivia—and as one usually must with men in general, who tend to be prickly regarding their authority.

I suppose you would just as soon I not go into this, Isabel, but I cannot leave it out because it is an aspect of your father that you should know. Before he was with me, Rodrigo believed that youth and vigor were all that was needed at the hour of making love, a very common error. I was surprised the first time we were together in bed; he rushed along like a lad of fifteen. I attributed that to his having waited for me so long, loving me in silence and without hope for nine years, as he had confessed to me, but he was equally awkward on the nights that followed. Apparently your mother, Eulalia, who loved him passionately, had not taught him anything. That task became mine, and once I was over my anger with Valdivia, I took it on with pleasure, as you can imagine. I had done the same with Pedro de Valdivia years before, when we met in Cuzco. My experience with Spanish captains is limited, but I can tell you that those I knew were ill informed in regard to lovemaking, although well disposed to learn. Don't laugh, daughter, it's true. I tell you these things just in case. I do not know what your intimate relations are with your husband, but if you have any complaints, I advise you to come to me, for after I'm dead, you won't have anyone to discuss them with. Men, like dogs and horses, have to be domesticated, but there are not many women capable of doing it, since they themselves know nothing unless they have had a teacher like Juan de Málaga. Besides, women are saddled with inhibitions; never forget Marina Ortiz de Gaete's famous nightgown with the embroidered keyhole. So you see, ignorance is multiplied, and tends to end the best-intentioned love.

I had been back in Santiago for only a few days, and was just beginning to cultivate pleasure and blessed love with Rodrigo, when the city was awakened early one morning by a sentinel's trumpet. A horse's head had been found impaled upon the same stake where so many human heads had been exhibited through the years. A closer inspection had revealed that it was the head of Sultán, the governor's favorite steed. Everyone who rushed there had choked back a cry of horror. A curfew had been imposed in Santiago, and Indians, blacks, and mestizos were forbidden to go about at night, under threat of a hundred lashes at the whipping post in the plaza, the same punishment applied when they held fiestas without permission, got drunk, or bet on games—all vices reserved for their masters. The curfew eliminated the mestizo and indigenous population, but no one could imagine that a Spaniard could be guilty of such a hideous act. Valdivia ordered Juan Gómez to use torture, as necessary, to find the perpetrator of that outrage.

Even though I had gotten over my hatred of Pedro de Valdivia, I still chose to see him as little as possible. Nonetheless, we inevitably ran into each other, since the center of Santiago is small and our two homes were not far apart, but we did not participate in the same social events. Friends were careful not to invite us at the same time. When we met in the street or the church, we nodded discreetly, nothing more. The relationship between Valdivia and Rodrigo, however, did not change; Pedro continued to place absolute trust in Rodrigo, and he responded with loyalty and affection. I, naturally, was the target of malicious comments.

"Why must people gossip and be so mean-spirited, Inés?" Cecilia asked.

"It bothers them that instead of taking on the role of abandoned lover, I have become a happy wife. They relish seeing strong women like you and me humiliated. They cannot forgive us that we have triumphed when so many others fail," I explained.

"I don't deserve to be compared with you, Inés. I am not as bold as you," Cecilia laughed.

"Courage is a virtue appreciated in a male but considered a defect in our gender. Bold women are a threat to a world that is badly out of balance, in favor of men. That is why they work so hard to mistreat us and destroy us. But remember that bold women are like cockroaches: step on one and others come running from the corners," I told her.

As for María de Encio, I recall that none of the "best" people received her, despite her being Spanish and the mistress of the gobernador. They treated her like his housekeeper. And the other woman, Juana Jiménez? They made fun of her behind her back, saying that her señora had trained her to perform the pirouettes in bed that she had no stomach for herself. If that was true, I have to wonder what vices she entangled Pedro in; I knew him as a man of healthy, direct sensuality. He was never interested in the curiosities in the little French books Francisco de Aguirre liked to show around, except during the period of poor Escobar, when he wanted to magnify my guilt by picturing me as a whore. And by the way, I should not fail to note in these pages that Escobar did not reach Peru, but neither did he die of thirst in the desert, as had been supposed. Many years later I learned that the young Yanacona who had gone with him had led him by secret paths to the village of his family, hidden among the peaks of the sierra, where both live to this day. Before he left, Escobar promised González de Marmolejo that if he reached Peru alive he would become a priest, because there was no question that God had pointed his finger at him when first he saved him from the gallows and then the desert. He did reach Peru, but did not keep his promise; instead he had several Quechua wives and mestizo children, choosing to spread the holy faith in this more intimate fashion.

But returning to the women Valdivia brought from Cuzco, I knew through Catalina that they prepared him brews of *yerba del clavo*. It may be that Pedro was afraid of losing his virility, which for him was as important as his courage as a soldier, and that was the reason he drank potions and called on two women to stimulate him.

He was not yet of an age for his vigor to decline, but he did not enjoy good health, and he suffered pain from old wounds. The two women came to a colorful end. After Valdivia's death, Juana Jiménez disappeared; it was said that the Mapuche captured her during a raid in the south. María de Encio turned into a cruel, evil woman who tortured her Indian serving girls. They say that the bones of those poor girls are buried in the house, which now belongs to the town council, and that at night you can hear their moans . . . but that is another story that I don't have time to tell.

I kept my distance from María and Juana. I did not intend ever to speak to them, but when Pedro fell from his horse and fractured a leg, they sent for me because no one knew more about those injuries than I. For the first time, I went into the house that had been mine, built by my own hands, and I did not recognize it even though the same furniture stood in the same places. Juana, a Galician woman, short, but well proportioned and with agreeable features, greeted me with a servant's bow and led me to the room I had once shared with Pedro. There I found María, sniveling and putting wet cloths on the forehead of the injured man, who looked more dead than alive. María rushed to me and kissed my hands, sobbing with gratitude and fear; after all, if Pedro died, her own fate was rather murky. I freed myself from her grasp, delicately, not to offend her, and went to the bed. When I turned back the sheet and saw the leg, broken in two places, my thought was that the best course would be to amputate it above the knee, before gangrene set in, but I have always been horrified by that operation and did not find myself capable of performing it on a body I had once loved.

I commended myself to the Virgin and set about treating the damage as best I could, aided by the veterinarian and the smith, since the doctor had long ago proved to be a useless drunk. It was one of those terrible fractures, difficult to set. I had to set each bone in place, groping blindly, and only by a miracle did it turn out more or less well. Catalina stupefied the patient with her magic powders, dissolved in liquor, but even in his doped sleep Valdivia bellowed. It took several men to hold him for each of the procedures. I did my job without malice or rancor, attempting to save him suffering, though that was impossible. I can honestly say that I did not even remember his ingratitude. Pedro thought so many times that he would die of the pain that he dictated his will to González de Marmolejo, sealed it, and sent it to be kept under lock and key in the office of the town hall. When it was opened after his death, it stipulated, among other things, that Rodrigo de Quiroga should replace him as gobernador. I recognize that Pedro's two Spanish concubines tended him diligently, and it is partly owing to their ministrations that he walked again, although he would limp badly for the rest of his life.

Juan Gómez did not have to torture anyone to find the guilty party responsible for the crime of beheading Sultán; within a half hour everyone knew it had been Felipe. At first I could not believe it, because the young Mapuche adored the animal. Once when Sultán was wounded by Indians in Marga-Marga, Felipe took care of him for weeks; he slept with him, fed him by hand, cleaned him, and treated his wounds until he recovered. The bond between the youth and the horse was so strong that Pedro was often jealous, but since no one looked after Sultán as well as Felipe, he chose not to intervene. The Mapuche boy's skill with horses was legend by then, and Valdivia meant to name him *yegüerizo*, keeper of the mares, when he was old enough, a very respected office in a colony in which breeding horses was fundamental.

Felipe killed his noble friend by opening the large vein in his neck, so he would not suffer, then cut off his head with a machete. Defying the curfew, and using the cover of darkness, he set the head in the plaza and fled the town. He left his clothing and his few belongings in a bundle in the blood-splattered stable. He left naked, wearing the same amulet around his neck he had worn when he'd arrived years before. I imagine him racing barefoot across the soft earth, filling his lungs with the secret fragrances of the forest—bay, *quillai*, rosemary—splashing through pools and crystalline streams, swimming icy rivers, with the boundless sky overhead: free at last. Why would he do something so barbarous to the animal he loved? The sibylline explanation from Catalina, who had never liked him, was accurate. "You do not see then, *mamitay*, that the Mapuche is going back with his own kind?"

I can imagine that Pedro de Valdivia exploded with rage at what had happened, swearing the most horrible punishment for his favorite stable hand, but he had to postpone his vengeance because he had more serious matters at hand. He had just negotiated an alliance with his principal enemy, the cacique Michimalonko, and was organizing a great campaign in the south to subjugate the Mapuche. The aged cacique, on whom the years had left no trace, had recognized the advantages of allying himself with the *huincas*, seeing that he had not been able to defeat them. Aguirre's ruthless attacks had left him nearly stripped of warriors; only women and children were left in the north, half of whom were mestizos. Between perishing and fighting the Mapuche of the south, with whom he had had problems in recent times because he had not kept his promise to destroy the Spaniards, he opted for the latter choice; that way he at least saved his dignity and did not have to put his men to working the earth and mining gold for the *huincas*.

I, however, could not get Felipe out of my mind. To me Sultán's death seemed a symbolic act. With those blows of the machete he had assassinated the gobernador; following that, there was no turning back, he had broken from us forever and taken with him all the information he had gathered through years of intelligent pretense. I remembered the first Indian attack on the growing town of Santiago in the spring of 1541, and found in it the key to the role Felipe had played in our lives. On that occasion, the Indians had covered themselves with dark mantles and crawled toward the town at night, unseen by the sentinels, just as the troops of the marqués de Pescara had done in Europe with white sheets in the snow. Felipe had heard Pedro tell that story more than once, and had transmitted the idea to the *toquis*. His frequent disappearances were not casual; they were linked to a fierce determination nearly impossible to imagine in a boy his age. He could leave the town to hunt without being bothered by the hostile forces that held us hostage, because he was one of them. He used his hunting trips as a pretext for meeting with his people and reporting on us. It was he who brought us the news that Michimalonko's men were gathering near Santiago, he who had helped prepare the ambush to send Valdivia and half our defenders away from the town, and he who advised the Indians of the propitious moment to attack us. And where was Felipe during the attack on Santiago? In the uproar of that terrible day we forgot about him. He had hidden or gone to help our enemies; perhaps he contributed to setting the fires, I don't know. For years Felipe had devoted himself to studying horses, breaking them and breeding them; he listened attentively to the soldiers' stories and learned about military strategy; he knew how to use our weapons, from a sword to a harquebus to a cannon; he knew our strengths and our weaknesses. We believed that he admired Valdivia, his *taita*, whom he served better than anyone else, but in truth he was spying on him, while deep inside he nourished his bitterness against the invaders of his land. Sometime later we learned that he was the son of a *toqui*, the last of a long line of chiefs, as proud of his warrior ancestors as Valdivia was of his. I imagine the terrible hatred that darkened Felipe's heart. And now that eighteen-year-old Mapuche, strong, slim as a reed, was running naked and swift toward the humid forests of the south where his tribes awaited him.

His real name was Lautaro, and he became the most famous *toqui* in the land of the Araucans, a feared demon to the Spaniards, a hero to the Mapuche, a prince of the epic war. Under his command, the undisciplined hordes of Indians were organized, like the best armies in Europe, into squadrons, infantry, and cavalry. To stop a horse without killing it—they were as prized by them as by us—they used *boleadoras*, two stones tied to the ends of a rope that was thrown around the horse's hooves to bring it to the ground, or around the rider's neck to dismount him. Lautaro sent his men to steal horses, and devoted himself to breeding and breaking them, as he bred and trained the dogs. He trained his men and made them into the best horsemen in the world, copies of himself, and the Mapuche cavalry came to be invincible. He replaced the old heavy, clumsy clubs with shorter, more efficient ones. In each battle, he captured the enemy's weapons in order to use and copy them. He set up a system of communication so efficient that the very last of his warriors received their *toqui*'s orders instantly, and he imposed an iron discipline, comparable only to that of the celebrated Spanish tercios. He turned women into ferocious warriors, and used children to transport provisions, equipment, and messages. He knew the terrain, and preferred to hide his armies in deep forests, but when necessary he built *pukaras* in inaccessible sites, where he prepared his people while his spies informed him of each move by the enemy so that he would have the advantage. He could not, however, change his warriors' bad custom of, after every victory, drinking chicha and *muday* to the point of insensibility. Had he achieved that, the Mapuche would have exterminated our army in the south. Thirty years later, the spirit of Lautaro continues to lead his armies, and his name will resound through the centuries; we will never defeat him.

We learned about the epic Lautaro a little later, when Pedro de Valdivia marched south to found new cities, with the dream of extending the conquest to the Strait of Magellan. "If Francisco Pizarro conquered Peru with a little over a hundred soldiers to fight the thirty-five thousand men of Atahualpa's army, it would be embarrassing if these Chilean savages stopped us," he proclaimed to a meeting in the town hall. He had two hundred well-outfitted soldiers, four captains, among them the valiant Jerónimo de Alderete, hundreds of Yanacona bearers, and, in addition, Michimalonko riding the horse Valdivia had given him and leading his undisciplined, but brave, bands. The horsemen wore full armor, the foot soldiers breastplate and sword, and even the Yanaconas had helmets to protect their heads from the formidable clubs of the Mapuche. The only jarring note in this military panoply was that Valdivia had to be transported on a litter, like a courtesan, because the pain in his fractured leg, not yet completely healed, prevented him from riding. Before setting out, he sent the fearsome Francisco de Aguirre to rebuild La Serena and found other cities in the north, which had been nearly depopulated by the exterminating campaigns that same Aguirre had carried out earlier, and by the mass withdrawal of Michimalonko's people. Valdivia named Rodrigo de Quiroga to be his representative in Santiago, the one captain unanimously obeyed and respected. Thus, by one of those unexpected turns in life, I was again the gobernadora, a responsibility I have always borne, though the title was not always legitimately mine.

Lautaro flees Santiago on the darkest night of summer, unseen by the sentinels, and unbetrayed by the dogs, which know him. He is running along the banks of the Mapocho, invisible in the high reeds and ferns. He does not use the rope bridge of the *huincas*, but throws himself into the black waters and swims, with a yell of happiness in his breast. The cold water washes him inside and out, leaving him free of the odor of the *huincas*. With long strokes, he crosses the river and emerges on the other side, reborn. *Inche Lautaro!* he yells. I am Lautaro. He waits motionless on the bank as the warm air evaporates the moisture on his skin. He hears the screech of a *chon-chón*, the spirit with the body of a bird and the face of a man, and replies with a similar call, then feels very close by the presence of his guide, Guacolda. He must strain to see her, although his eyes are already adjusted to the darkness, because she has the gift of the wind; she is invisible; she can pass through enemy lines and the men do not see her or the dogs smell her. Guacolda, five years older than he, his betrothed. He has known her since childhood, and knows that he belongs to her, just as she belongs to him. He has seen her every time he escaped from the town of the *huincas* to deliver information to the tribes. She was his contact, his swift messenger. It was she who led him to the city of the invaders when he was a boy of eleven, with clear instructions about the role he was to play, learning about the *huincas*, she who observed from nearby when he attached himself to the priest dressed in black, and followed him to town. In his last meeting with Guacolda, she'd told him to flee on the next moonless night, because his time with the enemy was ended; he knew everything he needed to know and his people were waiting for him. When she sees him arrive that night without his *huinca* clothing, naked, Guacolda greets him—*mari mari*—then for the first time kisses him on the lips, licks his face, touches him as a woman touches to establish her claim on him. *Mari mari*, Lautaro replies; he knows that the moment for love is approaching; soon he will steal Guacolda from her *ruka*, throw her over his shoulder and run away with her, as is their way. This he tells her, and she smiles, then leads him in a swift race toward the south, always the south. The amulet Lautaro never takes from his neck was given him by Guacolda.

Days later, the young people finally reach their destination. Lautaro's father, a much-respected cacique, presents him to the other *toquis* so that they may hear what his son has to say. The enemy is on the way; they are the same *huincas* who conquered the brothers to the north, Lautaro explains. They are approaching the Bío-Bío, the sacred river, with their Yanaconas and horses and dogs. With them is the traitor Michimalonko, and he is bringing the rest of his army of cowards to fight against their own brothers in the south. Death to Michimalonko! Death to the *huincas*!

Lautaro speaks for several days; he tells them that the harquebuses are pure noise and wind, that they need fear the swords, lances, hatchets, and dogs more; the captains wear coats of mail, which no wooden arrow or lance will penetrate; with them clubs must be used to stun and lassos to drag them from their horses, and once on the ground they are lost; it is easy to drag them down and hack them to pieces, because beneath the steel they are flesh. But take care! They have no fear. The foot soldiers have protection only on the chest and head, arrows will work with them. But take care! They, too, have no fear. The arrows must be poisoned so that the wounded do not come to fight again. The horses are crucial; we will try to capture them alive, especially the mares, for breeding. Boys must be sent by night to the outskirts of the camps of the *huincas* to throw poisoned meat to the dogs, which are always chained. We will set traps. We will dig deep holes and cover them with branches and the horses that fall in will be impaled on pikes set in the bottom. The Mapuche advantage is numbers, fleetness, and knowing the forest, says Lautaro. The *huincas* are not invincible; they sleep more than the Mapuche; they eat and they drink too much; they need bearers because the weight of their supplies is too much for them to carry. We will buzz around them every minute, like wasps and horseflies; first we will tire them, then we will kill them. The *huincas* are people, they die as the Mapuche die, but their ways are the ways of demons. In the north they burned alive entire tribes. They want us to accept a god that is nailed upon a cross, a god of death; they want us to submit ourselves to a king we do not know, who does not live here; they want to occupy our land and have us as their slaves. Why, I ask my people? For no reason, brothers. They do not appreciate freedom. They do not understand pride; they obey, they put their knees to the ground, they bow their heads. They do not know justice or retribution. The *huincas* are madmen, but they are evil madmen. And I tell you, brothers, the Mapuche will never be their prisoners, we will die fighting. We will kill the men, but we will take children and women alive. The women will be our *chiñuras*, and, if we wish, we will trade their children for horses. It is just. We will be silent and swift, like fish; they will never know we are near until we fall upon them and take them by surprise. We will be patient hunters. The battle will be long. Let our people prepare.

While the young general Lautaro organizes strategy by day and by night hides with Guacolda in the thicket to make love, the tribes choose the war chiefs who will be in charge of the squadrons, and who in turn will be under the orders of the *ñidoltoqui* who is *toqui* of *toquis*: Lautaro. The afternoon air is warm in the clearing of the forests, but as soon as night falls, it will be cold. The tourneys have begun with weeks of anticipation, the candidates have competed and one by one have been eliminated. Only the strongest, with greatest endurance, only those with most courage and will, can aspire to the title of war *toqui*.

One of the strong braves leaps into the ring. *Inche Caupolicán!* he calls out. He is naked except for a short apron covering his sex, but he wears the thongs of his rank tied about his arms and his brow. Two husky youths walk to a felled oak—the *pellín*—they have trimmed and prepared, and with difficulty lift it, one at each end. They display it so that those gathered there can appreciate it and calculate its weight; then they carefully place it on the strong shoulders of Caupolicán. The man's waist and knees yield as he accepts the tremendous load, and for a moment it seems that he will be crushed beneath it, but he immediately straightens. The muscles of his body tense, his skin gleams with sweat, the veins of his neck stand out, near bursting. A quiet *hunh* escapes the circle of spectators as Caupolicán begins to walk, taking short steps, measuring his strength so he will last the necessary number of hours. He must win over others as strong as he. His one advantage is his fierce determination to die in the test before ceding first place. He intends to lead his people to combat; he wants his name to be remembered; he wants children with Fresia, the young woman he has chosen, and they must carry his blood with pride. He settles the trunk against the nape of his neck, bearing its weight on his shoulders and arms. The rough bark digs into his skin and fine threads of blood run down his broad shoulders. He takes deep breaths of the intense scent of the forest, feels the relief of the breeze and the dew. The dark eyes of Fresia, who will be his woman if he is winner of the competition, bore into his, with no trace of compassion, but with love. In that gaze she urges him to triumph; she desires him, but she will wed only the best. Bright in her hair is a copihue, the red flower of the forests that grows in the air, a drop of the blood of Mother Earth, a gift from Caupolicán, who climbed the highest tree to bring it to her.

The warrior walks in circles, bearing the weight of the world on his shoulders, and saying: *We are the dream of the Earth; she dreams us. Also in the stars are beings that are dreamed, and that have their own marvels. We are dreams within dreams. We are married to nature. We greet the Holy Earth, our mother, to whom we sing in the tongue of the Araucaria and the cinnamon, of the cherry and the condor. Let the flowering winds bring the voice of the ancestors so that our gaze may be hard. Let the courage of the ancient* toquis *flow through our blood. The ancients tell us that it is the hour of the hatchet. The grandfathers of the grandfathers watch over us and sustain our arms. It is the hour of combat. We must die. Life and death are but one . . .*

The warrior recites this endless rogative for hours, all the while balancing the tree trunk on his shoulders. He invokes the spirits of nature to defend his land, its plentiful waters, its dawns. He invokes the ancestors to turn the arms of his men into lances. He invokes the mountain pumas to lend their strength and courage to the women. The spectators grow weary, the night mist falls upon them; some burn small campfires for light; they chew grains of toasted corn; others sleep or leave, but later return, amazed. An aged machi spatters Caupolicán with a branch of the cinnamon tree dipped in sacrificial blood to give him fortitude. She is afraid, this woman, because the night before in her dreams the snake-fox, *ñeru-filú*, and the serpent-rooster, *piwichén*, appeared to tell her that much blood will flow in the war, that the Bío-Bío will run red to the end of time. Fresia pours a gourd of water over Caupolicán's dry lips. He sees the hard hands of his beloved on his chest, touching his stone muscles, but he does not feel them, just as he no longer feels pain or exhaustion. He keeps speaking, in a trance; he is sleepwalking. And so the hours pass, the entire night, and the dawn comes, as light sifts through the leaves of the tall trees. The warrior floats in the cold mist rising from the ground; the first golden rays of sun bathe his body, and he continues with a dancer's tiny steps, his back red with blood, his words flowing. *We are in* hualán, *the sacred time of the fruit, when the Holy Mother gives us food, the time of the* piñon *and the young of animals and women, sons and daughters of* Ngenechén.

Before the time of rest, the time of cold and of the dream of the Mother Earth, the huincas *will come.*

Word has traveled across the mountains, and warriors of other tribes are appearing and the clearing in the forest fills with people. The circle Caupolicán is tracing is growing smaller. Now they urge him on; again the machi sprinkles him with fresh blood. Fresia and other women wash his body with wet rabbit skins; they give him water; they put a portion of chewed food in his mouth so he can swallow without interrupting the poetic flow of words. The elder *toquis* bow before the warrior with respect; they have never seen anything like this. The sun warms the earth and burns off the mist; the air fills with transparent butterflies. Above the treetops, large against the sky, is the imposing figure of the volcano, with its eternal column of smoke. More water for the warrior, the machi orders. Caupolicán, who long before has won the competition but does not put down the trunk, continues walking and talking. The sun reaches its zenith and begins to descend, disappearing among the trees, and still he does not stop. Thousands of Mapuche have gathered and the multitude occupies the clearing, the entire forest; others arrive from the hills; *trutrucas* and *kultrunes* resound, announcing the feat to the four winds. Fresia never takes her eyes from those of Caupolicán; they sustain him, they guide him.

At last, when it is again night, the warrior stoops, lifts the tree above his head, holds it there for a few instants, and tosses it far away. Lautaro has his lieutenant. Oooooooohm! Oooooooooohm! The deafening cry races through the forest, echoes among the mountains, travels across all Araucanía, and reaches the ears of the *huincas* many leagues away. Oooooooooooohm!

It took Valdivia nearly a month to reach Mapuche territory, and during that time he was able to mend enough that occasionally he could ride, though with great difficulty. As soon as they made camp, the daily attacks began. The Mapuche swam the same rivers that blocked the Spaniards, who could not cross without boats because of the weight of their armor and supplies. While some of the Indians confronted the dogs, bare chested, knowing they would be eaten alive but willing to perform the mission of slowing the dogs, others threw themselves against the Spaniards. They left dozens of dead, led away the wounded who could still stand, and disappeared into the forest before the soldiers could organize to follow them. Valdivia gave the order for half of his reduced army to stand guard while the other half rested, in shifts of six hours. Despite the harassment, the gobernador pressed forward, winning each skirmish. He plunged deeper and deeper into Araucan territory without encountering large parties of Indians, only scattered groups whose explosive surprise attacks tired his soldiers but did not stop them; they were used to facing an enemy a hundred times their size. The only uneasy person was Michimalonko; he knew all too well whom they would soon be dealing with.

And it happened. The first serious confrontation with the Mapuche took place in January 1550, when the *huincas* had reached the banks of the Bío-Bío, the line that marked inviolable Mapuche territory. The Spaniards had camped beside a lake of crystalline water, in a well-situated place where their backs were protected by the clear icy waters of the lake. They had not considered that the enemy would come by water, quick and silent, like sea lions. The sentinels saw nothing, the night seemed calm, until suddenly they heard the clamor of the dread *chivateo*: yells, flutes, and drums, and the earth shaking with the beat of the naked feet of thousands and thousands of warriors: Lautaro's men. The Spanish cavalry, which was always prepared to strike, rode out to meet them, but the Indians did not flee as they always had before the charge; instead they stood their ground with a wall of upraised lances. The horses reared and their riders had to fall back, as the harquebusiers loosed their first volley. Lautaro had advised his men that it took a few minutes to reload the fire-breathing weapons, during which the soldier was defenseless; that gave them time to attack. Undone by the total fearlessness of the Mapuche, who were fighting hand to hand against soldiers in armor, Valdivia organized his troops as he had in Italy: compact squadrons protected by breast armor, raised lances and swords, while Michimalonko and his forces took up the rear. The ferocious combat lasted until night, when Lautaro's army retired, not in precipitous flight but in an orderly withdrawal at a signal from the *kultrunes*.

"Never in the New World has there been anything like these warriors," a debilitated Jerónimo de Alderete commented.

And Valdivia added, "And never in my life have I met such ferocious enemies. I served his majesty for more than thirty years, and I have fought against many nations, but I have never seen such tenacious fighters as these Indian Mapuche."

"What do we do now?"

"We found a city right here. It has all the advantages: a safe bay, broad river, wood, fishing—"

"And thousands of savages as well," Alderete pointed out.

"First we build a fort. Everyone except the sentinels and the wounded will be assigned to cutting down trees and putting up barracks and a wall with a moat—which we will need. We will see if these barbarians dare come after us."

They dared, of course. The Spaniards had scarcely built the wall when Lautaro appeared with an army so enormous the terrified sentinels calculated that there were a hundred thousand men. "There are not half that many, and we can handle them," Valdivia encouraged his people. *"Viva España!"* He was impressed more by the boldness and mindset of his enemy than by their numbers. The Mapuche marched with perfect discipline in four divisions under the command of their war *toquis*. The *chivateo* they used to terrify their enemy was now reinforced with flutes made from the bones of Spaniards who had fallen in the previous battle.

"They will not dare cross the moat and the wall. The harquebusiers will stop them," was Alderete's proposal.

"If we take shelter in the fort, they can lay siege and starve us out," Valdivia countered.

"Lay siege? I don't think they will think of that; it is not a tactic the savages know."

"I'm afraid they have learned a lot from us. We must go out and meet them."

"There are too many of them; we can't beat them that way."

"We can, with God's blessing," Valdivia replied.

He ordered Jerónimo de Alderete to ride out with fifty horsemen to confront the first Mapuche squadron, which was steadily marching toward the gate despite a first round of fire that had left many on the ground. The captain and his soldiers prepared to obey without comment, even though they were convinced they were riding to a sure death. Valdivia bid his friend farewell with an emotional embrace. They had known each other for many years, and together had survived uncounted dangers.

Miracles do happen. That day there was a miracle, there is no other explanation, as will be told through century after century by the descendants of the Spaniards who witnessed it, and as the Mapuche will tell through generations to come.

Jerónimo de Alderete took his place at the head of his fifty-horse formation, and at his signal the gates were opened wide. The monstrous *chivateo* of the Indians greeted the cavalry as it rode out at a gallop. Within minutes a mass of warriors surrounded the Spaniards and Alderete instantly realized that to go farther would be suicidal. He ordered his men to regroup, but some of the horses were hampered by the *boleadoras* Lautaro's warriors had wrapped about their feet. From the wall, the harquebusiers fired the second volley of shots, but that did nothing to discourage the attackers' advance. Valdivia was poised to go out and back up the cavalry, even though that meant leaving the fort undefended against the remaining three Mapuche divisions, for he could not allow fifty of his men to be killed without going to their aid. For the first time in his military career, he feared he had committed an irreparable tactical error. The hero of Peru, who had defeated the army of Gonzalo Pizarro in masterly fashion, was stymied by savages. The war cries were horrendous; no one could hear orders and in the confusion one of the Spanish cavalrymen was killed by a shot from a badly aimed harquebus. Suddenly, when the Mapuche in the first squadron had won their ground, they began to retreat helter-skelter, almost immediately followed by the other three divisions. In a matter of minutes the attackers had abandoned the field and were fleeing back to the forests like hares.

Dumbfounded, the Spaniards could not imagine what the devil was happening; they were afraid that this was some new enemy tactic, since there was no other explanation for a precipitous retreat that ended the battle before it had barely begun. Valdivia did what his experience as a soldier dictated: he ordered a pursuit. This is how he described the action to the king in one of his letters: "And barely had the men on horseback ridden out when the Indians turned away, and the other three squadrons did the same. Fifteen hundred or two thousand Indians were killed; many others were killed by lances and some we captured."

Those who were present swore that the miracle was visible to everyone, that an angelic figure, brilliant as lightning, descended over the field, flooding the day with a supernatural light. Some believed they recognized the person of the apostle Santiago, Saint James, riding upon a white steed, and that he faced the savages, delivered an eloquent sermon, and ordered them to surrender to the Christians. Others saw the figure of Nuestra Señora del Socorro, a resplendent lady robed in gold and silver, floating high in the air. The Indian prisoners confessed they had seen a flame that traced a large arc in the sky and exploded with a great noise, leaving a trail of stars in the air. In later years scholars have offered different versions; they suggest that the "miracle" was a celestial meteor, something like an enormous rock that had broken away from the sun and fallen to earth. I have never seen one of those meteors, but I marvel that they take the form of Santiago or the Virgin, and also that one should fall precisely at a time and a place that so greatly favored the Spaniards. Miracle or meteor, I do not know, but the fact remains that the Indians fled in fear and the Christians were left masters of the field, celebrating an undeserved victory.

According to the news that reached Santiago, Valdivia took around three hundred prisoners—although he admitted only two hundred to the king—and ordered the following punishment: he had their right hands hacked off with hatchets, and their noses with knives. While several soldiers forced a prisoner to place his arm upon a block of wood and black executioners wielded their sharp hatchets, others cauterized the stumps by submerging them in boiling oil. That prevented the victim from bleeding to death, so he would be able to carry the lesson to his tribe. Then a third group mutilated the faces of the hapless Mapuche warriors. The Spaniards threw hands and noses into baskets as blood soaked the earth. In his letter to the king, Valdivia said that after dispensing justice, he called the captives together and spoke to them, for among them were caciques and other important Indians. He declared that he had done that "because he had sent messages many times with conditions for peace, and they had not been answered." On top of their torture, then, the Indians had to endure a harangue in Spanish. Those who still could stand went stumbling off toward the forest, to show their stumps to their fellows. Many of the amputees fainted, but then came to their senses and followed, filled with loathing, and not giving their victimizers the pleasure of seeing them beg or moan in pain. When the executioners were so weary and nauseated they could no longer lift the hatchets and knives, soldiers had to take their place. They threw basketloads of hands and noses into the river, where they floated down to the sea, carried by the bloody current.

When I heard what had happened, I asked Rodrigo what the purpose of that carnage had been; in my eyes it seemed that it would bring horrible consequences because after such an event we could not expect mercy from the Mapuche, only the worst vengeance. Rodrigo explained that sometimes these things were needed to frighten the enemy.

"And would you have done the same?" I wanted to know.

"I think not, Inés, but I wasn't there, and I cannot judge the captain general's decisions."

"I was with Pedro for ten years, Rodrigo, through good and bad times, and this does not sound like the person I knew. Pedro has changed greatly, and I must tell you that I am happy we are no longer together."

"War is war. I pray to God that it will soon end, and that we can found this nation in peace."

"If war is war, we can also justify Francisco de Aguirre's massacres in the north," I told him.

Following the brutal object lesson, Valdivia collected what food and animals were left to confiscate from the Indians and took them back to the fort. He sent messengers to all the towns, announcing that in fewer than four months, with the aid of the apostle Santiago and Nuestra Señora, he had made progress in imposing peace in the land. I thought he was a little quick to sing victory.

In the three years he had left to live, I saw Pedro de Valdivia very seldom, and had news of him only through other people. While Rodrigo and I were prospering almost without realizing it, and wherever we looked our herds were flourishing, our crops were multiplying, and gold was leaping from the rock, the gobernador was devoting himself to building forts and founding cities in the south. First he would plant the cross and the flag, and if there was a priest, they would hold mass. Then he would erect the "tree of justice," or gallows, and begin to cut trees for building a defensive wall and dwellings. The most difficult part of the venture was to find people to populate the settlement, but little by little soldiers and their families would arrive. That was how, among others, Concepción, La Imperial, and Villarrica came about, the latter near the gold found on a tributary of the Bío-Bío. Those mines produced so generously that gold dust was used to buy bread, meat, fruit, vegetables—anything for sale, since gold was the only currency. Merchants, tavern keepers, and vendors went about carrying scales for buying and selling. The conquistadors' dream had come true, and now no one dared call Chile the "country of *rotos*," or the "graveyard of Spaniards." The city of Valdivia was founded at that time, so named at the insistence of the captains, not because of the gobernador's vanity. Its coat of arms describes it: "a river and a city of silver." Soldiers told that hidden in the depths of the cordillera was the famed City of the Caesars, all gold and precious stones, defended by beautiful Amazons—in other words, the persistent El Dorado myth—but Pedro de Valdivia, a practical man, did not waste time or manpower looking for it.

Numerous military reinforcements came to Chile by land and by sea, but they were never enough to occupy that vast territory of coast, forest, and mountain. To win his soldiers' loyalty, the governor distributed lands and Indians with his usual generosity, but these were empty gifts, poetic intentions, since the lands were virgin and the natives indomitable. The Mapuche would work only when brutally forced.

Valdivia's leg had healed, and though it was always painful, he could now ride a horse. Tirelessly he traveled across the vast south with his small army, penetrating dark, humid forests where a high canopy of green was pierced by araucaria pines that traced an austere geometry against the sky. The horses' hooves sank into soft, fragrant humus as the riders slashed their way through the at times impenetrable growth of ferns. They crossed streams of frigid water where birds often could be seen trapped in ice along the banks, the same waters in which Mapuche mothers submerged their newborn infants. The lakes were pristine mirrors of the intense blue of the skies, so calm that one could count the pebbles on the bottom. Spiders wove their dew-pearled lace among the branches of oaks, myrtles, and hazel trees. Forest birds chirped their chorus: finches, crown sparrows, linnets, ringdoves, and thrushes, even the "carpenter bird," the woodpecker marking time with his eternal drumming. As the soldiers passed, they flushed clouds of butterflies, and curious deer came near enough to greet them. Light filtered through the leaves, projecting patterns onto the ground, and mist rising from the warm earth wrapped the world in a mysterious vapor. Rain, more rain; rivers; lakes; white, foaming waterfalls: a liquid universe.

And always in the background, the snow-capped mountains, smoking volcanoes, drifting clouds. The autumn landscape was gold and blood red, bejeweled, magnificent. Pedro de Valdivia's soul escaped his body, captured among slim, moss-covered tree trunks as soft as velvet. The Garden of Eden, the promised land, paradise. Mute, his face wet with tears, the conquered conqueror was coming to know the place where the land ends: Chile.

On one occasion, Valdivia was riding with his soldiers through a forest of hazel trees, when bits of gold began to rain from the treetops. Speechless before such a marvel, the soldiers jumped from their horses and rushed to collect the yellow nuggets, while Valdivia, as astounded as his men, attempted to instill order. The enthralled Spaniards, quarreling over the gold, looked up to find themselves surrounded by a hundred Mapuche archers whom Lautaro had taught to aim at the vulnerable parts of the body not covered by armor. In fewer than ten minutes, the woods were strewn with dead and wounded. Before the survivors could react, the Indians had disappeared, as stealthily as they had moments before materialized. Later the Spaniards found that the lure had been river pebbles covered with a thin layer of gold.

Some weeks later, another detachment of Spaniards, exploring the region, heard female voices. They rode forward at a trot and parted the ferns to be met by the seductive scene of a group of girls bathing in the river, their heads crowned with flowers, their long black hair their only covering. These mythic Undines continued their frolic with no signs of fear as the soldiers spurred their horses and charged toward the river with yells of anticipation. The lust-filled, bearded satyrs did not get far before their horses sank up to their flanks in the swamp bordering their side of the river. The men dismounted, intending to pull the animals toward solid ground, but imprisoned in their heavy armor they, too, began to sink, at which point Lautaro's implacable archers had appeared and riddled the Spaniards with arrows while the naked Mapuche beauties celebrated the carnage from the far shore.

Valdivia soon realized that he had come up against a general as skillful as himself, someone who knew the Spaniards' weaknesses, but he was not overly concerned; he was certain of triumph. The Mapuche, however warlike and cunning they might be, could not measure up against the military might of his experienced captains and soldiers. It was only a question of time, he said, before the land of the Araucans would be his. It did not take long to learn the name traveling from mouth to mouth. Lautaro, the *toqui* who dared defy the Spaniards. Lautaro. It never occurred to Valdivia that the famed warrior was his former stable boy Felipe; he discovered that the day of his death. He would stop in the isolated hamlets of the colonists and preach his invincible optimism. Juana Jiménez accompanied him, as I once had done, while María de Encio stewed in her own juices in Santiago. Valdivia wrote letters to the king, reiterating that the savages understood the need to accept the designs of his majesty and the blessings of the Christian faith, and that he had tamed that most beautiful, fertile, peaceful land in which all that was lacking were Spaniards and horses. Among those messages, he interspersed requests for new favors, which the emperor ignored.

Pastene, the admiral of a flotilla composed of two ancient ships, explored the coast from north to south, and back north again, fighting invisible currents, black waves, and proud winds that shredded his sails, in a vain search for the passage between the two oceans. It would be a different captain, in 1554, who would locate the strait Magellan had discovered in 1520. Pedro de Valdivia died before it was found, and before fulfilling his dream of extending the conquest to that point on the map.

In Pastene's pilgrimage, he sailed to idyllic places he described with Italian eloquence, omitting the abuses others reported. In one remote inlet, his sailors were welcomed with food and gifts by friendly Indians, whom the Spaniards rewarded by raping the women, killing many of the men, and capturing others they took in chains to Concepción, where they exhibited them like animals in a fair. Valdivia believed that this incident, like so many in which his soldiers behaved badly, did not merit paper and ink. He did not mention it to the king.

Other captains, like Villagra and Alderete, came and went, galloping through valleys, scaling mountains, disappearing into forests, sailing the lakes, leaving marks of their harsh presence all through that enchanted region. They would from time to time tangle briefly with bands of Indians, but Lautaro was careful not to show his true strength while he was meticulously laying his plans in the heart of Araucanía. Michimalonko had been killed in an encounter with Lautaro, and some of his warriors had allied themselves with their brothers, the Mapuche, but Valdivia was successful in retaining a good number of them. The gobernador insisted on pushing his conquest toward the south, but the more territory he occupied, the less he could control. He had to leave soldiers in each city to protect the settlers, and assign others to exploring, punishing the Indians, and stealing cattle and food. His army was divided into small parties that might go for months without communicating among themselves.

During the raw winter, the conquistadors took refuge in the settlements, which they called towns; it took enormous energy for them to move heavy supplies across swampy ground, even more when exposed to rain and dawn frosts and the bone-penetrating winds off the snows. From May to September the earth rested; everything grew still and only the raging rivers, beating rain, lightning, and thunderstorms interrupted the winter's sleep. In that time of rest and early dark, Valdivia was haunted by demons, and his soul was beset with premonitions and regrets. When he was not on his horse with his sword at his side, his mood was dark, and he convinced himself that he was pursued by bad fortune. In Santiago we heard rumors that the gobernador had changed greatly, that he was aging rapidly, that his men did not honor him with the blind trust of the early days. According to Cecilia, Valdivia's star rose when he met me and began to decline when he left me behind, a frightening theory because I do not want the glory for his successes or the guilt for his failures. Each of us is master of his or her own destiny. Valdivia spent those icy months indoors, bundled in wool ponchos, warming himself before a brazier, and writing his letters to the king as Juana Jiménez served him his *mate*, the bitter tea that helped him bear the pain of his old wounds.

In the meantime, Lautaro's warriors, invisible, were watching the *huincas* from the undergrowth, as their *ñidoltoqui* had ordered.

In 1552 Pedro de Valdivia traveled to Santiago. He did not know it would be his last visit, but he must have suspected because he was again tormented by black dreams. As he had before, he dreamed of massacres and awakened trembling in Juana's arms. How do I know? Because he was taking *latué* bark to frighten away the nightmares. Everyone knew everything in this land. When he arrived, he found a festive city awaiting him, prosperous and well organized because Rodrigo de Quiroga had governed wisely in his place. Our lives had improved in that couple of years. Rodrigo's house on the plaza had been renovated under my direction, converted into a mansion worthy of the teniente gobernador. As I had energy left over, I had built another residence a few blocks away, with the idea of giving it to you, Isabel, when you married. In addition, we had very comfortable houses on our summer *chacras*; I liked large rooms with high ceilings, galleries, orchards of fruit trees, medicinal plants, flowers. I kept domestic animals in the third patio, well guarded to protect them from being stolen. I made sure that the servants had decent quarters; it makes me angry when I see that other colonists treat their horses better than the people who serve them. As I have never forgotten that I come from humble origins, I have no problem getting along with our servants, who have always been very loyal to me. They are my family.

During those years, Catalina, still strong and healthy, tended to domestic matters, though I kept an eye on things to assure that my own servants were not abused. There were not enough hours for me to perform all my chores. I was involved with a number of businesses, with building and helping Rodrigo in his affairs, in addition to my charities—never enough time there. The line of impoverished Indians who ate in our kitchen every day wound around the Plaza de Armas. It was so long that Catalina complained about the crowds and the dirt, so I decided to inaugurate a kitchen on a different street.

A black Senegalese woman named Doña Flor had come to Chile on a ship from Panama. She was a magnificent cook, and she took on that demanding task. You know who I mean, Isabel, the same woman you know. She came to Chile with no shoes on her feet, but today she wears brocade and lives in a mansion envied by the most prominent señoras in Santiago. Her cooking was so delicious that prominent señores began to complain that indigents were eating better than they were. Then Doña Flor came up with the idea of financing the food for the poor by selling her creations to the wealthy, and earning a little for herself in the process. That was how she became rich; it was good for her, but it did not solve my problem because as soon as her purse was filled with gold she forgot about the beggars, who soon were back at my door. And they are still there today.

When Rodrigo learned that Valdivia was on his way to Santiago, it was clear that he was worried. He could not think how he would handle the situation without offending someone, torn as he was among his official responsibilities, his loyalty to his friend, and his desire to protect me. It had been more than two years since we had seen my former lover, and we had been very happy in his absence. Once he arrived I would no longer be the gobernadora, and I wondered, with amusement, whether María de Encio would be up to the challenge. It was difficult for me to imagine her in my place.

"I know what you are thinking, Rodrigo. Don't worry, we won't have any problem with Pedro," I told him.

"Maybe it would be best if you took Isabel to the country . . . "

"I don't plan to run away, Rodrigo. This is my city too. While he is here I will not do anything connected with matters of government, but I will live the rest of my life as I always do." I laughed. "I am quite sure that I will be able to see Pedro without getting weak in the knees."

"You can't help running into him all the time, Inés."

"It will be more than that, Rodrigo. We will have to give him a banquet."

"A banquet?"

"Of course. We are the second-highest authority in Chile, and it is our place to lionize him. We will invite him and his María de Encio and, if he wishes, the other woman as well. What is the Galician woman's name?"

Rodrigo stood gazing at me with that querulous expression my ideas tended to provoke, but I planted a quick kiss on his forehead and assured him that there would not be a scandal of any kind. If truth be known, I already had several women stitching tablecloths, while Doña Flor, contracted for the occasion, was gathering the ingredients for the meal, especially the gobernador's favorite desserts. Ships brought us molasses and sugar, which, while costly in Europe, in Chile were exorbitant, but not every dessert could be made with honey, so I resigned myself to paying the asking price. I intended to impress the guests with an array of dishes never seen in our capital. "You would be better to be thinking what you will dress yourself in, then, *señorayy*," Catalina reminded me. So I had her iron an elegant dress of iridescent, coppery silk that had only recently arrived from Spain. It accentuated the color of my hair. All right, Isabel, I do not need to confess to you that I kept it that color with henna, something I learned from the Moors and the Gypsies. But you already know that. The dress was a little tight, it is true, since a happy life and Rodrigo's love had soothed my soul and relaxed my body, but at least I would look better than María de Encio, who dressed like a harlot, and her enterprising servant, who could not compete with me. Don't laugh, daughter. I know that may sound vicious, but it's true: those two were very common women.

Pedro de Valdivia made his triumphal entrance into Santiago beneath arches of leaves and flowers, cheered by the council and the whole town. Rodrigo de Quiroga, his captains, and his soldiers, in polished armor and plumed helmets, formed in the Plaza de Armas. María de Encio, in the doorway of the house that once was mine, stood awaiting her master, squirming with coquettish little laughs and hand flutterings. What an odious woman! I was careful not to be seen; I observed the spectacle from afar, peeking through a window. It seemed to me that the years had suddenly caught up with Pedro; he was heavier and he moved ponderously—I don't know whether out of arrogance, added weight, or the fatigue of the journey.

That night, I suppose, the gobernador rested in the arms of his two women, but the next day he went to work with suitable zeal. He received Rodrigo's complete and detailed report on the state of the colony and the town, reviewed the treasurer's books, heard the council's complaints, and dealt one by one with citizens who came with their petitions or hopes for justice. He had become a pompous, impatient, haughty, and tyrannical man. He could not tolerate the slightest contradiction without spewing threats. He no longer sought counsel or shared his decisions but behaved as if he were a sovereign. He had been too long at war, accustomed to being obeyed without a word from his soldiers. It seems that he gave his captains and friends the same peremptory treatment, but he was amicable with Rodrigo de Quiroga; obviously he intuited that Rodrigo was a man who commanded respect. According to Cecilia, whom nothing escaped, Valdivia's concubines and servants were terrified of him, and he vented all his frustrations on them, from aching bones to the obstinate silence of the king, who never answered his letters.

The banquet in honor of the gobernador was one of the most spectacular events I presented during the course of my long life. Just making the list of dinner guests was a task, since we could not include all five hundred townspeople. Many important people were left waiting for an invitation. Santiago was buzzing with talk; everyone wanted to come to the banquet, and I received unexpected gifts and profuse messages of friendship from persons who the day before had barely looked at me. None of it mattered; we had to limit ourselves to the captains who had come with us to Chile in 1540, the king's representatives, and members of the council. We brought in additional Indians from our country houses and dressed them in impeccable uniforms, though we could not get them into shoes. The evening was brilliantly lighted by hundreds of candles, tallow lamps, and pine-resin torches that perfumed the air, and the house was splendidly decorated with flowers, large platters of seasonal fruits, and cages of songbirds. We served a good Spanish wine and a Chilean one that Rodrigo and I had begun to produce. We sat thirty guests at the head table, and another hundred in other rooms and in the patios. I made the decision that the women would be seated with the men that night, as I had heard was the style in France, instead of on cushions on the floor, as they did in Spain. We butchered pigs and lambs, to offer a variety of dishes in addition to stuffed fowl and fish from the coast that had been transported live in seawater. There was one table with nothing but desserts: tortes, pastries, meringues, custards, puddings, and fruit. The breeze carried the aromas of the banquet through all the city: garlic, roast meat, caramel. The guests came in their gala clothes; they seldom had reason to pull their finest from the depths of their trunks.

The most beautiful woman at the fiesta was Cecilia, of course, in a sky blue dress with a gold belt and adorned in an array of her Inca princess jewels. She had brought a young black who stood behind her chair and fanned her with a feather fan, an urbane detail that left all the rest of us with mouths agape. Valdivia brought María de Encio, who did not look all that bad, I am forced to acknowledge, but not the other woman; it would have been a slap in the face to our small—but proud—society had he presented himself with a concubine on either arm. He kissed my hand and praised me with the flattery demanded by such occasions. I thought I detected in his gaze a mixture of sadness and jealousy, but that may just have been in my head. When we sat down at the table, he lifted his glass to toast Rodrigo and me, his hosts, and delivered some deeply felt words comparing the hard days of hunger in Santiago, only ten years before, with the present abundance.

"In this imperial banquet, my beautiful Doña Inés, only one

thing is lacking," he concluded, his glass held high and his eyes misty with emotion.

"Say no more, Your Mercy," I replied.

At that moment you came in, Isabel, dressed in organdy, wearing a flower and ribbon wreath on your head and carrying a silver tray covered with a white linen napkin on which was one empanada for the gobernador. Loud applause celebrated the moment, because everyone remembered the lean times, when we made empanadas from anything we had at hand, including lizards.

After the meal there was a ball, but Valdivia, who had been a lively dancer, with a good ear and natural grace, did not take part, blaming his refusal on the old hip injury. Once the guests had gone and the servants had distributed the remains of the banquet among the poor, who had come from the Plaza de Armas to listen to the sounds of revelry, after the house was closed up and the candles extinguished, Rodrigo and I fell, exhausted, into bed. I laid my head on his chest, as I always did, and slept without dreaming for six hours, which for me, a chronic insomniac, is an eternity.

The gobernador stayed in Santiago for three months. During that time, he made a decision that he had surely thought over carefully: he sent Jerónimo de Alderete to Spain to deliver sixty thousand gold pesos to the king, the *quinto* owed to the Crown, a ridiculous sum when compared to the gold-laden galleons that sailed from Peru. He carried letters for the monarch with assorted petitions; among others, that he, the gobernador of Chile, be granted a marquisate and also the Order of Santiago. Valdivia had changed; he was no longer the man who prided himself on disdaining titles and honors. Worse, once a person repelled by slavery, he requested permission to import two thousand black slaves without paying the tax. The second part of Alderete's mission was to visit Marina Ortiz de Gaete, still living in the modest home in Castuera, give her money, and invite her to come to Chile to act as gobernadora at the side of her husband, whom she had not seen for seventeen years. I would give anything to know how María and Juana welcomed that news.

I regret highly that Jerónimo de Alderete did not get back with a positive answer. He was gone nearly three years, as I recall, partly because of the delays of crossing the ocean, and partly because the emperor was not a man given to haste. During his return, as he crossed the isthmus of Panama, the captain contracted some tropical plague, and was dispatched to a better life. He was a very good soldier and loyal friend, that Jerónimo de Alderete. I hope that history will reserve the place for him he deserves. In the meantime, Pedro de Valdivia had died without learning that finally he had been granted the favors he requested.

When Marina Ortiz de Gaete received her husband's invitation to travel to this kingdom, which she imagined as another Venice—who could know why—along with the seven thousand five hundred gold pesos for her expenses, she bought herself a gilded throne, an imperial wardrobe, and came to Chile accompanied by an impressive retinue that included several members of her family. The poor woman came all that way to learn she was a widow, and additionally, that Pedro had left her as poor as a church mouse. To crown her bad fortune, before six months had passed, all of her nephews, whom she adored, had died in the war with the Indians. I can only pity her.

In those months that Pedro de Valdivia was in Santiago, we saw each other very little, and always at social gatherings where there were many other people; malicious eyes followed our every move, hoping to surprise some gesture of intimacy, or attempting to divine our sentiments. In this city no one could take a step without being spied on and criticized. Why did I put that in the past? Now, in 1580, people gossip as devotedly as ever. But though I had spent the most intense years of my youth with Pedro, I felt strangely indifferent toward him; it seemed that the man I had loved with desperate passion was a different person. Shortly before he announced his return to the south, where he planned to visit new cities and continue his search for the elusive Strait of Magellan, González de Marmolejo came to see me.

"I wanted to tell you, daughter, that the gobernador has asked the king to name me bishop of Chile," he told me.

"Everyone in Santiago knows that, Padre. Tell me why you have really come."

The priest laughed. "How bold you are, Inés!"

"Come on, speak, Padre."

"The gobernador wishes to talk with you privately, daughter, and clearly it cannot be in your house, or in his, or in a public place. We must maintain appearances. So I offered him my residence. . . ."

"Does Rodrigo know about this?"

"The gobernador does not think it necessary to bother your husband with such trifles, Inés."

I found the messenger, the message, and the secrecy suspicious, so I told Rodrigo that same day, to avoid problems, and from him learned that Valdivia had asked his permission to meet me alone. Why, then, did he want me to hide it from my husband? And why hadn't Rodrigo mentioned it to me? I suppose that the former wanted to put me to the test, but I do not believe that of the latter; Rodrigo was not capable of such deviousness.

"Do you know why Pedro wants to talk with me?" I asked my husband.

"He wants to explain why he acted the way he did, Inés."

"That was more than three years ago! And he's coming with explanations now? I find that very strange."

"If you don't want to talk with him, I will tell him that myself."

"It doesn't bother you that I will be alone with him?"

"I trust you completely, Inés. I would never insult you with jealousy."

"You do not act like a Spaniard, Rodrigo. You must have some Dutch blood in your veins."

The next day I went to the home of González de Marmolejo, after mine, the largest and most luxurious in Chile. The priest's fortune was obviously of miraculous origin. His Quechua housekeeper received me, a very wise woman who knew a lot about medicinal plants, and such a good friend she did not have to hide from me that she had for years lived as wife with the future bishop. She led me through several salons linked by double doors, carved by an artisan the priest had had brought from Peru, to a small room where Marmolejo had his desk and most of his books. The governor, elegantly dressed in a dark red doublet with slashed sleeves, greenish breeches, and a black silk cap with a dashing plume, came forward to meet me. The housekeeper discreetly withdrew and closed the door. When I found myself alone with Pedro, my heart raced and I could feel blood pounding in my temples. I thought I would not be capable of meeting the look in those blue eyes whose eyelids I had often kissed as he slept. However much Pedro had changed, at some moment he was the lover I had followed to the ends of the earth. Pedro put his hands on my shoulders and turned me toward the window, to observe me in the light.

"You are so beautiful, Inés! How can it be that time does not change you?" he sighed.

"You need spectacles," I told him, stepping back from his grasp.

"Tell me that you're happy. It is very important for me to know that."

"Why is that? Perhaps a bad conscience?"

He smiled, then he laughed, and we both took a deep breath of relief; the ice was broken. He told me in detail about the trial in Peru, and La Gasca's sentence; the idea of wedding me to someone else had come to him as the only way to save me from exile and poverty.

"When I proposed that solution to La Gasca, it was a dagger in my breast, Inés, and I am still bleeding. I have always loved you. You are the only woman in my life; the others are nothing. Seeing you married to someone else causes me unbearable pain."

"You were always jealous."

"Don't mock me, Inés. I suffer from not having you with me, but I am happy that you are rich and that you have married the finest hidalgo in this kingdom."

"That day when you sent González de Marmolejo to bring me

the news, he hinted that you had chosen someone for me. Was it
Rodrigo?"

"I know you too well to try to impose anything on you, Inés,
least of all a husband," he answered evasively.

"Then for your peace of mind, I will tell you that your inspiration was excellent. I am happy, and I love Rodrigo very much."

"More than me?"

"I no longer love you with that kind of love, Pedro."

"You are sure of that, Inés of my soul?"

Again he took my shoulders and pulled me toward him, seeking
my lips. I felt the tickle of his blond beard and the warmth of his
breath; I turned my face and softly pushed away from him.

"The thing you always most appreciated about me, Pedro, was
loyalty. I still have it, but now I owe it to Rodrigo," I told him,
sadly, because I sensed that at that moment we were saying good-
bye forever.

Pedro de Valdivia set out once again to continue his conquest and
to take reinforcements to the forts and seven recently founded cities. Several mines with rich veins had been discovered, and they
had attracted new colonists, including some from Santiago who
chose to leave their fertile haciendas in the Mapocho valley and
take their families to the mysterious forests in the south, dazzled
by the prospect of gold and silver. Twenty thousand Indians were
working the mines, and the production was almost as good as it
was in Peru. Among the colonists who left was our constable,
Juan Gómez, but Cecilia and his children did not go with him. "I
am staying here in Santiago. If you want to bury yourself in those
swamps, you go," Cecilia told him, never imagining that her words
were a foreshadowing.

When Rodrigo de Quiroga said good-bye to Valdivia, he advised
him not to take on more than he could handle. Some of the forts
were maintained by only a handful of soldiers, and several of the
cities had no protection.

"There is no danger, Rodrigo, the Indians have given us very few problems. The territory is won."

"It seems strange that the Mapuche, whose reputation for being unconquerable reached us in Peru before we ever began the conquest of Chile, have not put up the battle we expected."

"They have realized that we are too powerful an enemy, and have dispersed," Valdivia explained.

"If that is the case, it is a good turn of events, but be on your guard."

They embraced each other with real affection, and Valdivia left without a concern for Quiroga's warning. For several months we had no direct news of him, but we heard rumors that he was living the life of a Turk, lolling on pillows and growing fat in the house in Concepción he called his "winter palace." It was said that Juana Jiménez was hiding the gold from the mines, which was transported on large trays, to avoid having to share it or declare it to the king's officials. And jealous tongues added that between the gold he had amassed, and that still in the Quilacoya mines, Valdivia was wealthier than Charles V himself. That shows how quickly people judge their neighbors. I remind you, Isabel, that when Valdivia died, he did not leave a maravedí. Unless Juana Jiménez, instead of being kidnapped by Indians, as everyone believed, had stolen that fortune and escaped somewhere, Valdivia's treasure never existed.

Tucapel was the name of one of the forts built to discourage the Indians and protect the gold and silver mines, although no more than a dozen soldiers were posted there, and they spent boring days staring at the surrounding forest. The captain in charge of the fort suspected that the Mapuche were plotting something, even though the relationship between Spaniards and Mapuche had been peaceful. It was always the same Indians who brought provisions once or twice a week to the fort, and the soldiers, who by then recognized them, usually exchanged friendly greetings in sign language. There was, nevertheless, something in the Indians' attitude that motivated the captain to take several of them prisoner and, under torture, extract information about a great uprising the tribes were planning. I myself would swear that the Indians confessed only what Lautaro wanted the *huincas* to know, because Mapuche have never yielded under torture. The captain requested reinforcements, but Pedro de Valdivia attached so little importance to that information that all he sent to the Tucapel fort in the way of aid was five soldiers on horseback.

It was spring 1553 in the aromatic forests of Araucanía. The air was warm and the five soldiers rode through clouds of translucent insects and waves of birdsong. Suddenly an infernal racket broke the idyllic peace and the Spaniards found themselves surrounded by hordes of attackers. Three of them were run through with lances but two managed to whirl around and gallop at breakneck speed toward the closest fort to seek help.

In the meantime, the Indians who always brought the foodstuffs appeared in Tucapel, greeting the soldiers with the most docile air in the world, as if they knew nothing about the torture their fellows had endured. The soldiers opened the gates of the fort and allowed them to come in with their bundles. Once inside, the Mapuche unwrapped the packs, pulled out hidden weapons, and assaulted the soldiers. Once recovered from their surprise, the Spaniards flew to get swords and breastplates and defend themselves. In the next minutes a large number of Mapuche were slaughtered, and many were taken prisoner, but the stratagem was successful, for while the Spaniards were occupied with the Indians inside the fort, thousands had surrounded it. The captain rode out with eight of his men to take them on, a courageous but futile decision, for the enemy was far too numerous. At the end of a heroic battle, soldiers with any life remaining retreated to the fort, where the unequal battle continued the rest of the day, until finally, as it grew dark, the attackers fell back. Six soldiers were left in the Tucapel fort, the only surviving Spaniards, along with numbers of Yanaconas and prisoners. The captain took a desperate step to frighten away the Mapuche, who were waiting to attack again at dawn. He had heard the legend of how I had saved the town of Santiago by throwing the heads of their caciques toward the Indian warriors, and decided to duplicate that move. He had the captives decapitated, then threw their heads over the wall. In response came a long roar, swelling like a terrible wave on a stormy sea.

As the night passed, more and more Mapuche surrounded the fort, so many the six Spaniards realized that the only possibility of salvation was to try while it was still night to break through the enemy lines on horseback and head for the nearest fort, which was in Purén. That meant abandoning the Yanaconas, who did not have horses, to their fate. I have no idea how the Spaniards reached that audacious decision, because the forest was choked with Indians summoned from great distances by Lautaro for the great insurrection. It seems likely that he had some duplicitous reason for allowing them to escape. In any case, with the first light of dawn, the Indians who had been waiting all night burst into the abandoned fort and there in the courtyard found the bloody bodies of their companions. The unfortunate Yanaconas still in the fort were massacred.

The news of that first victorious attack reached Lautaro quickly, thanks to the communication system he himself had created. The young *ñidoltoqui* had formalized his union with Guacolda, after paying the traditional dowry. He had not participated in the warriors' drunken celebration because he had no love for alcohol, and he was also too busy planning the second phase of his campaign. His objective was Pedro de Valdivia.

Juan Gómez, who had reached the south the week before, did not have time to think about the gold mines that had induced him to leave his family, for as soon as he'd arrived, he received the cry for help from the fort in Purén, where the six surviving Tucapel soldiers had joined the eleven already there. Like every encomendero, Gómez had the obligation to go to war when called, and he did not hesitate to do so. He galloped to Purén and took charge of the small detachment. After hearing the details of what had happened in Tucapel, he felt sure that this was not a skirmish, like so many in the past, but the beginnings of a massive uprising of the southern tribes. He set up the best defense he could, but there was not much he could do in Purén with the meager materials at hand.

A few days later, at dawn, they heard the familiar *chivateo* and the sentinels sighted a Mapuche squadron at the foot of the hill; strangely, they whooped and yelled but did not attack. Juan Gómez calculated that there were five hundred enemies for each of his men, but he had the advantage in weapons, horses, and the discipline for which Spanish soldiers were famed. He had a lot of experience in fighting Indians, and knew that the best way to combat them was in open country, where the horses could maneuver and the harquebusiers were at best advantage. He decided to leave the fort and confront the enemy with what he had available: seventeen mounted soldiers, four harquebusiers, and two hundred Yanaconas.

The doors of the fort were opened and the detachment went out, with Juan Gómez in the lead. At his signal, they rode down the hill at a full gallop, swinging their terrible swords, but this time they were surprised when the Indians did not scatter as usual but held their formation. And now they were not naked; they wore protective pads on their torsos and sealskin headgear as hard as Spanish armor. They were carrying seven-foot lances pointed at the horses' breastbones, and their heavy wooden *macanas* were more manageable than the clubs they had traditionally carried. The Indians did not give way but took the charge of the horses head-on, impaling them on their lances. Several horses were killed but the soldiers quickly adjusted. Despite the fearful numbers of Mapuche killed by Spanish iron, they were undaunted.

An hour later, the Spaniards heard the unmistakable *tam-tam* of the *kultrunes*, and the warriors fell back, fading into the forest and leaving the field strewn with dead and wounded. The Spaniards' relief lasted only minutes before another thousand warriors came to take the places of those who had withdrawn. The Spaniards had no choice but to keep fighting. The Mapuche repeated this same strategy every hour: the drums sounded, the tired warriors disappeared and fresh ones took the field, while the Spaniards had no respite at all. Juan Gómez realized that it was not possible to combat that skillful maneuver with his reduced number of soldiers. The Mapuche, divided into four squadrons, rotated; while one group fought, the other three awaited their turn. Gómez was forced to give the order to return to the fort; his men, nearly all wounded, could not continue without rest and water.

In the last hours of the day they treated the wounded as best they could, and ate. At dusk, Juan Gómez considered the possibility of a new attack, to interrupt the enemy's rest during the night. Several of the wounded men said that they would rather die in battle; they knew that if the Indians got inside the fort, death would be inevitable, and without glory. By this time Gómez had only a dozen horsemen and half his foot soldiers, but that did not deter him. He lined up his men and addressed them with passion, he commended himself to God and to Santiago, the patron saint of Spain, and then ordered the attack.

The clash between iron and club lasted less than half an hour; the Mapuche seemed spiritless, they fought without the ferocity of the morning and, earlier than the Spaniards could have hoped, retired to the summons of their *kultrunes*. Gómez waited for the second wave to come, as it had that morning, but that did not happen, and though confused, he ordered the soldiers back to the fort. He had not lost a single man. During that night, and the day that followed, the Spaniards awaited the enemies' attack, not sleeping, clad in armor and holding their weapons, and still there was no sign of the Mapuche. Finally, convinced that they would not return, they knelt in the courtyard and gave thanks to Santiago for such a bizarre victory. They had defeated the enemy without knowing how.

Juan Gómez determined that they could not stay in the fort without communications, on edge, and waiting for the sound of the *chivateo* that would signal the return of the Mapuche. The best alternative would be to take advantage of the night hours, during which Indians rarely moved because they feared evil spirits, and send a couple of hard-riding messengers to Pedro de Valdivia, informing him of their inexplicable triumph but also warning him that a total rebellion of the tribes was forthcoming, and if it was not immediately crushed they could lose all the territory south of the Bío-Bío. The messengers galloped as quickly as the undergrowth and darkness permitted, fearful at every turn that the Indians would rush them, but that did not happen. They were able to travel without problem, and reached their destination at dawn. They had felt all during the night that the Mapuche were watching, hidden among the ferns, but as their foe had not attacked, they attributed the feeling to their own nerves. They could not imagine that Lautaro wanted Valdivia to receive the message and for that reason had let them through, which is just what he did with the messengers who carried the return letter from the gobernador, in which he told Gómez to join him in the ruins of Tucapel fort on Christmas Day. The *ñidoltoqui* had planned carefully; he had learned the contents of the letter through his spies, and he smiled with satisfaction. Now he had Valdivia where he wanted him. He sent a squadron to lay siege to the Purén fort, to prevent Juan Gómez from leaving to carry out those instructions, while he put the finishing touches on the trap he had set for his *taita* in Tucapel.

Valdivia had spent the lazy winter months in Concepción, playing cards and watching it rain, well looked after by Juana Jiménez. He was fifty-three years old, but lameness and excess weight had aged him before his time. He was good at cards and always lucky in the game; he nearly always won. Envious companions claimed that he added what he had won from other players to the gold from the mines, and that the sum ended up in Juana's mysterious trunks—which to this day have not been found. Spring had burst forth with buds and birds when the unconvincing news of an Indian uprising reached Valdivia, something he considered an exaggeration. More to fulfill a duty than out of conviction, Valdivia took fifty soldiers and reluctantly set out to join Juan Gómez in Tucapel, prepared to crush the brazen Mapuche, as he had done before.

He started the fifteen-league journey with his fifty horsemen and fifteen hundred Yanaconas at a slow pace, for he had to fit his progress to the speed of the bearers. Before long, however, he grew worried about how slowly they were moving; his soldier's instinct warned him of danger, and he could feel eyes watching from the undergrowth. For more than a year his own death had been much on his mind, and he had a presentiment that it would happen very soon; he did not, nevertheless, want to worry his men with his suspicion that they were being spied upon. As a precaution, he sent a party of five soldiers ahead to check out the route and he continued at the original pace, hoping the warm breeze and intense aroma of the pines would soothe his nerves. When a couple of hours had gone by and the five horsemen had not returned, his premonition grew sharper. Another league along the way, a soldier, with a cry of horror, pointed toward something hanging from a tree branch. It was an arm, still in the sleeve of a doublet. Valdivia ordered the party to proceed with weapons drawn. A short distance farther they saw a leg, still in its boot, it, too, hanging in a tree, and then every so often other trophies: legs, arms, heads . . . bloody fruit of the forest. "Revenge!" the outraged soldiers shouted, ready to gallop off in search of the assassins, but Valdivia forced them to rein in their anger. The worst thing they could do would be to break into smaller units; they had to stay together till they reached Tucapel.

The fort sat at the top of a barren hill; the Spaniards had cut down the trees to build the wall and the fort, but the base of the hill was all virginal forest. From the fort there was a view of a swift river. The cavalrymen rode up the hill and were the first to reach the smoking ruins, followed by the slow-moving lines of Yanaconas with the supplies. In accord with Lautaro's instructions, the Mapuche had waited till the last man reached the top to announce their presence with the blood-chilling sound of the flutes made from human bones.

The gobernador, who had barely had time to dismount, peered between the charred tree trunks of the wall and saw Indian formations of compact squadrons protected by shields, with their lances upright, resting on the ground. The war *toquís* were at the front, protected by a Praetorian guard. Astonished, Valdivia marveled that the savages had somehow instinctively discovered the ancient Romans' method of fighting, which was the same the Spanish *tercios* employed. Their general could only be that *toquí* they had heard so much about during the winter: Lautaro. Valdivia was shaken by a wave of anger as he realized that his body was bathed in sweat. "I personally will see that that damned savage dies an atrocious death!" he exclaimed.

Atrocious death. How many of those have there been in our kingdom? They will weigh forever on our consciences. I must, as an aside, say that Valdivia was never able to carry out his threat against Lautaro, who would die fighting at Guacolda's side a few years later. Within a short time, this military genius sowed panic through the Spanish towns in the south, forcing their evacuation, and succeeded in leading his armies to the very outskirts of Santiago. By that time the Mapuche were decimated by hunger and plague, but Lautaro continued to fight with a small, very disciplined army that included women and children. He directed the war with masterly cunning and arrogant courage for only a few years, but they were enough to inspire the Mapuche insurrection that lasts to this day.

According to what Rodrigo de Quiroga told me, there are very few generals throughout history who can compare to this young leader who converted a pack of naked tribes into the most feared army in America. After his death, he was replaced by the *toqui* Caupolicán, as courageous as he but not as astute, who was taken prisoner and sentenced to die seated naked on a pike. It is told that when his wife Fresia saw him being dragged along in chains, she threw their infant son at his feet, crying that she would not nurse the offspring of a conquered man, but that story seems to be another legend of the war, like that of the Virgin who appeared in the heavens in the midst of a battle. Caupolicán bore without a sound the hideous torture of the sharpened pole slowly penetrating his entrails, as is told in the verses of young Zurita—or was it Zúñiga?

God help me, names are escaping me; who knows how many errors there are in this account. Thankfully, I was not present when they tortured Caupolicán, just as I have not had to see the oft-applied punishment they call *desgobernación*, in which half the right foot of rebellious Indians is hacked off. Not even that discourages them: lamed, they keep on fighting. And when they cut off both hands of another cacique, Galvarino, he had weapons tied to his arms so he could return to the battle. After such horrors, we cannot expect mercy from the Mapuche. Cruelty engenders more cruelty, in an eternal cycle.

Valdivia, that decisive day, divided his men into units led by soldiers on horseback and followed by Yanaconas, and ordered them down the hill. He could not send the riders at a gallop, as was customary, because he knew that they would be speared on the lances of the Mapuche, who obviously had learned European tactics. First he would have to disarm the lancers. In the first encounter, Spaniards and Yanaconas had the advantage, and after a brief, intense, and merciless fight, the Mapuche fell back in the direction of the river. A shout of triumph celebrated their retreat, and Valdivia ordered his troops back to the fort. His soldiers were confident that the victory was theirs, but Valdivia was uneasy because the Mapuche had left in perfect order. From the top of the hill, he could see them drinking and washing their wounds in the river, a solace his men did not have. And then he heard the dread *chivateo*, and new troops emerged from the forest, fresh and disciplined, just as they had in Purén against Juan Gómez's soldiers, information that had never reached Valdivia. For the first time, the captain general gave new thought to the situation; until that moment he had thought himself master of the land of the Araucans.

The battle continued the rest of the day. The Spaniards, wounded, thirsty, exhausted, in each turnover faced a rested and well-fed Mapuche horde, while those who had quit the field refreshed themselves at the river. The hours went by, Spaniards and Yanaconas fell, and still Juan Gómez's hoped-for reinforcements had not arrived.

There is no one in Chile who does not know the events of that tragic Christmas in 1553, but there are several versions, and I am going to tell you the one I heard from Cecilia's lips. While Valdivia and his reduced troops struggled to defend themselves in Tucapel, Juan Gómez had been captive in Purén, to which the Mapuche had laid siege until the third day, at which time there was no trace of them. The whole morning, and part of the afternoon, went by in anxious waiting, until finally Gómez could not stand the suspense any longer and rode out with a small party to reconnoiter the woods. Nothing. Not an Indian to be seen. He suspected then that the siege of the fort had been a maneuver to distract them, and to keep them from joining Pedro de Valdivia, as ordered. So while they were trapped in Purén, the governor was waiting for them in Tucapel, and if that fort had been attacked, as Gómez feared, their situation must be desperate. Without a moment's hesitation, Juan Gómez ordered the fourteen healthy men under his command to select the best horses and follow him immediately to Tucapel.

They rode the entire night, and the morning of the next day found them at the fort. They could see the hill, smoke from a fire, and scattered bands of Mapuche, drunk from war and *muday*, waving human heads and limbs, the remains of the Spaniards and Yanaconas defeated the previous day. Horrified, the fourteen men realized that they were surrounded, and that they could meet the same fate as Valdivia's men, but the intoxicated Indians were celebrating their victory and did not challenge them. The Spaniards spurred their sweating mounts up the hill, slashing their path through the few drunken Mapuche who stood in their way. The fort was reduced to a pile of smoking wood ash. They looked for Pedro de Valdivia among the corpses and quartered bodies, but did not find him. They sated their thirst, and that of their horses, from a large basin of dirty water, but they had no time for anything more because now they could see thousands and thousands of Mapuche swarming up the hillside. These were not the intoxicated warriors they had first seen; these had come from the woods, sober and orderly.

The Spaniards could not defend themselves in the ruined fort, in which they would be trapped, so they got back onto their long-suffering mounts and galloped down the hill in an attempt to burst through the enemy ranks. Within instants they were surrounded, and a cutthroat battle ensued that would last the rest of the day. It is impossible to imagine how men and horses that had galloped from Purén all through the night could fight hour after hour that fateful day, but I have seen Spaniards in battle, and I have fought alongside them. I know what we are capable of. Finally, Gómez's soldiers had thrust their way to a point where they could flee, hotly pursued by Lautaro's hordes. The horses were on their last legs, and the forest presented fallen trees and other obstacles that slowed the soldiers, but not the Indians, who darted among the trees and easily overtook the horsemen.

Those fourteen men, bravest of the brave, decided then to sacrifice themselves one by one and hold back the enemy while their companions attempted to get away. They did not discuss it; they did not draw lots; no one ordered them. The first one yelled his good-byes to the others, reined in his horse, and turned to face the pursuers. He struck sparks with his sword, determined to fight to his last breath; it would be a thousand times worse to be taken alive. Within minutes a hundred hands pulled him from his horse and attacked him with the very swords and knives that had been taken from Valdivia's vanquished soldiers.

Those few minutes that hero won for his friends allowed them, briefly, to pull ahead, but soon the Mapuche had caught up again. A second soldier decided to forfeit his life; he, too, called a last good-bye and turned toward the mass of Indians avid for blood. And then a third. One by one, six soldiers fell. The remaining eight, several of them badly wounded, continued their desperate flight until they came to a narrow pass where yet another must sacrifice himself if the others were to escape. He was dead within minutes. It was then that Juan Gómez's mount, drained and bleeding from arrow wounds in its flanks, dropped to its knees. It was completely black in the forest, making it nearly impossible to go forward.

"Climb up behind me, Captain!" one of the soldiers shouted.

"No! Ride on, don't stop for me!" Gómez ordered, knowing he was badly wounded and calculating that the horse could not bear the weight of two riders.

The soldiers had to obey him and ride on, and so feeling his way through the darkness, disoriented, he plunged deeper into the undergrowth. After many terrible hours, the six survivors reached the fort at Purén and warned their comrades before collapsing with fatigue. They stayed there long enough to stanch the blood from their wounds and give a rest to their mounts, before undertaking a forced march toward La Imperial, which then was only a village. The Yanaconas carried anyone with a breath of life in hammocks, but they had to give the dying a quick and honorable death so that the Mapuche would not find them alive.

In the meantime, Juan Gómez was sinking into mud up to his ankles; the recent winter rains had turned the area into a swamp. Though he was bleeding from several arrow wounds, depleted, thirsty, without food for two days, he did not give in to death. Unable to see, he laboriously felt his way through trees and rank growth. He could not wait till dawn, night was his only ally. He could hear the Mapuche's cries of triumph when they discovered his fallen horse, and he prayed that the noble animal that had accompanied him through so many battles was dead. The Indians often tortured wounded beasts to wreak revenge on their masters. The smell of smoke indicated that his pursuers had lighted torches and were searching for him in the thick vegetation, certain that he could not have gone far. He took off his armor and clothing and buried them in the mud, and naked, walked deeper into the swamp. By now the Mapuche were very close; he could hear their voices and glimpse the flare of their torches.

It is at this point in her narration that Cecilia, whose macabre sense of humor seems entirely Spanish, doubled over with laughter as she told me about that horrible night. "My husband ended up buried in a swamp, just as I warned him he would," the princess said. Juan Gómez cut a reed with his sword and submerged himself completely in the putrid ooze. He did not know how many hours he lay there, naked, with open wounds, commending his soul to God and thinking about his children and Cecilia, the beautiful woman who had left a palace to follow him to the end of the world. Mapuche brushed by him several times, never imagining that the man they were searching for lay buried in the mud, clutching his sword, gasping for breath through the hollow reed.

At midmorning of the following day, the men marching toward La Imperial saw a nightmarish vision covered with blood and mud pushing his way through the heavily wooded forest. By his sword, which he had never let go of, they recognized Juan Gómez, captain of the famed fourteen.

For the first time since Rodrigo's death, I slept restfully for several hours last night. In the halfsleep before dawn, I felt a pressure in my chest that weighed on my heart and made it difficult for me to breathe. I did not feel any anxiety, only a great calm and a sense of blessing because I realized it was Rodrigo's arm, and that he was sleeping at my side, as he had in the best of times. I lay without moving, with my eyes closed, grateful for that sweet weight. I wanted to ask my husband if he had at last come for me, to tell him how happy he had made me through the thirty years we shared, and that my one regret had been those long periods when he was away at war, but I was afraid that if I spoke he would disappear. During these months of solitude, I have learned how timid the spirits are. When the first light of dawn sifted through the chinks of the shutters, Rodrigo went away, leaving the mark of his arm on me and his scent on the pillow. By the time the servants came in, there was no trace of him in the room. Despite the happiness that unexpected night of love gave me, I must not have looked well when I awoke because the women went to call you, Isabel. I am not ill, daughter, I have no pain; I feel better than ever, so don't look at me with that dreary face. I will, though, stay in bed a little longer; I feel cold. If you don't mind, I would like to use the time to dictate to you.

As you know, Juan Gómez came out of that ordeal alive, although it took several months to recover from his infected wounds. He gave up the idea of the gold, returned to Santiago, and is still living with his magnificent wife, who must be at least sixty, though she looks thirty. She has no wrinkles, no gray hair, and whether that's by a miracle or witchcraft, I couldn't tell you. That fateful December was the beginning of the Mapuche uprising, a merciless war that has gone on for forty years and seems to have no end. As long as one Indian and one Spaniard are left, blood will flow. I should hate them, Isabel, but I can't. They are my enemies, but I admire them because I know that if I were in their place, I would die fighting for my land, as they are doing.

For several days I have been putting off the moment of telling about Pedro de Valdivia's death. For twenty-seven years I have tried not to think about it, but I suppose the time has come to do it. I would like to believe a less cruel version, that Pedro fought until he was clubbed on the head and killed, but Cecilia helped me discover the truth. Only one Yanacona escaped the disaster at Tucapel and told what happened that Christmas Day, but he knew nothing about the gobernador's fate. Two months later Cecilia came to see me and told me that a Mapuche girl who had just come from Araucanía was serving in her house. Cecilia knew that the girl, who did not speak a word of Spanish, had been found near Tucapel. Once again, the Mapudungu I had learned from Felipe—now Lautaro—was useful. Cecilia brought her to me and I was able to talk with her. She was a young girl of about eighteen, short, with delicate features and strong shoulders. Since she did not understand our language, she seemed slow-witted, but when I spoke to her in Mapudungu, I realized she was very bright. This is what I was able to find out from the Yanacona who survived Tucapel, and the Mapuche girl who was present at Pedro de Valdivia's execution.

The gobernador was in the ruins of the fort, fighting desperately with his handful of courageous soldiers against thousands of Mapuche; the enemy troops were regularly replaced with fresh squadrons, while the soldiers could never put down their swords.

The whole day passed in fighting. At dusk, Valdivia lost any hope that Juan Gómez would arrive with reinforcements. His men were totally drained, the horses were bleeding as profusely as the men, and new enemy detachments kept obstinately ascending the hill to the fort.

"Señores, what do we do?" Valdivia asked the nine men still standing.

"What would Your Mercy have us do but fight and die?" one of the soldiers replied.

"Then let us do so with honor, señores."

Those ten tenacious Spaniards, followed by any able-bodied Yanaconas, went forward to fight and die face-to-face with the enemy, swords held high and with the name of Santiago on their lips. Within minutes, eight soldiers had been pulled from their horses by *boleadoras* and lariats, dragged across the ground, and massacred by hundreds of Mapuche. Only Pedro de Valdivia, a priest, and one faithful Yanacona were able to break through the lines and flee along the one route open to them; the others were blocked by the enemy. One other Yanacona was hidden in the fort; he endured the smoke from the fire beneath a pile of rubble, and two days later escaped with his life after the Mapuche had withdrawn.

The way open to Valdivia had been carefully prepared by Lautaro. It was a dead end, leading through the dark forest to a swamp in which the horses bogged down, exactly as Lautaro had planned. The fugitives could not turn back, for the enemy was close on their heels. In the afternoon light, they watched hundreds of Indians come from the trees and underbrush as they sank deeper and deeper into that foul mud, which emitted the sulfurous odor of hell. Before the swamp swallowed them up, the Mapuche rescued them; that was not how they planned to end the Spaniards' lives.

When Valdivia saw that all was lost, he tried to negotiate his freedom, promising that he would abandon the cities he had founded in the south, that the Spaniards would leave the Araucans' lands forever, and, in addition, that he would give them sheep and other

rewards. The Yanacona tried to translate, but before he could finish, the Mapuche beat him then killed him. They had learned to
distrust the promises of the *huincas*. The priest, who had formed a
cross with two sticks and was trying to administer the last rites to
the Yanacona, as he already had to the gobernador, was clubbed to
death. And then began the martyrdom of Pedro de Valdivia, their
most despised enemy, the incarnation of all the abuses and cruelties imposed upon the Mapuche people. They had not forgotten the
thousands of dead, the burned men, the raped women, the slaughtered children, the hundreds of hands that had floated down the river,
the sliced-off feet and noses, the whips, the chains, the dogs.

They forced the captive to witness the torture of the Yanaconas
who had survived Tucapel, and the profanation of the Spaniards'
corpses. They dragged Valdivia by the hair, naked, to the settlement where Lautaro was waiting. Along the way, stones and sharp
branches tore his skin, and when he was deposited at the feet of
the *ñidoltoqui*, he was a rag soaked in mud and blood. Lautaro
ordered that he be given something to drink, to rouse him from
his stupor, then had him tied to a post. As a symbolic insult they
broke Valdivia's Toledo steel sword, his inseparable companion, in
half and drove it into the ground at his feet. Once the prisoner was
conscious enough to open his eyes and realize where he was, he
found himself staring at his former servant. "Felipe!" he cried with
hope; at least this was a familiar face, someone who could speak
Spanish. Lautaro's eyes bored into his with infinite disdain. "Don't
you recognize me, Felipe? I'm your *taita*," the captive persisted.
Lautaro spit in his face. He had been waiting for that moment for
twenty-two years.

At an order from the *ñidoltoqui*, the inflamed Mapuche filed
before Pedro de Valdivia with sharpened clamshells, gouging out
pieces of flesh from his body. They built a fire, and with the same
shells cut the muscles from his arms and legs, roasted them, and
ate them before him. That macabre orgy lasted three nights and
two days before Mother Death took pity on the miserable prisoner.
At last, on the morning of the third day, when Lautaro saw that

Valdivia was dying, he poured molten gold into his mouth so he would have his fill of the metal he loved so much, and that had caused the Indians so much suffering in the mines.

What pain, what pain! These memories are like a lance here in my own breast. What time is it, daughter? Where has the light gone? The hours have flown backward, it must be dawn again. I believe it will be dawn forever . . .

The remains of Pedro de Valdivia were never found. They say that the Mapuche devoured his body in an improvised ritual, that they made flutes from his bones, and that his skull is used to this day as a vessel for the *muday* of the *toquis*. You ask me, daughter, why I hold to the terrible version of Cecilia's serving girl instead of the other, more merciful one: that, as the poet wrote, Valdivia's skull was crushed in; after all, that is a custom among the Indians of the south. I will tell you why. During those three ominous days in December 1553, I was very ill. It was as if my soul knew what my mind still did not. Horrendous images passed before my eyes like a nightmare I could not wake from. I thought I saw baskets filled with amputated hands and noses in my house, and in my patio impaled and chained Indians. The air reeked of burned human flesh, and the night breeze carried the sound of cracking whips. This conquest has cost enormous suffering. No one can forgive such cruelty, least of all the Mapuche, who never forget an injustice, just as they do not forget favors received. I was tortured by memories; it was as if I were possessed by a demon. You know already, Isabel, that except for an occasional flurry with my heart I have always been a healthy woman, thanks to God's grace, so I have no other explanation for the illness that afflicted me those three days. While Pedro was suffering his gruesome death, my soul accompanied him from afar, and wept for him and for all the other victims of those years. I lay prostrate, with such violent vomiting and burning fever that they feared for my life. In my delirium I clearly heard Pedro de Valdivia's screams, and his voice telling me good-bye for the last time.

"Farewell, Inés of my soul . . ."

*Chronicles of Doña Inés Suárez, delivered by her daughter,
Doña Isabel de Quiroga, to the Church of the Dominicans
to be conserved and safeguarded, in this month of December
in the year of our Lord 1580.*

Santiago de la Nueva Extremadura

Kingdom of Chile

Author's Note

THIS NOVEL is a work of intuition, but any similarity to events and persons relating to the conquest of Chile is not coincidental.

The feats of Inés Suárez noted by the chroniclers of her era were nearly ignored by historians for more than four hundred years. In these pages I narrate events as they were documented. My hand merely strung them together with a fine thread of imagination.

MY FRIENDS Josefina Rosetti, Victorio Cintolessi, Rolando Hamilton, and Diana Huidobro aided me in researching the period of the conquest of Chile, especially in regard to Inés Suárez. Malú Sierra reviewed the material related to the Mapuche. Juan Allende, Jorge Manzanilla, and Gloria Gutiérrez copyedited the manuscript. William Gordon cared for me and fed me during the silent months of writing.

I am grateful to those few historians who mention the importance of Inés Suárez; their works allowed me to write this novel.

Bibliographical Note

THE RESEARCH for this novel took four years of avid reading. I did not keep a record of each of the history texts, works of fiction, and articles I read to saturate myself in the period and in the characters because the idea of adding a bibliography came only at the end. When Gloria Gutiérrez, my agent, read the manuscript, she told me that without a bibliography this account would appear to be the product of a pathological imagination (something I am often accused of). Many episodes from the life of Inés Suárez and from the conquest of Chile seem beyond belief, and I want to demonstrate that they are historical fact. The following are some of the books I consulted, a number of which are still piled in my studio at the back of the garden, where I write.

For the general history of Chile, I was able to call upon two classic studies: *Crónicas del reino de Chile* (El Ferrocarril, 1865) by Pedro Mariño de Lovera, and Diego Barros Arana's essential *Historia general de Chile* (1884); the first volume of Barros Arana's study records episodes from the period of the conquest. A more contemporary account is found in *Historia general de Chile* (Planeta, Santiago de Chile, 2000) by Alfredo Jocelyn-Holt Letelier.

Among a sizeable number of works about the Conquest, I found helpful *Estudio sobre la conquista de América* (Universitaria, Santiago de Chile, 1992) by Néstor Meza; *La era colonial* (Nascimento, Santiago de Chile, 1974) written by Benjamín Vicuña Mackenna, a name closely associated with Chilean history and historiography; and also *El imperio hispánico de América* (Peuser, Buenos Aires, 1958) by C. H. Harina. To assure the authenticity of the Spanish background, I consulted histories of Spain by Miguel Ángel Artola (Alianza Editorial Madrid, 1988; vol. 3) and Fernando García de Cortázar (Planeta, Barcelona, 2002), among others. And to learn more about the conquistadors, I turned to, among others, *Conquistadores españoles del siglo XVI* (Aguilar, Madrid, 1963) by Ricardo Majó Framis; *Los últimos conquistadores* (2001) and *Diego de Almagro* (third edition, 2001) by Gerado Larraín Valdés; and *Pedro de Valdivia, capitán conquistador* (Instituto de Cultura Hispánica, Madrid, 1961) by Santiago del Campo.

The bibliography of the Mapuche universe is impressive; among many titles, I want to make special mention of *Los araucanos* (Universitaria, Santiago, 1914) by Edmond Reuel Smith; the more recent *Mapuche, gente de la Tierra* (Sudamericana, Buenos Aires, 2000) by Malú Sierra; José Bengoa's *Historia de los antiguos mapuche del sur* (Catalonia, Barcelona, 2003); along with a more specialized work, *Folklore médico chileno* (Nascimento, Santiago de Chile, 1981) by Oreste Plath.

Among these readings, two excellent historical novels should not be overlooked: *Butamalón* (Anaya-Mario Muchnik, Madrid, 1994) by Eduardo Labarca, and *Ay Mamá Inés* (Andrés Bello Santiago de Chile, 1993), the work of Jorge Guzmán. To my knowledge, it is the only previous novel about my protagonist.

And last, a special mention for two works from the period: *La Araucana* (1578), an epic poem published in countless editions (I used the Santillana), including the very beautiful 1842 volume from which the illustrations for this book have been taken, and *Cartas,* the letters of Pedro de Valdivia. Two editions of the latter are particularly noteworthy: the Spanish version by the Editorial Lumen and the Junta de Extremadura (1991), under the direction of the Chilean Miguel Rojas Mix, and the 1998 Chilean volume published by the Compañía Minera Doña Inés de Collahuasi.